THE MOMENT OF TRUTH

With Tremayne's shirt in her hands, the task of repairing it seemed more daunting. Still, she would try.

Ellie felt something in the breast pocket. Something rigid, a square of cardboard. She withdrew it and the shirt fluttered to the ground while she grasped the cardboard between both hands, staring with numb disbelief.

Her own likeness stared back at her.

How well she remembered the day the photograph had been taken. And since the day it had arrived from the photographer, it sat imprisoned in an ornate silver-gilt frame atop her father's desk. Jonathan McKittrick's sole reminder of his runaway daughter— and he'd given it away, like the drawings of escaped convicts he passed out to his trackers.

With blinding clarity she realized Tremayne's true purpose. And yet she'd ignored her instincts and dared to trust him . . . to believe in him . . . to burn for him.

Also by Donna Valentino

Conquered By His Kiss

Available from
HarperPaperbacks

Harper
Monogram

Mirage

DONNA VALENTINO

HarperPaperbacks
A Division of HarperCollinsPublishers

HarperPaperbacks *A Division of* HarperCollins*Publishers*
10 East 53rd Street, New York, N.Y. 10022

Copyright © 1994 by Donna Valentino
All rights reserved. No part of this book may be used or reproduced in any manner whatsoever without written permission of the publisher, except in the case of brief quotations embodied in critical articles and reviews. For information address HarperCollins*Publishers,*
10 East 53rd Street, New York, N.Y. 10022.

Cover illustration by Vittorio

First printing: July 1994

Printed in the United States of America

HarperPaperbacks, HarperMonogram, and colophon are trademarks of HarperCollins*Publishers*

❖ 10 9 8 7 6 5 4 3 2 1

For my mother, Florence McNeil
because I love her,
and because she didn't bug me too much
when I wanted to stay inside
and read
instead of playing outside
with the other kids

And for Colleen and Jacki,
who read and reread
without complaining
until I got it right

Mirage

Prologue

Fort Smith, Arkansas
July, 1877

Ellie McKittrick shivered, bone cold while a desultory morning breeze, heavy with summer heat and humidity, teased the edge of the breakfast room's fine lace curtain. She shivered, even though her elegant charcoal wool mourning gown was better suited to winter temperatures, even though its stifling, voluminous folds concealed yet another gown beneath it, trembling despite the three layers of stockings fattening her legs until they bulged like sausages. Her toes cramped from the grip required to hold the overlarge boots she'd stolen from the gardener. Sweat beaded Ellie's forehead, and again she shivered, fear striking her cold to the pit of her soul.

She heard her father's stolid, measured tread

descending the stairs, and flinched when a creaking board announced that he'd stopped as usual before the hall clock to check it against his personal timepiece. He entered the breakfast room, his slight smile hinting he felt gratified to find her in place, and she was grateful she'd sat shivering there for two hours, making sure she arrived before he did because she feared her legs might buckle if she tried to walk.

A sorry plight, since she meant to leave him this day.

"Here's your coffee, Warden McKittrick," said the maid, placing a steaming cup before him. "Tea for you today, Miss Eleanor?"

"Yes, thank you," Ellie whispered. She doubted she could swallow a drop, but if she could manage it, it might abate the cold gripping her.

With a slight broadening of his smile, Father swept his closed hand next to her plate. When he moved his hand, her Sunday locket lay gleaming in a golden heap near her fork.

She didn't dare touch it, didn't want to touch it, felt faint at the sight of it. She kept her hands clasped in her lap, and bowed her head, quelling the shivering wracking her soul, praying her thundering heart couldn't be heard while she waited for Father to begin saying grace.

Father always talked straight to his Lord, disdaining to share in conversation with his earthly companions. He'd placed the locket next to Ellie's plate, and it would be in his so-called prayer where she'd learn his reasons for doing so.

She silently whispered a prayer of her own. She'd

been so careful to keep her plans secret. She prayed the locket didn't portend something gone awry.

"You see your daughter Eleanor looks properly penitent this day," Jonathan McKittrick thundered. "I, your most humble servant, have been encouraged by her submissive acceptance of her lot since you saw fit to remove the contagion from her life."

Ellie's hands clenched, her fingernails cutting deep into her palm at hearing him desecrate her dead mother's memory.

But she couldn't lash out. Not on this day. The last time she'd defied him, daring to stay at her mother's sickbed after he'd ordered her to go to sleep, he'd locked Ellie in her room for forty days and forty nights.

"You saw fit to bless me with this daughter, O Lord," Jonathan intoned. "I have held her close, knowing you meant her life to be devoted to me. You have made your choice for her clear to all, O Lord, by striking her only friend with a disfiguring affliction. You taught her the nurturing skills, O Lord, by punishing her ungrateful mother with lingering sickness, so that Eleanor would be prepared to comfort me if you should deem a similar earthly punishment for me, your most humble of servants. I thought a reward might be in order, O Lord." Jonathan seemed oblivious to her distress, concluding his prayer with a satisfied, smug-sounding "Amen" far quicker than she expected.

The locket, his quick prayer . . . something was amiss.

She stared at the locket while he gulped his water,

realizing with a dull sense of surprise that she scarcely knew what her father looked like anymore, she'd spent so much time studying her clenched hands to avoid affording him a glimpse of the rebellion in her eyes.

When he spoke to her, his voice lacked the thunder of his prayer. "I specifically instructed Hannah to set out your rose gown for you to wear this morning, Eleanor."

It was beginning. Ellie sipped at her water, grateful that the trembling inside her didn't transmit itself to her hands and set her glass knocking against her teeth.

"She did, Father. I carelessly snagged the gown upon the edge of an open drawer, ripping the skirt away from the waist. I didn't want to be late for breakfast so I substituted this one."

The lie came easily. The sight of her rose-colored gown laid out over the bed, with her mother dead only two weeks, had sent waves of fury through her. How dare her father attempt to cut short the time she meant to wear mourning for her mother! But she couldn't risk punishment by openly defying his choice, not today. Ripping the offending rose gown's seam apart had relieved some of the anger, but she'd had additional motives for substituting dresses. Her most serviceable gown, the charcoal wool, would hold up well throughout the long trip to Kansas.

Interminable moments later, she heard the clink of his silver against china and felt like sagging with relief.

"You see your locket next to your plate."

"Yes, Father."

"You know how it has grieved me to deny you the pleasure of wearing it except when I am on hand to keep watch."

"I have witnessed your pain," she managed through clenched teeth.

"You know why I have done so, Eleanor."

"Yes, Father."

Years ago, the diamond had fallen from the setting of her mother's bethrothal ring. Jonathan had immediately confiscated all of his wife's jewels, all of his daughter's baubles, producing them only when social occasions demanded they appear in public adorned. *He's afraid we'll sell them to get the money to run away,* Ellie's mother Angeline had whispered. *And he's right.*

"Have you prayed to God to cleanse you of your mother's careless ways?"

"I have, Father." It came out barely more than a whisper, so tightly did her throat clench around the despicable words, ominous in their allusion toward Angeline's lost diamond.

"You heard me tell God I believe it is time you were rewarded. You may henceforth wear the locket throughout the day, here in the home. You will of course turn it back over to me every night, until you prove yourself trustworthy."

He would expect some show of gratitude. She forced herself to look at him, pasted a false smile upon her lips.

"Thank you, Father."

He stared back at her, stolidly chewing his morning rasher, a magnanimous, self-satisfied smirk distorting the broad contours of his face.

"You look quite pale, Eleanor."

Her pallor, evidence of her tension, could be exploited.

"Actually, I'm feeling a bit headachy, Father. I wondered if you might ask Hannah to fetch some headache powder for me."

She'd taken the precaution of dissolving the household's supply of powder in her washing water. She laid the empty packet on the table alongside her locket as proof of her need. Getting Hannah out of the house was essential to escaping unnoticed.

"You may send her yourself. Hannah!"

The serving woman, Ellie knew from experience, always stood just beyond the dining room door awaiting just such a summons.

"Hannah, please go at once to Doc Halliburton's and fetch some headache powder for me." Ellie issued the order calmly, waiting without surprise while Hannah's gaze flickered to Jonathan for his silent nod of approval before dipping her head and slipping noiselessly back through the door. The servants had been forbidden to take direct orders from Ellie and her mother.

"You may put on the necklace, Eleanor."

Ellie fastened it about her neck, having a little trouble managing the clasp, her fingers felt so numb. The gold lay gleaming against the sober color of her gown. She lifted the locket, feeling it cold against her fingers. So glittering, so appealing in appearance, and yet its insignificant weight felt like an anchor dragging her beneath the water while she vainly struggled toward the sky.

She would sell it at the first opportunity.

The thought tugged her lips into a little smile.

"I see you are pleased."

"Yes, Father." Let him think what he would. "But the headache has robbed me of my appetite and kept me from sleeping last night. I would like to retire to my room for the day. Hannah could slip the headache powder beneath the door. That way, if I manage to fall asleep before she returns, she won't disturb me." If he consented, she might gain hours before her disappearance was discovered. His office in the jailhouse compound was a good half mile away, and she could slip from the back door unnoticed once he left for work.

"Very well. I will tell her to let you rest. You will, of course, join me for dinner this evening."

She nodded and rose, carefully sliding her chair back into place, a wild, thrilling excitement churning through her. Things were going better than she'd dared hope.

She'd nearly reached the door when he called out to her.

"Just one more thing, Eleanor."

The fanciful notion that it was only the many layers of stockings keeping her legs stiff enough to support her nearly caused her to burst into a nervous giggle. She couldn't force herself to turn and look at him.

"Yes, Father?"

He took his time over answering while she let her

hand against the door support her weight, dreading what he might say.

"We are better off now. Your mother was an ungodly woman. You see how pleasant it can be, with you getting your jewelry back and assuming command over the servants. So no more long faces, hmm? And you will mend the rose gown for tomorrow?"

"I pray to God you will never see me frown again, and that you will nevermore have the opportunity to question my attire," Ellie said.

The closed carriage waited at the end of the avenue. The door flung open at her approach; Ellie clutched her light cloak more tightly at her throat and hurled herself through the opening. Her teeth chattered so, one might have thought she suffered from a cold. Instead she felt heated, feverish, frantic with the sense of urgency.

Lauretta, bedecked in black from head to toe, pulled Ellie into her seat. "Here, Ellie, change your cloak. Cousin Andy swore not to tell anyone he drove us to the train station, but we don't want anyone else recognizing you." Lauretta handed her a black garment identical to her own. A broad-brimmed black hat and concealing mourning veil waited on the seat.

Lauretta had thought of their disguises. Nobody, she asserted, would pay the slightest bit of attention to two women bedecked in widow's weeds, but they couldn't hope to escape unnoticed if people recognized the everyday bee bonnet that shielded Lauretta's pock-ravaged face from prying eyes.

"You have the tickets?"

"Of course I have them." Lauretta fumbled in her reticule to produce one. Ellie ran her fingers over her ticket, awed to think that such a near-weightless paper scrap would send her on her way to freedom.

"And the money? Oh, let me see the money, Lauretta."

Lauretta pressed a small stack of greenbacks into Ellie's hand. "Lordy, Ellie, you act like you've never held paper money before."

"I haven't," Ellie whispered, embarrassed that a twenty-three-year-old woman would have to admit to such a thing. Father had never entrusted his womenfolk with more than a few pennies. She felt her mother's loving presence surround her, fancied she could feel her mother's joy singing through her veins. This money, this means of escape, was Angeline's triumph beyond death. Ellie wondered what life would be like if things ever got matched up properly, if by some miracle the right man and the right woman somehow managed to find each other. She would never know. She'd never risk involvement with any man. The chances of making a mistake were too great; the price a woman had to pay far too steep, the men far too capable of exacting that price.

A sharp rap at the roof drew their attention, and Lauretta's Cousin Andy called, "Train station coming up."

Ellie drew the widow's veil tight around her neck. Her vision dimmed. How did Lauretta stand this day after day?

A covered breezeway was all that separated them from the train steaming and huffing at the other side of the station. The car doors were folded open, beckoning them to enter. The air smelled sulfurously of burning coal. Fine grit crunched beneath their feet with each step.

The veil distorted everything, and gusts of steam drifted from the waiting train to cloud her vision further. Her blood seemed to pick up speed inside her, rushing faster and faster until her head roared. The breezeway seemed endless, plank after plank stretching forever. Safety lay beyond those planks; if her father suspected what she was up to, one of his men would leap out from behind a corner and stop her before she gained the train. Her knees threatened to buckle and Lauretta placed a firm, steadying hand beneath her elbow, lending her strength to climb the steps leading into the car. They collapsed onto the first empty bench they found.

If he knew, Father would strike now.

It seemed an eternity before she heard the conductor's muffled, "'Board!" A moment later the train lurched, nearly spilling them from their seats. Ellie had to press her feet against the floor to keep from sliding when that first lurch was followed by a second, and then quickly by another, and then another, until they were moving fast enough to overcome their inertia. She looked outside and even through the veil's obscuring folds she could see the landscape rushing past.

Unbidden, laughter bubbled up within her throat.

Lauretta looked at her and giggled.

The train's wheels roared louder than the noise in her head, each revolution taking her farther and farther away from Fort Smith and its hellish United States Court. Her father wouldn't dare come after her now; a man charged with upholding the law wouldn't dare try forcing a grown woman away from her lawfully owned land. He wouldn't. He . . . wouldn't. She laughed again and found she couldn't stop. She laughed and laughed until tears began seeping from her eyes, and wondered why her sides weren't aching from laughing so hard, wondered why her lungs strained and gasped for air.

Lauretta closed a hand over hers. "It's all right, Ellie. It's all right."

1

**Fort Smith
Barracks Courthouse Jail**

During his last surreptitious examination, Tremayne Hawthorne had found the jailhouse compound's east gate discouragingly unbreachable, snug in its stout wooden frame, its oaken planks so finely fitted that not even a glimmer of light seeped through from the other side. Force of habit, an undying conviction that one day he would find a weakness, kept his gaze skimming the walls as he'd done, fruitlessly, each day for the past five months.

But today . . . today, the east gate hung ever so slightly askew.

His fellow inmates labored on, oblivious to the minuscule gap that sent his pulse racing. It took every bit of strength he could muster to keep his grip on the hoe, to continue the mind-numbing chopping, to pretend weary attention to the back-breaking chore. *Run!* his mind screamed as he hacked a weed from its root. *Go! Go! Go!* some demon within him urged. His rational self argued that it would be insanity to bolt now, while the mounted overseer's watchful eye ranged over the miserable group.

He changed rows, bringing him several steps closer to the gate. Score marks, so fresh they gleamed silver-white against the weathered hasps, showed where an ax or wedge had wrenched the mangled hinges from the wall. Someone had pried the six-inch screws from their moorings, had left the gate so slightly ajar that only one with a morbid interest in its normal position would notice. It smacked of a trap, a tempting invitation designed to lure someone into a cleverly designed ambush.

Trapped animals sometimes cowered in the corners of their cages, too frightened and suspicious to move when the doors were accidentally or purposely left open. Those who dared venture into the unknown sometimes earned their freedom.

The overseer yawned, motioning for one of the sweat-grimed inmates to bring him water. He leaned down to accept the proffered dipper, leaving him vulnerable and off-balance, his attention diverted. *Go now, go now, go now.* Tremayne crouched, though the half-grown corn offered little concealment. Gripping the hoe midhandle, he lunged for the gate.

A choking sputter followed by the warning crack of a bullwhip told him the overseer had caught sight

of him. One hundred paces, at least, to the gate. He
would never make it at less than an all-out run. He
abandoned the crouch, freeing his long legs to attain
full stride. Cornstalks whipped his chest as a ragged
cheer rose from the other inmates. His legs pumped;
his heart surged, its thunderous thumping deafening
his ears to all save his instincts urging speed, more
speed.

The gate loomed. Without pausing, he swung the
hoe, its metal head biting deep into the loosened
hinge. The impact shuddered the length of his arms.
Setting his heels, he wrenched back, widening the gap
between gate and wall by several inches. Enough for a
cat to squeeze through, or a small dog. Or one exceptionally large man, so hell-bent on escape he could
ignore the splintered wood tearing at his skin, the
rough stone wall scraping his flesh, as he clawed and
squirmed his way to freedom.

He stumbled through, his weight coming down
hard on the wrist of his hastily braced hand, but he
ignored the pain shafting up his arm. The woods
beckoned, the trees blurred as if the intervening quar-
ter-mile-wide field had stretched to a league or more.
Safety lay beyond that field; once within the woods,
he could hide, he could dodge. His lungs screamed
for air; he drew it in with great, gasping gulps, hearing excitement wheezing through him. Hearing, too,
the dull thunder of hoofbeats against summer-baked
earth, the swish of a well-thrown lariat snaking
through the sky.

An ambush, just as the saner half of his mind had
warned. One set with deliberate cruelty, as if the trapper

had gauged just how far he could let Tremayne run, how high his hopes might rise, before bringing reality crashing down around him.

A whistling noose settled over him, trapping his flailing arms tightly against his torso. Tremayne fought the rope, staggering forward, his balance thwarted until a second noose joined the first and pulled him to a stop.

Another noose whistled over his shoulders, drawing taut across his chest. A fourth settled round his neck, closing snug with a final tug against his windpipe, reminding him of the futility of fighting against his complete and utter helplessness.

The open field, a moment ago rendering the woods so distant and unreachable, took on its true proportions. With only a few more ground-eating strides he might have attained the cool, sheltering darkness, might have eluded Jailer McKittrick's trackers. The air reverberated with the low, triumphant snicker that he knew without looking belonged to his nemesis, Silas Stringer.

And it was Stringer's heavy, ungentle hand that controlled the noose encircling Tremayne's neck. Stringer twisted the rope around his fist, forcing Tremayne's jaw upward, tearing his gaze away from the woods until he had nowhere to focus except upon the tracker's exultant expression.

"Got you again, woman killer." Stringer's thin lips, grinning with wolfish delight, stretched over yellowed teeth.

Rage shook Tremayne. His forearms flexed and he surged against the ropes, mindlessly intent upon wrapping his hands around Stringer's neck and putting an end to that mocking sneer.

Stringer merely tugged at his lariat, drawing an embarrassing, strangled wheeze from Tremayne's throat, leaving him lightheaded and weak-kneed from lack of air.

Stringer slid his boot from his stirrup. He drew back his foot and with swift, brutal force, buried the sharp-pointed toe deep into Tremayne's belly. Breathless agony seized Tremayne; only by sheer force of will did he prevent his knees from buckling.

"God damn if I didn't call it right," Stringer jeered. "I knew you'd poke your nose through that hole, just like a rat sniffing fresh garbage. English nobleman, my ass. Earl of pig shit's more like it." He gestured to the unseen men whose ropes held Tremayne motionless as an unbranded calf awaiting the iron. "You can all take a turn at His Highness here, boys, but be a mite careful. Boss McKittrick don't want no trouble from him, but he wants to see him alive."

"Ain't you gonna beat on him with us, Silas?" asked one of Stringer's henchmen.

Stringer blew lightly across his fingernails and polished them against his greasy shirtfront. He peered at them, as if admiring his reflection in their dirt-rimmed surfaces. "Don't want to mess myself up, boys. McKittrick's sending me to bring back his runaway girl soon's we're done here. She's holed up somewheres in Kansas. Easy pickings."

A chorus of ribald suggestions greeted Stringer's pronouncement. Then the men turned their attention to Tremayne, leaving him no pity to spare on the jailer's luckless daughter.

Magnolia, Kansas

"It kind of looks like a cave, doesn't it?" Lauretta marveled, holding a lantern aloft.

Ellie nodded. A cave . . . or the inside of a grave. For a moment, it seemed as if the dirt walls darkened to a deeper black, swallowing the faint sunlight illuminating the room's one small window. A shudder coursed through her. She hadn't expected it would be so dark. She would have to keep a candle or lantern alight, always.

The prairie wind howled and whistled through the unprotected doorway as they stood near the center of the crowded dugout. Despite the lantern's yellow glow, Lauretta's face bore an ashen pallor as she held the lamp high, turning it slowly to give the two women their first look at the inside of their homestead.

Ellie could touch what passed for a ceiling with her fingertips, which made the room no more than six and a half feet tall. The floor, which had been dug two feet below ground level, sported warped, twisted, wooden planks. The rear wall, which backed into the slight rise of the prairie, oozed wetly. Sod blocks added height to the front and side walls, the whole thing topped off with a layer of plank rafters as contorted as those on the floor. Tufts of dried prairie grass and cornstalks poked through the rafters.

"Someone actually lived here," Lauretta whispered. "I can understand why they didn't make their payments to the railroad."

"Well, we're going to live here, too, and *we're* going to keep up our payments," Ellie vowed.

The earthen walls swallowed her voice, dulled the sounds of their breathing, absorbed the lamplight.

Ellie turned in a circle. The light fell upon an earthen hearth taking up most of the right wall. It danced over stacked crates meant to hold their household goods, past two nail kegs, serving as chairs, which rested beneath the plain pine table.

She touched the table. It rocked, with only two legs at a time finding purchase on the buckled wooden floor. "I thought a wooden floor was a great asset," she said, frowning at the twisted boards, imagining how easily one might stub a toe.

"It is," Lauretta agreed. "The railroad man said we won't have as many fleas as the folks living on dirt floors. He said we might encourage a toad to take up residence under the wood, which will help keep the bedbugs down, too."

"That's a comfort," Ellie said faintly.

She thought they'd surely kill themselves trying to navigate across such a toad-concealing, uneven surface. A sudden thrill chased through her. *She* could tear up the floor and recover it with straight, clean-smelling planks without seeking anyone's permission. She could do anything she liked, and nobody would prevent it.

"Oh, look, Ellie!" Lauretta dropped to her knees before the primitive hearth. A small, soot-encrusted bake oven crouched amidst the debris littering the grate. "My grandmother had an oven just like this! It baked the best biscuits."

"I hope your grandmother taught you how to use that oven, because I don't see a stove." Ellie said, her voice tight as a trickle of dirt sifted down from the ceiling onto her head.

No physical comforts at all, for that matter, but a long-dormant hope raised its head, lifting spirits battered into submission. If comforts were all that mattered, she'd have been content staying home with Father.

It would certainly take some doing to make a home of this black, cold, cheerless hovel. Yet Ellie felt a whimsical smile tugging at one corner of her mouth. She curled her arm around her middle for warmth as she studied the possibilities. Lauretta's biscuits would be a start; the scent of baking might help dispel the earthy, cloying dampness.

"I'll mix up a batch right now," Lauretta said as if Ellie had spoken aloud. "Soon's I start a fire. There are plenty of chips in that box next to the hearth."

"Chips?" Ellie swung her gaze to the box. "Where?"

"Right here, silly." Lauretta crouched next to her, pulling several brownish clods from the box and tossing them atop the cold ashes clogging the hearth. "Don't you remember me telling you the railroad man said we'd find them all over the prairie?"

"Chips? Those . . . those dried up old turds are *chips?*"

Merriment danced in Lauretta's eyes. "What—did you think chips were something that fell from trees?"

"Why, I suppose I did," Ellie admitted. And then they both burst into laughter.

"Look at what we've gotten ourselves into, Lauretta," Ellie gasped at last. "I swore I didn't care what sort of house we'd find when we got here, but I never suspected we'd be holed up in a burrow like a couple of jackrabbits."

"Don't you like it?"

"I hate it!" Ellie's voice softened. "And I love it. How I wish Mama could have seen it. She'd have loved helping us make a home of this place."

"She'll watch over us while we have a fine time building up this homestead." Lauretta blew gently upon a tiny spark.

The flames rose grudgingly, casting a rosy glow over Lauretta's skin and upswept blond hair. She'd discarded her widow's bonnet at the door. Ellie couldn't remember the last time Lauretta had felt so free to bare her face, exposing the scars marring her delicate features. Scars alone, though, wouldn't have forced someone like Lauretta into spending a lifetime behind a veil; the smallpox had ravaged her eyelids in a most horrendous manner, thickening them, obliterating her lashes, grotesquely framing beautiful sky blue eyes in a way that caused people to gape and cringe away.

But here, with their closest neighbor four miles distant, Lauretta could bare her face to the sun. And here Ellie could pretend to be brave, and tear up old boards and let her hair hang free, and wear whichever of her two gowns she pleased, and never again avert her eyes to disguise her true feelings.

A low, sinister scraping sounded near the door. Lauretta reached for her veiled bonnet, Ellie for the shotgun she'd bought in Wichita, as they sidled toward the yawning doorway. Poking the gun barrel out first, Ellie gathered a deep breath, summoning her courage to confront the intruder.

"Hold on, there! Don't shoot!"

The quavering cry of alarm sent both their heads peeking curiously around the door frame. A gaunt, bedraggled man, his dark hair and youthful frame belying his old-sounding voice, stood on the stoop with raised hands. Upon close inspection, it seemed evident he couldn't be more than twenty-five years old. His head jerked at the sight of them. He gaped at their black-cloaked forms, his hands coming to rest at his hips. "Wimmin! Why, I'll be . . . "

"You'll be dead if you come any closer," Ellie said, the shotgun giving her confidence to speak above the leaden hammering of her heart.

He shrugged as if being threatened by gun-toting women meant nothing to him. "I don't mean any disrespect, ma'am, but who the hell are you? You ought not to be holdin' a gun on me. Everyone knows this claim's been abandoned, but I got squatter's rights, bein' here six months or so."

"Squatting for six months and this place in such condition? You're not very industrious, are you, sir?" Lauretta sniffed.

"Name's Hiram Espy, ma'am, and I'm about as industrious as they come in these parts. I been shakin' on an' off with the ague. Can't hardly work till it settles down some, can I?" He drew himself up, obviously highly offended at Lauretta's insult.

"We bought this claim from the railroad," Ellie

said, anxious to quell Lauretta before her comments provoked the interloper's anger. "You go on your way now."

"Aw, ma'am." He shook his head and remained where he stood.

Something about the way he postured there, his feet so defiantly planted in *her* dirt, stirred smoldering resentment within Ellie. Remembering the Wichita gunsmith's admonition that the shotgun pulled to the right, she aimed far to Hiram Espy's left and squeezed off a warning shot. A puff of dust and splintered hay kicked up far closer to him than she'd expected.

"Jeezus!" He yelped, leaping back. He scowled toward them. "No need to shoot at me, ma'am. My ague's just about run its spell. I could help out around the place if you'd let me roll out a pallet in the barn. Just fer a couple days."

"We don't need any help. Be on your way."

"Ellie . . ."

Ignoring Lauretta's tug at her sleeve, Ellie brought the gun to eye level and peered down the barrel in what she hoped was a convincing manner.

Throwing up his hands in defeat, Hiram Espy heaved a huge sigh and turned on his heel. He stalked away, casting occasional, wistful glances back at them while his long strides carried him swiftly out of their vision. Lauretta stared after him, her form still and mournful.

"We don't need a man hanging around, Laurie," Ellie said, horribly conscious that the crumbling dugout, their neglected acres, could use all the help they could get. "He'd overhear our conversations, and I'd just as soon not have anyone know I ran away from home. Word could get back to my father."

"You're right." Lauretta sighed. "Besides, I'd have to keep my bonnet on all the time if he stayed."

The sky and prairie suddenly loomed impossibly huge around them, an endless vista, casting the two of them into insignificance. The intoxicating rush of freedom to act as she pleased, the successful ending of the confrontation with Hiram had fleetingly raised her spirits; now they crashed about her. Ellie felt some small measure of the delight and satisfaction she'd found in taking possession of their new home slip away. She lowered the rifle stock to the floor and balanced her weight against it, glad of the support it offered her suddenly quaking limbs. The familiar, uneasy dread that had haunted her from the moment she stole away from her father crept back, lodging itself around her heart.

Rough hands shoved him into the room. Tremayne strove for balance, his equilibrium shattered by the nooses still binding his arms to his waist, by the trailing ropes tangling his legs. His head pounded, his entire body aching and quivering from being pummeled and then dragged like a sack of flour behind Stringer and his men while he did his desperate best to avoid their horses' flailing hooves.

"Good God—what have you done to him!"

Oh, Christ, not again. Tremayne groaned. The polished, clipped tones belonged to his father's solicitor and general adviser, Jessop T. Farnsworth, who stood next to Jailer McKittrick, witnessing this new humiliation.

McKittrick frowned as his stare assessed the damage to Tremayne's hide. "It would appear Mr. Stringer approached this assignment with more vigor than I anticipated. There was no need for him to rope you down like a steer. I shall have a word with him over it."

Tremayne didn't bother trying to withhold his disbelieving snort. Though McKittrick never lifted a finger against his charges, he likewise did nothing to eliminate or reduce the brutalities his henchmen took such delight in inflicting. Nor did he do anything to alleviate the inhumane conditions that had earned the Fort Smith Barracks Courthouse Jail its reputation as the most brutal of the U.S. territorial prisons.

"Believe what you will, Hawthorne. Stringer was instructed to bring you here at Mr. Farnsworth's request. I had no time to devise a punishment for you. Indeed, I would have preferred delaying this meeting. I find myself preoccupied today with more urgent matters."

Such as finding his runaway daughter, Tremayne assumed.

As always, Tremayne found himself taken aback by his jailer's voice, so high-pitched did it sound, coming from a man who stood about six feet tall. The bald top of McKittrick's sparsely fringed head came to just about the level of Tremayne's eyes. Lots of muscle gone to fat, which didn't lull Tremayne into respecting his strength any less. He'd tussled a time or two with fat men who'd known how to use their weight to overpower someone quicker and fitter. What was interesting was the way the jailer had gone to fat, with narrow shoulders crowning the rounded sugges- tion of breasts at his chest, hips wide, thighs plump.

His face bore a sort of prissy look about it, his lips red and pursed, with nary a hint of whisker upon smooth, fleshy cheeks. Maybe McKittrick had the habit of shaving several times throughout the day; even so, he must possess the world's slickest razor. Tremayne's own face hadn't looked so peach-fuzzy smooth since hair had sprouted in his armpits.

Tremayne had seen such a build on a male once before—on a London dock, he'd watched while a similar-shaped, hard-eyed eunuch herded a half- dozen veiled concubines aboard a Turkish pasha's private ship.

He wondered if Jessop Farnsworth had witnessed a comparable sight while waiting to board the ship that had brought him here today. The solicitor squinted hard at Tremayne, as if to reassure himself some imposter hadn't stepped in to take his place since Farns- worth's last visit.

Tremayne, amused by Farnsworth's perusal, merely straightened, the motion freeing one of the nooses to puddle round his feet. No words were nec- essary. Despite the mud and blood coating his skin, Tremayne Hawthorne knew he would forever carry the noble lines and bearing of Reginald Bavington, the sixth earl of Chedgrave, upon his tall frame. His mother's ultimate revenge: While Chedgrave's legal wife had produced but one sickly boy child, the ille- gitimate Tremayne developed into an exceptionally

robust duplicate of the earl, from the thick tawny hair
crowning his head to the mud-encrusted toes of his
feet, from the uncompromisingly straight carriage of
his shoulders to the impressive bulges threatening to
pop the buttons of his homespun jailhouse shirt, from
the wintry blue Bavington eyes to the husky, cultured
accent of his voice.

Tremayne subsided against the wall, pressing his
full weight back, ignoring the agony when the wallpa-
per adhered to his torn flesh, taking perverse pleasure
in imagining his rusty silhouette greeting McKittrick
every time he stepped into this dismal room.

Farnsworth tilted a barely polite nod toward
McKittrick, his lip curling as if he shared Tremayne's
distaste for the jailer. "Let me preface this conversation by saying I would much prefer conducting it in
private. Mister McKittrick, however, has refused this
slight courtesy."

McKittrick looked not at all abashed. "We can call
Mr. Stringer in to take my place, or we can bring this
interview to an end now. Under no circumstances will
I leave a criminal of his repute unguarded. As I told
you, I have an urgent matter to attend. Besides, this
man has no secrets from me."

Farnsworth sighed and visibly stiffened his spine.
"Very well. His lordship asked me to remind you once
again, Tremayne, how you spurned him when he sent
me to offer his assistance five months ago, after he'd
heard about your, er, little spot of trouble."

Little spot of trouble? Tremayne felt his shoulders
shake with mirth. "Such a masterpiece of understate-
ment, Farnsworth. An allegation that could lock a

man away for the rest of his natural life is indeed a bit of an inconvenience. I'd prefer hearing that my father is stricken with remorse over his shabby treatment of my mother, including his failure to acknowledge her death." More than his bruised throat lent huskiness to his voice. Grief and guilt burned within him.

"His lordship regrets many things," Farnsworth said, his manner appropriately subdued. "And that is why he sent me again, to try to set things to rights."

"He missed his opportunities."

Farnsworth proceeded as though Tremayne hadn't spoken. "Young Richard, your father's legitimate heir, recently succumbed to fever. And I'm afraid your father's capability for siring another son to inherit Chedgrave is, shall we say, another missed opportunity. The title and estates shall revert to the Crown upon your father's death, which would leave your stepmother and your half sister penniless."

"I can't pretend to offer sympathy," Tremayne said, though he felt an odd twisting near his heart to think that the half brother he'd once wished ill now lay dead, that his half sister would find herself homeless. "You can tell my father he left it too long. With my mother dead, I have no need to hear apologies for his reprehensible behavior."

"Hawthorne, listen well." Farnsworth's well-modulated voice betrayed no emotion as he recited the words Tremayne had ached to hear long ago. "His lordship, the earl of Chedgrave, wishes to publicly acknowledge his former liaison with your mother and claim you as his natural son."

A triumph, the realization of all his mother had

ever wanted. Tremayne tasted naught but bitterness. Had his father's admission of the truth come about three years earlier, Margaret Hawthorne would have been alive to savor the moment.

"Do you understand, Hawthorne, that this action serves to acknowledge you as Chedgrave's legal issue, establishing your status as heir to an earldom?" Farnsworth continued in the stark silence.

For one stunned, bewildered instant, Tremayne imagined the noose still choked him, that the events of the past few moments were naught but the ravings of a head beaten near senseless. He blinked, certain he'd find Stringer's malicious sneer peering back at him once he reopened his eyes, but Farnsworth's sober countenance continued to regard him; McKittrick's broad, suety face turned impatiently from one to the other, anxious to bring this strange interview to an end. Tremayne heard an odd little laugh, something between humor and disbelief, and realized the sound had come from himself.

He raised a hand, marveling that it trembled not at all, and pointed toward the fretting McKittrick. "He might have something to say about that. It's his job to keep me here, to stand trial for the murder of my wife and son."

If this blunt admission startled Farnsworth, he didn't show it. McKittrick's words breached the tension.

"This is all very touching, gentlemen, but Hawthorne speaks the truth. You may tell your earl his son's here for the duration. I'd not have wasted my time if I knew you meant to discuss something this preposterous. Now, I'd see this interview finished."

"I have been authorized by his lordship to offer several thousand pounds to grease the prison doors open. He understands that a lack of operating funds has caused this delay in bringing Hawthorne to trial." Farnsworth spoke so low, none outside their small circle could have heard.

McKittrick reacted with annoyance. "A bribe? Use your head, man. The court may be unfunded at present, but I have wealth to spare. Why would I jeopardize my good name over—"

"I'll fetch your daughter back home for you."

Tremayne scarcely recognized his own voice, so hoarse and swift was his outburst. To think that a chance comment overheard while he was being pummeled into near unconsciousness might provide him with the opportunity for freedom, to set things right! Feelings, stifled deliberately over the past months, poked tentative fingers into his heart: hope, excitement, a surging awareness of his strength and ability.

McKittrick's face blanched. "How do you know of my daughter's disappearance?"

"Stringer's been announcing it to all and sundry," Tremayne stretched the truth a bit. "He makes no secret of how he relishes the assignment."

McKittrick's face managed to turn even paler. "I specifically swore him to silence." An angry red mottling replaced his pallor. "You have a hell of a nerve suggesting such a thing—you're nothing but a cold-blooded murderer, Hawthorne. The minute these gates swing open for you, you'd bolt like a jackrabbit. And I'd be a laughingstock."

"Not if you held Farnsworth hostage as assurance

against my return," Tremayne interjected, nodding toward the Englishman.

Farnsworth's eyes all but popped from his head. I . . . no! . . . absolutely not . . . unthinkable!"

"Stringer said your daughter's hiding in Kansas. I know the territory," Tremayne said, his mind working furiously to devise a feasible plan. McKittrick was a man like any other, a fact easy to forget under the circumstances. As such, he would want assurances. "The way it stands now, my case won't be heard for months yet. I'd need only a little time away from the jail. Time to collect some vital information I left behind in Caldwell before I fetch your girl."

"Collecting vital information? Bah. Anyone can fetch information. You're looking to run away or murder again." McKittrick's lips formed a thin, uncompromising line.

"If I'm not back, ready and willing to stand trial before anyone has the chance to miss me, you can cut Farnsworth's throat and place the blame upon me." Tremayne ignored Farnsworth's strangled-sounding gasp. "Say I killed him and then escaped. Hell, save face and blame me for your daughter's disappearance—tell everyone I kidnaped her when I escaped. Use that bribe my father offered you to post a reward. Every lawman and bounty chaser in the country would be after me. I wouldn't stand a chance."

"Preposterous," McKittrick said, his voice scarcely above a whisper as he groped for a chair to settle into. He blinked several times, staring at nothing, before beginning to talk in a low tone, as if to himself. "Eleanor was so prostrated with grief over her mother's death that she didn't act rationally. My daughter inherited some rather distressing tendencies from her mother. The girl's completely incompetent. Some might even call her lunatic. I suspected she was up to something like this when I heard her pock-faced freak of a friend purchased passage for two to Kansas."

"I refuse to be a party to this," Farnsworth stated.

"It seems you ought to be willing to do anything to effect a reconciliation between my father and me," Tremayne challenged the solicitor, who closed his jaws with a snap. "After what you've told me today, I'd say the stakes are rather high. I cannot entrust this information I need to anyone else. You must act as hostage until I return. Otherwise, McKittrick risks losing his daughter, and my father will be burying another heir. It seems a fair trade to me."

"'Tis God's will!" McKittrick shouted suddenly, startling Tremayne and drawing a sharp yelp from Farnsworth. A fanatical light sparked the jailer's eyes. "You return my daughter to me, and I return the earl's son to him." With each word he spoke, his concerned-father veneer slipped a little, revealing an icy animosity. "They thought nobody would report back to me that they bought homestead land from the railroad agent. I know exactly where the little chit's gone."

Tremayne felt apprehension at the malice revealed in McKittrick's voice. Never before had the man exposed anything of his nature save for a cold professionalism that had earned the inmates' grudging respect despite the inexplicable unease they felt in his presence. Of course, it was suspected that the excessively harsh discipline meted out by Stringer and his ilk had McKittrick's silent approval, but nothing had ever been proven. The jailer always seemed dismayed when some poor soul's broken body found its way to the infirmary. Hadn't he, just moments ago, sworn to take Stringer to task for hurting Tremayne?

Tremayne shook his head. McKittrick's lapse had an explanation: The girl had run off in a fit of grief, and the man was naturally upset and concerned over her safety. Look at what lengths his own father was willing to go to achieve a reconciliation.

"If you suspected her intentions, you might have stopped her, then, and saved us all this trouble," Farnsworth groused.

McKittrick's venomous chuckle called forth the image of a coiled snake timing its deadly strike. "No, Mr. Farnsworth, if I'd have stopped her before she got away, she'd have never ceased plotting another escape. But to drag her home after she thinks herself safe . . . ah, she'll know there's nowhere to run where I can't find her. The lesson's better taught when the student thinks he's fooled his teacher, and the switch across his ass tells him otherwise."

"Why not fetch her yourself?" Farnsworth persisted.

Tremayne leveled a smoldering glance at the solicitor, intending to pummel him into silence if he made one more protest. "Bloody hell, Farnsworth. You act as if you fear I don't intend to honor my word."

Farnsworth scowled, an embarrassed blush staining his cheeks. "I just want to know why a man wouldn't go after his own flesh and blood."

"Why didn't my father come after me?" Tremayne asked.

McKittrick's amiable expression dissolved into swirling, bitter anger, as if annoyed that their conversation had drifted away from him. "Your father has the right attitude, Hawthorne. Going after her myself would give my darling daughter an undeserved sense of importance. Eleanor erred grievously in leaving her place. She must be brought to heel, like any whining bitch who can't learn to obey her master. Having a murderer drag her back will help her realize the extent of her mistake. She knows where she truly belongs. Here. With me. But I'd not have her mistreated, and I'll admit there's that risk with Stringer involved. It seems God himself has presented this opportunity. You have three weeks to take care of your business in Caldwell and bring Eleanor home."

"We'll want this arrangement legitimized on paper, of course," Farnsworth stated, accepting the terms on Tremayne's behalf.

McKittrick shot him a look fraught with incredulous scorn. "I bend the rules far enough as it is by allowing men like Hawthorne to work outside in the fields. If Judge Parker heard about *this* little arrangement, I'd be hauled up before him myself. You're as mad as my daughter if you think I'll commit any of this to writing."

"But what guarantees will I have about my safety?" Farnsworth blustered in protest. "And we must notify

the earl! He is waiting to hear when he might antici-
pate Tremayne's arrival."

Tremayne raised a silencing hand. "No scrap of
paper could hold me on course if I choose to run. Nor
could one force McKittrick to stand by an agreement
so obviously detrimental to his position. It's apparent
none of us trusts the other, and yet none of us is in a
position to bypass this opportunity. I have given my
word. So perform your duty, Farnsworth, as befits a
command from the heir to Chedgrave."

Farnsworth closed his eyes, and gave Tremayne a
curt nod. "Yes, my lord."

No rusty lock need be pried open. No forbidding
wall breached. No need to strain one's ears forevermore listening for the sound of bloodhounds baying
at his heels. To a man who'd sometimes despaired
over the hand dealt him by fate, it seemed almost too
easy to believe.

Such a simple thing, to haul a headstrong, runaway
miss back to her loving father. Though Tremayne
fleetingly wished McKittrick's almost maniacal diatribe revealed more caring and less vindictiveness, his
own incarceration in the Barracks Courthouse jail
proved intense emotion often made a man behave in
ways alien to his nature.

Yes, putting an end to Eleanor McKittrick's grief-
provoked flight was an opportunity too good to be
missed. After all, if Tremayne declined the assignment, McKittrick would only send Stringer after the
girl. She'd be brought back one way or another. To a
luxurious, if somewhat dreary home, to a cold-
natured father with power and money to spare. Not

unlike what Tremayne's own future held in store.
He'd waited a decade to make peace with his father;
perhaps in exchange for bringing her back, he could
spare the unknown Eleanor those long years of gut-
churning anger, and regret.

"I'll need some money," Tremayne said. "And
some regular clothes."

"Done," said McKittrick. "Praise be to God!"

Jessop Farnsworth heaved a resigned sigh.

The next morning, Silas Stringer groaned, pressing
the heel of his hand into his temple to stop the incessant banging that threatened to shatter his skull. No
relief. The hammering continued, each thud driving a
dull wedge deeper into the whiskey-soaked mess last
night's revels had made of his mind. He rubbed his
hand over his forehead, feeling little bumps throb
against the tight skin. Damn that son of a bitch
Englishman. If he hadn't stuck his goddamned British
nose in McKittrick's business, Stringer would be
clutching the boss's daughter instead of his hung-over
head. Just the thought of what he'd missed out on
raised another insistent flurry of pounding, and he
swore, recognizing the noise as someone beating on
his door.

"Stringer!" There was no mistaking his boss's irate
voice. "Open this door immediately."

Shee-it. He'd hoped McKittrick wouldn't catch
him out so soon in the day. But the hell with him.
Knowing McKittrick, and the delight he took in tormenting people for no good reason, he'd probably

jumped at the chance to snatch the plum job away from him. Stringer groaned again at another barrage of pounding. Aiming a wavering foot at the wooden bar haphazardly jammed in brackets, he kicked the makeshift lock free, springing the door open for McKittrick to enter.

The jailer's beefy frame blocked most of the sunlight eking through the door, but Stringer winced at the golden brightness. McKittrick's red, puffy lip curled with derision, his piggish nose twitching at the reek that always filled Stringer's bunkhouse for a few days following a night like the one before.

"You said you didn't have anything for me to tend to today," Stringer said, his mood as sour as his mouth tasted.

"Correction. I said you could forgo your normal duties in favor of looking after our hostage."

Stringer scowled. "I told you I ain't no goddamned governess. Besides, I locked old Farnsworth out in the pigsty. Stuck-up son of a bitch ain't never been around hogs before. He's so scared of that old boar, he ain't budged but two feet in any direction."

"Indeed?" McKittrick lifted a skeptical brow. "And when was the last time you checked on him?"

"Right after Hawthorne left. . . . Hell, maybe it was last night. I don't remember." Stringer eased himself up until he reclined on his elbows, the bunk's rusted springs squealing like the pigs guarding Jessop Farnsworth.

"You don't remember." McKittrick's beefy face darkened, taking on a mottled cast Stringer had seen once on a man who'd dropped dead of an apoplectic fit. "He's gone, you drunken whoremonger. While you were debauching yourself with spirits and loose women, he overcame his so-called fear of hogs. The Lord sent him to me, and your satan-inspired behavior—"

Stringer groaned again, closing his ears to the Bible-thumping diatribe. McKittrick's voice grew shriller, his color heightening, leading Stringer to entertain the hope that the jailer might after all have that apoplectic fit. But then the federals would appoint another jailer, one less inclined, perhaps, to condone the sort of work Stringer took such pleasure in performing. Stringer unashamedly played upon McKittrick's unstable sanity and religious delusions, even played upon his vanity by granting him the inflated title of warden, with the side benefit that McKittrick thus believed that Stringer was some sort of angel of vengeance, sent to wreak punishment against those who had wronged innocent people. McKittrick embraced the notion with a fervor that left Stringer certain the jailer wouldn't mind meting out some of those overblown punishments himself.

"The Lord giveth, and the Lord taketh away." Stringer mumbled the only faintly biblical phrase he could muster, anxious to calm McKittrick down and earn a little quiet for his aching head. "Get off your high horse, Warden. I'll track him down for you. A hoity-toity British lawyer stinking like pig shit shouldn't get too far."

"Oh, no. That will never do." McKittrick's eyes took on the fanatical light that usually accompanied his rapt attention when Stringer described some particularly satisfactory form of punishment. "This is a sign. The bargain I struck has met with the Lord's displeasure. It stands no more. Forget the lawyer, he means nothing. You go after Tremayne Hawthorne. He is on his way to his former homestead near Caldwell, Kansas. I shudder to think what harm he might cause. Oh, to think I set the man free! I shall surely burn if he kills again. He is the devil's instrument, preying on my weakness to tempt me into flouting the laws of our land, while he roams free for God alone knows what nefarious purposes."

"Should of stuck to the original plan," Stringer agreed, still annoyed that Hawthorne had beat him out of chasing down McKittrick's daughter.

"You are being tested, too," McKittrick said.

Stringer sighed. But the jailer's next words added a tiny curl of dread to the morning-after discomfort already churning in his guts.

"I have noticed a distressing decline in your abilities, Stringer, which I directly attribute to your drunkenness and penchant for fornication. The Silas Stringer I've known for these many years would never have permitted a hostage to escape him. Perhaps God induced me to allow Hawthorne time enough to tend to his own business before fetching my daughter so you may prove your worthiness to continue in this work. You stop him, Stringer, before he causes any more harm. If you cannot return Hawthorne, you will be marked as unworthy by the Lord. You have already failed me by forcing me to depend upon outside sources to learn my daughter meant to leave home. And now you have let your sinful ways provide the opportunity for Farnsworth's escape."

Stringer bit back an angry retort. McKittrick had never let Stringer get so much as a glimpse of his precious daughter; how was he supposed to keep her from running away? Well, maybe he had slacked off over Farnsworth, but he wouldn't have been drinking away his annoyance if Hawthorne hadn't suckered McKittrick into letting him go after the girl.

Stringer remembered his first glimpse of Tremayne Hawthorne and the instant dislike he'd taken to him. Held himself like a goddamned king, and though Hawthorne had never made an issue of it, some of the inmates had discovered he'd been born on the wrong side of some English nobleman's blanket. As if that made a difference here. But it had been one more thing turning Stringer against the man.

Now the son of a bitch could cost him his job. Stringer tightened his jaw. Hawthorne would pay.

"He don't have but a one-day head start. I'll bring him back to you, Warden," he vowed. "It shouldn't be too hard to catch up with him, 'specially after that beating he took. You care if he's dead or alive?"

"No."

That sweetened the task somewhat. Maybe there was something to McKittrick's incessant blathering about the will of God—dislike him as he might, Stringer could never have killed Hawthorne outright while he remained on territorial courthouse grounds.

But maybe not. Though Farnsworth had squirmed free, the fact that he'd agreed to act as a hostage hinted at Tremayne Hawthorne's importance. It seemed foolish to kill a man who might be worth something alive. Maybe more than a little ransom money could be squeezed from the Englishman's family, if the right pressure—such as holding a knife against Hawthorne's neck—could be applied.

"I'll get him. And I'll pick up your daughter along the way."

A worry line puckered McKittrick's brow. "You mustn't do anything to Eleanor—"

"Hawthorne, that, uh, watchacallit, instrument of the devil, is the one who put that idea into your head, Warden." It felt good to turn McKittrick's words against him. But as for promising not to do anything to the mysterious Miss McKittrick . . . well, a man was entitled to some reward for his troubles.

"I'm sure the Lord will inspire my behavior once I catch up with your daughter," Stringer added with an anticipatory smile.

2

Magnolia, Kansas

Dawn came fast on the prairie, and its first faint glimmer peeped over the horizon. Tremayne spared a moment to remember how he'd relished greeting the sun each morning, tipping his face to the sky, while his wife Darla had preferred pulling the blankets over her head to snatch another hour or two of sleep. Greeting the dawn—just one of many pleasures they'd never shared. He forced the memory from his mind. He would return to it later, when he could pull it out and examine it at length, when he could let his rage and fury build to explosive levels. Oh, yes, he'd travel to England and deal with his father. But first he meant to finish what he'd started *here,* before they'd caught him and clapped him into chains.

For now he need only concentrate on the miserable homestead growing visible beneath the brightening sky, and figure how best to capture the prey cowering within. The low-slung dugout sat off to his right. A few hundred yards of trampled, grassless dirt marked their yard and separated the dugout from a half-eroded sod barn. Warped cottonwood rails formed a shaky corral next to the barn, holding in two skinny mules. Bloody hell—the place looked so pitiful, he ought to try introducing himself and stating his purpose. If Eleanor McKittrick had any sense at all she'd rush straight into his arms and beg to be taken home.

The horse he'd hired from the Wichita livery looked asleep on its hooves. Nonetheless, Tremayne looped the reins around a low-hanging cottonwood branch. The women might scream, rousing the beast and sending it stumbling across the prairie.

Light illuminated the dugout's only window, the steady glow of a lantern. So they were early risers, Miss Eleanor McKittrick and her friend Lauretta Myers. That would save him the trouble of ordering Eleanor into clothes suitable for traveling.

He knew their lantern light would transform the single window pane into a mirror casting back their own reflections should one of them glance outside. Still, he crouched low as he ran, glad his feet made no sound on the hard-packed dirt leading to the dugout.

The eastern sky gleamed a watery grayish white that illuminated the makeshift dwelling. Whoever built it had hacked into a low-rising prairie swell and no doubt dug down to create the floor, since the front wall rose little more than five feet above the ground.

He would have to stoop to enter. There was no door to batter down, merely a moth-ridden buffalo hide tacked to the wooden frame that didn't quite seal the entire doorway.

He waited for the wind to send the hide flapping and timed his entry to its rhythm, slipping through the gap so quietly, so unobtrusively, that they didn't notice his presence at once.

He held himself absolutely still, scarcely daring to breathe, as he studied the surroundings, seeking what he might use to his advantage. Though the lantern burned, it seemed scarcely brighter within the shelter than outside in the predawn gloom. The dugout walls glistened in the dim light, moisture oozing down their crumbling surface. No more than twelve feet square, the dark, low room contained little more than day-to-day necessities. They used a carton for a table, nail kegs for chairs. They probably shared the lone bed, a boxlike affair consisting of rough boards pounded into the dirt wall to support one side, set atop chunks of tree trunk to keep it above the floor. He imagined the cords threaded over the boards groaned in protest each time they settled their slight weight onto it, that the mattress stuffed with prairie hay would do little to prevent the tight-stretched rope from digging into their bodies as they tossed and turned.

Any doubts Tremayne felt over taking Eleanor back home receded. No sane person would want to live this way.

One female form, clad from head to toe in bee-keeping gear though she tended a primitive bake oven, could only be Lauretta Myers.

The other woman had to be Eleanor McKittrick.

He touched his pocket, feeling the familiar stiffness of the photograph McKittrick had given him to help identify her. Faced with the living, breathing woman, he felt stunned by the inadequacy of the photograph. Until this moment, he'd fooled himself into believing the jailer's daughter was no more real than the pale, flat photographic image.

She stood near the bed, folding a blanket with that supremely gratified expression some women conveyed when occupied with household tasks they enjoyed, oblivious not only to him but to the smear of mud cresting the curve of her cheek, to the dust dimming the chestnut gleam of her hair. Her charcoal-colored gown appeared stained a deep black from ankle to knee. Like a lamp wick, it had probably absorbed moisture from the ground. Tremayne shook his head slightly. He understood all too well the constant, futile battles with dirt and water that plagued dugout living. He wondered how Eleanor McKittrick exuded such obvious pleasure while literally burying herself in Kansas mud.

His motions caught Lauretta's attention. Swiveling her veiled head toward him, she let loose with an ear-piercing shriek of such intensity that not even the sound-deadening dugout walls managed to absorb it. Eleanor dropped the blanket and whirled about, her eyes widening at the sight of him.

And then the jailer's incompetent, insane daughter pulled a shotgun from the folds of her gown, leveled it at his gut, and fired.

*　　　*　　　*

"Oh, Lordy, Lordy, you shot him, Ellie. You shot him dead!" Lauretta's excited babbling managed to sound both admiring and fearful as she rushed to the intruder, who'd fallen as if he'd been poleaxed.

"I did not," Ellie denied, coughing a little and waving her hand in a futile attempt to dispel the choking smoke that had followed the shotgun's retort. "Well, I did shoot him—but I couldn't have killed him. I aimed for his arm."

"You've been telling me for days that you keep missing those practice targets because the gun pulls to the right. You shot him dead, Ellie. I'll bet you got him right in the heart."

"Nonsense." She couldn't have killed a man, wouldn't have killed a man, even though he'd invited any manner of punishment by sneaking up on them like that. She pressed a hand to her heart to still the fearful fluttering that had commenced the moment she caught sight of him, but the sensation only seemed to worsen seeing him lying there, so ominously still.

Lauretta crouched beside him. "I can't see where the bullet went in." She poked the man's chest, drawing forth a low moan. With a frightened squeak she scurried back, diving like a child for safety behind Ellie's skirt.

"You see? I told you he wasn't dead." Relief washed through Ellie, along with a realization of her responsibilities. She'd shot him—now she'd have to tend his wound and send him on his way. And she'd have to comfort Lauretta.

Hard to credit now how Ellie had believed

Lauretta's freedom granted her a suave worldliness, an invulnerability to the terrors Ellie found so all-pervasive. The past few days had taught Ellie that her own business sense was keener, her own handling of day-to-day activities more sober and mature. In some ways, Lauretta was little more than a child—a warmhearted, playful child determined to live every day to the fullest; in many ways like Ellie's mother, needing protection and assurance that everything would turn out all right, but loving her wholeheartedly in return.

"Fetch a pillow so we can get his head up off the ground." Ellie dropped to her knees beside the man after first making certain her shotgun stayed within reach.

In her usual quick manner, Lauretta was stuffing the pillow beneath the stranger's head before Ellie had done little more than unfasten one button of his worn homespun shirt. While Ellie's fingers hovered over the next button, Lauretta withdrew her hand and stared, dumbfounded, at the crimson blood smearing her skin.

"Oh, Lordy," she whispered. "You shot him in the back of the head."

"How could I shoot him in the back of the head when he was facing me?" Ellie asked. She glanced at the low-hanging door frame and saw a strand of tawny hair dangling from a splinter. She understood at once what must have happened. "I shot him in the arm, and the impact knocked him back against the doorway. He just cracked his skull against the lintel. Look, I'll bet there's not a mark on him."

Her fumbling fingers had made little progress with his buttons. Eager to prove her point, she simply wrenched his shirt open, and both of them gasped in astonishment.

She was not completely ignorant of the way a man's chest might look. Many times she had watched from the window while her father's laborers worked in the distance, stripped to the waist. Her favorite book, *Art Treasures of Italy,* had featured Michelangelo's *David* from the waist up. But those far-off figures, that perfect marble-sculpted image, didn't quite measure up to the warm, breathing flesh filling her vision. She folded the shirt wider apart to reveal the full extent of those broad, flat, muscular planes. His middle, narrower, but projecting the tensile strength of steel, rippled with each faint breath, revealing tight bands of muscle. Perfection. *David* in the flesh—except for the hideous marks of violence despoiling him from waist to neck.

What looked like rope burns creased his torso and encircled his neck in a parody of a necklace. Bruises blossomed over his stomach and abdomen like sinister flowers, deep purple at their centers, fading to sickly greens and yellows near the edges. He'd endured a beating, there could be no doubt, and perhaps more than one well-aimed kick. Abrasions marred his flesh, scabbed over but obviously little more than a few days old. But no fresh blood. Not a drop. She wasn't responsible for any of this.

With shaking fingers, she pulled the edges of his shirt together, fastening the buttons she hadn't torn off all the way up to his neck, as he'd worn them. It shouldn't matter to her, but she felt certain he would hate having his injuries exposed to them like this.

"Maybe he's a brawler," Lauretta suggested, peering over Ellie's shoulder. "One of those boxing fellows."

"I don't think so. Not with that nose." Boxing had been one of her father's passions; he'd arranged matches between willing inmates and regaled his wife and daughter with sordid accounts of the bouts. Proud and straight, this man's nose had never been broken during a boxing match.

"Maybe he's a murderer. A debaucher of women. A . . . a bounty man!" Lauretta gulped, then broke the stoic silence they'd maintained concerning the fear dogging them since leaving home. "Oh, Lordy, you don't think your father sent him after us, do you, Ellie?"

"I don't know." Each day, Ellie tried to think up a new reason to convince herself that her father wouldn't dare come after her. But she remembered all too well how he'd terrorized her and her mother, how he'd relished describing the agonizing punishments they would suffer at the hands of his trusted tracker if either of them dared leave him—a man her father called too sadistic to ever be appointed a bona fide U.S. Marshal. Ellie had actually seen the man once. Wakened by a midnight commotion, she'd peered through her window to see her father speaking in low tones to an apparition in black, a tall, forbidding carrion crow of a man, a malevolent figure who even now haunted her dreams. "I told you about the man

who runs my father's . . . errands. He doesn't look
like that man."

"Silas Stringer," Lauretta responded promptly.
"Tall and skinny, greasy haired and ugly. No, I don't
guess this is that Stringer fellow." She chuckled, a
surprisingly ribald sound, as she returned her attention to the prostrate stranger. "This sure is one fine-
looking man."

"I suppose so." Actually, Ellie thought he looked
entirely too menacing for one knocked unconscious.
With each shallow breath, his shirt buttons strained,
the homespun pulling tight across his chest. That
proud straight nose topped a chin that jutted with
remarkable firmness in repose. Long lashes, much
darker than his hair, spiked low over his cheeks. A
day's growth of bristling beard sculpted his features.
And surrounding it all, thick tawny-gold hair framed
his head, rather like a rough-cut lion's mane.

His breath stilled, and then he gasped, a harsh,
pain-wracked sound bursting from him as his chest
heaved. "The mission!" he bellowed before falling
silent save for the harsh, rasping sound of his breath.

"A priest?" Lauretta sounded doubtful. "He
doesn't look like one."

"No, he doesn't," Ellie agreed.

His arms thrashed and she saw the blood then.
She'd been right; for once her aim had struck true.
Her shotgun pellets had gouged shallow, bloody
channels along his left forearm. She gave herself a
mental shake. How could they have stood there gaping at him while his life's blood soaked into their
floor?

No—how could they have forgotten how skillfully he'd come up behind them? Though her mind raced, she couldn't imagine one honorable purpose for such behavior, only sinister intent. What had Lauretta suggested—that he might be a murderer, a debaucher of women? This apparent helplessness could be a ruse. Like a lion feigning sleep, waiting for a curious antelope to come and investigate, he might even now be bunching his muscles for a lightning-quick, lethal leap.

"No time to waste," he muttered.

She could make no sense of his ranting. His voice grated, rough as if from disuse, or from inner damage caused when that rope had been wrapped around his neck tight enough to leave a burn.

"Maybe we should tie him up." She wondered anew what he had done to merit the beating he'd taken.

Lauretta must have shared some of Ellie's fears, for she nodded. "But don't you think we should at least drag him over to the bed? This floor's so awful damp since you pulled up the cottonwood boards."

"We'll tie him first."

She used the sash of her dress to bind his wrists, uncertain that such a flimsy length of wool would prove much of a barrier if he sought to twist his huge, callused hands apart.

They tried moving him to the bed, their exertions proving only that his stupor was no sham, for surely no conscious man would silently endure such rough tugging, such ineffectual wrenching of his wounded limbs. "He'll just have to lie there," Ellie gasped, bracing herself against the doorway to catch her breath, noting sourly that his position hadn't shifted by more than a couple of inches.

"We need help," Lauretta agreed. "I'll go get some."

"Lauretta, we're four miles away from our nearest neighbor. It will take hours to fetch help. *I'm* not staying alone with him—what if he wakens?"

"Well . . ."

They'd been friends for so long that the tilt of Lauretta's bonneted head revealed as much to Ellie as most people's facial expressions. "Well?" she prompted, certain Lauretta's cheeks blazed scarlet beneath her bee veil.

"I could ask Hiram to help us," Lauretta whispered, her head hanging low.

"Hiram? That squatter? He's just lucky I chased him off before I learned how to shoot well enough to hurt him, too!"

The mere thought of how forcefully she'd run off the skinny, malaria-plagued wretch was enough to ease Ellie's apprehensions over dealing with the stranger lying at her feet. For a moment—and then her stomach knotted again. What if, like Hiram, the golden-haired stranger had simply blundered in on them, innocently assuming he could enjoy a few hours' sleep in an abandoned dugout, only to be shot?

"Oh, God." Ellie groaned, covering her eyes with her hand.

"Don't be mad," Lauretta implored. "You heard him promise to help out whenever the shakes don't grab him too hard." At Ellie's baffled stare, she continued. "Hiram, Ellie. I found him camped out by the creek when I was out looking for blue gum logs for my bees. I just felt so sorry for him, he looked so downhearted and lonely. I know you said he had to leave, but I told him he could stay in that old falling-down soddie barn across the yard."

"Lauretta." Ellie's reprimand clogged in her throat. Lauretta's hands were clasped before her; her small form bobbed up and down on her toes. That blasted bee bonnet projected such a jaunty tilt, the veil itself quivering with excitement. Hiram Espy—now she understood why, despite their isolation, Lauretta continued shrouding herself in her veil.

Ellie swallowed her disapproval. This wild, lonely prairie existence suited her just fine, but Lauretta, staunchly ignoring the pitying stares and whispered comments, had been accustomed to a broader social life, a continual mingling with other folks. No doubt she found herself lonely with only Ellie for company, so starved for companionship that she welcomed the presence of one man knocked unconscious and one shaking with the ague.

"I'll go fetch Hiram," Lauretta trilled, taking Ellie's silence for acquiescence.

"I'm here, Miss Lauretta."

The buffalo hide swept aside to admit Hiram Espy. His narrow chest heaved with exertion. Sweat filmed his pale forehead, plastering his dark, rough-shorn hair against his skull. He clutched a gnarled cottonwood branch, probably for balance as much as protection. "I heard the shot and come runnin' fast as I could. You ladies hurt?"

Lauretta's entire frame beamed a welcome. "No, we're fine, Hire. Ellie protected us. This fellow's hit his head, though. We'd like to get him up off the floor."

Hiram cast one quick, nervous glance toward Ellie. "Yer aim's improved some, ma'am." Setting the cottonwood branch against the wall, he assigned one of the stranger's brawny ankles to each of them before taking position at the man's head. Showing surprising, wiry strength, he easily hefted the intruder's solidly muscled upper body while Ellie and Lauretta groaned beneath his weighty legs.

They settled the stranger on the straw-stuffed mattress, making him as comfortable as they could despite those ridiculously long legs dangling over the edge of the bed.

"You ladies think you'll be all right now?" Hiram asked. "You need to fan yerselves or drink tea or somethin'?"

Ellie's face heated, embarrassed that the man she'd run off was proving to be so protective and thoughtful. Lauretta giggled, seeming pleased and proud and not at all angered that Kansas men showed a penchant for barging into their home every five minutes.

Keen disappointment knifed through Ellie, probing at each of her flaws. She'd misjudged Hiram. Shot—perhaps fatally—a man—perhaps innocent. Her own company wasn't enough for Lauretta; her strength had failed its first test, not even equal to that of an ague-wasted, half-starved squatter. Perhaps her father had been right to keep her under lock and key all these years—she couldn't manage on her own. And then she shook her doubts away, angry that she'd let such muddled thoughts enter her mind at all.

"Thank you, Hiram."

His happy smile lifted her spirits just a little.

"We'll be fine," she added, just as the stranger's hand shot out, his fingers encircling her wrist like manacles of welded steel.

3

Tremayne's thumb decided of its own accord to trace the petal-soft skin pulsating delicately at the juncture between her palm and wrist. Only one feminine wrist warmed his grasp, but two winsome women peered down at him. Twins! Their chocolate-brown eyes widened in matched motion. Women . . . good God, how bloody long had it been since he'd reveled in the sight and scent of a beautiful woman?

At his delighted grin, their identical oval faces first pinkened, then paled; tumbled masses of chestnut-brown hair tangled together, spilling over their shoulders, beckoning a man to bury his fingers in silken softness. He tried. Found it frustratingly impossible to lift his right hand without letting loose of the wrist he grasped in his left. A garbled protest burbled from his throat, and then the women parted their curved lips.

"LLLettt mmmmeee gggooo. . . ."

The twin beauties spoke as if submerged below water, their words bubbling discordantly against his ears. White-hot pain shafted through his skull; he gasped aloud at the strength of it, sending the twins weaving against one another, merging, blending, until his eyes ached from the effort of keeping them straight.

A second set of twins—two decidedly scrawny, wary-looking farmers brandishing clubs—swam into view.

"God damn bloody hell," Tremayne whispered, closing his eyes when understanding at last burst within his throbbing skull. He remembered Eleanor lifting the rifle. The searing pain knocking him back against the wall. His head knocking against the door frame. A goddamned concussion. He'd once acquired one during a childhood scuffle, experiencing the same slow-wittedness, the same double vision, the same helpless weakness gripping his limbs. It all trickled back now: his surroundings, his mission.

He held Eleanor McKittrick quite literally in the palm of his hand, and he could do nothing about it. For now.

He couldn't even hold on when she wriggled herself free. Her movements, though light and gentle, roused an excruciating stinging along his arm. She'd shot him. And no doubt bound his wrists, if the half-numb, half-tingling sensation in his fingers was any clue. He tried to raise his hands to the spot pounding at the back of his head and saw his wrists were indeed inexpertly shackled with a flimsy length of charcoal wool.

How McKittrick would laugh; how Stringer would gloat to see him laid low by a crazy woman; how they both would chortle over the failure of Tremayne's strategy.

Tremayne didn't, for a single minute, trust McKittrick. He knew the jailer expected him to travel first to Caldwell. Most men would, considering that failure to obtain certain information could doom Tremayne to an intimate acquaintance with the gallows. So instead he'd headed straight for Magnolia to fetch Eleanor. He'd hoped the detour would throw off any pursuers, and enable the worst of his bruises to heal. Now, here he lay with a wounded arm and concussed head added to his physical woes.

"Who're you, mister? What're you doin' here?" asked the club-wielding man.

Tremayne might have asked the same questions. How had the women managed to find a protector in such a short space of time? They couldn't have been here for more than a week. He opened one eyelid the narrowest measure, giving the blinding sunlight only a tiny slit to work its damage, so he might assess the unexpected obstacle.

"Hiram—" Lauretta cautioned.

Hiram. An apt name for one so obviously suited to homesteading life. Tremayne's practiced gaze appraised Hiram's lean, stringy frame. Hidden strength there, a body toughened by long hours of heavy work. Though certainly no older than his midtwenties, he stooped around the shoulders, hinting at countless hours spent hunched over a plow. Bucking a plow helped a man develop an iron-hard belly, one impervious to any but the most thundering fists. Not a man Tremayne felt capable just now of confronting, even though Hiram bore the sweat-slicked, feverish countenance of one suffering from the ague.

He swiveled his narrowed glance toward the women standing together at the foot of the bed. Lauretta, looking foreign, clung to Eleanor, her bee-keeping clothes lending her an otherworldly air. Her slight frame shivered with a mixture of excitement and apprehension.

Eleanor McKittrick stood with one arm protectively wrapped about her friend. Her other arm rested at her side, her hand gripping the business end of her shotgun. She held herself with the regal bearing much prized by the women he'd known in England, imparting such an aura of strength and confidence that one could easily be fooled into missing the agitation gleaming in her eyes, the pulse frantically hammering at the base of her throat. His gaze swept to the gun, noting her white-knuckled grip round the barrel. She'd shot him once; with him lying prone at her feet, her aim could be more accurate if she leveled the gun at him again.

It didn't seem like the right time to tell her why he'd come.

But Hiram persisted. "Well, mister?"

"I've come . . ." Damned if his tongue didn't stall, his mind drained empty like a cistern during drought season. He needed but one excuse, one feeble reason to explain his presence, and he could dredge nothing from his scattered wits save his true purpose in being there.

"Yes, tell us why you've come."

Eleanor's voice washed over him, cool and quiet now that the clanging within his skull had dimmed, so soothing he forgot to be careful of the sunlight and opened his eyes wide. Her chin lifted a notch when he winced away from the pain skewering the backs of his eyeballs.

"A job," he murmured, his aching head tempering any amusement he felt at telling her such an ambiguous truth.

"My father didn't send you?"

"Who's your father?" he equivocated, taking no pride in his clever evasion when he saw her brow smooth, her shoulders relax.

"Oh, Ellie, this is perfect!" Lauretta turned all aflutter at Tremayne's statement. Like a nest-building wren in search of the right materials, she dashed to Hiram and squeezed his hand; she whirled back to Eleanor and gripped her forearm; and despite a fearful tremor quaking her arm, she gave Tremayne's knee a hesitant, delicate pat, her quick gestures somehow binding all of them together. "Hiram said he'd build us a sod house, Ellie, except it's a job for two men. Now we have two and we can get one—two men, I mean, and one sod house. Botheration! I'm so excited I can't speak straight!"

Hiram took a protective stance in front of the women, rather like a scrawny stallion standing guard

over his mares. He fixed a ferocious scowl upon
Tremayne. Tremayne wished he could answer with
the intimidating glower that had served him well in
the jailhouse, but any movement of his facial muscles
set his head pounding. He would have to watch for
signs that the sickly farmer might have developed a
troublesome infatuation for Eleanor McKittrick. If so,
the man might try putting up a fight when Tremayne
plucked the woman away.

"You know anything about homesteadin'?" Hiram
jutted a challenging jaw toward Tremayne.

"Enough." Ironic to think that with a single word
he could so easily dismiss the most tumultuous years
of his life.

"There, you see! He's an experienced hand. Just
what we need to help Hire." Lauretta clapped her
hands.

"Lauretta, we should talk about this."

Eleanor McKittrick was her father's daughter, all
right. She'd pitched her voice low, a trick her father
often employed to draw the attention of those bent on
mayhem. The jailhouse inmates usually fell into com-
pliant silence. But on the days when hot tempers prevailed, those who waited too long to obey knew the
quieter McKittrick's voice, the harsher the punishment Stringer later meted out . . . and his daughter
Eleanor's voice sounded ominously quiet as her fingers stroked the gun barrel.

"Now, mister, why don't you tell us your name?"
she said when the room echoed with naught but silent
tension.

"Hawthorne." There seemed no point in refusing

to answer such a reasonable question, but he'd be damned if he'd let the chit grill him while he lay flat on his back. Forcing his body upright, with the gain of a few inches and a grunt punctuating the space between each name, he got it out in full: "Tremayne. Bavington. Hawthorne."

Weak as a newborn babe. He'd have to catch his breath before attempting to stand.

"Yer from England," challenged Hiram. "Yer sort don't know nothin' about farmin'."

Eleanor compressed her lips before speaking. "I'll ask the questions if you please, Mr. Espy."

"Yes, Hiram, do hush up—you're not even supposed to be here, remember?" Lauretta whispered.

Hiram lapsed into silence, sneaking a red-faced look at Eleanor. Tremayne grunted to himself. He'd pegged the man right, already more than half in love with the admittedly attractive but bossy-natured Eleanor. He wondered how many suitors she'd chased off with that fine, proud tilt to her head. Tremayne could have told those foolish, inexperienced swains that they had it all wrong—it was the meek, submissive, clinging women who could ultimately drive some men to murder.

The damned concussion certainly had made a messy muddle of his mind, delving deep to stir up these particular demons, reminding him of what he'd done, of what he had yet to finish. Agony raged through his skull as he quelled memories better left buried. Buried deep, along with his wife and infant son.

"We have to tend to those wounds, Mr. Hawthorne,"

Eleanor said, misunderstanding the true source of his pain.

If only you could, his addled mind whispered.

"What about the sod house?" Lauretta chirped.

"Hell, he don't know nothin' about buildin' sod houses," Hiram chimed in, lending Eleanor his support.

"You have no idea what I'm capable of doing," Tremayne said, irritated beyond reason.

Damn his temper! He wished to call back the words, fearful that the provocative comment might alert Eleanor to his purpose. Instead, everybody seemed to think he meant that he possessed the skills to help them build their damned sod house.

"Lauretta, I just don't think this is a good idea." Eleanor sounded aggrieved.

With a loud, drawn-out sniff and a quiver of her bonnet, Lauretta conveyed the stricken attitude of a martyr. "You're right. We don't need a sod house when we've got a perfectly fine dugout, even though you tore out the wooden floor and we have to walk around in mud all day. I don't really mind the fleas. 'Course, you're only twenty-three and I'm much too close to thirty—I guess the dampness doesn't strike your bones so hard as mine, Ellie, even though I see you racing out into the sun first thing every morning just like me. I purely don't know how I'll warm myself up in the morning once winter sets in."

Tremayne slumped back against the wall, dimly aware that his blood saturated the straw mattress, but unable to stifle the grin prompted by Lauretta's bla-

tant conniving. He peered toward Eleanor to see how
she would put the bonneted minx in her place, and
realized she was completely taken in by Lauretta's
posturing.

Gentleness settled over her features, revealing
what a rigid mask she normally made of her face.
Regret darkened her eyes, subtly altering the shade to
a rich, melting chocolate. A tremulous quiver shook
her lush lower lip. The softness and vulnerability
lasted but an instant; he'd have missed it completely
had he not been studying her covertly.

"I didn't realize, Laurie," she whispered, her words
awash with guilt though her expression betrayed it
not a whit. "I just wanted—"

"You just wanted to do everything around here by
yourself." Lauretta, gracious in victory, curved an
arm around Eleanor's shoulders and gave her a quick
hug. "It's all right to depend on other people sometimes. Now, let's go pick out a nice site for our new
house."

"Look at him, Laurie. He can barely sit up. We
have to do something about his bleeding before you
start pacing off the dimensions of a house you expect
him to build."

"Do you want me to tend him? I'm real quick at
winding bandages." Lauretta obviously had no intention of abandoning her agenda, but seemed amenable
to a slight delay.

Eleanor shook her head. "No, you go on with
Hiram and look for a place. I shot him. I'll clean up
the mess."

It felt curious, listening to himself being discussed

as if he were a side of beef awaiting fileting. But she'd pegged him right—he was indeed a mess, judging by the strange sensation that came over him when Eleanor's eyes met his. Almost as though by keeping his purpose a secret he was lying to her . . . and that it mattered.

He could deal with that easily enough. A man suffering concussion had every reason to keep his eyes closed.

"You're sure you ain't scared to be all alone with him, ma'am?" Doubt fairly dripped from Hiram's voice. Tremayne felt certain that if he opened his eyes he'd see the homesteader hopping from foot to foot in agitation over walking out on his ladylove.

"You don't look like you're up to causing much harm, are you Mr. Hawthorne?" Lauretta added.

No, he meant Eleanor no harm. He'd be doing her a favor by wresting her away from this miserable place and returning her to the oppressive luxury of the jail keeper's well-appointed home. Harm her? When he had everything to gain by returning her safe and sound?

"I wouldn't hurt a hair on her head," he vowed. And he meant it, provided she didn't kick up too much of a fuss on the way back home.

Near Caldwell, Kansas

Stringer crouched and brushed a thick layer of dust from a darkened spot on the abandoned cabin's floor. Dim light filtered through the only window's broken shutter, picking out the stain's rusty color and splattered dimensions. Blood. Spilled months ago. More than a woman's body would hold, it seemed, as Stringer's gaze followed its dark, rusty trail across the rubble-strewn floor and up the walls.

He swallowed, unsettled by the evidence of past savagery. Though Tremayne Hawthorne had often showed flashes of temper, Stringer had always dealt with him from a position of strength, surrounded by the trappings of justice, backed up by a handful of tough, experienced men who brought Hawthorne's raging under control before any harm could be done.

This time, once he caught up with Hawthorne, it would be just the two of them. Man to man. But now Stringer would face him with his mind recalling the image of this charnel house where Tremayne Hawthorne had brutally slaughtered his wife and child.

A black fly flitted through the doorway and buzzed around Stringer's face, showing no interest in the dried blood. And who could blame it—the stains had to be at least five months old. Strange, though, that after all this time no squatters had taken possession of the sturdily built cabin, or that the contents hadn't been hauled off to grace some lesser furnished home.

Maybe the cabin's isolated location had something to do with it. Caldwell, renowned as the Border Queen, marked the boundary between whatever civilization Kansas boasted and the wilds of Indian Territory. As a result, the town held strong appeal for the rough element, since it was easy to slip across the border and virtually disappear whenever the law made an infrequent appearance. The town's motley collection of shacks barely qualified to be called a settlement, and the nearest rail station, Wichita, lay a good sixty miles away.

Despite its bad reputation, the area attracted its share of homesteaders. Rich bottomland lined the banks of the Chikaskia River, the Fall Creek, and Bluff Creek. Hawthorne's homestead lay well outside of town with a view of the Chikaskia, and his land, despite his long absence, testified to its fertility with a heavy crop of weeds.

Stringer felt a contemptuous smile curl his lip. Superstitious farmers were probably afraid to enter where violence had ruled; most likely they thought the contents cursed or haunted by the ghosts of Darla Hawthorne and her infant son.

"What are you doing here?"

Hawthorne! The low, menacing voice, coming hard on Stringer's musings over ghosts, almost bowled him over. His fine-honed instincts took effect a split second later, whirling him to his feet with his pistol in his hand, ready to face whoever had spoken.

"Shee-it," he muttered, seeing a lean, stoop-shouldered old man standing in the doorway, his only weapon a wide-tined hay rake.

"Well?" the old man challenged, taking a step into the cabin.

He pronounced the word *vell*, with a trace of German accent. Stringer had heard that those immigrants known as Pennsylvania Dutch favored this part of Kansas, and the old man's sober appearance seemed to fit the mold. His thin, shoulder-length hair called to mind the streaky color of pissed-on snow. His eyes might once have been as blue as Hawthorne's; now, one wandered, a milky cast marking it as sightless, while the lid squinted so tight over the other Stringer doubted the man could see more than two feet in front of him.

"Was this Tremayne Hawthorne's place?" Stringer asked, keeping his gun trained upon the old man despite his harmless appearance.

"Still is. He proved up on it before he went away. What's it to you?"

"You might say I've been sent to look him up," Stringer said. "He been around here lately?"

"Does it look like anyone's been here?" the old man countered. "You are wanting to see Tremayne, you'll be finding him at Fort Smith. You see him, you tell him old Gus is taking good care of his property till he's found innocent."

"Fort Smith, huh?" Stringer pretended surprise, taking his time to study Gus. The Dutchman's demeanor projected a profound sadness, with nary a hint of deception. If what he said was true, McKittrick had guessed wrong about Hawthorne coming straight to Caldwell after being sprung from the jailhouse. What an irritating, unpredictable bastard.

"Must've done something real bad to get sent up in front of ol' Hangin' Judge Parker," he added, making a sweeping gesture he wasn't sure Gus could see. "There's blood and busted furniture all over this place. What'd he do—kill someone?"

Mistrust and eagerness warred over the old man's face, as if he longed to tell the story but held back out of loyalty. Eventually he sighed and shook his head. "Someone else will be telling you if I don't. They say he killed his family."

"They *say?* Don't you believe it?" Stringer prodded.

Gus sighed again, his shoulders drooping even more. "Tremayne never admitted to it, but what else can a man believe? The law had been alerted and they burst in here and found him sitting on that bed, covered with blood, and mud, from the burying. Not a word would he ever say about what happened that night, so the sheriff is having no choice but to send him to prison for trial."

"Well, he must've done it, then. An innocent man would have defended himself."

"Perhaps." Gus peered at him with his squinty eye. "Were you saying you was Tremayne's friend?"

"An acquaintance," Stringer said. "We've sort of lost touch, but I mean to correct that straightaway."

Gus studied him for a long moment, a dubious frown creasing his forehead. "You will be looking him up at the jailhouse?"

"Sure. I'd be real happy to catch up with him at the jailhouse." Stringer grinned.

"Well, maybe you could be taking him some of his smaller things," Gus spoke with great reluctance, as if he'd been saving up the request and now hated making it. "A man should have his own spoon and razor, but he had no time to gather them up before they hauled him away. I've been keeping watch, but I'm getting older and can't do so good anymore. I would have sent him some things, but it is so hard for me to get to the train at Wichita and the freight, it is costing so dear, you understand?"

"I sure do. It'd be a pleasure for me to deliver Tremayne's things for you."

Gus looked like he wished he could take back his request, so Stringer struck up a lighthearted whistle. The old Dutchman cast a final, doubtful squint in Stringer's direction before leaving the cabin.

Hawthorne's possessions were almost laughably poor, considering his blue-blooded heritage. Stringer found his mind analyzing the old man's information as he searched. Interesting, that the law had been alerted to Hawthorne's crime before the man had had a chance to clean himself up or stick his spoon in his shirt pocket. Interesting, that while Hawthorne had never denied guilt, he'd apparently never admitted it, either—but that was no concern of his.

Stringer scattered the cabin's meager contents about, heedless of maintaining any sort of order. After sitting empty so long, he doubted the cabin would still hold anything of value or import. And yet there was a silver coin, right on the mantel for anyone to see, and there, wedged beneath the mattress, a leather-bound diary, with feminine handwriting scrawled flowery and vivid across its cheap yellowing paper.

He flipped the diary open to a page near the end and read: "I swore to keep his name secret but I find myself possessed of the urge to say it again and again.

Cato, Cato, Cato Crowden. Dare I write it out in full: Darla Crowden."

And on the next page:

"After a month's absence, Cato came for an hour today. These endless days without him have convinced me it's no use pretending anymore. Tomorrow I'll ask Tremayne if he'd mind my leaving."

It was the journal's final entry.

Stringer's low chuckle echoed off the blood-spattered walls. No wonder Hawthorne hadn't wanted to talk about what happened. No man wanted to admit being cuckolded. And no wonder he was so anxious to get out of jail and personally collect this information instead of entrusting it to another. The jury might well see things Hawthorne's way if he conceded the truth and entered this Cato's name into the mix when his case came to trial. No jury could fault a man for murdering a fornicating wife.

It occurred to him, then, that there had been no mention of a man being murdered, only Hawthorne's wife and son. The man must have escaped Hawthorne's killing spree.

Well, it looked like Hawthorne had outsmarted himself by letting the journal fall into Stringer's hands. He stroked the leather greedily, wondering what Hawthorne might be willing to pay to get it back. And maybe more than one party might be interested in its contents—Cato Crowden, for instance.

Gus had disappeared from the yard, his lanky form a barely discernible dot against the horizon. Considering how protective the old man seemed of Hawthorne, he might not be the best source of infor-

mation about the mysterious Cato. But Stringer knew
how to find out information about mysterious men.
He tucked the diary in his shirt pocket, mounted his
livery horse, and spurred it toward Caldwell.

The first whore he asked threw him out of her
room, screeching, "You come across that two-timing
liar Cato Crowden, you tell him he still owes me five
dollars!"

The second refused to speak at all, and as she
turned away, Stringer noticed her touching a thin,
jagged scar marring her neck.

The third smiled wistfully, and after pulling in a
deep breath of resolve, spat on the floor.

The fourth stared at him with eyes that bore the
wounded look of a woman still in love with a rogue.
"He went to Indian Territory," she whispered. "He's a
'breed, you know. You find him, you tell him Mary
Sue's still waiting."

Indian Territory, that vast, lawless expanse to the
south of Kansas, attracted more than its share of
those who'd run afoul of the law. Stringer had no
time to track Cato Crowden there, not even to satisfy
his curiosity. And if Hawthorne had gone after
Crowden into that wild wasteland, he might never be
found.

But Hawthorne couldn't know Jessop Farnsworth
had escaped. And if he wanted to save the solicitor
and return to England to claim his birthright, he'd
have to bring Eleanor McKittrick back home. And
though Stringer had no real idea where Hawthorne
might be at this moment, he knew exactly how to find
Eleanor McKittrick. All he had to do was go to her

place in Magnolia and wait for Hawthorne to show up.

Of course, more than eighty miles of hard riding lay between Caldwell and Magnolia. A man developed a powerful thirst chasing across country that way. Lucky thing Wichita lay smack in his path. Not even Boss McKittrick could say he wasn't entitled to spend a day or two enjoying the big city's delights while he replenished his liquid reserves.

Lauretta and Hiram left the dugout to pace out the sod house's dimensions. Ellie clamped her lips hard to keep from calling them back when Tremayne Hawthorne lurched to his feet a scant moment later. He'd sworn he wouldn't harm her and, truly, he didn't look capable of wreaking much havoc just now, except maybe crushing her to death if his swaying frame toppled over on top of her.

There was so much of him.

He straightened slowly, as if he feared knocking his already-injured skull against the low ceiling. A wise precaution, since the top of his head nearly skimmed the rafters. His bootheels surely accounted for some of his height, but before Ellie glanced at his feet, she found herself distracted in a most unseemly manner by the way his worn homespun britches hung low over his hips and hugged his well-formed legs.

Sunshine filtered through the flour-sack curtain, striking burnished sparks from his long, unruly hair. His hand went to his shirt pocket, his movement drawing the cloth tight against his bulging upper arm. One blunt finger touched the frayed corner of what looked like a photographic cardboard protruding from his pocket. He ran his hand over his head, prodding gingerly and wincing when he found the spot where skull had met door frame. His shredded shirt sleeve, stained harsh crimson, barely covered the mangled mess she'd made of his forearm. At the sound of her indrawn breath, he opened his eyes.

"No apology?" he asked.

"Only for ruining your shirt," she answered. She would *not* beg forgiveness for defending herself against his unannounced intrusion. "I'm afraid that sleeve can't be mended."

"Luckily, what lies beneath it can. I judge it to be no more than a flesh wound." An unfamiliar light glittered briefly in his eyes; his lips parted, their edges twitching in what she would swear was the prelude to a smile. But before his expression softened into anything resembling friendliness, he clamped his jaw tight, his eyes frosting with glacial indifference. With but the slightest inclination of his head, he somehow managed to convey the full-blown image of a polite but uninterested courtier bowing his way clear of an unwanted lady's attentions. "Perhaps it is just as well that there need be no apologies between us."

"Your arm should be tightly bound," Ellie said, swallowing her annoyance. In truth, she'd been expecting some gentlemanly expression of regret from him. "I know something of nursing."

"How did you gain your experience?"

He had some nerve, questioning her abilities. But

then Father had always disparaged her nursing skills, claiming any camp follower could have done better. "I could fetch Lauretta, if you'd prefer. She has actual hospital experience tending men who were wounded during the war. All I did was ease my mother's suffering during her last days," she said through stiff lips.

"I see." His voice thawed a bit, and though he seemed no friendlier, he leaned closer, peering at her, as if he found their mundane conversation intensely interesting. "Caring for loved ones can be a most demanding chore. And when someone you love . . . dies . . . despite your best efforts, it can make you lash out in ways quite out of character."

"That's true. I about went crazy from grief when she passed on," she admitted.

"And what did you do upon your mother's death that you would call 'out of character,' madam?" he asked.

"Well, I . . . I came here." Ellie wondered what it was about his rumbling voice that prompted her to speak so freely. She sternly clamped her lips closed, remembering how she'd warned Lauretta against telling anyone that she'd run away from her father. And here she stood, ready to blurt out that very information to a complete stranger!

A slight curve at the edge of his lips hinted at a smile. "So you wouldn't have gone homesteading if your mother hadn't died?"

"Of course not," Ellie answered, affecting a light tone, thinking how she'd vowed to remain at her mother's side until the end. How glad she would have been to run off years ago, if only her mother hadn't been too sick to come with her. Tremayne seemed set upon questioning her; perhaps that was a side-effect of his head injury. She would safely steer the conversation away from such personal observations by giving him a reason why she and Lauretta had taken to the prairie. "My mother always dreamed of homesteading, so I'm doing it in her memory. Now, Mr. Hawthorne, that wound needs tending immediately."

Her prevarication worked; he looked supremely satisfied by her comments. He said nothing more, merely pressed his wounded arm against his belt. The movement parted his shirt near his waist, exposing a section of firm, bruised skin. It seemed improper to stare at his near-naked belly, so she ventured a glance upward and caught him looking warily at her once again, his wintry eyes narrowed and suspicious as he glared downward at her, not so different from the way a man might regard a balky, unpredictable mule. There he stood, virtually dwarfing her, the air humming with his temporarily abated strength, and he looked as though *he* were afraid of *her,* as if he feared she might be some sort of mad dog apt to bite off his injured arm. She stifled her annoyance, remembering the wounded arm, the blow to his head, which she had caused. She'd had good reason to protect herself; he had equally good reason to question every move she made.

"I'll have to tear up this curtain," she said, lifting the flour sack from the nails holding it against the window. "I washed it yesterday so it's clean—or as clean as anything can be in this place."

"You have no bandages?" He seemed astonished at her lack.

"No." Medical supplies topped the steadily growing list of items she and Lauretta meant to purchase, as soon as Ellie felt safe enough to venture into town.

"Carbolic acid?"

"No. Nothing."

"No carbolic against infection? What about laudanum? Or—good God—don't tell me you women are homesteading here without quinine?"

She tilted her chin, her cheeks burning as embarrassed resentment surged through her. He had no right to lecture her! "We've been here less than a week. Lauretta and I are simply bursting with good health."

"Madam, don't you realize the tiniest pinprick can burst any bubble?" He spoke scarcely above a whisper, advancing upon her until she felt compelled to take one step back, and then another, until she backed up against the table. "You claim to know something of nursing. Have you never seen what can happen if you carelessly tread upon a nail? No doubt half this county suffers from ague and summer complaint. How long do you think your bursting good health will survive intact in this lice-ridden, plague-infested backwater?"

"There's no plague in Kansas."

He shook his head at her, a grimace creasing his forehead when the movement apparently roused some pain. His lips settled into a grim, exasperated line. "It was only a figure of speech."

"As was my comment. Now, will you cease prattling about a situation I mean to correct at the first opportunity, and let me tend that arm for you?"

She challenged him, twisting the flour sack in her hands while she met his icy, superior glower with the cool, calm blankness that had so often served her well when dealing with her father. And it worked. He left off criticizing her to fumble with his wrist buttons.

He pushed the torn, bloodied material up past his elbow, and extended his wounded arm with a rueful grin. And something happened to the air inside the dugout.

Lauretta had tucked the buffalo robe to one side when she left. Fresh breezes gusted through both doorway and window now that no robe or flour sack offered a barrier. Yet Ellie felt as if all the air had been sucked from her lungs, that she might never fill them again unless she matched her breath to the rise and fall of Tremayne Hawthorne's broad chest.

Except for her father, she'd never found herself alone with a man in such small confines. She wondered why her mother had never told her how a man's presence overwhelmed his surroundings. Her senses reeled; it seemed no matter where she looked, her meager belongings served as mere background framing Tremayne. She knew the wind sang outside; knew the kerosene lamp hissed and sputtered; but heard only Tremayne's light breathing. The cloying, earthen dugout smell receded, replaced by a heady scent composed of honest sweat and horse and something primitively masculine.

"Shall I cut the cloth, madam?"

"Oh." She groped over the tabletop for their knife,

and though a warning flared within her, she handed it to him with only the briefest hesitation. Folly to arm a stranger when they were so alone, but cutting the flour sack would occupy his attention, stifling conversation. And somehow she feared a knife in his hands less than the husky edge of his voice. A knife could cut her skin. His voice, too, somehow pierced her skin, striking deep within her, rousing a sweet, aching pain unlike anything she'd ever felt.

He used the hand of his uninjured arm to make quick work of the flour sack. Its stout threads parted like custard before his strength. Each movement he made, from his easy grip on the knife to the tension in his arm as he ripped through the cloth, outlined different bunches of muscles along his forearm.

Dampening a section of cloth, Ellie dabbed the drying blood away from the edges of the shotgun wound. Fine golden hair gilded his arm, so different from the crisp, curling strands showing near his neck. Large, ropy veins mapped him from biceps to the back of his broad hand. Carefully, with great concentration, she began at his elbow and covered every muscle bunch, every vein, every golden hair, with strips of grayish flour sack.

"You'll have to sit so I can see to your head." Her voice sounded scarcely above a whisper.

Scorning the nail kegs, he propped himself against the table, bending slightly at the waist to bring his great, shaggy head to the level of her breast. "There isn't a great deal of blood, just a lump," she told him. The blood had turned sticky, matting his hair, making it difficult to clean, forcing her to stand closer than she liked. She tried to be gentle, but at her touch his breath whooshed from him, warm and heavy, penetrating the charcoal wool and stroking over the crowns of her breasts like a heated, invisible caress.

When she finished, he straightened and held the knife toward her, handle first.

She'd forgotten all about the knife. She accepted it, withdrawing it gently, lest the sharp blade slice his hand. She felt suddenly weak-kneed, remembering the warmth of his breath, realizing how vulnerable she'd left herself by standing so close while he held a knife, how he'd done much the same by relying upon her to tend his wounds.

She tried scolding him back into bed, but Tremayne waved the offer aside, sour distaste churning in his gut. His stomach found it difficult to digest the notion of depriving Eleanor of her bed so he could wallow in its dubious comforts with the specific purpose of regaining his strength to force her home to her father.

"I'll bunk with that Hiram fellow," he said.

"The barn's little better than a falling-down mud heap."

He cast an appraising eye around the dugout, clearly conveying his contempt for the damp, sagging structure. "You can't consider this much better?"

"Please don't mock my home," she said with quiet dignity. "I know it's not much, but it's mine and I love it." After a pause barely brief enough to allow Tremayne to feel a stab of remorse, she continued. "I have to keep those wounds clean if they're to heal. It would be much easier to tend you if you slept here."

She spoke with dispassion, her unflinching gaze daring him to come up with one good reason for thwarting her. He permitted a small, humorless smile to play over his lips. "Are you offering to share your bed, madam?" he asked, his voice growing husky at the image suddenly flooding his mind.

A rosy flush suffused the tender skin above her collar. Tremayne found his attention riveted to its slow progress, his mouth turning dry as the delicate blush stained upward. Eleanor took a deep, deliberate breath, and when next her gaze met his, her expression had been smoothed blank, the enchanting blush dampened down as thoroughly as embers doused by a full bucket of water.

He'd never witnessed anyone—man or woman—successfully exercise such rigid control over her emotions. If he'd been blessed with similar skill, his temper might not have wreaked such havoc throughout his life.

"The barn is outside, I presume?"

Eleanor quirked an amused brow, driving home the inanity of his comment. Bloody hell, his wits must have drained out along with his blood. Well, damn her and her smug, superior smile; damn this distasteful situation. He'd sleep in her damned barn and regain his damned strength and finish the damned mission and be rid of them all and get on with his own damned life. Summoning the shreds of his dignity, he squared his shoulders and took his first step toward the doorway. A severe lightheadedness struck him with something like pain, robbing him of his balance, threatening to send him crashing to the floor.

But she was there. Somehow, she'd sensed his peril and balanced his sagging weight against hers, ignoring his moan of anger and frustration. She inclined her head toward the bed. "No," he rasped.

"Lean on me, then." She pulled his arm round her shoulder. At his humiliatingly weak attempt to withdraw it in protest, she clamped her hand over his, holding it in place.

"I'm strong," she said. "Very strong."

"Not strong enough," he whispered. Another of his inane comments? Or his subconscious taunting him with the knowledge that no amount of strength could withstand the devastation he was about to wreak?

She shrugged, not understanding what he meant, not knowing her misplaced trust in him meant the destruction of her dreams.

They made slow progress across the yard, her slight form bending but not buckling beneath his weight. He felt like a vulture hulking over her, a hidden scavenger awaiting its chance to feast on her defeat.

He shook off the image, cursing the concussion that had rattled his brain. He couldn't let these inappropriate twinges of guilt divert him from completing his mission. Farnsworth's life would be forfeit, and McKittrick would send someone else. Someone else to beat her down and drag her home.

Curse this concussion that seemed set on turning him maudlin! Or maybe it wasn't to be cursed. If this concussion proceeded like the last, he'd spend most of the next few days sleeping off its effects. Oblivion. What a delightful prospect.

"Well," she said when she settled him atop the uncertain comforts of a straw heap. "Perhaps we *can* trust one another."

She stared at him as if she expected he would smile, perhaps issue a word of acknowledgment, at least show some slight breach in his unfriendly attitude. Instead, he responded with unexpected bitterness.

"No, madam. You mustn't trust anyone. Not ever."

4

The barn's thick sod walls kept its interior cool and dim, no matter what the outside temperature. Even so, a light sheen of sweat moistened Tremayne Hawthorne's brow. Ellie settled herself onto the low milking seat next to him. She drenched a strip of cloth in the water bucket, wrung it out, and laid it across his forehead. Though his eyes were closed, she detected motion behind the lids.

"What is your name?"

"If you women don't know it by now, there's no sense in repeating it."

Ellie hid a smile; Lauretta had decreed a course of treatment she'd learned while acting as a field nurse during the War between the States. Tremayne hadn't been permitted to sleep longer than two hours at a stretch, and each awakening had been accompanied by a brief list of questions to ensure the proper working of his injured head.

His answer this time wasn't exactly right, but it hinted that his brain was working just fine.

"Your age?"

He slitted his eyes open. "Ninety-seven."

"Minus how many years?"

A brief smile hovered over his lips. "Minus sixty-seven."

"Your place of birth?"

A pause greeted the question, stretching long enough to cause her alarm. "England. You know that."

"Where in England?" He'd always given the same vague answer. His increased coherence piqued her curiosity.

"Can't we talk about something else?"

Invalids often turned peevish. She proceeded with care lest she agitate him. It was important that he remain calm, but more so, she longed to question him, and feared any outburst on his part would send her scurrying back to the shelter of the dugout. "What would you like to talk about?"

"Anything but bees. I've already learned the fine points of distinguishing wildflower from clover honey, the approved technique for capturing a swarm, and the advantages of manufactured hives over traditional straw skeps or the blue-gum logs favored by the thrifty pioneer."

Ellie couldn't help a burst of laughter. Lauretta did love her bees, and as Tremayne's primary nurse, she'd spent many more hours conversing with him than Ellie had—one-way conversations, to judge by Tremayne's comments. Her laughter sounded a little shrill to her, but he didn't seem to notice, so she gathered a fortifying breath and plunged into her question.

"Why are you here? What brought you to this place?"

His casual pose atop the pallet turned rigid. She stiffened in accord, scarcely daring to breathe, wishing she could be more trusting, like Lauretta. Hadn't she already quizzed this man once, asking him straight out whether he'd been sent by her father? She wondered if any response would satisfy her. Given her suspicious nature, he might spend every waking hour declaring honest intentions, and she'd still doubt him.

Only the soft, feathery rustle of a scratching hen marred the silence that stretched between them. And after what seemed an eternity, when Ellie's nerves were stretched so near fraying that she almost wished he'd flat out admit he'd come to kidnap her, Tremayne shifted himself into a reclining position.

"You shouldn't stare at me like that," she said, scandalized by the excited tremble that shook her as his eyes swept her from head to toe.

"Turnabout seems fair to me. The two of you have been gawking at me as if I'm some sort of oddity."

"Well, you are a . . . a medical specimen," Ellie said, and then caught herself blushing. The covert glances she'd cast at him, admiring the rangy length of him stretched out over his pallet, drawn to the way his clothes clung to a musculature so different from her own, had had little to do with her nursing duties. "I'm sorry if we've made you feel uncomfortable."

Surprisingly, gentleness settled over his features. "Actually, it's been . . . rather different. I'm not accustomed to soft glances from a woman."

Ellie stifled her impulse to tell him she found that hard to believe. "You've changed the subject."

"Ah, yes, why am I here?" He propped his head on his braced fist, causing his unbuttoned shirt to fall away from the lower portion of his chest. "My reason is not unlike your own."

For a moment, she felt only blankness, and then remembered their brief conversation while she'd bandaged his arm. "I'm here because of my mother," she said.

He nodded. "Eleven years ago, I left England for my mother's sake."

"Did she come with you?"

Again, he nodded. "As far as Philadelphia. She stayed on there while I went homesteading. She died several years ago."

Tremayne's instincts issued a warning whisper urging him to end the conversation. Despite Ellie's and Lauretta's excellent nursing, he still found himself disgustingly weak, not at all equipped to carry on with his mission. Discussing his past could only lead to explaining the present.

One sharp retort, one dismissing comment, and she'd withdraw behind her smooth mask of indifference, leaving him and his secrets at peace. He felt oddly reluctant to bring it about.

"And your father?" Her voice shook upon the last word.

"We left England because of . . . something he'd done." For a moment he cursed his revelation; the next moment, he felt a calm sensation of inevitability settle over him. The conversation suited his purposes entirely. If he could convey to her one scintilla of the pain and betrayal his father's abandonment had caused, perhaps she might return to her own parent with renewed heart.

"What did he do to you?" Her question sounded softer than a summer breeze, but he could hear the curiosity mingled with apprehension layered beneath it.

Her vulnerability touched a spot within him, a place so deeply buried it ached to bring it to light, but he found himself helpless to stop himself from exposing it to her.

"It happened on my ninth birthday," he said. "I was only a child, so I'd never questioned why my father kept my mother and me sequestered on his most remote estate, or why he stayed with us so infrequently. On my ninth birthday, we expected one of his rare visits. My mother, Margaret, had been in a frenzy of primping and blushing for days. My father never made an appearance."

"I can see where a small boy might consider that a tragedy," Ellie said, her compassionate eyes glowing like warm chocolate.

"That's not the whole of it."

He stopped speaking, swallowing against the sudden dryness of his throat. She made no demand that he continue; he found himself powerless to remain silent.

"My father's solicitor, a man named Jessop Farnsworth, arrived in his stead and shattered my world as I had known it. For all my life, I'd been living in a mirage, a false paradise. On my ninth birthday, I learned that my mother had earned our lonely luxury by serving as my father's occasional mistress. For the first time I heard the term bastard applied to me. Farnsworth carried papers notifying my mother that my father was ending their illicit arrangement. He intended to marry a woman with bloodlines equal to his own, a real *lady* who might find it offensive to learn my father disported himself with a commoner. We were evicted at once."

"How could he do that to you?"

"It was my mother who suffered most. For ten long years afterward we stayed in England, enduring the snide remarks, the smug glances slanted her way, while trying our best to live with some semblance of dignity. To no avail. Mother's relatives seemed gratified that she'd gotten her comeuppance instead of the marriage she'd always hoped against hope might occur. We were left to our own devices to survive as best we could. Mother took in sewing, which barely covered our living expenses; I was always large for my age, and I'd found work early on, but it took me until I reached nineteen to save enough to buy our passage to America. My mother died still clinging to the hope that one day my father would realize that it was she he truly loved, that I was his first . . ."

Dismayed at his volubility, Tremayne let his explanation trail to an end before revealing that by taking

Ellie home, he would make reality of his mother's life-long dream.

"It was a cruel, cruel thing to do to an innocent child." Ellie's quiet comment struck close to the heart of his pain.

Cruel, yes, but being branded a bastard had meant little to him. It was the callous casting aside, the rejection by one to whom he'd given unconditional love, that had embittered his soul. At the age of nine, he had sworn never to expose his heart to anyone in a position to hurt him, a strategy that had served him well—for the most part.

Her hand fluttered over his, and after a moment's hesitation, her fingers brushed against his skin in a gesture of comfort he hadn't felt in years.

"Can you tell me why your body bears so many marks of violence?"

Should he tell her he'd endured the beating at the hands of her father's men? That its aftereffects, leaving him aching and uncertain of his strength, had caused him to alter his plans so that he'd traveled here first, rather than directly to Caldwell as he'd planned? He'd believed the side trip to Magnolia would be the easy part of the journey; he'd been wrong.

"I find myself fatigued now, madam." He dropped back onto the pallet, spurning her hesitant touch, and wrapped his arm over his eyes. He found himself thick-throated, unable to continue speaking, and he couldn't bear it if he glanced toward her and found pity marking her features. He ignored her soft good-bye and listened while she gathered her supplies and left him alone with his thoughts.

And he hoped she would remember his uncharacteristic soul-baring and realize how fortunate she was that her father truly cared for her when she learned he'd come to take her home.

Had it really been only three days since Tremayne Hawthorne stumbled upon them? Lauretta wondered. And now another visitor, a mule-mounted stranger, approached their dugout. Perhaps it wouldn't be so lonesome on this prairie as she'd feared.

Ellie, not having the benefit of a bee bonnet, had to shade her eyes against the sun. "Heavens! It looks like a woman, Laurie. Do you want to put a pot of coffee on to boil?"

Lauretta shot Ellie an appreciative smile for tactfully offering her a chance to hide if she didn't feel up to showing off her bee bonnet yet. "I'll be fine. You make better coffee than I do anyway."

"How do!" hollered the unfamiliar woman. "Don't yew gals get skeered! I'm Mattie Murrow, yer five-mile neighbor. I heard tell there was two gals took up this place. I had to come myself 'n' make sure my leg wasn't bein' pulled."

While Mattie dismounted, Lauretta dragged the nail kegs from inside the dugout to the stoop and sat, fanning her face through the veil, hoping their first female caller might think it was the heat that had her so flustered. She breathed a sigh of relief when Mattie Murrow planted her generous behind atop the other keg without splintering it or disparaging its rough-hewn condition. Mattie sighed contentedly, as though the rough cask nestled her bottom like an upholstered armchair, and gazed about her with frank curiosity.

"Why, yew gals're gettin' this place goin', ain't yew! And is that Hiram Espy I see over there near yer team?" she asked.

At Lauretta's murmur of agreement, she bellowed, "Yew get on over here and visit, Hire. Quit lurkin' around them mules." Without turning toward Lauretta, Mattie whispered from the corner of her mouth, "I can't abide lurkin' men. 'Less, a' course, one a' *those* kind was to lurk around me." Surprise heightened her words and her posture perked considerably as Tremayne Hawthorne stalked from the barn.

"Now, who on earth might that be?" Mattie wondered aloud.

"Oh, he's just a man Ellie shot a few days ago," Lauretta said. Then, realizing how awful her comment made Ellie sound, she rushed to explain. "Soon as he feels better, he's going to help us build a sod house. I know it's not exactly appropriate to have two single men living on the premises."

There—she'd admitted the one thing guaranteed to shred any woman's reputation. She gripped the rim of her nail keg, anxious to hear how Mattie would react.

"Hmm. Honey, 'round here we don't worry much 'bout what's appropriate. Here, a woman's got to do what she's got to do."

It sounded like an excellent philosophy to Lauretta.

"Coffee's nearly done," Ellie called from the dugout.

"Take yer time," Mattie hollered back. "We're just settin' here admirin' the view."

Lauretta stifled a giggle, amused and inordinately

relieved at Mattie's tolerant attitude. Tremayne
Hawthorne did provide interesting viewing, suppos-
ing you liked your men huge and ominous and bad
tempered.

She preferred a gentler sort herself. Like her
fiancé, Michael, had been, before his lingering war
wound claimed his life. She'd caught the smallpox
that destroyed her face while tending him during his
last days. So few caring nurses, so many suffering
men, forgotten victims of a war long ended. She
touched the bee veil again, her finger trembling,
knowing she wouldn't trade one minute of the time
they'd shared for a return of her smooth, creamy
complexion.

She knew some people thought her flighty and irre-
sponsible, as if the tragedies she'd known should have
beaten down her spirits. Instead, she understood how
fleeting beauty could be—physical beauty as well as
love's singular perfection—and she'd vowed to spend
the rest of her life relishing each moment. And if that
meant reacting with childlike delight to things she
found astonishing, well, anyone who didn't like it
could just whistle in the wind.

"Yew ever take that hat off?" Mattie asked, putting
an end to Lauretta's wistful musings.

Nobody back home had ever been bold enough to
ask such a question right out, but Mattie's wide face
was creased with such kindly concern, Lauretta
couldn't take offense. "Never. Not during the day,
that is. I take it off to sleep."

"What's yer misery?"

"Pockmarks. Real bad."

"Folks'd get used to seein' yew, ye know. Heck, yew're prob'ly better lookin' than half the gals around here. All in all, I guess us Kansas folks are 'bout the ugliest I've come across, what with the ague 'n' losin' teeth over the winter 'n' all. Look at me, all fat 'n' windburned 'n' gray 'n' not even forty years old."

"I don't mind wearing the bonnet." Lauretta hoped her firm tone would discourage Mattie, but the busy-body persisted.

"Yew'll have to take it off for the dance. If yew don't, it'll just fall off, what with all the kickin' 'n' such."

"What kicking?" asked Ellie, stepping from the dugout, balancing steaming tin cups on the wooden plank that served as their tray.

"Bud 'n' Ruthie Naylor's havin' a big to-do! I'd say they're about six-mile neighbors from here, other direction from my place." Mattie stared from Lauretta to Ellie with wide-eyed astonishment. "It's on Saturday, two days from now. Don't tell me nobody invited yew gals yet?"

"I guess we haven't been here long enough to get invited." Ellie held the tray toward Mattie and then offered it to Lauretta, casting an uncomfortable glance toward Hiram and Tremayne before sitting down on the stoop. "You're our first real guest, more or less."

Lauretta lifted the edge of her veil just enough to enable her to sip at her own drink, grimacing when the bitter tang of Freeman's Coffee Essence attacked her tongue.

Mattie, in the midst of a slurp, choked when the

hot beverage scalded her throat. "Why, yew gals can't stay away from Naylor's!" Her heavy chins quivered. "Folks'd think yew gals just ain't neighborly."

Ellie's stricken gaze met Lauretta's own, leaving Lauretta uncertain over whether she should laugh or cry. Hurtful taunts beyond number had been hurled at her since her illness, and she knew some of the terrible things Ellie's father had often said about her. Yet none of the insults, none of the invective, had ever created such a sensation of loss, of dread, as this simple, kindly homesteader telling them they weren't neighborly.

Back in Arkansas, it didn't matter whether you spoke to your neighbors. But here, a good neighbor might make the difference between survival and defeat. She'd heard all kinds of tales about grasshopper plagues and prairie fires and any number of disasters lurking over the horizon. The success of their homestead could well depend upon their neighbors' good will.

Ellie, still fearful that her father had someone stalking her, wouldn't want to go to the dance; Lauretta would just have to convince her. They had to meet their neighbors sometime, and what better way to do it? A dance! A little thrill curled in the pit of her stomach. She knew a special knot she could tie that would anchor her veiled bonnet so tight no manner of kicking or carousing could knock it loose.

"We can't go—" Ellie began.

"We *have* to go," Lauretta interrupted, hoping to soothe some of Ellie's fears. "If we plan to make our living by selling honey and hay to the folks around here, we'll have to start making some friends."

Sheer panic glazed Ellie's eyes and vanished, so quickly Lauretta felt sure Mattie must have missed it.

"Really, Ellie, it will be all right."

Lauretta wished she knew what else to say to help calm Ellie's skittish nerves, but platitudes had never been a big part of their friendship. Nothing Lauretta could say would have made life with Ellie's father easier to bear. Nothing Ellie could say would ever erase the scars from Lauretta's face. In her heart, Lauretta knew Ellie could talk for three years straight and never make her completely understand what it had been like to live under Jonathan McKittrick's tyrannical rule. No more could she ever explain to Ellie the soul-deep ache that struck Lauretta each time she looked in the mirror or met a nice fellow like Hiram Espy and knew she'd never have a husband, a home, a family.

Some things just plain couldn't fit into words. Few and treasured were the friends who respected one's silences.

"Don't mind her, Mattie," Lauretta said, covering up Ellie's decided lack of enthusiasm. "She's just a little nervous, since she doesn't know how to dance."

"Aw, that won't matter. Them boys'll be so glad to see two new gals in town, they won't care how rough yew stomp on their toes. Now, I'd best be goin' 'n' let yew gals get on with yer day's business." She swallowed her remaining coffee and hauled herself to her feet. "Hiram knows the way t'Naylor's. I see yew gals got yerselves a team a' mules. Yew already done better than half the folks round here. Yew'll have to bring Hire along with yew 'less that boy scraped up enough money 'n' got himself a mount. Heck, be sure to bring both a' them fellas along with yew. I wouldn't mind takin' a spin or two with that big 'un."

Tremayne strode over the prairie after discouraging Hiram's offer to accompany him. Swinging a hammer, he reveled in the simple pleasure of his limbs moving without pain, at the sun heating his skin, at the blessed, blessed quiet. Strength surged through him, marking an end to Espy's bleating solicitousness and Lauretta's whirlwind visits where she'd flipped him to and fro like a gutted mackerel, poking at his wounds, badgering him with bee lore.

Eleanor hadn't visited since yesterday's pathetic outpouring of past history that would have been best left buried. He'd regretted the confession ever since. But life had taught him regrets couldn't mend broken hearts, or restore life to a knife-hacked corpse, or undo impulsive actions. He'd blundered in revealing so much about himself; he would simply hold himself more aloof in the future, and do his best to forget the compassion in her eyes, the gentleness of her tentative touch.

He found a likely spot and hunkered into the grass, the hammer balanced over his right knee. His belly growled, so to kill his appetite he reminded himself of the pasty oatmeal and brittle corn dodgers Lauretta had served for breakfast. He'd eaten better at McKittrick's jailhouse. How Espy endured the fare he didn't know, and if he didn't get Ellie back to her father soon, her slim form would fade into nothing. His eyes raked over the prairie, noting the faint rabbit runs crisscrossing the dry grass. Bloody hell, just thinking of a plump rabbit set his digestive juices rumbling again. He hefted the hammer, balancing its weight for throwing. He'd stew the goddamned rabbit himself, so they could enjoy one edible meal before they left.

After spending three days traveling here and another three nursing his concussion, almost one third of his allotted time had elapsed. He had no more than fifteen days left to complete his mission before Farnsworth's life was forfeit.

It was time to take Eleanor away from here. Not this day, with morning all but gone, but tomorrow, for certain.

Tremayne curled his fingers round the hammer, judging the readiness of his stiff muscles. The concussion-enforced bed rest had worked a minor miracle, restoring him beyond expectations. He'd be more than a match for Espy, should he be so foolish as to put up a fight on Eleanor's behalf. More than a match for Eleanor. For McKittrick himself, should the jailer dare to renege on his promise. Fit and ready—and eager—to cancel a few debts owed him by others, and then on to deal with his father.

Trilling, feminine laughter drifted through the air. He caught a flash of pink from the corner of his eye, and he lost interest in hunting for the moment, his attention inexorably drawn to the two women cavorting over the prairie.

Hunting bees, as Lauretta's cheerful chatter had informed him. They meant to support themselves by keeping bees and growing clover for the bees to feast upon, giving them two cash crops, honey and hay. A body tired quickly of the molasses that was the staple sweetener on the frontier, and quality horses and cattle fared poorly grazing on nothing but tough prairie grass. Customers would vie for the chance to buy or barter for their honey and hay. Two puny women could never hope to farm a traditional homestead, but they could tend bees, and they could hire men to cut and bale their hay on shares. Hell, one blushing request from Eleanor and Espy would leap at the opportunity to stay on to handle the chores.

Tremayne shook his head in wonderment. The scheme sounded profitable to him, so sensible it was hard to credit women conceiving of it. Particularly when one of them had been wrongly dubbed a helpless, indecisive lunatic by her own father.

He'd warned Lauretta about the hidden dangers lurking on the prairie, but she'd passed off his cautions as the ravings of an addled mind, telling him they had to trap bee swarms to build up their colony. They darted over the prairie now, dancing free and unfettered as butterflies. Lauretta wore her bonnet as always, its ends tucked safely into her light gray gown. Tremayne hadn't caught the slightest glimpse of her face over the past days.

Ellie wore a soft pink cotton dress instead of her usual charcoal wool. Far too large for her delicate frame, it should have hung like a flour sack over her;

instead, its soft folds clung like a second skin to her shoulders and breasts, molding her legs as she ran.

A luckless rabbit, perhaps frightened by the women's antics, chose that moment to dodge from its burrow. Tremayne let the hammer fly, sitting back on his heels and sighing with satisfaction when it thunked solidly against the rabbit's head. He rose to fetch the carcass. He gripped it by the neck, his fingers gripping the soft, warm fur. His hand grew still. If he were a fanciful man, he could cast Ellie in the role of rabbit, himself as hunter.

"Hiram! Tremayne! Look what we found!"

He finished securing the rabbit to his belt, the sudden lurching of his stomach at hearing Lauretta's shout having nothing to do with the anticipation of a savory stew.

"Hiram! Tremayne!" Lauretta called again, breathless after her long dash across the prairie.

Like a shadow, Ellie followed several paces behind. Her face betrayed no sign that yesterday's intimate discussion left her feeling awkward in his presence.

Tremayne, on the other hand, felt like a ham-handed laborer working beneath the scrutiny of a foreman who suspected he didn't know his job. He pretended great interest in his blood-encrusted hammer, bending on one knee to rub it against a tuft of grass while the women paused several steps away from him. "What is it?"

"I don't know, silly. That's why we're asking you. Show him, Ellie." Lauretta plopped down in the grass. Ellie likewise dropped to her knees across from him, holding her hands before her like a supplicant, with a fragile length of tissue-thin beauty draped over them.

"It's a snake skin. A rattler."

She gave a little gasp and dropped the skin. Hoping he might have erred in calling it a rattler's, he reached out to run a finger along the pattern's intricacies, never expecting Ellie might do the same. Their fingers brushed and they jerked apart so quickly, so clumsily, that a fragment of the delicate snake skin broke away. The prairie wind picked it up and carried it aloft.

He clenched the hammer, thinking how easily Ellie might have stumbled over the real snake instead of its discarded skin while she and Lauretta chased bloody, goddamned bees. He imagined the reptile sinking its fangs into Ellie's luminous skin, imagined her swelling and screaming with pain. His quiet, serene nurse, dying on the prairie, while her mindless murderer slithered away.

My lunatic daughter, McKittrick had called her, this woman who'd shot him and then supported his weight; who subordinated her own wishes to gratify her friend; whose tranquil voice and gentle touch soothed emotional wounds he would have sworn had been scarred over. McKittrick had lied, and Tremayne couldn't help but wonder why, and couldn't help cursing the position he found himself in.

By his own words, he was sworn to take her back. Staking his honor upon it, he'd hinged another man's life to the bargain. Impetuous and hotheaded as always, he'd accepted a limit on the time he had to accomplish this job that left no margin for sitting back and judging whether or not he was doing the right thing. Tomorrow. He had to tell her what he meant to do, and start off with her tomorrow.

Something deeper than fear twisted in his gut. He pounded the hammer into the snakeskin until it was nothing more than shreds mingled with grass. He must look like a madman to her, but he hammered the snakeskin one last time, thinking what a fine thing it would be if he could deal similarly with all the hidden dangers threatening her.

But he was one of those dangers, wasn't he? Tremayne Hawthorne, the hunter, concealing himself with deadly intent. Ellie, the gentle rabbit, glorying in her freedom, unaware that the hunter meant to strike from an unexpected quarter.

"You have no sense, madam." Anger at her vulnerability, anger at his own impossible position, lent undue harshness to his voice.

With an outraged gasp, she leaped to her feet. He squinted up at her. Her hair tumbled over her shoulders, the sun's golden glow washing over her. High color raged in her cheeks; her breasts heaved, her eyes snapped a challenge. He found himself spellbound, locked with her in visual combat. And then she calmed, her face an unreadable mask erased of all expression, her breath shallow. She stood before him, and yet she'd somehow disappeared.

One shoulder of her pink dress slipped, baring smooth, ivory skin, skin that quivered with the force of the emotions she otherwise successfully controlled. A stray chestnut curl nestled against her throat.

Tremayne found he couldn't look away, and he busied himself tucking the hammer into his belt to still the unseemly impulse that urged him to smooth the curl against her skin.

"That wasn't a very nice thing to say, Mr. Hawthorne," Lauretta chided, rising to lend support to her friend. "Why, I've half a mind to tell you you'll have to go traveling by yourself."

Somehow, a bar of molten lead wedged itself in Tremayne's throat. "What do you know about my plans for traveling?"

"Forget your plans." With a self-satisfied tilt to her bonnet, Lauretta put her arm through Ellie's. "We've been invited to a big to-do at the Naylor homestead. They're our six-mile neighbors, you know."

Hiram Espy chose that moment to puff to a halt next to Tremayne. "Heard you call, ma'am, and got here fast as I could. You talking about Naylor's dance day after tomorrow? I saw Mattie Murrow setting with you earlier and figured she'd invite us. Should be a slap-up time."

Tremayne glared at Hiram, who seemed entirely too eager to expend his meager strength on entertainment. A lecherous lout no doubt lurked beneath that sickly demeanor, anxious to get his hands on the area's most attractive single woman. Of a certainty, he had to spirit Eleanor away from Magnolia before she'd made friends among the settlers, friends who might block his efforts to take her home. Tremayne's hand tightened around the hammer grip. "You cannot go. It's too dangerous."

"Dangerous?" Lauretta quivered in indignation.

"It's just a dance. Besides, Ellie's never been to a dance."

It seemed like such a ludicrous statement, that he wondered whether Lauretta had somehow sniffed out his intentions and dreamed up this reason for delaying. But Ellie's murmured, "Lauretta," her embarrassed flush, convinced him of its truth.

Tremayne couldn't think of a single thing to say. In his experience, women of Ellie's age and social position were veterans of hundreds of dances, forever repeating boring accounts of who wore what, of who danced with whom, of which young beauty snared whatever wealthy male. Eleanor McKittrick was a beautiful woman, one who should have dazzled the onlookers at balls beyond counting. What had prevented her from attending?

Eleanor's silent, amenable posture took on new meaning. Could she be looking toward the pathetic Hiram with a soft, tremulous smile curving her lips, the color in her cheeks the palest echo of the pink she wore? A shy girl anticipating her first dance, her first escort a half-starved, ague-stricken homesteader, her first ball gown an ill-fitting length of cheap pink cotton, with dancing slippers fashioned of clumsily cobbled boot leather peeping from beneath the hem.

He doubted any woman could look more fetching than she did at that moment. Or that any man could deny her another two days of freedom, one night of dancing, before hobbling her dreams.

5

The sun-seared prairie thirsted beneath the sun's unrelenting glare, heat shimmers distorting the vista, every browned blade of grass begging for water—and Ellie felt seasick.

Again and again, the wagon wheels rolled up and over huge clumps of prairie grass, coming down on the other side with a resounding thud, rousing creaks of protest from the wagon itself, drawing inadvertent grunts from Lauretta and Hiram, and prompting a sickly churning within Ellie's stomach. Any one of the jolting bumps landed with force sufficient to crack a tooth, so she had to sit with her mouth gaping open in a most unladylike manner. No one seemed to notice— Lauretta and Hiram huddled together on the wagon seat, chattering like jays, while Tremayne Hawthorne, who'd scorned sharing the back of the wagon with her, trailed after them on his horse.

Tremayne. Perhaps it was best he rode alone, considering the mere touch of his fingers, brushing hers, could make her warm inside. That his breath against her skin could raise shivery bumps, sending her senses reeling. That the rich, husky timbre of his voice could cast such a spell upon her that she'd felt compelled to touch him, to let him know she understood his pain, only to have him recoil from her silent offer of friendship.

"Ellie? *Ellie!*"

Lauretta's call caught Ellie with her hand clapped over her mouth, swallowing hard against her stomach's reaction to a particularly sickening wagon lurch. The low, miserable moan escaping through her fingers apparently convinced Lauretta she'd captured Ellie's attention.

"I told him I couldn't believe it! I told him we'd have to see it for ourselves!" Lauretta, twisted around to face Ellie, clung tight to the back of the wagon bench, excitement vibrating from her with the intensity of a tuning fork. "You won't mind, will you, Ellie? Hiram says it will only add half an hour to the trip."

"That's right. Thirty minutes. Mebbe just a tad more." Hiram craned his neck, turning his hopeful face back toward her.

"What are you two talking about?" Ellie whispered, just to be polite, since she felt certain nothing on God's earth could induce her to prolong the agony of this trip.

"Hire's got himself a claim!"

"One hunnert sixty acres a' prime Kansas prairie,"

Hiram agreed, quiet pride suffusing his face. "I'd sure be proud to show it to Miss Lauretta, and you, too, ma'am."

Lauretta's bonnet brim dipped shyly.

Ellie felt a bittersweet ache flash through her accompanied by a shameful stab of jealousy, a sudden premonition of loneliness. Could it be that Hiram and Lauretta . . . ? Might Lauretta have traveled all this way to find a man capable of seeing beyond the veil to the vibrant, loving woman within? Lauretta and Hiram. Ellie and . . . no one.

Was she being disloyal to feel apprehension over Lauretta's friendship with Hiram? No. Lauretta had sworn she'd never bare her face to anyone, especially a man. She feared pity; she feared someone might think her wits as damaged as her skin and seek to take advantage. They knew next to nothing about this man, except that he'd taken advantage of an empty homestead. Might he be poised to prey on Lauretta's tender emotions?

"Why were you squatting on our place if you have a claim of your own?" Ellie asked, her suspicions taking precedence over her delicate stomach.

"Ain't got a house on my place yet," Hiram answered over his shoulder. "Meant to build me one, and then the ague struck me down. I'll tend to it soon's me 'n' Hawthorne get yer soddie built for you."

Your soddie. Not yours and Lauretta's, assigning sole occupancy to Ellie as though he'd already made plans for Lauretta's future. Tremayne, of course, wouldn't be around long. He'd made it clear her com-

pany held no charm for him, and she couldn't afford
to pay him a wage beyond the time it took to build the
sod house. Ellie pictured her solitary home rising
from the prairie, the sod bricks rough and bristling
outside, warm and smoothed with plaster within. Just
the way she wanted to be—a tough exterior shielding
a comfortable soul. But how much of that sturdy
facade would crumble once Lauretta left with Hiram,
once Tremayne rode off after earning a few coins to
provision his journey?

Lauretta knelt facing her, her knuckles bone white
from gripping the rough wooden seat back while she
waited for Ellie's approval. Ellie wondered if Hiram's
touch sent Lauretta's pulse leaping, if the heat from
his body warmed her through the veil. And if it did,
whether she had any right to interfere.

"I'd like to see your place, Hiram." Ellie sighed,
pulling hand over hand to reach the back of the
wagon. "I think I'll walk alongside for a while,
though."

Tremayne cursed his softhearted—and softheaded—
impulses. So what if she'd never attended a dance?
They could have been halfway to Arkansas by now
instead of standing in the midst of an empty, wind-
whipped prairie. He dismounted to investigate their
reason for stopping, and witnessed Espy blushing
furiously while pacing off imaginary walls. "It'll go
somethin' like this. Sixteen by twenty. Plenty a' space
to section off inside, so's the bed . . . so's the
kitchen's . . . separate."

Tremayne joined the women. At his questioning look, Ellie blushed and explained. "This is Hiram's claim. He wanted to show it to us."

Hiram nodded. "So, ladies, it'd make a nice place for one a' you to live, wouldn't it?"

Espy's absurd question prompted a sassy retort from Lauretta. "Why would either of us want to live here? We have our own place."

"Aw." Espy ducked his head, kicking at a tuft of grass. Tremayne couldn't tell whether the red skin showing through Espy's sparse, lard-slicked hair was sunburn or another of his endless blushes, and he didn't care. Fury raged through him. He knew what the farmer was about; he sought to impress Ellie.

"C'mon. I'll show you where I started diggin' the well." Espy gestured.

"I'll come with you, Hire. Ellie's looking peaky." Lauretta lifted her skirts a few inches to pick her way daintily across the prairie in his wake. Though Ellie had begun to follow, she stopped, her gaze traveling somewhat nervously from Lauretta to Espy.

"Yes, you two go on ahead," Ellie called, and to Tremayne's eyes, her staying behind sent Espy's shoulders slumping.

Though she didn't follow, her worried gaze tracked their progress. She sounded unsure as she asked, "The well seems awfully far away from the house, don't you think?"

She was anticipating, no doubt, a long trek in hauling water for cooking and cleaning if she should wed Hiram Espy. Tremayne stifled the urge he felt to tell her she needn't worry that far into the future.

"Water's scarce on the prairie, madam. He'll likely dig the well first and site the house next to it."

"Scarce? Then why doesn't he just set it beside that lake?"

She gestured toward the horizon, her arm forming a graceful arc framing a glistening, shimmering mirage that looked so real one might expect a large trout to leap from its rippling surface.

"It's a mirage," he said. "A trick of the sunlight merging with the heat rising from the prairie."

"Oh." Now that Hiram and Lauretta had moved farther away, she seemed more comfortable speaking to him. "I thought one saw mirages only in the desert."

"No, madam. People are forever imagining things that aren't truly there, especially if they want something badly enough."

Her attention swiveled back to Hiram when a sudden burst of laughter trilled from Lauretta. Tremayne mentally tipped his hat to Espy. The farmer's patently obvious attempt at rousing Ellie's jealousy by devoting his attentions to Lauretta seemed to be working. Only Tremayne knew the ploy to be a wasted effort.

"You say you know something of homesteading, Mr. Hawthorne."

He nodded. Espy wasn't the only man who could boast ownership of a choice piece of ground. America had seemed to offer so much once: opportunity regardless of a man's circumstances of birth; a classless society more concerned with hard work than social position; an ocean separating him from the father who'd cast him aside.

"Would you say this place shows potential?"

He realized, to his surprise, how much he missed intimate contact with the land. At her question, he squatted, working through the grass to press into the earth with practiced fingers, and ran a judgmental eye across the prairie's rolling contours. No harm in offering his opinion, even though she wouldn't be around long enough to learn whether he spoke the truth. He fought down an unexpected aversion at giving credit to Hiram Espy. "It's a fine piece of property. Any man would be proud to own this land."

"But is it enough?" She seemed fretful, her attention continually drawn toward Espy and Lauretta. "I've never known anyone who farmed for a living. Do you know if a man can provide for his wife, raise his children, with nothing to depend on but this piece of land?"

"If he wants to, he can." Tremayne rose, brushing his fingers against his thigh. "I did it."

The tiny worry lines smoothed from her forehead, though he felt certain he'd said nothing to ease her concerns. Her expression began its transformation into its customary unreadable blank mask, but for the first time, didn't quite succeed. A tiny tremor quivered over her lips. Something like embarrassment darkened her eyes, a blush staining her cheeks as she glanced toward his hands. Her long, slender fingers pressed into her belly, as if to quell a sudden pain.

"You have a family?"

"Not anymore."

Most women would have pounced upon his deliberately ambiguous admission with the ferocity of a terrier worrying a rat. He braced himself to deflect the expected onslaught of questions from her.

She asked nothing, merely stared at him with wide, startled eyes, her lips parted as if they'd just expelled a wounded cry.

And he found himself casting aside all his earlier regret about telling her so much about himself. He rattled on without provocation, as if the words had been aching to spill from his lips. "My mother was content to settle in Philadelphia after we left England. I wanted more, but lacked funds. The Homestead Act said a man had to be twenty-one years old or head of a household before he could claim a section of land. I was only nineteen, so I joined forces with a woman from a neighboring community who shared my interests. Or so I thought. We were together nearly ten years, more than long enough to prove up on the claim."

"Children?"

"A boy. He's gone, too."

"Gone . . . as in dead?"

He gave a quick, curt nod. Ellie didn't press him for further clarification, which was just as well, for his throat had gone tight. Thank God. What had come over him, filling her ears—again—with things best left unsaid?

The brief mention of the past conjured forth a long-suppressed image, the memory of the lone, unmarked grave desecrating a remote spot far from his Caldwell land. He'd buried Darla and Bobby with his wife's faithless arms wrapped around the boy's tiny corpse, telling no one where the bodies might be found. He'd thought it a final, though far-too-late kindness; Darla would have hated for others to see what had been done to her in death.

His refusal to turn over the bodies had proven the finishing nail in the coffin consigning him to hell on earth—awaiting trial at the United States Court at Fort Smith, where "Hanging Judge" Isaac Parker presided. They'd said his silence all but admitted his guilt, but they would leave it to the Hanging Judge to order the noose; they'd said the Hanging Judge knew what to do with a man who obviously held no respect for the sanctity of human life.

They'd been right about him, too. Otherwise, he wouldn't be assuring a marriage-minded woman of the worth of her suitor's land while secretly chafing at the delay in abducting her away from it. Damn it all, she'd better enjoy this dance tonight. He'd make certain she did, even if he had to see to it himself.

"We'd best be on our way," he said, his voice gruff. He swung himself up onto his horse, leaving it to Ellie to summon Hiram and Lauretta back to the wagon.

The rusty scrape of a poorly tuned fiddle drifted over the prairie. The sound prompted a quickening of the team's sluggish pace, accompanied by a wheezing bray from one of the mules. Ellie's lips quirked. The notion of a mule responding to a fiddle lifted her spirits, which had unaccountably plummeted after her conversation with Tremayne.

It wasn't learning he'd been married that stirred up this unwarranted melancholy. A man who looked like

Tremayne, whose entire being radiated such . . . such masculine vitality, was bound to attract a mate at an early age. He hadn't spoken the names of his dead wife and son. Had that nameless woman trembled at his touch the way Ellie had? Had she felt his breath sear her skin, responded to the low, husky murmurs of his voice? Of course she had—she'd borne him a son. And he'd mentioned her coming and going from his life as casually as he might have discussed a former business partner, acknowledged their deaths without a glimmer of pain shadowing his expression.

As her father had done, continuing his life without pause after the death of her mother. Men. They were a heartless lot, despite their sometimes flirtatious, intriguing ways, and any woman with sense would be wise to steer well clear of them.

And then Tremayne appeared at the foot of the wagon, adjusting his horse's pace to theirs while Hiram guided the team into the motley group of conveyances surrounding Naylor's sod house. Tremayne dismounted and sauntered toward them, leaning forward into the wagon bed.

"Madam?" He braced his sound arm against the floor, and extended his bandaged arm toward her. She placed her hand in his reluctantly, seeing no gracious way to refuse his assistance, and her resolve to steer clear of him vanished at the jolt of pleasure his touch aroused. He drew her toward him with fluid, effortless strength, his arm an unwavering rock lending solid support while she gained a tremulous foothold at his side.

"You'll need to stand steadier on your feet if you

mean to enjoy this dance," he murmured when her hip brushed against his.

"It's the wagon ride," she hurried to explain. She pressed her free hand against her belly, marveling at her fluttery breathlessness. "It made me feel a bit queasy."

He nodded, more soberly than their vapid conversation merited. "It strikes some people that way, especially if they've never traveled across open prairie before. Roads make for a smoother ride."

He'd tied his hair back in a casual queue, lending a strong sleekness to his rugged profile. His eyes, usually so cool and guarded, burned like blue flames through the sooty grate of his lashes. His heated gaze raked over her, sweeping from head to toe, and then he tilted his head toward the music, concentration lining his forehead. She realized suddenly that she'd never seen true happiness brighten his features; realized, too, that he still gripped her hand within his, that she'd been leaning against him with brazen abandon.

"Lordy, Ellie, doesn't that fiddle sound grand!" Lauretta frolicked into view, holding her skirt up while her feet stepped out a complex pattern. Hiram stood close behind her, an off-tune humming rumbling from his throat.

Tremayne dropped Ellie's hand and stepped away.

A breeze stroked Ellie's side, its coolness marking the place where she'd rested against Tremayne's solid warmth. How warm would she feel if he danced with her, enfolding her within his brawny arms? She clutched at her dress, a delicious tingle running through her fingers to find his heat still present within the cloth folds.

A piercing whistle, followed by raucous, masculine shouting, caused her head to whip around toward Naylor's soddie. Men—a veritable river of men—flowed through the door, headed in their direction.

"Wimmin!"

"Two a' them!"

"First dibs on the little 'un with the hat!"

The men surrounded them, sweating and smiling, their faces whisker-covered blurs, their voices an indecipherable babble of introductions, questions, and demands. Like chickens converging at feeding time, they crowed and pecked and scratched, trampling over each other to get close. Ellie caught Lauretta's hand. Panic rose; they had her surrounded, with no visible means of escape, almost as bad as finding herself locked in the dark. She fought against releasing a shameful whimper, struggling to regain her composure. She could deal with this, if only they would stand aside so she could see her way free.

Huge, sun-bronzed hands gripped the shoulders of the two men closest to her, heaving them aside to give her space to breathe.

"Tremayne," Ellie whispered. Tears nearly sprang to her eyes, her hands ached to grab hold of his shoulders, so absurdly grateful was she for his intervention when he wedged his big body between the clamoring horde and her.

"Gentlemen!" he bellowed, shocking them all into surprised silence. Hiram positioned himself next to Tremayne, his arms crossed over his chest.

"Gentlemen," Tremayne repeated in a normal voice. "The ladies won't be able to dance with you if you trample them to death."

Now that they'd quieted, she was able to count them. Goodness—eighteen or nineteen, aside from Tremayne and Hiram. Most ducked embarrassed faces and twisted their hats in their hands, but one belligerent fellow swaggered forward to face Tremayne.

"Them wimmin yer wives?" he challenged.

"No." Hiram and Tremayne answered simultaneously.

Ellie found herself wishing they'd lied. And felt a stab of annoyance at herself for thrilling to the notion of Tremayne Hawthorne calling her wife. She hadn't come so far, risked so much, merely to exchange one form of bondage for the one represented by a ring around her finger.

"Well, we all want our chance to dance with 'em," said the challenger, prompting a chorus of nervous nods from his fellow, would-be dancers.

"You'll all have your chance," Tremayne assured them.

"You don't mean to hog 'em up for yerself?"

Tremayne glanced back at Ellie. It seemed regret flared briefly in his eyes before he turned back to the men. "I'd say there are enough of you fellows here to give them the time of their lives tonight. I won't have to dance with them at all."

Ellie had learned, years before, the trick of guarding her spirit. Her face could portray a bright, interested smile; her body project the image of intense concentration, while her true essence floated free as if on a distant cloud, observing what was going on about her corporal body, but keeping *Ellie* unaffected, unharmed.

For the first time since mastering it, the trick failed her. She shuddered with a mixture of mortification and self-disgust while the men capered and tossed their hats in the air. They celebrated her shame; while she'd cast sense aside and trembled like a green girl in anticipation of a dance with Tremayne, he'd looked upon it as a chore to be eagerly shed at the first opportunity.

"I mean to claim my share of dances," Hiram announced, a roguish grin creasing his face.

"I thought you might," Tremayne muttered.

"Music's playin' and time's a-wastin'!" someone shouted, rousing an answering, affirmative roar. Like lemmings, the men rushed toward the soddie, drawing Ellie and Lauretta in their wake.

"Oh, Lordy, Ellie, ain't this fun!" Lauretta cried.

Ellie didn't answer, couldn't answer over the aching constriction in her throat. Despising herself for doing so, she slanted a glance back at Tremayne. He stood silhouetted against the darkening prairie, his legs splayed to support his tall frame, his arms crossed over his chest. Alone, in the midst of a crowd. It must have been a trick of the setting sun that made it seem as though his shoulders slumped, that a bleak desolation shadowed his face, before he turned and strode away.

Hiram waited until they neared Naylor's soddie. Amazing himself by his own boldness, he gripped

Lauretta's upper arm gently, lest her headlong rush be brought to a too-abrupt halt. He held her near his side while the others forced their way through the door.

"Miss Lauretta?" he croaked once they stood alone, embarrassment and sickly humors conspiring to make his voice crack like a boy's. God, how he hated his infernal illness!

Lauretta peered inquiringly at him, and he knew she had to be disgusted by what she saw. He hoped her looking at him through her veil might soften the rough edges of his homely face, maybe dim the red-rimmed weepiness burning in his eyes. This bout of ague had nearly run its course, he could tell, though he didn't know whether he'd last out a whole night of dancing. And that would surely make a good impression—collapsing smack in the middle of Naylor's dirt floor.

He wanted to tell her that on his good days he could manage the stubbornest ox team, he could plow a full acre of virgin prairie, and still bring home enough wood for cooking and bath water. But when she looked at him, when he knew the minute she stepped through that door every unattached male within three counties would converge upon her, he couldn't find the words to convince her of his worth.

"Miss Lauretta. Ahem. You're . . . you're a mighty sprightly gal," he managed to say.

"Why, I suppose I am." She tilted her head toward where his hand still clutched her arm.

"Kinda soft," he said with an embarrassed chuckle, reluctantly letting go of her.

"That, too," she agreed. Then, to his astonishment, she curved her fingers around his upper arm and squeezed. "Hmm. A little stringy, but I'd bet you've lifted more than a few bales of hay."

"I sure have, ma'am," he assured her fervently.

"Well." Lauretta leaned toward him, and lowered her voice to a conspiratorial whisper. "I hear that sometimes at these dances, a fellow will swing a lady up so she can kick the ceiling."

"Yes, ma'am!" Sweat broke out over Hiram's forehead; his cursed ague, or a reaction to imagining her waist caught between his hands, her weight straining his arms, her skirts swirling about her while a dainty foot knocked a few clods loose from Naylor's ceiling?

"I'll save that dance just for you, Hiram." She giggled and turned toward the door.

"Miss Lauretta!"

She peeked over her shoulder. The position drew the bee veil tight against her face, outlining a pert nose, a curving cheek, a determined chin.

"Ma'am." He shuffled in an agony of embarrassment. "I was wonderin' . . . what color is your hair?"

She grew very still and he wished he could call back the question—anything to restore the vibrancy that drew him to her the way the scent of flowers drew her precious bees.

But when she spoke, his heart lightened. He could tell by the thoughtful, yet pleased, tone of her voice that he hadn't offended her. "It's sort of yellow, Hire," she said. "Almost like the bottom end of a ripe corn tassel. Not the brown part that sticks out—the part that's inside the shuck."

Hidden inside the shuck, like Lauretta within her veil. He imagined silky, soft strands of pale gold, coiled and tucked beneath the hat brim where no man could ever see. Ever since meeting her he'd tried imagining what lay beyond that veil. What was it she hid?

"Thank you, ma'am," Hiram said. "I'll sure be lookin' forward to that dance."

As she squeezed into the soddie, Hiram wondered if he truly wanted to see the face she guarded so well, wondered if he were man enough to love a golden-haired woman who couldn't bear others looking upon her in the light of day.

6

From the moment her first partner swung her onto the floor, the dancing brightened Ellie's darkened spirits.

She'd been worried that her woeful inexperience would annoy anyone risking a dance with her. Mattie Murrow had been right; nobody cared that she didn't know how to dance. Regardless of the fiddler's bawled instructions—"Scamperdown!" "Double Shuffle!" "Texas Swing!"—whoever partnered her at the moment generally kept a firm arm clamped about her waist, leading her in a somewhat inelegant but oddly satisfying clumping and stomping that roused a great deal of dust from Naylor's floor. Faces swam into range through the gritty haze: friendly, smiling faces, sweaty and flushed from exertion, but beaming with the same silly delight she felt tilting her own lips.

With men outnumbering women by at least three to one, an endless line of partners awaited every woman present, from a barely nubile young miss to an arthritis-cricked old matron. Mattie Murrow waved an exuberant hello to her as she stomped past. How nice it would be if some of the other female faces were more than blurs passing in the dance, but Ellie doubted the eager men would stand aside long enough for her to make the acquaintance of any of the other women this night.

Still, mindful of Lauretta's instructions to gain introductions that could prove valuable for their business, she tried asking the names of her first few partners. She gave up when they all began looking and smelling alike: sweat-matted hair, bewhiskered cheeks, faded blue shirts turning dark near the armpits, the scent of perspiration mingled with the yeasty odor of beer.

She judged she'd been dancing for at least two hours when someone pressed a glass of raspberry cordial into her hand. Her throat, dry from the exercise and breathing in the choking dust, clamored for relief. She tossed the liquid back, nearly dropping her glass when the sharp alcoholic sting seared her throat and drew tears from her eyes.

It settled warmly in her stomach. Ellie smiled.

"Would you like to marry me, ma'am?" asked her partner, his face pinched with eagerness.

"I don't think so." She strived to decline this, her fifth unexpected proposal of the night, with dignity.

"Well, then you want another glass a' spirits, ma'am?"

"I believe I do."

Simply walking to the refreshment table was an impossibility. One, two, three—clump. One, two, three—slide. They made a round of the dance floor and her partner fished another glass of cordial from the table in passing and offered it to her. She swallowed it quickly and plunked the glass down on the table before they stepped beyond reach, grimacing and screwing her eyes shut against the fiery trail the cordial left, but enjoying the warmth seeping through her blood.

She found herself regretting her unmarried state when the man who'd confronted Tremayne earlier squeezed into the narrow space between Ellie and her partner. He waved another cordial before her, a wet, beery leer distorting his face.

"My turn!" he thundered, stiff-arming her startled partner into a stumbling heap.

"Sh—Sh—sure thing, Griff," stuttered the fallen dancer, scrambling out of reach.

There was no way to evade him in the close-packed room. Griff stepped closer than she liked and forced Ellie's fingers around the glass. "Saw you puttin' away the booze and figgered it'd be a good time to take over. Drink up."

The fiddle sawed on, the crowd of dancers pressed close, and the pleasant, giddy feeling brought on by the cordial dissipated like frost kissed by sunlight. Ellie's stomach churned, the back of her neck tingling with apprehension. Griff's mean little eyes glared redly at her, his fleshy tongue darting out to catch a sweat bead dripping from his mustache. Surrounded by merriment, she felt menaced, and trapped, so completely penned in she couldn't even turn away.

"I don't want the drink," she said, pushing it back at him. "And I've had enough dancing for now."

He tightened his fingers cruelly over hers, and with scarcely a ripple showing his effort, exerted a numbing force on her wrist. "Yer gonna drink it, and then yer gonna follow me outside, and then we're gonna—"

"You should plan on spending a solitary evening, *sir*. You forget the lady came with me."

Relief nearly buckled Ellie's knees when she recognized Tremayne's cultured British tones.

Though Tremayne's words sounded agreeable, frigid fury blazed from his clear arctic blue eyes. He towered a full head over Griff, leashed power and barely contained rage surrounding him like armor. With a motion so quick it was little more than a blur, he clapped a hand over Griff's elbow. Ellie couldn't see what Tremayne did, but Griff uttered a pained yelp and the pressure on her wrist eased. The cordial glass dropped to the floor and a passing booted heel crushed it into the dirt.

Tremayne curved his arm around her waist, drawing her close until her cheek pressed into the shirt stretched over his chest, his proprietary stance and the tilt of his clenched jaw daring Griff to raise an objection.

"Thought ya said ya didn't want her," Griff mumbled, scowling toward the floor.

"You never heard me say I didn't want her."

Ellie clung to him, absurdly relishing his protection while disparaging herself for not standing up to Griff on her own. Tremayne wouldn't be around the next time a Magnolia homesteader threw a dance party. She would have to learn to fend for herself, but, oh God, such a thrill coursed through her to have Tremayne handling the chore just this once.

"Well, I ain't gonna arguefy with someone bigger 'n me." Griff rolled his shoulders and winced, grabbing his elbow. His malevolent stare embraced them both. "Specially when I can see how much ya like ta win."

"I wouldn't say I like to win," said Tremayne. He leveled his hooded gaze upon Griff. "It's more that I hate to lose."

Spoken with utter ruthlessness, his clipped words carried a rapier-sharp edge of resolve. Griff's mottled complexion shifted into a pasty white mask of fear. Without another word, he blundered into the crowd and disappeared from Ellie's view.

Ellie felt, then, a tremor in the solid arm wrapped about her waist. She peeped up through her lashes and saw a tic leaping in the firm ridge of Tremayne's jaw, his eyes narrowed over flaring nostrils as his greater height let him track Griff's progress through the room. Beneath her cheek, his chest heaved like bellows stoking a smoldering flame. He wanted to run after Griff and beat him to a bloody pulp; she could feel him fighting for restraint with every pulse of the vein throbbing at his neck. How well she understood the struggle.

"Tremayne?" she whispered, daring to rest her hand against his arm. He shuddered at her touch and drew in a surprised breath, his attention immediately diverted from Griff to her. She snatched her hand away, remembering his bruises, thinking they still might pain him, but more afraid that his reaction would be a replay of the recoil that he'd shown the last time she'd touched him.

A dangerous man, as evidenced by his battered body and easy mastery over Griff. So why did she feel so well protected nestled against him, why did she long to soothe the tension from his limbs and put a smile upon that haunted, enigmatic face?

"He didn't do anything to me, Tremayne. Please ignore him."

He shook his head, but not from stubborn determination to see Griff punished; it seemed more a clearing of his mind. His expression took on a distant cast, as if he looked far into the past. "I hope I didn't frighten you with my damnable temper. I saw him bothering you. I know how sometimes a woman can be coerced into doing things that backfire upon her later."

"That man can't compare to . . . to someone I know when it comes to coercion," she said, amazed she could speak of her experiences so lightly. "I learned long ago how to deal with it."

"Much the same way as I learned the value of mastering my temper, I suppose."

Before Ellie could wonder at the odd thickening of his voice, someone jostled her from behind, shouting an inebriated apology. Tremayne caught her against him, and they both stumbled when yet another twirling couple crashed into them. "You'd best git dancin' or git outta the way," a flushed, near-breathless dancer hollered helpfully.

"Two fleas couldn't squeeze through this mob. So it seems we're meant to dance together after all," Tremayne murmured, subtly altering his hold upon her, and hers upon him. "I'll aim us for the door."

One, two, three—stomp. One, two, three—slide. Just as she'd been doing all evening. But unlike the rough clumping of the simple farmers she'd been dancing with, Tremayne moved with the lithe grace of a panther, his body alternately retreating and meeting in a sinuous arc against hers.

Her hand rested against his shoulder, and her pulse raced in response to the feel of his shirt sliding against his firm, muscle-ridged skin. To Ellie's horror, she felt the tips of her breasts tighten into sharp little nubs when he swept his chest over hers and then drew her hard against his out-thrust, steel-thewed thigh.

When she ventured an embarrassed glance upward, she found his hot stare boring back into her eyes, unblinking, solemn, almost as though his provocative movements were carried out with no conscious thought.

A dangerous man.

She looked away, an unfamiliar warmth rising from her loins, melting into a searing heat rising from his. With a pressure so light, so brief, she almost thought she imagined it, he slid his hand down her spine, molding her breasts, her waist, her hips, against him, and then he stepped away.

"We're out of their way now," he said.

She nodded to see that they indeed stood at the fringe of the crowd. A peculiar mixture of disappointment and relief knifed through her. Well, he'd admitted to not wanting to dance with her. She shouldn't be disappointed that he'd brought it to a halt as soon as he could. She wrapped her arms around herself when he abandoned his hold, suddenly chilled in the sweltering soddie.

"Shall I leave you to another partner?"

She shook her head, curiously certain that any other man's grip would be sweaty beyond endurance, that any other man's clumsy form brushing up against her tingling body would make her want to retch. "What I'd really like to do is go over to the creek and soak my feet. I think I've had enough dancing for one night."

He frowned, as if her abandoning the dance displeased him. "Are you're certain you've enjoyed the night to the fullest?"

What a strange question! "I've had my fill."

His brooding gaze studied her for a moment. "Very well. I shall keep watch over you. Gatherings of this sort usually end up with the men drinking more than they should and causing all manner of mischief. They're usually no danger to anyone but themselves, but one never knows."

He was so careful of her, rescuing her from Griff's unwanted attentions, and now this show of concern. It felt rather nice, having someone worry about her safety. Griff might be lurking outdoors, and Tremayne himself had warned her and Lauretta about snakes and prairie dog holes and a thousand other dangers waiting to bring down the unwary. She felt not the slightest pang of fear. She wondered if he'd stand

behind her like a silent sentinel or if he'd walk alongside her, turning his proud, aristocratic head from
side to side, alert for any peril.

Either way, she would be alone with him, away
from this roistering, bothersome crowd. Alone with
Tremayne.

She could not let him see how he affected her.
He'd cursed his temper, yet held it under control; she
could do no less with her wayward emotions. She
strove to regain her familiar shield of composure and
followed him out into the night.

Stringer helped himself to a big swallow of beer,
using the mug to shield his interest from the half-
drunk, card-playing crowd crammed into the sorry
excuse of a saloon. This Delano section of Wichita
certainly squeezed more than its share of rowdiness
within its limits, and Stringer intended to spend a few
days sampling all its wares before buckling down to
business.

A scrawny cow-kicker, looking lopsided until
Stringer realized the hair'd been scalped from his left
side, squirmed up to the bar, directing a bold, curious
glance at Stringer. "What outfit you riding with?"

"Ain't ridin'. Lookin'."

The newcomer nodded as if he'd expected the
answer. He leaned toward Stringer with a conspiratorial tilt to his head. "Lots a' interesting things to see
here in Delano. Lots that don't get seen, neither."

Stringer savored another swallow of the sour,
tepid brew, mulling the stranger's tentative hint. Hell,

might as well ask for a little information before his brain got too blistered with Delano rotgut. "You seen a man by the name of Tremayne Hawthorne? Big son of a bitch, English accent."

"Can't say as I have," said the cow-kicker, eyeing Stringer's mug.

"Don't drink with a man 'less I know his name," Stringer said.

"Jackson. Name's Ralph, but folks tend to call me Half-Scalped." Jackson ran a self-conscious hand over his scarred head.

Stringer waved the barkeep over and ordered a round for them both. While his newfound buddy gulped his with enthusiasm, Stringer fished in his shirt pocket, drawing out Darla Hawthorne's journal. He thumbed through to the last written page and ran a dirty fingernail over the script. "How's about someone called Cato Crowden? Last I heard, he was headed toward Indian Territory but it can't hurt to ask."

Jackson choked on his brew, wasting a good half mouthful. "You're saying it all wrong," he managed at last. "Ain't *Cat*-o *Crow*-den like some goddamned animals and birds. It's Kay-toe. And Crowd-en, like a crowd a' people."

The barkeep caught Stringer's head motion and served fresh rounds of beer.

"You know him, then?" Stringer pressed.

For the first time, Jackson showed a hint of nervousness. "Might. What's it to you?"

Stringer pretended nonchalance. "Just thought he might like to know this Hawthorne's in the area.

Anyone could get word to him could be doing *Cato Crowd*en a big favor."

Jackson concentrated on his beer for several long moments. "You gonna be around town for a while?"

A bosomy gal decked out in a too-tight satin gown brazenly stared at Stringer's gun belt, before flicking her gaze lower, her lush lips tilted in a practiced smile.

"I'll be around for a day or two," Stringer said.

Tremayne led Ellie to the creek.

"There's room enough for both of us," she said, gathering her skirts against her legs as she patted the grassy bank.

He declined her offer with a silent shake of his head and then he retreated beneath the trees, hoping the leafy darkness would help him rein in his rampaging sensibilities.

God knows he had reasons enough to loathe his very existence. But none could surpass his vile behavior on this night. On the morrow he would truss her up like a Christmas goose, if need be, and take her home to the man she'd hinted was a master of coercion. Yet tonight he'd beheld trust shining from her wondrous eyes and gloried in it; inflamed beyond reason by the feel of her within his arms, he'd deliberately provoked and relished her innocent responses, woman to man. No man possessing even a shred of decency would toy so with someone he meant to betray.

Betrayal. Such an ugly word. Merely thinking of

what he meant to do doused his raging body as effec-
tively as if he'd plunged into the creek where Ellie sat
splashing her tired feet in the water.

He should have dallied in Wichita with a willing
wench before seeking out Eleanor McKittrick. It
seemed incredible now that he hadn't, though perhaps his aching ribs had tempered his lusts. His baser
urges had plagued him so while in prison that he'd
deliberately squelched the memory of how long it had
been since he'd had a woman, but he started calculat-
ing now. Five months in jail. And at least four years
before that since he'd visited Darla's bed.

No wonder he found Ellie's presence so intoxicating.

Like any drunkard unable to resist what he craved,
he found himself unable to stay away from her. He'd
stood beneath the trees for no more than ten minutes
before he moved to the edge of the clearing where he
could see her again. She'd hiked her skirt up to her
knees, splashing her feet in the burbling water. The
sound must have masked his approach for she seemed
unaware of his presence. Moonlight illuminated her
movements as she bent and captured water in her
cupped hand, lifting it to trickle in silvery streaks
down the length of her bared calf. She'd freed her
hair from its loose knot, and it swirled around her like
a dark cloud, her ill-fitting dress slipping from her
shoulders and bagging around her, doing little to con-
ceal the slim, supple form within. His hands tingled,
remembering the feel of her firm, slender waist twisting rhythmically beneath his touch.

"Madam," he called softly, after a long, long
moment.

She paused, water glistening as it dripped through her fingers. Without looking back, she reached into the creek for another measure. "Please don't call me that."

"Eleanor." He tried the name her father used to address her, though saying it aloud fairly clogged his throat.

A shudder rippled through her. "Don't *ever* call me that. My name is Ellie."

Ellie. He'd tried so hard to think of her always as *Eleanor,* McKittrick's lunatic daughter. Or *madam,* a vague presence, no more interesting than the hired gelding he rode. There were any number of reasons why he'd failed to keep her distant: his long abstinence; the crack on his head that had befuddled his brains; the natural human inclination to look fondly upon one who nurses one to health. He should have stopped in Wichita. And it was Ellie's fault his mind had been scrambled, and that she'd looked so fetching while tending his wounds.

Tremayne went and crouched next to her, noting with grim satisfaction that she reacted to his nearness by tucking her dress snugly against her leg and leaning infinitesimally away from him. Good—she'd grown wary of him again.

A leaden heaviness blossomed in his chest.

"Have your feet recovered enough to brave the dance again?"

She shook her head, not meeting his eyes. "I think I'll stay out here. I'm . . . I'm not used to crowds."

"I could fetch Lauretta and Hiram and tell them you'd like to return. To the dugout."

He couldn't call it home, not when he meant to take her away from the homestead in the morning.

"Don't do that." She kicked at the water. "Lauretta's having the time of her life. I don't mind waiting. Besides"—she glanced around, averting her gaze quickly when she accidently met his—"it's much nicer out here than in the dugout. It's dark outside, but it's a different kind of darkness. I can't wait to get out of the dugout. I'll be so glad once you and Hiram put up our sod house."

His winced at the reminder of yet another way he'd deluded her, but his self-loathing diminished somewhat at her admission that she didn't like living in the dugout. Deep down, she really didn't want to be here, living out her mother's dream.

It helped to believe that, especially when she turned and faced him square on, her eyes glowing with luminous shyness, the moonlight bleaching the color from the blush darkening her cheeks. "I never thanked you properly for agreeing to help Hiram. And I should have properly apologized that day for shooting you, not just for ruining your shirt."

"I had another," he mumbled, losing a bit of his self-righteousness to think that *she*, dreaming happily of a sod house that would never be built, should be apologizing to *him*, when, once she knew the truth, she would have wished for better skill with the shotgun.

The breeze heightened, chilled from flowing over the swift-running creek. It lifted a strand of Ellie's hair and sent it stroking Tremayne's skin. He caught it between thumb and finger, finding it insubstantial yet silky smooth against his roughened skin. Drawn by an irresistible impulse, he smoothed it back into the curling chestnut mass framing her face, his eyes locked with hers, his fingers brushing ever so gently against the smooth shoulder bared by her slipping dress. She'd touched him, that day when he'd told her about his past, and again tonight, when she'd pressed a restraining hand against his arm. He doubted she knew how deeply those gentle pressures had struck, or the craving they'd prompted to touch her in return.

"You're cold," he whispered, stroking a heated trail against her skin.

"A little." She bent her head and sent her hair tumbling over her shoulders, burying his hand within its fragrant weight. "I . . . I didn't think you liked touching me, Tremayne. I don't think it's right."

"I know," he said, though no power on earth could have forced him to move his hand just then. He closed his eyes and drew a deep, rasping breath that did nothing to cool the fevers raging within him. Her skin pulsed beneath his fingers, shattering what little control he retained.

The only way to protect her from himself was to rouse her hatred so that she would turn away from him in disgust. Tell her what he was about now, while she was still flushed with the triumph of her first dance, with no curious eyes to witness the betrayal. Tell her that not only did he mean to take her back, but that it had been his idea to come after her in Stringer's place. He found he needed a fortifying breath before speaking.

"I shouldn't be touching you like this, not when I've offered my services—"

"Oh, goodness, I didn't mean it that way!" She caught his offending hand between both of hers and rose to her knees. "All that 'hired hand' and 'employer' nonsense belongs back East, not out here on the prairie. Why, I think Hiram has plans, but it's not for me to be the first one to speak of his intentions."

Her voice trailed off as she set his hand gently atop his outstretched thigh. It seemed a fit punishment to Tremayne, that her brushing touch against his leg should rouse his manhood into bursting, aching need while she knelt before him blushing at the mention of another man's honorable intentions.

He should have stopped in Wichita.

Honorable intentions and guilt be damned.

He swiveled to his knees, and leaned toward her, tucking the hand she'd so recently dismissed round the back of her neck.

"Ellie." He said her name, her *real* name, and reveled in the surge of pleasure that jolted through him as he drew her swaying figure into his embrace.

"Ellie." He murmured it again, burying his lips against the silken skin at her neck. She stiffened briefly, then melted against him when he yielded to the overwhelming urge to press his tongue to her skin, tasting her, before trailing another round of heated kisses along her throat, her cheeks. "Ellie." A woman who'd never gone dancing might never have kissed, and her lips parted hesitantly beneath his, their tender quivering bespeaking innocence, and shared passion.

He delved his hand past the too-wide neckline of her dress, his fingers tracing the contours of her breast and finding the nipple already engorged for him. Locked to her with lips and hands he throbbed for more, and somehow eased her flat on the grass without losing hold. "Ellie." She sighed at hearing her name, her breath a soft caress against his lips, maddening him even more as he molded her slender length against his brawn.

A flurry of cracking gunshots rent the air, penetrating his passion-crazed mind, restoring his senses before he claimed her right there on the prairie. "Bloody hell," he whispered, forcing himself up and away from her, cursing the interruption, cursing his loss of control.

"Lauretta and Hiram are still back at the soddie." Ellie cringed when, with whoops and hollers, the perpetrators fired off another round of shots. "Do you think they're in trouble?"

"I doubt it. It's just a bunch of drunken homesteaders intent upon mischief." And he was no different.

She smiled with relief as she lay in the grass looking up at him, her hair in wild disarray, her gown askew, her lips swollen and dark. Her breasts rose with her light, fluttering breaths. One hand plucked at dry turf; the other lifted as if she meant to reach for him and draw him back. Her lips parted in a tremulous smile. He touched a finger to them, tracing their delicate swell, feeling the moist heat with which he'd tried to brand her as his. Her eyes mirrored the frustration surging through him, mingled with a wondering awe.

He wished he could engrave this image of her on his mind, for he knew with sick certainty she would never look upon him like this again.

"Forgive me, madam. For everything."

She flinched at his deliberate distancing, and he thought he might never outlive his shame for causing the hurt, baffled embarrassment that replaced her joyous ardor.

Swallowing against the pain, he nodded toward where the noisy gunfighting continued. "I'll go see if I can help break that up before anyone gets hurt. And I'll send your friends to help you to the wagon—the dance is bound to break up once this sort of thing starts."

He left her without a backward glance, knowing each step he took placed more than physical distance between them.

7

He didn't come back.

Across the prairie, Ellie heard loud manly voices challenge the gun-happy drunkards. A moment later, indulgent male laughter and back-slapping sounds drifted through the night. She assumed he'd helped bring about a satisfactory conclusion to the drunken shooting spree. But Tremayne didn't return to her. And she couldn't bring herself to seek him out to assure herself of his safety, for she didn't think she could bear to have him look at her just then.

She burned, everywhere he'd touched her. And in some places where he hadn't.

A twig snapped behind her, crunched by a heavy booted foot. Her heartbeat commenced a riotous hammering, only to settle into a leaden thud when she whirled about and found Hiram and Lauretta making their way along the moonlit path.

"There you are, ma'am. Tremayne said we'd find you here."

"Yes, here I am!" she answered with false brightness, leaping to her feet as if she'd been eagerly waiting for Hiram and Lauretta, and none other, to join her. But she couldn't help asking after him. "He didn't . . . didn't get hurt during the commotion, did he?"

"Oh, Lordy, no," Lauretta reassured her.

"I expect he learned how to steer clear of buckshot since he met up with you," Hiram added.

Ellie kept her face averted. Tremayne had left her, and he hadn't come back, but her lips still felt the pressure of his possession, her tongue remembered the taste of his, her nose seemed filled with his heady scent, her body tingled, missing the press of his weight. The sharp-eyed Lauretta would certainly spot some lingering evidence of the wanton stranger Ellie harbored within.

"Tremayne said we should go on ahead. He has some business to take care of." Lauretta tucked her hand through Ellie's arm and the three of them found their way to the wagon.

From somewhere, Ellie summoned the strength to murmur politely interested responses to Lauretta's excited chatter. Inside, her mind seethed with confusion. What business could Tremayne have that required his attention tonight? Why had he left her? Why had he dared take such liberties, and why had she permitted them?

She should have remembered the way he always flinched from her touch. Instead, she'd ignored his blatant aversion, much as she'd spent long years deflecting her father's criticisms of her womanly charms. Maybe her father had been right all along—no man would want a skinny, wild-haired woman like her.

Five men had offered for her hand during the dance, but that meant nothing, given the severe shortage of women. Maybe she should have accepted one of them. The short, stout one with black hair and brown eyes, so completely unlike Tremayne. She didn't want to pay the high price of marriage, but there would be compensations. If she accepted someone's suit, she needn't worry anymore about her father's rights over her, since her husband's rights would take precedence. And as a married woman, when her love and desires would be firmly fixed upon her husband, she'd waste no time mooning over Tremayne Hawthorne's appealing presence, and it wouldn't strike so deep at her heart to know he found her unattractive.

She pretended to sleep during the long ride home, swallowing hard against the return of her seasickness, against the clogging ache in her throat. More times than she cared to admit, she found herself slitting her eyes open, raking the retreating prairie for a glimpse of Tremayne's gray gelding.

He didn't follow. And though she lay awake all night, staring into the candle's flickering flame, listening for the sound of his horse trotting into the barnyard, nothing but Lauretta's slumbering breathing broke the silence.

*   *   *

At the first pale glimmer of light, Ellie eased from the bed, shivers coursing along her limbs. Lauretta still slept, and Ellie tried her best not to wake her. Her friend needed the sleep, and she didn't feel like discussing the events of the night before, not just yet. She struggled with the fire, her jittery movements nearly dousing the banked flame before coaxing it back to life, heaping twigs and sticks upon the growing blaze until it burned wastefully hot. And still she trembled.

She missed her mother with a sudden, jolting ache. If only Angeline had lived, had dared to run away with her, perhaps she could have explained these sensations plaguing her. She would have been proud of Ellie and Lauretta, admired what they'd accomplished by acquiring the homestead, helped her see that Tremayne Hawthorne was nothing more than a hired hand, a necessary tool for this stage of their endeavors. Nothing more.

Draping her cloak around her shoulders, she stepped outside. Gazing over her land, breathing in great gulps of freedom, might soothe her soul.

The sky looked perceptibly lighter toward the east, brightening from black to gunmetal gray. A lone bird chirped, its single-noted song so different from the full-blown chorus that would have greeted her back in Arkansas. The mules weren't fooled by the lack of sunlight. Alert and hungry, they waited patiently next to the barn.

She heard someone moving about in the barn, heard the hiss of corn spilling into feed buckets, the rustle of hay. The noise brought two more inquisitive beasts toward the fence—Tremayne's gray gelding and a bay mare she'd never seen before. She gripped her cloak tighter to her neck, her apprehension warranted when Tremayne Hawthorne stepped into the yard, shirtless while she shivered.

She must have made some sound or movement for his head whipped around; indeed, his entire body swiveled, the lightening sky revealing clearly his wide-braced legs, the buckets supported by the strength of his sinewy arms.

Mere hours ago she had felt those brawny limbs surround her. His fingers had caressed her breast. And then he'd abandoned her. Ellie's face burned; her tongue seemed to swell, clogging her throat so that she couldn't speak to him even if she wanted to. She wasn't sure she should ever bring herself to speak to him again, since all her good sense seemed to desert her the minute he got near.

A tremor passed through him—a trick, no doubt, of the uncertain light. A hank of hair had escaped his queue. The hint of a beard sculpted his face, the dark stubble surprising, considering the sun-lightened gold of his hair. His wintry gaze blazed azure bright against the telltale smudges below his eyes, which proclaimed that, like her, he'd spent a sleepless night.

For some reason, she found that bit of knowledge quite cheering.

"Good morning, madam."

Though softly spoken, she could hear his gruff greeting clearly in the early morning quiet.

"I didn't hear those horses in the yard last night," she said. "I didn't know you'd come home."

"I let them loose in the corral and walked to the barn. And this isn't my home."

He seemed determined to project the cross demeanor of a grizzly bear, which perversely delighted her. In fact, her spirits seemed to be brightening in accordance with the sky as she watched his bare-torsoed form tend to the animals with quick, precise skill, every movement sending muscles rippling along his arms, his back, his chest.

She caught him peering at her over the back of the new mare.

"Why do you have two horses today, Mr. Hawthorne?"

It was a simple enough question, but his face blanched with the effort of answering it. "You said riding in the wagon makes you feel sick, so I bought it for you." He tore his gaze away as if his generous impulse embarrassed him, and then he caught both horses by their halters and led them toward the creek.

Giddiness swept through her. A horse! Buying it must have been the business he'd found so pressing last night. Perhaps he'd left her because he found himself as confused and uncertain as she, swept up by feelings neither of them felt comfortable acknowledging. He hadn't rejoined her at the creek, but he'd bought her a *horse*. Horses meant responsibility, stability. The implications of such a gift spun her mind into directions she'd never dared explore.

Hiram stumbled from the barn, yawning and scratching, squinting in the early morning light. With a halfhearted wave and mumbled greeting in her direction, he plodded toward the woodpile, no doubt intent upon stacking the day's cooking fuel near the dugout door. His gift to Lauretta, just as surely as Tremayne had gifted her with the horse. Lauretta would reciprocate with fresh-baked biscuits.

Ellie had nothing to give in return.

One of the horses whinnied. The gray gelding reared and she stared, captivated, watching Tremayne's quick, capable actions bringing the animal under control. He stood silhouetted against the sky, his lean, sinewy body gilded by sunlight, and a quick thrill of excitement rippled through her.

There *was* something she could do for him.

His shirt, the one he'd worn when she'd shot him—she could mend it for him. She might need to cut back the sleeves, and some of the bloodstains might have set permanently, but surely something could be salvaged. She would wash it, and repair it, using every bit of her skill as a needlewoman. The pleasure of performing a pleasant domestic task for him settled warm around her heart while she ran into the barn.

She found the homespun shirt stuffed haphazardly beneath the thin, grass-stuffed pillow that cradled his head at night—his impression still lingered. She ran her fingers over the outline, wondering if she figured in any of the dreams his tawny head conjured there, fancying a trace of his heat warmed her sewing hand.

Back in the sunlight, her task seemed more daunting. Wrinkled, the sleeve nearly shredded, the body of it stiffened with rusty brown streaks, the shirt looked nearly beyond saving. Still, she would try. Tremayne had managed to repair her tattered self-confidence with his gift. Perhaps the simple, womanly gesture of caring for his things might mend one or two of the tears rent in his heart from his father's abandonment, his businesslike marriage.

She shook her head and laughed at her fanciful thoughts.

Once she washed his shirt, she'd have a better idea of where to begin. Knowing her own habit of forgetting little things in her pockets, she delved into the homespun pouch sewn over his chest. Something rigid, a square of cardboard. She withdrew it, casting it only a careless look . . . and the shirt fluttered to the ground while she grasped the cardboard between both hands, staring with numb disbelief.

Her own likeness stared back at her.

How well she remembered the day the photograph had been taken: her father's insistence upon the too-tight, childish gown that bound her blossoming curves; the hairstyle he'd decreed, Hannah scraping it so tightly back that it looked like dark skin painted on her skull; the flat, dead feeling crushing her soul, so eloquently captured by the photographer. Only one time had she posed. Only one photograph had been ordered. And since the day it returned from the photographer, it had sat imprisoned in an ornate silver-gilt frame. Atop her father's desk.

Jonathan McKittrick's sole reminder of his runaway daughter—and he'd given it away. Like the drawings he passed out to his trackers when inmates dared try escaping.

With blinding clarity she realized Tremayne's true

purpose in being there, remembering how he'd surprised them in the dugout, her initial misgivings that he'd soothed away with half-truths. At every turn he'd warned her off. *You mustn't trust anyone, ever. People are forever imagining they see things that aren't truly there.*

And yet, fueled by schoolgirl guilelessness and empty-headed dreams, she'd ignored her instincts and dared to trust him. To believe in him. To dance . . . and burn for him.

"Oh, Tremayne." She spoke his name, hearing the bleeding agony in her voice. She couldn't drop the damning evidence; her fingers grasped the photograph with a frozen stiffness akin to the grip of a dead woman clutching the rosary that would accompany her to the grave. Her heart, so recently singing with joy, seemed to have burst into a thousand jagged pieces, each one intent upon sawing its way through her ribs. Trembling, aching, she pressed the photograph against her breast, as *he* had worn it, while tracking her down.

"Ellie!"

She heard him call her as if from a great distance; saw his chiseled visage approach her through a watery haze. The look he gave her conveyed such bleak, infinite sadness—and grim, ruthless determination. A man who didn't so much like to win as he hated to lose.

"My father sent you."

"Yes."

Rage surged through her despair. Her conflicting emotions held her immobile when she would have lashed out; paralyzed her tongue when she would have used words as a weapon. How many nightmares had she endured envisioning this very scenario? How many hours had she fretted, quelling the sense of panic that arose at the mere thought of being forced home? Nightmares and hours beyond counting, especially weighed against even more hours—nay, days— spent convincing herself that she would succeed. She'd planned on quite literally fighting capture to the death, or on appealing to her captor's sense of justice to win him to her side.

She'd never counted on being stalked by someone like Tremayne Hawthorne, who'd bared his vulnerabilities in order to prey upon her own. It would have been easy to curl fingers into claws and attack the dark, hulking figure who haunted her dreams, or someone who leered or smirked in triumph, who manhandled with the intent to harm or subdue. She found it impossible to strike Tremayne in anger, to make him bleed when his touches had sent passion coursing through her veins. And so she stood immobile, stunned into defenselessness, by betrayal.

But not by his betrayal. The betrayal was all of her own making, for she had allowed a few kind words, a few stolen caresses, to batter down defenses she'd vowed to keep erected.

Something hot and wet streaked down her cheeks to splash against the hand curled round the photograph. Tears. She stared at the shimmering droplets with dull recognition. After eleven years of trying, her father had finally found the tool that could break her spirit and make her cry.

*   *   *

From the first Tremayne had agonized over how he would tell her what he meant to do. He'd never expected a simple yes would be all that was required. Or that saying it would scrape his insides raw.

He'd forgotten all about the damning photograph. Its pallid, insipid portrayal was such a pale shadow of Ellie that he'd forgotten it the moment he set eyes upon her. He should have remembered, should have taken care to destroy it once its purpose was served. But then if he'd been better skilled at covering his tracks, he'd never have found himself in her father's jailhouse in the first place.

And Silas Stringer would have been the one standing before Ellie now, watching the light fade from her eyes, the animation desert her face, a profound stillness settling over her as if she meant to turn herself back into that damned cardboard effigy.

"I never meant to hurt you."

She gave no indication that she heard.

"You're truly better off away from here. Your mother wouldn't have expected you to live out this dream for her. You don't know the first thing about homesteading. You don't even have medical supplies on hand, and you don't know how to protect yourself from men." He could have choked on his own words, so pious and self-serving did they sound, considering his despicable lack of control the night before. Ellie blushed, as if the same thought crossed her mind. "Had things gone according to plan, you'd be safe at home now—"

"But I shot you and disrupted your schedule by several days. How inconvenient of me." While she spoke, tears continued coursing down her face. She practiced none of the histrionics one might expect from a crying female: no loud weeping, no heaving bosom, no delicate dabbing of the eye with a dainty muslin handkerchief. He found her silent tears far more affecting. "I suppose that's why you felt compelled to exact payment from me last night."

He'd imagined she might think him a lecher or a cad, but never that his desire for her might have been construed as punishment. "My behavior last night was unconscionable. It was a mistake of the worst magnitude—"

"Yes," she whispered. "Nothing but a terrible mistake."

At that moment, Lauretta stepped through the dugout door, balancing a mixing bowl against her hip. "Hey, you two early risers, how many biscuits you want for breakfast?"

To think that such an ordinary question, delivered in such a cheerful, good-morning tone, should swirl about them now. Irrationally, Tremayne wished it were an ordinary day, that he could scowl with pretended dismay at the thought of gnawing on Lauretta's biscuits, that Ellie's stone-faced countenance would brighten with excited pleasure. But it wasn't an ordinary day—it was their last day here, and he had to prepare for their trip.

"Make an extra dozen, Lauretta," he said, thinking they'd need something to eat on the way to Wichita.

"I can't believe I heard you right," Lauretta said,

laughing as she scurried over. "I never thought I'd see the day Tremayne Hawthorne asked for extra biscuits—why, Ellie, what's wrong?"

"It's Tremayne." With excruciating precision, Ellie detailed his purpose. "He's the one, Laurie. He's here to take me back to my father."

"No!" For one interminable moment, silence reigned, and then with a piercing screech Lauretta flung her bowl at Tremayne. He ducked it, but wasn't quick enough to evade her flailing fury. She attacked him, kicking his shins, pummeling his chest with small fists.

Tremayne endured the blows, silently staring over Lauretta's furious form at Ellie's rigid stance. She should be the one reacting so, punishing him for his perfidy. Her dispirited acceptance of her lot reminded him of a young fox he'd trapped as a child. Despite his best efforts to coax the beast into eating, the fox had huddled in one corner and stared unblinkingly past the bars of its cage, until one morning Tremayne had found its rigid form, its nose pointing unerringly toward freedom even in death. Anger at the fox's passive stubbornness had filled Tremayne with righteous indignation, and he'd shaken the wasted carcass, wishing he'd tried forcing food down its throat and taught it to act like a regular dog.

With Ellie, he felt the stir of a similar frustration. He longed to shake away the submissive Eleanor McKittrick and bring back the wide-eyed young woman who delighted in dancing over the prairie, chasing honeybees. But to what end? So he could shatter her pride once more? Revulsion, directed at his own miserable motives, churned within him.

"You . . . you . . . you . . . *skunk!*" Lauretta shrieked. "You low-bellied snake! For God's sake, Ellie, don't just stand there—*run!*"

Ellie's eyes widened, an all-too-tiny spark flaring briefly to life. Hitching up her skirts, she commenced a stumbling, weaving parody of flight that twisted Tremayne's heart. Picking up Lauretta's thrashing figure and setting her aside, he loped after Ellie, catching up to her as easily as the hated Stringer had always run him down, just as she gained the corral.

"There's no sense in running, madam," he said, keeping his voice very quiet.

She had her hand on a rail. Her fingers tightened around the rough wood and he flinched, thinking of the splinters piercing her skin. The pain seemed to rouse her spirit.

"If I keep running, will you rope me down like a steer?"

"If I must."

"How do you propose getting me back there? I won't go willingly."

He glanced at her slender wrists, taking no satisfaction in realizing how easy her strength would be to overcome. "I'll bind your hands and feet if you force me to. We have a great deal of riding ahead of us."

"A great deal of riding." Her eyes raked the prairie, coming to rest upon the horses grazing near the creek. "So that's why you bought the mare."

"Working animals are scarce out here. Lauretta will have need of the mule team. It didn't seem fair to take the wagon only to abandon it once we're on the train for Fort Smith. And I didn't want you to get sick on the journey."

She shuddered. "So concerned over my welfare. I should have shot you dead. I could still shoot you, if I get my hands on my shotgun."

"If you do, your father will only send another in my place. He is determined to have you back."

"And if I tell you I am equally determined to stay here?"

He felt a great, aching weariness overtake him. "I'm afraid your determination cannot stand against his. Or my own."

"Such loyalty to my father. I'm certain he values it highly—and paid for it well. So, what reward will you receive in exchange for me?"

When he refused to speak, she leveled him with a withering glance. "I have a right to know. It's a tradition dating back to Christ himself, when he learned Judas betrayed him for thirty pieces of silver."

He couldn't deny the comparison. Like Judas, he was finding the promised reward loomed less sweet in his mind than anticipated. How would he ever enjoy his independence, his retribution, his triumphant return to England, knowing Ellie's freedom had paid for his pleasure?

"Your father prizes you highly. A man's life hangs in the balance."

"Oh, Tremayne, can't you see that mine does, too?"

Tremayne almost relented at the heartache piercing her words. And then he thought of the luxurious, if dreary, home awaiting her in Arkansas, Jonathan

McKittrick's near-frenzy to have her safely home, balanced against Jessop Farnsworth's life. "You will not die if I take you back to your father, madam. A man has pledged to forfeit his life if I fail to return with you. Your father has given me his word that Farnsworth will remain safe and well provided I return you to his care."

She cast him a glance of incredulous scorn. "And you believed him? My father will promise anything to get his way, but thinks nothing of doing as he pleases the moment one's back is turned. Surely a professional hired gun would demand more than my father's word."

"But I am not one of your father's trackers, madam. I am an inmate waiting to be tried for murder."

He remembered how McKittrick had gloated, anticipating her reaction when she learned he'd sent a murderer chasing after her, and he cursed the man for knowing his daughter too well. His admission, deliberately couched in the plainest possible words, sapped her restored spirit. She stared at him without breathing, her face a white mask of horror. His hand moved toward her and she flinched away.

"Arrested for killing whom?"

"My wife. And child."

She didn't move but it seemed as if she staggered. Her lips formed the word *no*, but no sound came from her.

"Now see here, Hawthorne, we're not gonna let some murderin' rascal haul Ellie off."

He turned, grateful for the interruption, to find Hiram holding Ellie's shotgun braced against his shoulder, Lauretta peering over his shoulder. Tremayne shook his head.

"How do you propose to stop me, Espy? By committing murder yourself?"

"If that's what it takes."

"Aim to the left, Hire, that gun pulls to the right," Lauretta urged.

Hiram squeezed off a shot and Tremayne winced reflexively, though nothing more resulted than the sound of hammer striking bare metal.

"I took the precaution of emptying the shotgun yesterday before we left for Naylor's. But even if it were loaded and you sent a bullet straight through my heart, it wouldn't matter. Jonathan McKittrick will only send another in my place."

Hiram flushed, redfaced with embarrassment over his failure. "Why don't you just hightail it outta here, Hawthorne, and leave Miss McKittrick be? We won't tell no one where you headed."

Tremayne's face heated; his gaze shifted, as he found himself too embarrassed to meet their accusing stares. "My own freedom will be assured once I return with the information I need to defend myself during my trial. Miss McKittrick must return to her father. I must complete this mission in its entirety before returning to England to reconcile with my own father. Once our differences are settled, I shall become the acknowledged heir to the earldom of Chedgrave. Among other things, peoples' livelihoods and ancestral lands are at stake. I will not be forestalled."

"We can't stand against him, Hiram. And he's right. Father will never relent." Ellie shivered, staring out over the prairie as if she meant to etch its beauty upon her memory. "What's next, Mr. Hawthorne? Must I meekly pack up my belongings and follow your orders like a proper hostage?"

"It will go easier with everyone if you do."

"Very well."

"Oh, Lordy, Ellie, don't let him do this!" Lauretta cried. "Hiram, you have to stop him."

"I won't be stopped, Lauretta. Whoever tries will only get hurt." Catching Hiram by surprise with his quick motion, Tremayne snatched the shotgun from his hands. Harmless as it was in its unloaded state, it still assuaged something within him to whip it over the prairie and watch it spin end over end before falling into the grass. "We'll be gone by the time you find it again."

"You know I will hate you," Ellie said softly. "With every breath I draw, I will curse your name, and hate you to the pit of my soul."

"I know." He thought of McKittrick's dreary parlor, and imagined Ellie trapped within, her true nature stifled beneath her carefully cultivated calm, hating him more with every tick of the clock. He stared at her, certain his own gaze mirrored the cold emptiness reflected in her chocolate brown eyes. "Nevertheless, it's time for us to go."

8

On the train ride carrying them to their homestead, Ellie and Lauretta had occasionally noticed strange, tobacco brown mounds dotting the landscape. When Ellie had spotted a similar mound at the farthest corner of their homestead, she'd urged Lauretta to explore it with her. She remembered how they'd run from it, trailing exaggerated, girlish shrieks when they realized the mound was composed of grasshopper carcasses, harmless remnants of the descending horde which had devastated Kansas crop-land over the past several years. Dried, dead husks of once-living creatures, empty as the snake skin she had found, drained and devoid of life as she felt now. Which should suit Tremayne and her father just fine. They cared nothing for the soul and spirit of the woman she nurtured inside, only that her exterior shell be properly fed and clothed and placed where they wanted it to be.

Tremayne had tended to the tasks that would complete his successful day's trapping. He'd shoved her clothes into a pillowcase, dished yesterday's stew into a crock when Lauretta refused to bake biscuits, filled their extra jar with water for the journey. Ellie watched him pack it into the saddlebags, helpless to stop him. His superior strength would prevail even if she regained her ability to move. And he'd already proven his wits could best hers—a minor victory, since it seemed she had no sense at all.

Despair held her in its grip, so numbing and yet painful that she thought she might die from it. How could she ever have thought she might escape from her father's clutches? A woman had no rights—either she lived under her father's control, or married and subjected her will to her husband's. Her efforts seemed so pitiful now. Her father had probably known where she was headed long before she ever reached this place. How pathetic, in retrospect, her naive belief that becoming a landowner and establishing herself in a community would carry any weight against her father's wishes. No law in the land would stand against him. She should have found someone to marry her. No—she should have kept running.

She stood near the corral, her arms clasped tight over her middle, the blazing sun doing nothing to chase the chill that held her frozen in place. Lauretta sat rocking back and forth on the stoop, little hiccupping sobs sounding muffled through her veil. Hiram paced in the yard, quaking with frustrated impotence, glowering while Tremayne traipsed between the dugout and the horses, making everything ready for their trip.

Tremayne ran a practiced hand over the gelding's side, checking cinches, tying flaps. He did the same with the mare, his strong, capable fingers pressing and probing for weaknesses. Staring at his hands, Ellie felt her face flood with all the heat denied the rest of her body. Had his caresses the night before been nothing more than the same cool, businesslike assessment he used now to judge the mare's fitness?

Knowing what he meant to do to her this morning, he'd exercised his practiced hands and lips to kiss her and rouse her passions last night. His touch had sparked dreams best left dormant; he had slipped past her carefully erected wall of self-control with heady ease, stirring the long-dead hope that there might indeed be one man worth trusting, worth loving. She would never forgive him for that.

Never.

He patted the mare's neck and then flicked his gaze over to her. "I'm ready. Say your good-byes, El—Miss McKittrick."

Lauretta hurtled across the yard, wrapping her arms around Ellie's waist and burying her head against her shoulder. "Don't go, Ellie, please. I don't know what I'll do without you. Maybe the three of us could gang up on him and beat him up!"

Hiram, too, made his way to her side. His face flamed scarlet while he shot venomous looks at Tremayne. "This ain't right. There's gotta be somethin' we can do, ma'am. It just happened so sudden-like, I can't think of anythin' right off."

"Nor can I, Hiram. Nor would it matter if I could. My father has every legal right to do this." With a final squeeze of Lauretta's shoulders, Ellie took a step back, wondering when—or if—she'd ever see her friend again. "Please don't cry, Lauretta. We tried our best. It's not your fault we didn't succeed. I . . . I'll be all right."

"No you won't," Lauretta said tearfully. She turned toward Tremayne, her stance projecting trembling fury. "You take her back to her father and you'll be killing her just like you did your wife and child. I don't see how you can live with yourself, Mr. Hawthorne."

"You exaggerate, Miss Myers. I've lived under her father's rule for five months. He's a harsh taskmaster, but fair." At his comment, both Ellie and Lauretta gasped their surprise. But no flicker of remorse crossed his face; he flinched not at all before Lauretta's vehemence. He swung his attention to Ellie. "Are you ready now, madam?"

A poor horsewoman, Ellie had always had diffi-culty mounting unassisted. Today, with leaden despair weighing her limbs, raising her foot to the stirrup seemed an impossibility. Tremayne, seeing her difficulty, gripped her around the waist. Her traitorous body shivered in response to his firm touch, to the warmth of his breath stroking her cheek. She turned on him, her fingers curled like talons, out-rage suffusing her with a madness more akin to insan-ity than anger.

"Don't you ever dare touch me again!"

He stepped back at once, raising his offending hands in mock surrender, his dispassionate eyes sweeping over her as if planning where he might grip her should she fly at him in a shrieking rage.

She wouldn't give him the satisfaction of losing control in front of him. Nor would she let Hiram assist her into the saddle. Such a gesture might weigh on Hiram's soul later. With grim determination lending her strength, she heaved herself atop the mare, settling somewhat inelegantly into the saddle, gathering the skittish beast's reins in her shaking fingers.

Ellie glanced at Lauretta and nearly lost her resolve. Lauretta's head tilted up, the sun striking through her veil against the shimmer of tears. The dugout loomed low behind her, the outside of the primitive structure crumbling against the elements. As she would, if she gave way to her emotions. Ellie's throat tightened. "Take care, Lauretta."

"Ellie." Lauretta's indrawn breath caught on a sob. "I'll keep things going here, I swear. I'll keep up the payments to the railroad. The homestead will be ready for you when you come back. You got away from your father once, Ellie. You can do it again."

"Good-bye," Ellie whispered. She quelled the irrational hope that leaped through her at Lauretta's words. She eased the mare's head around and nudged with her knees, deliberately aiming so that one iron-shod hoof trod Tremayne Hawthorne's bloody shirt into the dust.

* * *

She could tell he chafed at their slow progress. Every so often he urged the horses into a trot or slow canter; equally as often, Ellie nearly lost her seat.

"We should have taken the wagon," he muttered, when once again only his quick hand hauling her back into the saddle prevented her from tumbling to the earth. "Wichita's another twenty miles yet. We'll not reach it before nightfall at this pace."

"I'm not in all that great a hurry. And you never asked if I could ride," Ellie said, drawing some slight amusement from disrupting his schedule.

"All proper young ladies know how to ride."

"Perhaps they do in England, Mr. Hawthorne, which should please you no end once you turn me over and make your escape to claim your precious ancestral lands."

He hadn't looked her in the eye once since Lauretta and Hiram's waving forms disappeared in the distance. He didn't look at her now. Only the thinning of his lips betrayed the fact that she'd found her mark with her cutting words. With a little click of his tongue he urged a faster walk from his horse, giving her a view of his broad back. She made a gruesome face at it.

Well done, Ellie, she chided herself. Perhaps she could insult him to death. But Father would only send another man, one with even thicker skin.

The mare she rode seemed a docile, amiable animal bearing no more enthusiasm for this trip than Ellie herself. Without Tremayne's gelding alongside to keep pace with, the mare's gait dawdled until they fell a few lengths back, and Ellie realized she could enjoy a head start if she tried to escape. The poor mare found its head jerked roughly to the side, its tender flanks pummeled with the stout heels of Ellie's stolen gardener's boots.

"Ellie!" Tremayne bellowed.

"Faster," Ellie urged, hugging tight to the startled animal's neck, losing the reins while she desperately tried to maintain her balance. The saddle horn prodded her stomach, threatening to poke straight through her back. Her heart beat in accord with the mare's pounding hooves, her spirits lifting like strands of the mare's mane blowing in the breeze.

From the corner of her wind-whipped eye she could see Tremayne hunched low over his gelding's neck, the gray animal's long strides eating up the distance between them. "Faster!" she cried, the mare's mane slapping against her face, the stinging pain drawing hot, salty tears. "Faster!"

The gelding raced in a wide circle, coming around to meet Ellie's mare. Tremayne positioned his horse sideways. The mare skidded to a halt with a confused-sounding snort, and Ellie nearly pitched over its head.

"That was stupid," he said roughly. "You've cost us two miles and nearly winded your mount. You might have been hurt."

"I wish I'd broken my neck," she muttered. Damn the sound of his voice! He'd just run her to ground the way his precious English countrymen hounded a fox, and the rich resonance of his voice echoed deep within her, somewhere below her heart. "How dare you act as though you have some concern for my well-being!"

"I do."

Her eyes flew open at his words, taking in his haggard expression, the mauve shadows beneath his eyes, the beard stubble he'd not taken time to shave off darkening his lean cheeks. For one fleeting second, she fancied he might care for her, just a bit, and then his blunt words shattered that tenuous hope.

"We will be spending two weeks together, madam. You'd best learn now that I won't be thwarted. My mission won't be complete until I've delivered you safely to your father. I'll control your reins so you can't try another trick like this."

The mare's neck stretched as far as it could before the animal was forced to take a step to keep up with Tremayne's gelding. The lurch nearly toppled Ellie and she gripped the saddle horn for support.

He spared one backward look and she met his annoyance with all the dignity she could muster, considering her ungraceful, unladylike seat astride the mare. He forged ahead like an ox hauling an overladen stoneboat, resigned to the task, caring not at all what he dragged.

Her mare trod upon a tuft, throwing Ellie's weight to the side. She slid off the saddle in an inelegant heap amid a whisper of cloth against leather and a small *oof* of surprise. Neither the mare nor Tremayne noticed. Wincing against the jolt to her bones, she opened her mouth to call out and then clamped her lips shut, watching the two nodding horses carry her captor ever farther away. It took but a moment to clamber to her feet, lift her front skirts as high as she dared, and begin running in the opposite direction.

Ellie loved the wide-open prairie, the endless vistas hinting at eternity, but just then she knew she would sell her soul to see a dense patch of forest, a cave-riddled mountain, anyplace where she might hide. A poor horsewoman, she was an even worse runner. Her lungs heaved, gasping for air; her head swam, sweat blurring her eyes; her legs ached, exhausted all too soon by the heavy gardener's boots, the heel-catching hem of her skirt, the slippery, grasping prairie grass.

The thundering in her ears might have been her heart hammering a protest over her exertions, but instead it was Tremayne, running her down yet again.

"You are determined to thwart me."

"I told you . . . I would not . . . go easily." Breathlessness stole some of the determination from her words.

He still towed the mare behind him; he positioned it in front of Ellie. He moved as if to dismount, and then stilled. "Mount up. I'll tie you to the saddle this time."

It had to be lack of air that made her ears roar so loud. She had to be imagining the note of grudging respect in his voice as he ordered her to submit to his bondage.

She gripped the saddle horn and steeled herself to mount. The mare's back seemed to loom ten feet above the ground, the stirrup at least as high.

She heard the creak of saddle leather as he dismounted and came up behind her. His hands, warm and solid, curved around her waist. She felt his weight shift as a prelude to lifting her. She turned in his grasp, her hand already raised, and she slapped his face with all the strength she could muster. The blow turned his face in profile and he dropped his hands from her waist.

And then she started running again.

She didn't know how many steps she'd taken, one, ten, or a hundred, before she felt his hand close around her upper arm. She struggled, trying to wrench herself free, hating the little whimper that rose from her throat at the burning twist hurting her flesh.

She managed another half step before he whispered, "Please, Ellie, don't do this to yourself." Brooking no further defiance, he drew her hard against his chest, stilling her struggles with one massive arm clamped tight around her shoulders.

The incessant prairie wind caught her high, keening wail of despair and dissipated it over the earth.

Lauretta stared blankly toward where Ellie and Tremayne had disappeared, her heart as empty as the horizon. "Oh, Lordy, I can't believe this. What will I do now?" she whispered.

Hiram settled himself onto the stoop next to her. The dull resignation in his voice matched her own. "You probably think I'm not much of a man, Miss Lauretta."

"Why? Because you didn't try to fight against someone who stands a head taller and outweighs you by a hundred pounds? A *murderer?*" Lauretta shook her head, absolving Hiram of guilt while she couldn't forgive herself. "He'd have killed you easy as swatting

a fly, Hire. And then . . ." And then she'd be finished
for sure, the thought of losing Hiram almost as hard
to bear as losing Ellie. Maybe, if she were honest with
herself, even a little harder, though in a different way,
a way that didn't bear exploring.

Hiram rested his elbows on his knees and propped
his chin on his fists, staring over the empty prairie.
"That's the funny part. He didn't seem like the killin'
type."

"Just the kidnaping type," Lauretta shot back.

"I don't know much about kidnappers, but a man
runs across his share of murderin' sons a bitches out
here on the frontier, pardon my language, ma'am."
Hiram's forehead creased with thought. "Hawthorne
sure had a fractious temper, but he kept it buttoned
up. Killers don't usually bother. They don't care if
they get out of hand. Kinda like actin' rowdy, as a
general rule."

"Well, I suppose that's why her father picked him,
knowing Tremayne could keep his murderous impulses
under control." Lauretta shivered. "He wouldn't hurt
her, would he, if Ellie's father's expecting him to bring
her home?"

"I don't believe he would harm her at all."

Hiram's confident assurance lightened Lauretta's
apprehension, but did nothing to lift her spirits. "It
doesn't seem right, us sitting here, while she's gone."

"No, ma'am, it don't. With Miss McKittrick gone,
it ain't at all proper for me to be stayin' on here, you
bein' a single lady and all. I do have a place of my
own."

Lauretta's breath left her in a little whoosh, as

though Hiram had dealt her a blow to the stomach. Her thoughts had been so consumed with concern for Ellie, so ridden with guilt for simply standing by wringing her hands while a murderer carried off the best friend she'd ever had, that she hadn't given a moment's thought to anything but how she might hold the homestead together until Ellie managed to return. Scarcely two minutes ago, she'd felt grateful Hiram hadn't tackled Tremayne and gotten himself killed. But his words sounded as if he meant to leave her anyway.

"It's not fair!" she cried, remembering the feel of his arms around her during last night's dance, the strength of his shoulder bumping up against hers during the long wagon ride.

"No, she doesn't deserve—"

"That's not what I mean. It's not fair that you have to leave me, too. I . . . I *like* having you here." She felt heat crawl from her neck clear to her forehead at her audacity, and next to her, Hiram's face flamed with the matching scarlet she knew her veil concealed.

"Well," he said. He cleared his throat. "Well."

"Oh, don't mind me, Hire." His obvious discomfort at hearing her declaration sent embarrassment flooding through her. "I'm just feeling all out of sorts after what happened."

"Well, darn it all, Miss Lauretta, if you don't go sayin' exactly what a man wants to hear and then take it back with the next breath."

There was a low, husky amusement to his voice that she hadn't heard before. She dared a peek at him from the corner of her eye and saw him looking at her in a speculative, somewhat possessive manner that sent a pleasant tremor skittering through her.

Standing alongside Tremayne Hawthorne, Hiram had seemed almost boyish in build; sitting next to her on the stoop, she felt rather nicely dwarfed by his greater bulk. Her waist tingled with the remembered feel of his hand, reminding her how tiny her fingers felt clasped within his, how her bonneted head had only come to his chin when they danced until he'd lifted her high to kick the ceiling.

Her bonneted head. What in heaven's name was she doing? Just minutes ago her best friend had been hauled off like a runaway slave, and here Lauretta Myers sat, all but flirting with a man who'd never seen her face! Flirting, when she should be mourning her friend! She closed her eyes, but it didn't banish the image that had haunted her dreams: Hiram's wide-eyed horror should she unveil her ruined face for him to see.

Everyone, except Ellie, reacted that way. She could steel herself against that initial revulsion, but what had sent her hiding behind the veil was the way people averted their eyes afterward, as if shamed by their own reaction. Most who saw her avoided her altogether rather than accept their own embarrassment in her presence. She wore the veil more for their sake than her own.

She couldn't bear it if Hiram turned away from her because of her scars. She'd sooner send him away now.

But before she could summon words of dismissal, his rough thumb pressed through the veil, tracing the contours of her chin.

"Yer gonna have to let me see you if we mean to do anythin' about the way we feel," he whispered.

"No." She gritted her teeth but couldn't for the life of her move away from his touch. "This isn't the right time for this sort of thing, Hire. Besides, I'm . . . hideous."

"That's funny. You feel kinda nice to me." He brushed her lips with a gentle finger. The lightweight veil seemed an insurmountable barrier denying her the feel of his skin against hers. "What color are your eyes?"

"Blue." She felt her breath caress his finger.

His hand dipped, reaching for the string securing the veil. She clapped her hand on top of his, her fingers so rigid they turned numb. She would fight to the death before she would let him strip the veil away, but he made no effort to continue. His fingers rested lightly against her neck.

"Will you describe yourself to me, like you did your hair last night?"

"No. Please, Hiram, don't do this. Not now."

Her teeth-chattering fear roused a sigh from him. "All right." They sat there a moment longer, his fingers against her pulse, before he spoke again. "I saw a blind man once, had the purtiest gal in six counties for a wife. Felt right bad for him, I did, thinkin' how it wasn't fair he couldn't even see his own wife's beautiful face. He told me he could see her just fine, like this."

His fingers moved, retracing her chin and lips, and then floating softly over the rest of her face, pressing the veil against her skin. When his finger reached the

crest of her cheek she ventured a glance at him, startled to see his eyes closed, intense concentration
creasing his brow. Her own thickened eyelids fluttered closed at his touch upon them. She felt his fingers hesitate and then linger on the coarsened,
pocked surface that had to be evident even with the
veil softening his touch.

"So that's it," he said thoughtfully.

"That's it."

"I can't rightly imagine how—"

"Don't try." She pulled away from him, sick at
heart to think of him trying to picture her face in his
mind. "Please, Hiram, I'd like to be alone for a little
while now."

"All right." He sat next to her for a heartbeat
longer. "You know, she's gone, Lauretta, and you're
gonna have to decide what you mean to do without
her." And then he rose, his long strides taking him to
the barn.

Lauretta waited for relief to flood through her at
his departure. Instead, an empty yearning gripped her
soul. She'd lost Ellie, and now she might lose Hiram
as well.

It wasn't fair. None of it. Tears trickled from her
eyes, washing away the feel of Hiram's fingers caressing her scarred skin.

9

Ellie's lungs strained with long, dragging gasps to make up the air she'd lost in her mad surge for freedom. Tremayne's weighty arm held her immobile, her cheek pressed hard against his shoulder. His scent pervaded her every indrawn breath; his broad, homespun-clad chest filled her vision. Her breath stirred the edges of his shirt, which gaped open from neck to breast, revealing tanned, sculpted planes crested with tawny gold curls.

Anyone chancing to pass by would think he meant to shield her from harm. She knew otherwise; his grip shackled her as thoroughly as the canvas restraints her father used to subdue violent inmates. Her throat ached with the effort of restraining another frustrated scream, quelling the urge to shout his betrayal aloud. It would be a frivolous waste of words. Nothing, not

even a bird, seemed to share the prairie with them.
None save the wind would hear.

"Are you through running, madam?"

"Yes." Her subdued whisper acknowledged his triumph. She closed her eyes briefly. Just last night he'd crushed her softness against his strength; she didn't need to stare at his finely honed muscles now to know she stood no chance against him. "Unhand me, if you please."

A true gentleman would have dropped his hands at once. She relaxed her rigid stance in anticipation. But Tremayne held her a moment longer, and her sudden suppleness brought her lower belly against his. When she sought to step back, her shifting hips pressed all the tighter against his.

His breath caught and then rasped above her ear. The hand wrapped round her upper arm tightened, but not painfully so, and then relaxed to slide slowly down to her elbow. The arm encircling her shoulders flexed, completing a subtle transformation in the way he held her from restraint to something altogether different. It seemed his entire body leaned into hers. A little thrill shot through her, an inner quivering that answered the sudden quickening of his breath. Her heartbeat hammered in her chest to match the visible pulsation at the base of his throat.

"Unhand me," she repeated.

"Ellie—"

"Are you measuring me to determine the length of the rope you'll need to tie me to my saddle?"

He shifted his hold, seizing her by both shoulders. He pushed her back to meet her gaze; his hot with frustration and something like remorse, hers as defiant as she could make it, unblinking, determined to stare him down. And she did. With a muttered curse he set her away from him and stalked to the grazing horses.

She could try running again, might even gain another fifty or sixty feet before he caught up with her. But a curious weakness descended upon her, as if she'd depleted her strength entirely over the past few moments. Her legs trembled and then buckled beneath her. She settled into a bedraggled pink heap, an insignificant blot of color on the endless, wind-swept prairie.

Her humiliating collapse must have caught Tremayne's eye. Ellie would swear she'd done little more than blink before he towered over her, hands on hips, glaring down upon her with a distinct lack of sympathy.

"How much sleep did you get last night?"

"About as much as you did, I daresay," she answered, boldly raking her gaze over his stubbled cheeks and dark-pouched eyes.

"You ate no breakfast."

She merely shrugged. Lauretta's biscuits sat heavy on one's stomach under the best of circumstances.

He heaved an exasperated sigh. "Stay there. I'll fetch our noon piece."

"Why so anxious to feed me, Mr. Hawthorne? Is my father paying you by the pound?"

"A lucky thing for me he's not, else I'd not earn enough for passage to England."

Her face flamed while he busied himself with

fetching the stew crock and water bottle. His insult reminded her of her father's taunts and helped her regain some of the strength in her spine. She straightened her posture and vowed to stiffen her composure as well. She should know better than to trade barbs with a man. Their mean-spirited natures lent them the advantage in arguments. Still, his comment rankled and she couldn't help wondering how her slight form compared to others he'd held clasped to his chest.

He squatted next to her and offered her a sip of water, which she declined with a shake of her head. He handed her the stew crock and a small metal scoop. "Eat your fill. I'll have whatever remains."

Ellie stared into the congealed brownish mass. Greasy fat globules dotted the thick gravy. "I can't eat it like this. It's barely edible when it's heated through."

"Espy told me there's been no significant rain for six weeks, madam. We can't light a fire. It's too dangerous." Tremayne caught a few wisps of prairie grass in his fist. He waved the brittle stems before her like a farmer tempting a mule with the season's new hay. "The slightest spark could send flames roaring back to your . . . to Lauretta's homestead."

His reminder that she no longer had a place to call her own robbed her of what little appetite she might have mustered. "I'm not hungry." She pushed the crock away.

He stared at the rejected crock for a moment and then treated her to a long, considering stare. He lowered himself into sitting position with one leg resting against the ground and the other bent at the knee. He braced one arm over his knee and lifted the crock. "Suit yourself," he said as he dug into the stew with the scoop. "You'll be more easily managed if you're weak from hunger."

He'd outmaneuvered her again! Ellie clapped her jaw shut before she could demand her share of the stew. He attacked it with unconcealed relish, taking quick, economical mouthfuls from the scoop without spilling a drop or smearing his lips. Someone—perhaps a nameless nanny back on his precious ancestral lands—had taught him excellent table manners.

As he delved deeper into the crock, the aroma of onions mingled with beef wafted through the air, setting up a ferocious rumbling in her traitorous stomach.

Perhaps the sound struck loud only against her own ears. Tremayne took no notice of it. He set the crock aside in favor of the water bottle. With his head tilted back, his tawny hair fell away from his face. He lifted the bottle to his lips and took several hearty swallows, the smooth column of his throat flexing rhythmically with each one. Replete at last, he leaned back to rest his weight on his elbows, reclining upon the prairie with a self-satisfied sigh as a Roman emperor might settle himself upon a silk-covered divan.

"There's a scoop or two left, if you're hungry," he said.

She shook her head, stricken mute by a sudden, disconcerting realization. Hunger indeed raged through her, but its unfamiliar appetite had been kindled by

the sight of Tremayne's lean, sinuous length outstretched before her.

He ignored her regard for as long as it took her to
regain the need to breathe. At her shuddering,
indrawn breath, he narrowed his eyes. They burned
blue, feeding on her hunger as a gaslight's insatiable
flame devoured its invisible fuel. He made no move
toward her, but a heated tension sprang up and siz-
zled between them, every fine hair on her skin rising
in response to it.

He need only beckon, or try once more to gather
her in his arms, and she'd press herself with wanton
abandon against every inch of him.

"I hate you," she whispered.

His hooded gaze flitted with impudence from her
lips to her breasts, and lower, studying her much as
she'd done him. Her face flamed, knowing her heaving, fluttering breathlessness made a mockery of her
declaration.

"You hate me. Perhaps that is for the best."

He rose, dangling the water bottle from his fingers.
He seemed taller than ever, broader, every inch the
aroused male. The wind blew his hair back, revealing
the determined clench of his jaw, the unslaked
hunger burning in his eyes. Ellie dug her fingers
through the tough prairie grass, burying them deep
into the dirt, as if only that grip on the earth could
keep her from flinging herself into his embrace.

"I'm going to find some water for the horses. Be
ready to travel when I return. And don't try running.
You won't get far."

She curled onto her side, facing away from him,

listening to the horses' muffled hoofbeats and his receding boots crunch through the dried grass. Never before had she felt so cold.

Tremayne strode blindly, hauling against the horses' reins.

His blood churned through his veins, heated by the way Ellie's delicate features revealed her newly awakened desire, her innocent invitation. The women he'd enjoyed in England had been bought with hard-earned coin. And though he and Darla had made a few halfhearted attempts at intimacy over the years, they'd been more embarrassed by than enamored of the result. For the first time in his life, a woman smoldered with desire for *him*, not because she'd been paid, not from a sense of duty. No matter his sins, he didn't deserve this agonizing punishment. How McKittrick would chortle if he knew the dilemma Tremayne had thrust upon himself!

It had gone beyond the simple rightness or wrongness of taking her back to her father.

Could he keep his hands off her, when her cool composure slipped and she revealed the hidden passions burning within her? Could he ignore the goading voice urging him to press her for more than she offered, knowing there were none to say him nay, knowing that Ellie herself might willingly accept him? He pictured her as she'd been the night before, her glorious hair surrounding her like a dark cloud, her skin warm and supple beneath his fingers, her lips swollen from his kiss. The image roused his blood all the more. What manner of man would force himself upon a woman helpless to deny him? But then, what manner of man would have maneuvered himself into this position in the first place?

Somehow, some way, he'd have to tame his desires until . . . until what? Until he completed this odious mission and straightened out the wreck that had been made of his life. Perhaps then . . .

No trees or green growth heralded a stream, but a long-abandoned buffalo wallow dipped into the prairie. The sides, hard packed from countless heavy hooves, stood bare, while a small pool of cloudy water puddled at the bottom. Though the horses eagerly sucked up the liquid, Tremayne decided against refilling their water bottle. They'd find a fresh-running stream somewhere between here and Wichita. He hunkered next to the puddle and splashed some of the water against his face, wishing the wallow were better filled. Perhaps submerging his entire body would dampen the fire raging within.

The sign marking the border between Indian Territory and Kansas struck Cato Crowden funny, as it always did: First Chance Saloon. He laughed when he spurred his horse into a gallop past it. He turned and laughed again at the Kansas side of the sign: Last Chance Saloon. Depending on whether you were coming or going, the sign had the right name.

He was still chuckling when he let himself into the saloon's private meeting shed. Rosalee, the bar girl who always set up his table with whiskey bottle and tumblers, lurked near the passage to the saloon. "Later, darlin'," Cato called, sending her sashaying away with a wink and a broad, appreciative smile that made her rabbity face squinch with delight. Hot damn, it was a simple thing to get between the legs of a homely woman.

Thinking on how he'd enjoy her more attractive features later that night kept the smile on his face when he settled down across from Half-Scalped Jackson, but the old skull-faced vulture wouldn't crack an answering smile. Probably because he was sweet on Rosalee and she wouldn't give him a tumble when Cato was anywhere near town. Women just naturally gravitated to him. Like a cat spotting the lone cat lover amidst a group of dog men, a lonely woman curled up on his lap for a little stroking and purring. Hard work and the struggle for survival preoccupied the minds of men trying to earn an honest living, leaving their needful, lovelorn womenfolk ripe for the plucking.

Mooning over Rosalee always led Jackson to drink, and he looked more than a little hung over, which Cato knew put Half-Scalped in a surly, unpredictable mood.

"You laughing about that stupid sign again?" Jackson whined.

"Ain't stupid. Wish I'd a' thought of it."

Quick as a striking copperhead, Jackson had his gun trained right for the center of Cato's forehead. "Told you I'd kill you if you didn't stop laughing at that sign."

"You ain't going to kill me over no sign. You're

just sore 'cause your gal likes me better." His own hand flashing with blurred speed, Cato closed his fingers around the gun barrel and pointed it toward the ceiling, shaking his head at Jackson's foolhardiness. "Hell, Half-Scalped, all the girls like me better."

They'd been through this before, this grim test of wills. Despite his beanpole appearance, Jackson possessed immense wiry strength. Cato had to employ every bit of the power hinted at by his wide shoulders and bulging arms. Teeth gritted, grunting, they tussled over the gun, sweat beading their foreheads, until the whiskey bottle shimmied near the edge of the table. Snatching it up before it fell gave them the opportunity to put an end to the matter without losing face.

Jackson laid the gun down alongside his tumbler. Cato drew his and duplicated the move. He smiled at Jackson and got an answering scowl in return.

"I hope your so-called news is important enough to make up for insulting my sense of humor," Cato said.

Jackson fished in his pocket and withdrew his tobacco pouch. "Important enough, considering it don't have much to make up for," he said, taking his time over setting up his pipe, sucking hard on the stem without spilling the news Cato was curious to hear.

"You trying deliberate to get on my nerves?" Cato, tired of humoring Jackson's bilious nature, added a layer of menace to his voice. He closed his hand over his gun. "You got the rest of your life to smoke that pipe and think about why you sent for me. I'm tellin' you that life'll be awful short if you don't talk to me right now." Cato leaned back, satisfied with his turn of phrase, and poured himself a good measure of whiskey.

Jackson's scowl deepened, ending in a wince, as if the movement of his facial muscles hurt. "I wouldn't stick in one place too long if I was you. There's a fellow asking after you up Wichita way. Fella by the name of Silas Stringer, looking for you and someone named Tremayne Hawthorne. Claims this Hawthorne escaped from jail and might be out for some kind of revenge against you."

"Goddamn!"

Hearing Hawthorne's name roused a deep-seated fear that had haunted Cato for months. Now, there was one time when he should have shooed the purring, lonesome house cat away. He was the first to admit he'd erred when dallying with Hawthorne's wife. No wonder Hawthorne had tired of her; the damned clinging bitch like to have suffocated him. Who'd have thought Hawthorne would take it so personal—the woman claimed her husband didn't love her, though Hawthorne's inexplicable behavior after Cato put an end to the affair seemed to contradict Darla's contention.

Cato had followed Hawthorne's arrest with interest, blessing his good fortune when the man ended up in jail to await trial without Cato's part in the tragedy ever coming to light. And by God, he'd kept himself clean since then—a little rustling, a few bank robberies, no killing except in Indian Territory—but he hadn't had another thing to do with any married woman.

Why the hell couldn't Hawthorne have stayed in

Fort Smith, or disappeared into the Territory like any normal person would if fortunate enough to escape from jail?

Cato flung his empty glass against the wall and immediately regretted it. He'd either have to drink straight from the bottle, and Jackson, ever the mimicker, would do the same, blubbering his slimy lips all over the mouth. Or he'd have to pay the bartender for another glass. Shit. This day certainly wasn't shaping up well.

"I got the feeling this Stringer's *interested* in you, but it's Hawthorne he's really after. Could be the two of you might want to team up against Hawthorne."

"That's not a half-bad idea," Cato admitted. He felt obligated to mutter a gruff thanks, which he hoped Jackson wouldn't hear. No such luck.

"My, but your manners have improved considerable." Jackson snickered. "Since you're so nice and polite, how's about I arrange a little meeting 'twixt you and Stringer so's you can both chase after this Hawthorne?"

"You do that," Cato said.

Though he spoke calmly, a squirrelly feeling chased up his spine. Damn, just thinking about anything bringing him face to face with Hawthorne made him thirst for another whiskey.

The self-satisfied smirk on Jackson's face raised the hackles along Cato's back. The idiot actually thought he'd done him a favor. Maybe he had. He hadn't paid Rosalee a visit in a couple weeks. And if he teamed up with Stringer and got rid of Hawthorne once and for all, he'd have one less worry in his life. The second

Jackson put his glass down Cato snatched it up, claiming it for his own. Jackson merely shrugged and raised the bottle to his lips.

Even though Ellie's poor horsemanship slowed them down, Tremayne thought they might have made it to Wichita before nightfall, if it had been the mare turning a foreleg in a prairie-dog hole.

But it was the big gray gelding that stumbled, nearly tossing Tremayne over its head. "Stupid nag!" he roared, frightening the gelding into attempting another step. After one painful lurch, the animal stood quivering with bowed head, its right hoof bent while it supported its weight and that of its rider on three legs.

"Oh, the poor thing!" Ellie cried as Tremayne dismounted to check the gelding's injury. "Did it break its leg?"

"No." Tremayne ran his hand down the foreleg, feeling no jagged edge of bone. He took little comfort in knowing the gelding suffered only a sprain. The animal would barely be able to walk, let alone carry Tremayne.

The mare, a delicate, fine-boned creature, could probably carry their combined weight over the miles they had yet to travel. They'd have to stop frequently, though, and their pace would be too slow to get them there before all the decent hotels were filled for the night.

Before Ellie thought of making another escape, he leaped up and caught the mare's bridle near the bit, drawing a surprised snort from the mare and a contemptuous glance from Ellie.

"You might have made her bolt," she said.

"Really?" he drawled.

Color blazed in her cheeks. "Yes, really. Lord knows which way she might have run, with me hanging on for dear life. Why, she might have gone for miles. . . ." Her voice trailed off, her expression abashed as her own words made her realize she'd missed an opportunity to escape.

Tremayne squinted into the sun, dismayed by its low position in the sky. He peered toward where Wichita lay beyond the horizon, hoping in vain that they might have covered more ground than he'd calculated, that the town's low-rising skyline might greet his questing vision. Nothing.

"Move up," Tremayne ordered curtly.

"What?"

"In your saddle. Move forward so I can get up behind you."

He tied the gelding's reins to the saddle horn while Ellie scooted forward. "Remove your foot from the stirrup." When she complied, he hoisted his own weight and swung a leg over the mare's broad rump, settling into the saddle with Ellie nestled between his legs.

He'd never ridden so. The unexpected intimacy jarred his sensibilities. She sat bolt upright before him, gripping the saddle horn with all her might. Again he cursed his failure to stop in Wichita before embarking upon this ill-conceived plan. He gritted his teeth, remembering his determination to exert control over his baser nature while in her presence. . . . Bloody hell, if she leaned back any farther, she'd be bound to think this saddle equipped with two horns! He shifted uncomfortably and gave the mare a light taste of his heels.

The wind lifted strands of Ellie's hair and sent stray tendrils to tease his skin, surrounding him with her clean, flowery scent. "Your hair's blowing into my face," he said, his harsh tone masking the desire he felt to bury his face in the thick, shining tresses.

"Good. Perhaps it will blind you and send you back to the homestead. I've vowed to always wear it loose."

"Tie it back, madam, or I'll hack it off an inch from your scalp."

Her breath caught, as if she stifled another retort, but she grudgingly gathered the chestnut curls in and pulled them over her left shoulder. Immediately he wished he'd held his tongue. Sunlight glimmered against her bared neck. Her gown gaped away from her slender frame, affording him an unobstructed view of the shadowed valley between the creamy, satin-smooth curves of her breasts.

Bloody hell! He tore his gaze away and concentrated briefly on the prairie framed between the mare's ears, and then found his attention riveted to the sight of Ellie's slender leg pressed against his. Her straddled position pulled her gown up past her knee, revealing a tantalizing glimpse of sweetly curving thigh, the slim expanse of her calf lying alongside his, her incongruously booted foot braced against his shin.

He didn't know what to do with his hands.

He usually rode with forearms resting easily along his thighs, or hands wrapped loosely over the saddle horn. He couldn't spend the next several hours with his elbows akimbo like some triumphant vulture flexing its wings. The best thing to do with them would be to encircle Ellie's waist, to let his hands rest in her lap . . . unthinkable.

"You're taking me to Wichita no matter what," she said, a wistful note to her voice.

"Yes."

"Is it far? This . . . this position isn't very comfortable."

He doubted she knew the depths of his discomfort. "It's easier when only one sits in the saddle," he admitted.

"I could adjust my position," she offered, squirming to show what she meant.

"No! You're fine." Tremayne drew several deep breaths. "Perhaps you could just shift over to the right a little. Rest your head against my shoulder." *So I can't look down the front of your dress.*

She tilted a skeptical glance through her lashes, but with great reluctance did as he suggested. He breathed easier as she grudgingly leaned against his arm. Her hair cascaded over her shoulder, her dress fitted against her neck, concealing all but her legs from his view. With all of her propped against one side, he could rest his left hand against his thigh.

Her warmth seeped through his homespun, stoking his skin into awareness. His arm tingled from the soft pressure of her breast.

"You should try to get some rest," he muttered.

"So concerned for my welfare," she answered tartly, though exhaustion laced her voice. Eventually her breathing slowed, until she no longer sounded like a wounded doe fleeing slavering hounds. By infinitesimal degrees she relaxed more fully against him, until his arms cradled her protectively, for all the world appearing as if he could safeguard her against any harm coming her way.

Tremayne clenched his jaw and spurred the tiring mare ahead.

The prairie rolled before them, unending, no trees to break the grassy monotony, no birdsong, only a ceaseless, sighing wind. Ellie shifted against him, her lips parting with a soft, sleepy sound. Asleep, she might tumble from her unconventional perch, and that was the reason, the only reason, he tightened his arm around her waist.

10

The cessation of movement stirred Ellie's mind from the numb, slumberous place where it had retreated. A light breeze tickled her neck and she huddled back against the wall of warmth surrounding her. With dawning dismay she realized she snuggled against Tremayne—her enemy—like a kitten dozing upon a sun-warmed patch of carpet. She struggled to sit upright.

"Why have we stopped?" she demanded.

"In a hurry all of a sudden?" With a humorless grunt of laughter, Tremayne slid from the saddle and then lifted her down to stand on unsteady legs beside him. "The horses could use some rest. I want to take the gelding's saddle off and see if he moves easier without the weight on his back."

Relief at the delay swept through her. She clamped her lips shut, lest she inadvertently say anything that would propel him once more toward Wichita. She wrapped her arms around the mare's neck, absurdly grateful to the tired beast for buying her a few more moments of freedom. She would spend every minute of the intervening hours between now and morning thinking of a way to escape Tremayne.

She stole a glance at him to see if he showed any sign of growing lax; after all, she had slept, astonishingly enough, while he'd remained awake. He seemed as vigilant as ever, unfortunately, glowering at her with a brooding blue-eyed intensity that seemed to pierce right into her thoughts.

"Will we be stopping here for the night?"

"It wouldn't be very comfortable if we did," he said.

"I don't mind," she hurried to assure him, willing him to tarry, but prompting nothing more than a mocking twist of his lips.

"I didn't plan on our spending this night in the open. We have no more food and there's nothing to protect us from the cold except what we're wearing and the clothes in the packs."

"And no fire, since the grass is so dry." She repeated his earlier warning like a well-schooled student. The words helped distract her attention from his tall, muscular form. Her back and arms still tingled from the heat he'd radiated while enfolding her against his chest. "It's July. I doubt we'd freeze to death."

He ignored her in favor of tending the horses.

He left their reins to trail, which seemed exceedingly careless to Ellie, since the animals could very

well tangle their legs in the thin leather. After unsad-
dling the gelding, he threw the smelly, sweat-stained
horse blanket on the ground and gestured toward it
as if it were a cushioned divan promising great comfort. She pretended not to notice, which drew another
mocking curl of his lip as he saw to the mare. Ellie
wrapped her arms around her waist. The sun, though
sinking lower into the sky, still burned with midsum-
mer intensity. There were hours to go until nightfall,
plenty of time to reach Wichita, hours that promised
to be sweaty and humid, unless those few odd-shaped
clouds dotting the sky managed to cast a little shade.
Instead, they scudded over, seeming to boil from the
horizon while the wind increased its intensity. The
mare nickered, dancing nervously, her flaring nostrils
drawing in great gulps of the west-blowing air.

He squinted a look toward the horizon and cursed.

Ellie felt like swearing, too, when she saw the mile-
wide cloud that prompted his cuss words. Clouds like
this one seemed common in Kansas, though she'd
never seen its like in Arkansas. Roiling thick and
black, it spouted from the edge of the horizon like a
gout of spilled tar. It raced toward them, impossible
to outrun, hugging low over the earth, casting a wide,
dark shadow over the prairie, the air between cloud
and ground fogged by misty rain. Within seconds it
caught them, but it seemed to hover over them for an
eternity, shedding the fattest, closest-packed raindrops Ellie had ever seen, before finally passing overhead, leaving them drenched and steaming beneath
bright sunlight.

With a muttered oath, Tremayne kicked the gelding's saddle. His hair lay plastered against his skull and neck in thick hanks; his homespun shirt clung tight across his back and pouched loosely in the front. Water streamed from a gap near a button, as if someone had poured a bucketful of water down the front of his shirt.

Ellie couldn't help it; she giggled.

He swung around to glare at her and she laughed all the harder, running her hands alongside her head to smooth back her own sodden tresses. Her gown seemed to have expanded with its soaking, the bodice managing to mold her breasts and still hang loose around her waist. Her hem must have lengthened by several inches, for it caught her heel the moment she tried to step back from Tremayne's murderous frown.

His expression softened, his eyes sweeping over her drenched form. His voice held no malice, only a gentle teasing when he spoke. "So you would laugh at me, Ellie?"

"I would," she retorted.

With a mumbled oath, he slung his arm around her waist and threw her over his shoulder.

"Put me down! I won't be hauled around like a sack of cornmeal!"

Tremayne clamped a hand over her thighs, holding her steady while she pummeled at his back and strove to push herself upright. "Would you rather I held you in front of me, madam, so you could wrap your lovely arms around my neck and give me a good view down the front of your dress?"

At once, Ellie held herself as rigid as a pair of tongs, considering she was bent at the middle.

"Let me down," she whispered.

"In a moment. We're nearing dry ground."

She could tell by his changing stride when they reached the edge of the area soaked by the cloudburst. Tremayne's steps lengthened, the long, flat muscles she pressed against on his back flexing rhythmically with each pace.

The rustle of parched grass beneath his feet confirmed they'd reached dry ground. Ellie wanted nothing more than to wriggle free of his grip, but she didn't dare squirm. He stopped, and Ellie considered leaning to the side, trusting to gravity to send her tumbling from his shoulder, when he made a grunting heave and she found herself sliding down his front.

He kept his hand pressed against her back as she slid, which stopped her from flopping backwards, but which also held her snugly against him. Her slow descent landed her on her feet with her thighs pressed right up against his, her hands gripping his wide shoulders. A wave of dizzy breathlessness caught her; there were any number of reasons for it, from getting unexpectedly drenched to being manhandled. Any woman in similar circumstances might find herself a little short of breath, grateful for strong, solid muscle to lean against. She told herself she would move away from him the minute her legs regained their steadiness.

She felt the cool caress of a breeze tickle the skin just above her knee and glanced down. Her hem had caught in his belt buckle; she could see her bare calf pale against his homespun-clad leg.

He towered over her. She hoped he couldn't see

past her sodden hair and drenched gown to the sight of her bare leg. She slid her hand down his shirtfront and nimbly freed her gown from his belt buckle before pressing her fingers over her mouth to stifle a pretend yawn. Unfortunately, the wet pink cotton continued to cling to his damp homespun, prompting a frustrated sound low in her throat, a sound not unlike one echoed by Tremayne. He pushed himself away from her, his gaze fortuitously riveted upon her own rather than the sodden length of pink cotton that stretched between them, threatening to bare even more of her legs, before flopping wetly back into place around her ankles.

"The gelding doesn't seem to be bothered by the weight of the saddle. I'm going to rig the horses back up and have them carry the saddles here to dry ground," he said.

"I was hoping they'd run away," Ellie said crossly. "Lucky for you they didn't—you left their reins trailing."

"Which is precisely why they haven't run off, as you would know, madam, if you understood the first thing about keeping livestock."

She remembered how he'd enumerated her lack of homesteading experience among the excuses to justify his taking her back to her father. As he turned and strode toward the peacefully grazing horses, she made another horrid face at his back. "At least I never got myself stuck out in the middle of the prairie with nothing to eat or drink and no shelter for the night!" she shouted.

"I apologize if you find my preparations lacking.

I've never had to plan the taking of an unwilling companion before."

"No. I suppose you've contented yourself with murdering women who cause problems for you."

She wished she could call back the words even before her waspish tongue finished flinging them. *I didn't mean it,* she longed to say. But why didn't she? He stared at her, rigid and threatening, his eyes frigid and unfeeling, the stance and eyes of a cold-hearted wife murderer, if the apprehension skittering down her spine could be trusted.

He turned, making no effort to discredit her statement.

She watched while he threw blankets and saddles over the horses' backs. Tremayne's shirt and britches clung as tightly to him as horsehide; each movement he made revealed sleek muscle flexing to conquer its assigned chore. He didn't bother cinching the saddles, but led the horses back toward her and dumped saddles and blankets into a heap at her feet.

"I'd suggest spreading out those blankets to dry. The horses would appreciate it. And you might want to change dresses while I'm gone." There was no hint in his voice that he'd given her vile accusation a second thought. It took her a moment to sort out his words and realize he meant to leave her.

All of a sudden, the prairie seemed darker. "Gone? Where are you going?"

He was busy tugging off his boots and woolen socks.

"I have to find water. It shouldn't take long. The rain should have filled one of the old buffalo wallows."

He narrowed his eyes, skewering her with his icy blue stare. "Can I trust you to stay here?"

Her gaze flickered over the endlessly stretching openness. She had no grasp of their location, no idea which direction she should take to find anything. "Do I have a choice?" she whispered.

His lips settled into a disapproving line. "You are determined to cast this into a bad light. You act as if I mean to take you back and lock you up in your father's jail, not his home."

"There is no difference, Mr. Hawthorne. None at all."

An unreadable expression flickered over his face. "I, too, chafed beneath my father's rule, until he turned his back on me entirely. You might be surprised, madam, to find that you'd miss what you now think is so intolerable."

"Never," she whispered, horrified at the misunderstanding, and pain, marking his words.

One disbelieving tawny brow tilted in accord with his supercilious grunt as he turned from her. He didn't get far; with a loud curse, accompanied by a one-footed hop, he stopped to pry a small stone from the mud encrusting his foot.

A stone no wider than her fingernail, no more than a quarter inch thick. Memory flooded Ellie's mind. "Give it to me," she said, her throat tightening.

"This pebble?"

"Yes."

His thumb brushed over it, dislodging some of the dirt before he dropped it into her upturned palm. Ellie worked her fingers over it, too, rubbing the mud from the small stone's smooth surface, wishing she could as easily brush away the agony she felt.

"Do you intend to stare at the pebble all day, madam?"

She supposed she looked a fool, clutching at the tiny stone, because he had no way of knowing that one similar to it had meant the difference between life and living death. Perhaps she could use the stone to make him understand.

"Do you know how difficult it can be to find a stone like this, Mr. Hawthorne?"

"I seem to stumble over them without problem."

Ellie's voice trembled. "I want to tell you about a stone, and my father, this man you called a harsh but fair taskmaster. Will you hear me out?"

Interest kindled in his eyes, indicating his willingness to listen.

She steeled herself to face memories stifled since her mother's death. She chose her words carefully, doing her best to paint a picture for Tremayne.

"On the day I'm going to tell you about, when I looked up I saw nothing but clouds spitting snow. If I looked down, there was nothing but dingy, icy slush covering the ground. And looking back toward the house—that was even worse. I knew my mother lay dying within."

The memory unfolded in Ellie's mind, and it was as though her voice, explaining it all, belonged to an interested observer while she found herself living it anew.

"What could my mother have been thinking? She

sent me, a grown woman, on a child's errand, to find a stone for her—before Father came home."

Not just any stone would do. To suit Angeline McKittrick's whim, the pebble's size must match exactly Ellie's smallest, well-trimmed fingernail. Its depth could not exceed the thickness of the locket Ellie was allowed to wear only to church. Smooth, it must be, like the fine wool of Ellie's gown, which showed the texture of its weave but presented no rough spots or snags.

Ellie had trembled while she searched, not so much from the cold as from the effort of holding back the rage bubbling within her. Who in all Arkansas would believe that Angeline, Jonathan McKittrick's outwardly pampered and adored wife, should beg with her dying breath for her daughter to find her a stone from the garden? Who would credit that Ellie—no, *Eleanor* McKittrick—their outwardly cosseted and indulged daughter, should long with all her heart to find the stone, because it would be the one and only gift she had ever been able to give her mother?

So numb were Ellie's fingers, so dismally certain was she of failure, so frightened was she that her mother might slip away before she found the right pebble, that she'd nearly cast aside the perfect stone.

It had rested cold in the palm of her hand, smooth and milky white, a dimple on one side keeping it from perfect symmetry. She ran back toward the house, praying Father's servants hadn't noticed her outdoor foray. Her thin-soled, satin slippers clung in soggy ruined shreds to her cold-cramped toes. She stripped them off lest she leave wet footsteps in her wake.

"I found one for you, Mama, and there's time to spare," she'd called softly as she stepped into the room and pulled the door closed behind her.

"Let me see."

Ellie knelt next to the bed. "Here, Mama." She closed Angeline's fingers around the white stone. Her mother's eyes widened, "seeing" the stone with her touch. Ellie felt a resurgence of her fury. It wasn't fair, that the disease wasting Angeline's body should have claimed her eyesight, too, just as she was about to die.

"Why, it's perfect, Ellie girl." Angeline groped for Ellie's hand and pressed the stone back into her palm. "It feels so cold, though. I don't think I could abide that. Drop it into my tea and set the cup near the fire to warm, and bring me a nice clean handkerchief."

"Yes, Mama." Ellie's heart plummeted as she placed a clean linen square into Angeline's hand, baffled by her mother's sudden obsession with the stone. It made no sound as it slipped into the inch of luke-warm tea and settled amongst the dregs. She set the teacup close to the fire, wondering why it was so important to Angeline that the stone be warm.

"Now, mind you don't look at me until I say so."

Ellie expected to hear her mother's hacking, ruinous cough. Instead, only a soft rustling from the bed, the metallic ticking of the clock filled the room.

"You can come here now, Ellie girl."

Ellie searched her mother's face, hoping to see some sign of improvement, and trying to burn Angeline's features into her mind, knowing in her heart that all too soon that beloved face would be gone from her sight forever. Her throat tightened with dread—already something seemed different about Angeline, some indefinable, subtle change had settled over the pale, pain-etched countenance.

Angeline moistened her lip with the tip of her tongue and then prodded beneath her upper lip. "It feels funny, going without it after all these years. Can't say it feels any better. I believe I must have grown accustomed to it."

"What are you talking about, Mama?"

A smile flickered over Angeline's lips. "You're not one for noticing, Ellie girl, not at all like your father. Now, you lift your hem, right where your right foot peeks out, and see that little pocket I sewed in there before my eyes went dark."

Thoroughly mystified, Ellie did as Angeline asked. It took her a moment to find a tiny square of wool, perfectly matching the pattern of her dress and no bigger than the tip of her finger, sewn with nearly invisible stitches on the underside of her hem. Only someone made aware of its presence would note it, its exquisite workmanship making it virtually disappear into the soft fabric.

"There's one just like it on every one of your dresses," Angeline said. "I never knew, you see, when my time would come, and with you so stubborn about staying here with me, I had to make certain you'd be prepared. I couldn't expect you to get away with what I did. He'd notice for sure."

"Mama, please, I don't know what you're trying to say." Ellie felt certain her mother's life ebbed with her wits.

"Look in my hand, Ellie girl. I don't know how it looks after being shoved up under my lip all these years. It used to sparkle right nice."

The skin above Angeline's upper lip, which for eleven years had bulged with the rounded contours of what Doc Halliburton had decreed a water cyst, lay smooth and unblemished, crowning Angeline's radiant, triumphant smile. And cradled atop the handkerchief in Angeline's palm, glittering in the flickering firelight, rested a diamond identical in size to the stone Ellie had been sent to find.

"This . . . this looks like your betrothal diamond," Ellie whispered, turning the sparkling gem in the firelight.

"It is. Now hide it, Ellie girl."

"But how can it be?"

Ellie had been only twelve when Angeline, white-faced and trembling with fear, admitted to Jonathan that somehow the stone had come loose from its setting, that she'd lost her betrothal diamond, the finest of its kind in three counties.

The resultant search had seen the house virtually torn apart. Jonathan had ultimately issued broom-straws, ordering everyone to poke into every crack and crevice, between floor planks, anywhere a fallen diamond might lie hidden. All to no avail, even though he'd repeated the all-out search sporadically over the years.

"Hide it, Ellie." Angeline shriveled back into her pillow. "I couldn't sew it into *my* dress—I knew he'd tear apart every stick of furniture and every stitch of my clothing to find that diamond, and he did. He figured out, you see, that I could sell it to get the money we needed to run away from him."

Ellie's fingers shook so hard she almost dropped the diamond, but she slipped it securely into the tiny hidden pocket in her dress hem. Angeline's hand felt for hers and Ellie caught it up, pressing it against her heart, knowing her mother would feel her thundering pulse, knowing no words need pass between them to acknowledge Angeline's imminent death and the gift of the diamond that would give Ellie the means to strike for freedom.

"Your father came back from the war so mean, I knew I'd have to do something to provide for you. I got the idea when a watermelon seed lodged itself up there and I didn't even notice until a day later. Doc Halliburton promised to play along. I found a nice smooth stone and used it until Doc told your father I'd developed a cyst. I switched it with the diamond. Your father would have suspected right off what I'd done with that diamond if my little lump showed up just when I lost it.

"I never explained your pa's secret to you, Ellie girl, the reason why he turned so sour. You see, when an injury to his private parts robs a man of his . . . virility, he needs to prove to himself that he's still a man. Your father—well, that war injury just warped his whole nature."

A quick flash of memory suffused Ellie's mind, a lightning image of a tall, smiling man tossing her high in the air, delighting in her childish squeals and giggles—a laughing, generous man who now seemed a figment of her dreams.

The Jonathan McKittrick she knew reserved his smiles for his business associates. No generous, loving husband and father, but a harsh tyrant who kept his wife and spinster daughter virtual prisoners in his home: beautifully clad but without a cent to spend on impulse; well fed but forced to account for every ounce of provender; spared all work but forbidden to issue a single order to servants loyal only to Jonathan. Living, breathing, doll-like creatures paraded for public benefit, but terrorized behind closed doors, their self-esteem slashed to ribbons by his vicious insults, their pride reduced to rubble by being forced to beg for the slightest privilege.

"Oh, Mama, all those years." Ellie's eyes welled with tears, remembering how Angeline would only accept kisses on her cheek, how her smiles sometimes turned to grimaces of pain. How must it have felt, to speak, to eat, to smile? The depth of her mother's love shook her profoundly.

"I always meant for us to strike out on our own, you and me and that diamond, Ellie girl, if only I hadn't took sick. I never planned for it to go on so long."

"I know." Ellie's throat ached. Ellie had flatly refused Angeline's unending pleas to run off on her own, despite her mother's furtive comments about providing the means for her escape. Never, ever, would she have left her mother alone to face Jonathan's wrath.

"Don't you let his servants touch me when my time comes," Angeline said. "You tend me yourself, Ellie girl. I don't want them prying around in my mouth and giving away my secret after all this time."

"I'll tend you, Mama."

Angeline gripped Ellie's hand with a strength made ominous by the fevered heat of her skin. Her voice, scarcely audible, nonetheless brooked no argument. "The minute I'm gone, you take that diamond to someone who will give you fair value for it."

"I will," Ellie promised, though she knew no amount of money could equal her mother's sacrifice.

"Well, then, give me that stone." A frown puckered Angeline's forehead. "What color is it?"

"It's sort of milky white—it's real pretty, like a moonstone."

"Ah, that sounds real nice. Go on, then, fetch it out of the tea."

"Kiss me first, Mama, good and hard."

Ellie wrapped her arms around her mother's neck, lifting the skeletal head, planting a firm but gentle kiss moistened with tears upon her mother's lips before helping Angeline slide the smooth, white stone into place.

The worn, pain-wracked face took on its normal contours.

Angeline's sightless eyes, chocolate brown like her own and with the pain of the past eleven years sealed behind them, seemed to burn into Ellie's.

"There's nothing to keep you here now. A woman should honor and respect the man she loves, but not even God would expect her to bend like a little puppet under a man's control. You know your father will keep you a prisoner in this house. He never meant for you to have a home or husband or children of your own. Go, Ellie. Promise me you'll go and find a good man to love. Someone strong enough to stand against your father."

Yes, she would go, somewhere far away, where she could grieve for her mother. Where her every moment need not be accounted for, where she could laugh for no reason, and wear what she liked, and loosen her hair and lift her face to the sun. But a husband . . . to willingly enslave herself, to subject her will to a man's whim . . . never.

"I'll go," Ellie had whispered, hoping her mother wouldn't realize she'd only made half a promise.

Ellie didn't know how long she and Tremayne stood silent once her tale ended, only that when she blinked, her eyelids felt gritty and dry, as if she'd spent an hour staring into the wind, and her throat ached with remembered sorrow and an unaccustomed amount of talking.

"I tended her when she died," Ellie said. "I could never kiss her again without causing her pain. She went to the grave with that damned lump above her lip. So Father wouldn't suspect anything. And I did just as she said. Lauretta sold the diamond and used the money to pay the railroad agent for the down payment on our land. There was enough left over to buy the mules and chickens."

At some point during her story Tremayne had turned away from her to stand in rigid profile, his arms crossed over his chest. The wind caught his hair and blew it straight back, revealing the sharp planes of his face set in stiff, uncompromising lines.

"If you take me back to my father, Tremayne, all of it will have been for nothing."

His head swiveled toward her. He impaled her with a smoldering blue stare. She fancied his bronzed skin had paled, that a flicker of indecision marred his resolve, and for a moment she dared to hope she'd touched his heart.

"Ellie. I wish . . ." For a brief moment, nothing but wind and the hammering of her heart could be heard. And then he said, "Change into your dry dress while I find water for the horses. Wichita's not far. I don't want you growing ill before we get there."

She had bared her most painful memory to him for nothing. He'd listened with the stoic boredom a churchgoer might bestow upon a long-winded preacher, betraying none of his inner thoughts by so much as a sigh or whisper. And now he gathered the horses' reins and strode over the prairie in search of water, leaving her feeling drained and shamed for daring to tell, and daring to hope that it might make a difference.

She rummaged through the saddlebags to find her charcoal wool and stripped off the wet pink cotton. She felt more vulnerable and exposed than she ever had, though she knew it was impossible for Tremayne to see her naked flesh. She yanked her dry charcoal wool dress into place, fastening the buttons with shaking fingers, with difficulty, because she still clutched the small stone in her hand.

Ellie aimed for Tremayne's departing back and threw the stone with all her might.

11

Tremayne made certain Ellie's seat was steady in the saddle before winding the horses' reins around his hands and setting out to walk to Wichita. The exhausted mare could no longer support the weight of them both; even if it could, something within Tremayne rebelled at the thought of riding with Ellie encircled in his arms.

The physically punishing pace set by jailhouse overseers had taught him the trick of toiling for endless hours with numb, mindless precision. His work-honed body easily recaptured that rhythm, his long-legged stride carrying him swiftly over the prairie, the muscles in his upper arm swelling with the strain of forcing the tired horses to match his desperate pace.

The wind whistled in his ears. Behind him, the horses huffed, their heavy hooves thudding against the earth, their tack jingling with musical merriment.

None of it was loud enough to drown out the memory of Ellie's grief-stricken voice recounting the story of her mother's diamond. A brown haze darkened the horizon, marking where Wichita lay. Dust, stirred up by thousands of cattle, drifted skyward, dulling the reddish streaks heralding sunset. If only the haze could dull the image of Ellie's face as she'd told her tale.

She had spoken the truth, he had no doubt of it. Her halting revelation portrayed a Jonathan McKittrick crueler than Tremayne had ever suspected. And an abiding mother love almost capable of transcending death, Angeline granting her daughter the ability to achieve her dream.

Angeline McKittrick's dream, to set Ellie free. Margaret Hawthorne's dream, to see Tremayne acknowledged as Chedgrave's heir. The dreams of dead women. To allow Angeline's to flower would mean abandoning Margaret's. To make Margaret's reality would mean destroying Angeline's.

Regardless of whose dream prevailed, Ellie would pay the price. If he took her back to her monstrous father, her spirit would wither and die. If he left her alone—whether to pursue his own ends or give himself up for failing to honor his part of the bargain—McKittrick would send another after her. Silas Stringer, or someone like him. He felt rage at the thought of what Ellie might suffer at Stringer's hand.

He couldn't leave her to that uncertain fate. To guarantee her safety, he would have to take her home.

Wichita beckoned, its buildings taking shape in the distance. Cattle called to one another, their deep lowing resonating with frightened exhaustion. Tremayne's pace slowed. As he'd feared, a large herd had arrived in town, meaning water, stable space, and decent hotel rooms would be nearly impossible to find, not to mention dozens of trail-weary cowboys roaming through town, looking for sport.

He noticed a neat, well-maintained homestead standing a half mile to their left. He turned toward it.

"Aren't we going into town?" Ellie spoke for the first time since telling him her story. The hope in her voice sent shame shaking through him. He spoke over his shoulder, unwilling to face her.

"We need water and a place to sleep, madam. Things might be a bit wild in town."

She made no response.

A lean, work-worn farm woman stood in the doorway. Two children clung to her skirts, wide-eyed, watching their approach. In answer to Tremayne's hail, she shooed the children into the cabin and stepped out to meet them.

"We ain't got any extry beds," she said. Her wind-burned face settled into sorrowful lines, as if she would have welcomed their company, and her voluble discourse confirmed it. "I keep tellin' Buck to forget growin' crops. We'd do better buildin' an extry room or two to rent out. Not many herds come into town anymore, but we could turn a few dollars when they do. I can let you have a bucket or two of water for your animals."

"We'll pay for the water," Tremayne offered, knowing how scarce the precious liquid could be in late summer.

"Well, that's right thoughtful of you, mister. I sure am sorry—oh, my, look at your poor wife!" With a matronly cluck, the woman headed toward Ellie's mare. "Why, you've been cryin', haven't you gal? Your face is white as milk."

"I never cry," Ellie said, contradicting her words by rubbing a grimy fist against a tear-streaked cheek.

"I'm sure you don't usually," the woman said soothingly. "'Pears you let loose a little today, though."

"And I'm not his—"

"She been fractious all day?" the woman asked Tremayne.

"She's upset because I'm taking her back East," Tremayne said. Ellie stared at him, openmouthed, no doubt startled that he'd brought their purpose out into the open. He'd done it deliberately, expecting she might have tried to win the farm woman's sympathies by explaining her plight. By introducing the subject himself, he'd disarmed her, but he felt no pride in doing so.

"Wish someone would take *me* back East," the woman said. "This place sure gets on a woman's nerves, what with the wind and cow pats and grasshoppers and all. There's no shame in going back, honey." She reached out a thin hand to squeeze Ellie's. "I'll tell you what. You folks seem like good people. I ain't got the room for you, but Sarah Reynolds has a nice rooming house. If she's full up with cowboys, you can ask after the snug little corn-crib out behind her place. It'll be empty this time of year, what with the corn not coming in till next month. You go on to Sarah's and tell her Bessie Engle sent you." She gave directions for the widow Reynolds's place, which lay a bit more than a mile beyond Wichita's town limits, and she described a route skirting the main street and avoiding the worst of the carousing cowboys.

Tremayne, grateful for the kindness, inclined his head toward her, which sent her into a blushing tizzy. Ellie gave an unladylike snort at Bessie's display, but held her tongue over the short ride into town.

Sarah Reynolds, smiling at the mention of her friend's name, directed Tremayne around the back of her house. She promised to send out a broom and bedding. "A candle, too," she added. "There ain't a bit of light gets into that place. Light ain't good for the corn. I won't charge you for the use of the corncrib, but you'll have to buy bait for your horses and pay for tonight's supper and breakfast in the morning."

"Could we buy a bath?" Tremayne asked.

A small cry of delight came from Ellie's direction.

"The cowboys interested in bathing go to the Douglas Avenue Hotel. And it seems like a temporary bathhouse springs up every now and again." Sarah cast a dubious glance toward Ellie. "'Course, your wife couldn't go there."

"How do you usually accommodate your female guests?" Tremayne persisted.

Sarah sighed. "Mister, I got fourteen cowboys roomin' here tonight. I can't guarantee I can keep them out of the kitchen long enough for your missus to tend to all that hair and such."

"Perhaps there's a lad for hire who might be will-

ing to haul the tub and water out to the corncrib,"
Tremayne suggested.

Sarah studied Ellie, and then her face crinkled into
a sympathetic smile. "Can't say as anyone ever bathed
in my corncrib before. I'll send my young 'uns out
with what you'll need."

Despite Sarah's warning about light being bad for the
corn, Ellie rejoiced to see that a single beam of waning sunlight found its way through a crack in the
corncrib's rear wall. The narrow shaft joined with the
light admitted by the open door. A thin layer of chaff
covered the floor. Ellie stared at the dust motes floating in the beam. So long as the sun shone, it wouldn't
be unbearable. The place certainly did need a good
sweeping out. The promised broom stood propped
against a wall, a quilt heaped against its straws. As far
as she was concerned, both items could sit there for
eternity. She'd wither up into a bloodless husk before
she'd lift a finger to make Tremayne Hawthorne comfortable for the night.

A fat tallow candle spiked onto a wide pewter
plate sat next to her. Once the sun set, only the candle's light would brighten this small space.

She wondered if Tremayne meant to act the gentleman and spend the night outdoors with the horses.
Or if he'd somehow sensed her fear of small, dark
places and meant to stand sentry over her after the
candle went out.

His wide-shouldered shadow appeared in the doorway, ending that fanciful notion.

"You deliberately let Bessie and Sarah believe we were married," Ellie said as he stepped into the corn crib.

"I did." He crossed the small room and grabbed the broom, dropping the saddlebags he'd carried over his shoulders. "Would you have preferred it if I'd told them we would be spending the night together without the benefit of marriage?"

Ellie felt her face heat. "I would prefer you spend the night outside with the rest of the animals."

"Would you give your word you won't try running away?"

Her indrawn hiss of breath was his only answer; he smiled, mockingly. "I thought not. Now, move yourself outside, madam. I, for one, have no intention of sleeping on a floor covered with rat excrement."

He applied the broom with skill, sending waves of dusty chaff pluming through the door, finishing just as a wiry boy arrived, an upside-down hip bath fitted over his head and shoulders like some strange medieval armor. His adolescent eyes raked over Ellie and then rolled up to stare at the edge of the tub hanging over his forehead. A blissful smile descended over his features. "Fer you, ma'am? You want I should set it down here?"

"Set it inside." Tremayne's blunt instruction raised a flush along the boy's cheeks.

Four young girls, each carrying a steaming bucket, ran chattering from the Reynolds's back door. Ellie waited until they reached the corncrib and then entered the small structure with them. Tremayne had arranged the bedding into two pallets on either side of the corncrib. Their saddlebags lay in a neat stack in one corner. It gave Ellie an odd feeling, to think of a man who murdered his family taking such care to sweep the place clean, to heap the bedding into such inviting piles. The tub separated the pallets. The arrangement seemed to amuse the girls, who darted interested glances from Tremayne to the pallets, giggling profusely as they poured their water into the hip bath.

Their fresh-faced happiness caused Ellie to feel a renewed awareness of her bedraggled condition. Her gown seemed to puff with dust at every movement. She smelled of horse, and sweat, and her eyes stung from spending too many hours facing the wind and sun, and maybe just a little from the tears she'd denied shedding.

She glared at Tremayne Hawthorne, who looked supremely unaffected by the day's trials. His clothes had dried against him like a second skin. His hair curled around his sun-bronzed face like a golden cloud, and when he smiled at the four giggling girls, his teeth gleamed white beneath eyes of bluest azure.

She hated him. There could be no other explanation for the furious hammering of her heart as she watched him herd Sarah Reynolds's children out of the corncrib.

He closed the door against the outside and leaned back against it, illuminated only by the fast-fading single sunbeam piercing the darkened structure. Steam from the bath rose between them, and through its blurring effect she fancied he looked as hopeless, as drained as she felt.

"Do you intend to watch while I bathe?" she asked.

"No, madam." He heaved himself away from the door. "There's a latch on the outside. I intend to lock you in here while I go into town and visit the public baths, and see about trading the gelding for an uninjured horse."

"You'd lock me in here?" Ellie's horrified whisper barely made it through her suddenly tight-clenched throat. The tiny building seemed to shrink in on itself, the lone sunbeam lighting the space suddenly dimming like an oxygen-starved lamp wick. Sunset. Within moments there would be no more natural light. Her pounding heart quickened its beat, thumping a warning, urging her to run, to beg him not to impose this dark confinement, to swear she wouldn't try running away if only he'd let her keep the door unlocked.

None of it would work. It never had with Father.

She could not let Tremayne see how this affected her. She willed her pulse to stop racing, her throat to unclench. Her mouth, dry with dread, could still form words. "Very well, Mr. Hawthorne. If you would please light the candle before you go."

He complied. "You should find everything you need in these saddlebags," he said, after rummaging through them and drawing out a change of clothes for himself. "I shouldn't be more than two or three hours."

Two or three hours. A tremor seized her and she whirled away from him, pretending great interest in the hip bath's cooling water. She clasped her hands, willing them to still, hoping Tremayne couldn't hear her panicked breathing.

He left her. She heard the door close with a muffled thud, heard the slide of metal entering wood as he engaged the latch.

Every cell in her body urged her to run to the door and test the latch. No doubt he waited outside for that very thing. How he would laugh at her impotent rattling of the door! No, better to ignore the locked door and pretend, for as long as she could, that she was in control of the situation.

She forced herself to stay where she stood, unfastening her gown with stiff, shaking fingers. She wouldn't permit herself even a glance at the door as she climbed awkwardly into the small hip bath. She wrapped her arms around her bent knees and buried her face against her thighs, quivering, waiting for the water's warmth to seep into her bones so she could stop shaking.

He couldn't do it. Tremayne fiddled with the latch, engaging it and then, remembering the look of trapped despair in her eyes, he slid the bolt free. He'd seen that look before, probably would have recognized it in himself, if he'd ever bothered looking into a mirror after suffering through one of Silas Stringer's more creative punishments. High-spirited inmates like himself who'd run afoul of jailhouse rules had sometimes found themselves lowered into a dry well, where they'd spend a week or two in near-total darkness reassessing their attitudes toward prison life.

He'd understood the punishment had been devised by Jonathan McKittrick.

Ellie, afraid of close quarters, afraid of the dark. It didn't bear contemplating how she might have gotten that way.

She would probably test the door the minute she believed he'd taken himself away. He imagined her cry of delight at finding the door unbarred. When he returned, she would probably be gone. Perhaps that would be for the best.

He heard the muffled splash of water from within, imagined Ellie naked in the flickering candlelight, lowering herself into the hip bath. He swallowed, a painful process with his throat gone suddenly parched. His hand found itself back upon the latch, his finger toying with the bolt, his mind urging him to shoot it home and keep her there, keep her safe. And then the memory of the look in her eyes returned. With a muttered curse, he left the latch undone and went to fetch the mare for the ride into Wichita.

A curious peace descended over him. Ellie held her fate quite literally within her own hands. He'd done his best to convince her of the dangers she faced. If she fled his protection, he would not pursue.

He dunked himself into the first empty chamber at a nondescript public bathhouse and used a slab of the Wichita Soap Factory's finest against the worst of the dirt. With every stroke of the washcloth, he thought of Ellie. Outside, boisterous cowboys shouted drunken, nearly incomprehensible renditions of trail songs. Tremayne stared at the slatted wooden walls, remembering the stark fear haunting Ellie's face when he'd told her he meant to lock her in. He closed his eyes, forcing himself to recount the chores he meant to complete. Visit the barber. Stop by the livery and arrange to trade horses. Purchase the supplies they would need for the sixty-mile trip to Caldwell.

He did none of the chores. While music and laughter and the scent of roasting beef prompted hunger pangs in his stomach, he became possessed by an irrational fear of his own, a baseless certainty that something had gone wrong, that he'd failed Ellie by giving her a choice. He plowed through his bath like a muskrat aimed for a bed of cattails and flung his still-dripping frame atop the sleepy mare.

Someone called to him from the door of Lawrence's Drug Store, claiming his reluctant attention.

"Well, if it ain't Tremayne Hawthorne! What're yew doin' here in town? Ellie and Lauretta and that Hiram Espy with yew too?"

So driven was he by the need to return to Ellie, Tremayne stared at the broad, kind-faced woman without a shred of recognition.

"Mattie Murrow," she provided helpfully. "Yew mighta remembered me some if yew'd a' danced with me out to Naylor's."

"Perhaps another time, madam. I'm quite busy tonight," Tremayne said before pressing his heels into the mare's flanks.

He arrived at the corncrib with his hair still wet against the back of his neck, his fresh shirt and britches clinging in damp patches to his skin. No light seeped through the crack in the corncrib door. She had found his gift of the unlocked door and fled, taking the candle with her.

So be it. No more struggling within his mind as to whether he should take her back or let her stay. She'd spurned him, and she had more cause than others had ever had. And if she possessed even an ounce of sense, she'd take herself far away, where her father couldn't find her. Perhaps the new territories out West, where vast, empty spaces promised endless hiding places. Great, sweeping stretches of loneliness, like the sensation overwhelming him at the thought of never seeing her again.

He flung the corncrib door open, letting it bang against the wall, steeling himself for the emptiness he knew he would find within.

She sat there in the inadequate little hip bath, her arms wrapped around her knees, a river of damp chestnut hair cascading over flesh pale and silver-gilded from the moonlight streaming through the door. She raised her head, her eyes dark and frantic and impossibly huge, her face moonstruck with a pallor suited to the grave.

12

The unexpected light sent shafts of pain through Ellie's eyes. And then Tremayne stepped into the doorway. He came between her and the penetrating moonbeams, just as he'd shielded her from the clamoring men at Naylor's and turned aside Griff, deflecting every threat. He protected her against everyone and everything—except from *his* purpose.

Still, an involuntary, glad cry escaped from her fear-frozen throat. It could have been a trick of her moon-blinded eyes, but she thought his face blanched at the sound.

Cursing, Tremayne crossed the intervening space in no more than three strides, scooping her up out of the frigid water and crushing her against his warm torso with one smooth motion. Until that moment she'd been too frightened to feel the cold; pressed against his heated frame, she began to shiver, her body blindly seeking the source of the blissful warmth.

He supported her weight with one arm while he knelt next to one of the sleeping pallets and drew a quilt around her shoulders. "Why in God's name were you still sitting in that water—and in pitch darkness?"

"My hair." Her voice came out a hoarse whisper, as if her throat had been injured by the silent screams she'd held back over the past hour. "The bath was so small . . . when I tried to rinse my hair the water splashed over the edge and drowned the candle . . . and I . . . it was so dark, Tremayne. I couldn't move from the tub. I wish . . . I wish you hadn't locked the door." A shuddering spasm accompanied the memory.

Tremayne muttered an expletive as he lowered her atop the pallet. He swiveled to leave her side; of their own accord, her arms reached out to hold him with her, but her nearly numb fingers could do nothing more than feel the cloth of his sleeve slip through. A soft cry, embarrassingly like a whimper, escaped her.

But he was gone for only a few heartbeats. She felt his return, his formidable shape looming even blacker than the stifling darkness. A scratching sound followed by the scent of a struck match filled her senses, and then the squat tallow candle stood lit, flickering brightly near her head.

Thank you. Her ingrained politeness urged her to say it aloud, but the retreating darkness released the stranglehold it had held on her will. Everything he did raised such paradoxes within her. His arrival had sent her demons fleeing. But there would have been no terrifying duel with the dark if Tremayne hadn't locked her in the corncrib. And she'd be damned if she'd feel gratitude toward someone who meant to return her to her father.

Tremayne crouched next to her. The candle glow illuminated the bold lines of his face, casting hollows beneath his cheekbones, shrouding his deepset eyes in mystery. His hair, freshly washed, had been gathered back in a loose queue, as if he'd hurried in tying it. His shirt gaped open, buttoned only at the waist, baring faded bruises and a thatch of tawny curls sculpting his chest. He'd shoved his sleeves up past his elbow, and along one arm she saw the healing tracks marking where she'd shot him. Another paradox. The only wound she'd inflicted upon him would soon heal and vanish, while the wound he meant to cause her would last a lifetime.

"The door wasn't locked, Ellie."

"It was. I heard you shoot the bolt home."

"No. I couldn't lock the door after I saw the look in your eyes. I know . . . a bit about fear of the dark."

It couldn't be true. If it were, she could have alleviated her terror at any time simply by crossing the tiny space and pushing the door wide. It meant she'd spent what seemed like an eternity of soul-numbing terror for no reason. It meant a suspected murderer, a man who might have slain his wife and infant son, possessed tender sympathies, that he'd sensed her fears and sought to allay them.

Or he could be tormenting her, now that she'd admitted to not knowing the door was open. Her father would have delighted in such a game. And Tremayne was her father's man.

"You're lying," she whispered, mortified that she'd revealed her weakness to him. "You locked it because you were afraid I'd run away."

"I *was* afraid you'd run away. But I didn't lock the door." He moved infinitesimally closer so she could see the clear, honest blue of his eyes, eyes that studied her face and dropped lower, reminding her that she lay naked beneath the quilt he'd wrapped around her. He raised one huge hand, and then his forefinger, blunt and callused, traced the delicate skin beneath her eyes and trailed down, brushing over her lips, settling against a place in her throat that pulsed in response.

"I never meant to frighten you, Ellie." He shifted closer, and his overwhelming presence should have marked his comment a lie, but she felt fear desert her. "I am cursed with bad luck in every endeavor. My intentions never seem to produce the desired results."

"And what is your intent now, Tremayne?" His name became a soft, breathless sound echoing through her mind. She felt a slight pressure from his fingers against her throat as he leaned forward without breaking his touch. She caught her breath, her gaze mesmerized by the full, proud curve of his lips as they descended to meet hers. The contact sent a sweet, hot shaft of pleasure coursing deep within her. Her lips parted, and she breathed in his essence, shuddering with sensual pleasure as his tongue probed and found hers.

The quilt slipped from her as she clasped her arms around his broad shoulders. Her bare breasts met his heated skin, her tender nipples stroked by the silky soft hair curling over his chest. She craved more; whimpering against his questing mouth, she pressed closer, closer.

With a ragged gasp, Tremayne pushed her away. "No!"

The objection came from her own lips; with stunned surprise, Ellie placed shaking fingers against her mouth lest she let loose with another wanton cry.

"This is wrong." Tremayne's eyes, smoldering with desire, burned into hers. "I have no right. This is unconscionable, to take advantage just because you turned to me for protection against the dark."

He turned his head. She could see the strong cords in his neck pulse with subdued frustration. His breath came in harsh gasps that set the edges of his shirt fluttering. His hands, tight around her shoulders, loosened their grip, and she sensed him withdrawing, marshaling his control. In a moment he would set her away, as he'd done on the creek bank the night before at Naylor's dance, assuaging some gentlemanly instinct within himself while leaving her honor intact.

She caught his hand as it left her shoulder and pressed it against her breast. He cupped her with an instinctive curl of his fingers, and she saw with shivering awe how perfectly God had fashioned a woman to fit to a man.

"Let us see whether your results can live up to my intent," she said, her bold words shocking her even as she spoke them. But she wouldn't, couldn't call them back.

His low groan told her he needed no further invitation.

He moved over her, pressing her back into the pallet's softness. His mouth claimed hers once again, more insistent, demanding bolder tongue play from her. He traced exquisitely sensitive patterns over the softness of her breasts. She felt the scrape of his unshaven cheek against her skin as he lowered his mouth to join his fingers, and she cried aloud when he caught her turgid nipple between his teeth and did something with his tongue that seemed to sizzle through her torso. And as if he knew how her body was misbehaving, he found a throbbing place with his finger and with gentle strokes transformed her into a quivering, moaning, bundle of sensation.

Oh, he was right, this was a terrible thing to do. Wrong to tremble at the touch of a man who some thought had killed his wife and child—but who'd left the door unlocked because he'd known she was afraid of the dark. Unconscionable to fit as many inches of her skin as possible against the man she should be running away from. Somehow, he'd managed to shed his clothes without letting her loose. Her still-damp hair curled in long strands over their entwined limbs, her dark tresses mingling with his of tawny gold. They lay belly to belly, his manhood rigid and pulsating between their heated skin, a sensation both unfamiliar and exciting.

He broke their kiss, but held her face against the warm juncture between his neck and shoulder. She could feel his heart thundering against hers and reveled in the heady scent of clean, warm male surrounding her. "Ellie?" he asked, his voice rumbling from his chest against her ear. "Are you frightened? Of the dark, of me?"

To think that the rugged, masculine timbre of Tremayne's voice should resonate with the same unutterable loneliness and uncertainty that sometimes threatened to overwhelm her. "I've never been afraid of you, Tremayne," she answered, hoping her admission would erase the horrible memory of her taunting him with his wife's murder. It seemed he forgave her; she thrilled to the soft, relieved rush of air he expelled, the almost imperceptible tightening of his arm around her.

Though her mind seemed curiously detached from the rest of her body just now, she realized that what she'd said was true. She'd never feared him, not when he first told her who he was or what he'd been accused of doing. His intentions never produced the desired results. . . . What did that mean when spoken by a man accused of killing his wife and child? Instead of yearning against him, she should be fleeing this man. Her lips brushed over his skin. She darted her tongue out, tasting him, and knew the only thing she feared was having him pull away from her again.

At the touch of her tongue, he groaned and pushed her onto her back, deep into the enveloping bedding. She watched him, thinking passion must cloud her mind to make her exult so in the smooth, muscled contours of his body gleaming in the candlelight as he poised over her.

"Oh, God, Ellie, I don't mean to hurt you, but I want . . . I want . . ."

She felt him move between her thighs, and though she'd never parted her legs in exactly this way, they curved naturally to embrace him.

She felt hardness where none but herself had ever touched, and then his huge frame dwarfed her, one hand cradling her head against his chest, his strong body piercing hers, his lips murmuring gentle sounds against her ear. She didn't mean to cry out from the pain, but she did, the sound muffled against his skin and soon forgotten in the alien sensation of something huge and hot and perfect moving inside her and the intoxicating feel of his weight crushing her.

Her mother had explained the nature of what men did with women, but not until this night did Ellie realize that pleasure accompanied the act.

And not until this night did she realize that it could be done more than once, and that the woman would welcome the repeating.

Eventually, she noticed with sleepy indifference that the candle had guttered out, and that impenetrable darkness lay outside the cocoon made of Tremayne's chest pressed against her back, his body surrounding hers. Her mind, still dazed, registered that she'd never felt so safe in her life as she did now, lying in the dark, with a murdering traitor's arms wrapped around her.

Tremayne felt the subtle change come over her as she drifted into sleep. Her weight settled against him, so soft, and melding with his flesh so perfectly, that she might have been boneless. Unable to resist the temptation she presented, he trailed his hand along her sleek skin from knee to breast. Three times he'd claimed her this night, surely enough to sate any man, and yet the feather-light feel of her warm skin against his fingers roused an aching tightness in his loins, a racing in his blood. He groaned and buried his face in her hair, lest she hear and think him a sex-starved fiend.

Though he successfully muffled the sound, there was no stopping the reaction brought on by caressing her. His manhood stiffened against her smooth bottom. She stirred.

"Again?" Her voice, heavy with sleep, held a husky, humorous edge.

"We shouldn't," he answered, tightening his arms around her. He'd never bedded a virgin, and Ellie's gift of her maidenhead created a torrent of emotions within him unlike anything he'd ever experienced: exultation; possessiveness; a fierce desire that seemed unassuageable just now.

Bloody hell, he was no better than his father, pursuing and using every advantage to take what he had no right to take. And taking it again, and again, driven by his own insatiable, inexplicable need, caring only for the sounds of pleasure she made and worrying not at all about the distress she might feel on the morrow. Physically or emotionally.

He owed her an apology, but he'd be damned if he felt like making it, not when every inch of him gloried in possessing her and clamored to take her again.

"Why shouldn't we do it again?" she asked, rousing him to aching need. He fought to rein in his passions and speak with some modicum of sense before he succumbed, powerless to resist her sweet temptation.

"You are inexperienced. Your body is not accustomed to such activity."

"This was not the usual way of things between men and women?"

He sought to calm the puzzlement in her voice. "What I meant was that I have not loved a woman for several years, Ellie, and fear I was not as considerate as I should have been."

"I see. You've been deprived of feminine companionship for far too long." She tensed, stiffening within his embrace so that while they still touched, their contact seemed less intimate.

He had to fight the urge to gather her back into soft, warm, submission, to tell her that any number of prostitutes had sashayed down Wichita's streets, beckoning him toward their beds and willing flesh, and he'd strode past them all, thinking only of her.

"You don't understand, Ellie. There is more to this. I acted with hasty disregard. For your inexperience. For our situation."

"Ah, yes. There's 'our situation.' I had hoped . . ." Warm, naked, entwined as they were, she managed with another subtle movement to distance herself, silently declaring her separateness from him.

He cursed himself for a fool. He'd begun to believe on the prairie that she desired him for himself. Her words proved she'd had a purpose in submitting to him after all, and a man didn't have to see it carved in stone to understand what it might be.

"You thought that lying with me would influence my decision about taking you home to your father."

She didn't try to deny his accusation, but tensed away from him. "You make me sound like a whore."

"Ellie." His superior strength easily overpowered

her rigid aloofness, but though he crushed her back against him as intimately as before, an invisible barrier seemed to hold them apart. Anger gripped him; curse Jonathan McKittrick and this impossible position he'd forced upon him. *Take her again!* taunted a devil in his mind. Mold her body to his, drive himself into her again and again, draw from her those wondrous moans and cries of pleasure until she melted beneath him and clasped him against her heart, separate no more.

To what end?

He buried his face into the cloud of her hair. "Don't you realize how this dilemma torments me? We have no choice, Ellie. Clearing my name and reconciling with my father are the least of my concerns right now. I must return to the jail or Jessop Farnsworth's life is forfeit. And if I don't bring you with me, your father will only send another in my place. Don't you realize I would set you free if I could? There is no place where you can shelter, no law that will question a father's right to force his daughter home."

"There is one."

For a moment neither of them breathed. Their silence throbbed in the stifling darkness. "What law do you speak of?" he asked at last.

"If I married, my father would have no further claim upon me. It is something I haven't been willing to consider until . . . until very recently."

The darkness rang with the validity of her comment. It was true; she was vulnerable to her father's will only because she remained unwed.

Unreasoning, senseless rage held him silent. Ellie, married? Hiram Espy's earnest, ague-twitching face swam in Tremayne's mind. Never. Bringing the two of them together would be as inappropriate as mating a blooded thoroughbred to a jackass.

Who, then? Himself? An escaped criminal who could expect the law to descend upon him the moment he disappointed McKittrick? A man who'd sworn to shield his heart against caring, whose first wife had found his self-imposed wall so daunting that she'd turned to another for the love she craved and found herself paying the ultimate price for her adultery?

"Tremayne? What . . . what do you think of that idea?"

"Doomed to failure," he stated flatly. "No matter how carefully you arrange the terms of such a marriage, sooner or later one of you will come to expect more than the other ever intended to give. My experience has soured me upon loveless marriages."

"Oh, I never even considered marrying *you.*" Her short laugh held a brittle edge. "*I couldn't* marry you. You have to return to the jail to save your Mr. Farnsworth. Why, my father would be apt to put a bullet right between your eyes the minute he found out we were wed, and I'd be just as bad off as I am now."

"He'd not find me such an easy target."

Ellie greeted his outburst with a disparaging sniff.

"I suppose you know other men better qualified to fend off your father's wrath?"

"Not necessary fend it off—merely to avoid it by staying well away from Fort Smith. A man from these parts, for instance. Women are so scarce out here. I daresay I can be wed within days. Do you know that five men, at least, offered for me yesterday at Naylor's?" Ellie sounded amazed, not at all gloating, as most women would over offering such proof of their desirability. "I could choose any one of them. I could."

Heavy-footed clodhoppers, the lot of them, not to mention that mean-spirited Griff who'd eyed her like a vulture circling a hamstrung doe. And yet they could offer her what he could not: a legitimate name that didn't carry the stigma of murderer; a future that didn't demand a quest for vengeance; a heart not callused by the mistakes of his past. But not so callused that he didn't despair over losing yet again.

"If you set me free to marry someone else, you'd make even better time retrieving the information you need, couldn't you?" She sounded tearful, as if thinking of Farnsworth biding his time with her father roused her sympathy.

"I could."

"Would this scheme work?"

"It might." He couldn't manage to string more than two words together around the ache clogging his throat, thinking of Ellie lying with another man.

Lest he go mad at the thought, he forced himself to dispassionately consider the peril surrounding her suggestion. Only two weeks remained before McKittrick would execute his hostage. Ellie spoke the truth: he had to return to McKittrick's office and remove Farnsworth from danger. More importantly, McKittrick had to accept that his daughter was married, and that

both daughter and son-in-law were well beyond his
reach. A letter or telegraph would not accomplish the
trick; someone must face McKittrick and convince him
that he no longer had any control over his daughter.

Would McKittrick quietly accept the news?
Tremayne heartily doubted it. Whether he returned to
the jail as Ellie's husband, or merely as the messenger
bearing unwelcome news, his future looked uncertain. McKittrick might very well kill him out of spite.
The information Tremayne sought in Caldwell might
not be sufficient to earn him an acquittal from
Hanging Judge Parker. But if Tremayne presented her
case well enough, Ellie would remain free. A man
who loved her could not deny her this chance.

"Will you let me go, Tremayne?"

I don't know if I can. He could not speak the
words aloud.

"I have been told my father is honorable in matters
of business. He couldn't blame you if you went back
and told him he'd sent you too late, that I'd already
become someone's wife."

She sought to soothe him, Tremayne knew, and yet
her words sent arrows to pierce his heart, making a
mockery of his unemotional analysis of the situation.
Someone's wife. Face McKittrick and tell him Ellie
had cleaved to another, that even as they spoke her
soft, passionate body warmed another man's bed, her
rare and glorious smile lit another man's life. There
was no explaining the jolting pain that knifed through
Tremayne's heart.

"You can act as my father's proxy and give me
away, if it would enable you to confront my father

with a clearer conscience," she said, her skin flushing hot, as if the suggestion embarrassed her.

Give her away. Lead her down the aisle of some creaking, rough-sawn clapboard chapel and hand her over to Espy or another of his ilk. Impossible. "My conscience needs no salving," he managed to say through gritted teeth. He held his breath, his ears straining, half-unconsciously waiting for her to press the point and ask why he felt no guilt over the state of his conscience.

"You'll let me go?" she asked instead. Her voice betrayed an odd little catch; her breath held expectantly as she awaited his reply.

"Damn it all, Ellie. I can't take you back to him."

Once he said the words, he realized he'd merely admitted aloud the knowledge that had been swirling through his mind for days now. He should feel relief that she'd come up with such a novel solution; he felt only a huge, unseen weight crushing his chest as a wordless sound escaped her, a completely feminine sound conveying utter joy.

"Oh, Tremayne, thank you!" In her excitement she struggled against the arms he held wrapped around her. Her strength was nothing against his; he kept her close with a fierceness that didn't bear inspection.

"Tremayne." She locked slender fingers around his forearm and tugged. "Let me up. This isn't right anymore. It's inappropriate that we stay like this. Not now, when you're setting me free to marry someone else."

"When. When will you do it? How soon?" He had to ask.

"At once. Women are so scarce out here. I daresay I can be wed within days."

A trickle of wetness scalded his forearm. Tears. *She's crying?* He'd heard women sometimes cried from happiness and Ellie proved it now, silently. The tears unlocked his embrace when he knew words never could. She slipped free, moving away, though not far for he heard no footsteps padding across the rough wooden floor. A sudden weariness gripped him. The floor, which he'd not noticed before, suddenly felt unbearably hard beneath his hip so he flopped over onto his back, staring wide-eyed through the dark at nothing.

He heard her tentative movements and imagined she must be looking for the clothing she'd discarded before her bath. He remembered how her skin had looked, satiny smooth and glowing like golden cream in the candlelight.

"Will you draw a map for me? I'm not sure I can find my way back across the prairie."

He could spend another day in her company, then. "I will take you back to the homestead."

"I'd rather you didn't."

His jaw flinched, as if it had been on the receiving end of a well-aimed roundhouse punch. "I saw one of your neighbors in town earlier. Mrs. Murrow. Perhaps I could locate her in the morning and ask her to ride with you."

"I'd like that."

He felt the quilt beneath him stretch as she moved farther away, her hand patting the floor. She shifted positions, searching near his head, and he draped an arm over his eyes. Though the darkness was nearly impenetrable, he didn't have one bit of trouble conjuring up the image of her nude form seeking her missing garments. A satisfied sigh told him she'd found something, and then she commenced patting again, her palm thumping against the floor. He felt the curve of her hip nudge his side, and before either of them could react to the unexpected contact, her blindly searching hand landed smack in the middle of his chest.

Her fingers briefly tightened amid the curls crowning his chest. She made a soft, startled sound and started drawing her hand away. But he was quicker. His hand closed around hers, flattening it against his chest. He could feel his own heartbeat coursing into hers and knew he had to place more than physical distance between them if he ever hoped to free her for the life she envisioned.

"I will agree to this preposterous idea only on one condition. I will be facing your father again in only two weeks. You must give me your oath you will marry at once."

"So eager to see me wed, Tremayne?"

He wasn't. If anything, he wished he had the right to ask her to wait, he wished he had more than vague hopes and the very real prospect of a life spent in widow's weeds to offer her. "The journey I must take isn't difficult, but it could be dangerous if the person I seek learns what I'm doing. I could be killed before I have the chance to face your father. But even if I live to confront him, he might dispatch another tracker to confirm what I tell him. You must be safely wed, the sooner the better."

He felt her pulse flutter against his fingers and shook from the effort of beating down the thought that within days some other man would hold her thus.

She said nothing for a long moment, did nothing to break his hold upon her. "Will I see you again before you return to England?"

The harsh sound he made had nothing to do with humor. "Why? To share tea and biscuits with you and your new husband? I think not."

"I thought you might . . . I thought you might want to make sure I carry out this plan."

"I'm not your father, Ellie. I trust you to hold to your word." His tone softened. "Besides, it wouldn't hurt to keep such information out of your father's hands. It's better if I don't know the name of the man you marry."

Better for his own sanity, he should have admitted. He might be able to endure the images he knew would forevermore haunt him if he had no name, no face, to assign to Ellie's husband.

He swiveled upright, pulling her to her knees before him. Despite the dark, his eyes had adjusted to enable him to see the pale blur of her face, the dark mass of her hair, the faint glimmer of tears. They knelt, she clutching at his chest with one hand and a scrap of cloth with another, while he ran possessive hands over her shoulders.

So much had been lost to him. The name he'd thought belonged to him at birth. The independence he'd forged with his sweat and strong back. And now Ellie, the cruelest loss of all, since the very circumstances conspiring to tear her away from him would swing him full circle, giving him back his lost name and independence, however temporary.

He lowered his head and claimed her lips until hers opened beneath his. One last time he molded her form to his, and felt his manhood rise with undiminished desire between them. He held her, their pulses, their breathing, throbbing in accord.

"Remember this, Ellie. I had you first. No matter who you give yourself to after this night, you first belonged to me."

His britches and shirt lay near at hand, easy to find once he reluctantly set her free. And then he found himself in a rush to escape her, to leave her alone with her excited anticipation of the as-yet-unknown man she meant to wed.

She swayed upon her knees, staring at him unblinkingly while he donned his garments with hands that would rather have been caressing her silken skin.

He didn't fully understand why, but it seemed right to leave her this way, with desire raging unquenched between them, with their passion a near-palpable thing in the dark.

He left his britches unfastened, his shirt unbuttoned, and carried his shoes and saddlebags in his hand as he paused by the door. "Never forget you were mine first," he told her. And then he left, making certain the door hung ajar so moonlight could keep her fears at bay.

13

Though last night's whiskey pounded mercilessly through his skull, Stringer couldn't prevent smiling at the sight of a tall, tawny-haired figure striding straight toward the group of women clumped in front of W. C. Woodman's dry goods store. He wore everyday clothes instead of jailhouse issue, and looked a sight cleaner than convicts usually did at this time of day. But there was no mistaking him, it was Tremayne Hawthorne.

Stringer tipped his hat brim lower, shielding his face from Hawthorne's sight and sparing his aching eyeballs the morning sun's piercing rays. With a sidling motion, he edged himself back into the narrow alleyway where he'd spent the night, intending to follow once Hawthorne crossed the alley.

But the clump of Hawthorne's booted heels stilled well before reaching the alley, and from the excited, giggling flutter arising from the group of women, Stringer realized his quarry had stopped to pass the time of day.

"Mrs. Murrow." The cultured voice stirred another round of giggles.

"Howdy do, Mr. Hawthorne."

Stringer pressed against the board wall, straining to hear.

"Do you plan to return to your homestead today, Mrs. Murrow?"

"Sure do."

"Would you mind a bit of company along the way?"

"Long's yew ain't got too many calves, I don't mind a bit if yew come along," Mrs. Murrow replied.

"Calves?"

"That's why yer here, ain't it, to pick up the calves the cowboys cut out a' the herd? Me and my middle boy is the only ones could come, the herd rode in so unexpected. We can't be takin' too many critters back with us."

"Ellie and I didn't come here to collect calves," Hawthorne assured her.

"Bet he'll find himself with one soon anyway," whispered one of the women, raising another storm of giggles.

"Me 'n' the boy'll be ready to head home in two hours," Mrs. Murrow said. "If yew 'n' Ellie want to ride with us, yew can meet us right here."

"Agreed." Hawthorne's face darkened and he hesitated a bit before speaking again. "She'll be looking for some female advice, Mrs. Murrow, concerning marriage. I hope you'll be able to accommodate her."

"Don't yew worry none, Tremayne. Me 'n' Ellie'll have us a real nice chat."

"Praise the Lord," Stringer whispered, mocking McKittrick's fanaticism. Maybe the warden had a point with all his will-of-God blathering. In two hours, without Stringer making the slightest effort to find her, Hawthorne would serve up Miss Eleanor McKittrick slick as one of the hog-tied calves the other woman was expecting. A low, rusty-sounding laugh bubbled from his throat, brought to a quick halt by someone plucking at his sleeve. With an instinctive skill so ingrained that even his alcohol-benumbed state couldn't diminish it, Stringer caught the person's neck in a breath-denying grip, and held his knife blade at the intruder's throat.

"Goddamn cow-kicker!" he cursed, recognizing Half-Scalped Jackson's terrified countenance.

"Don't kill me!" Jackson wheezed. "I brung Cato Crowden to meet you."

"Now?" Incredulous, Stringer heard the retreating clump of Hawthorne's measured tread. He'd have to move quickly to keep Hawthorne in his sights; there was no time to discover whether Crowden might be willing to pay to keep Darla Hawthorne's journal for himself. "I ain't interested in your Cato Crowden anymore."

"He's right there." Jackson jerked his maimed head toward the far end of the building. "I tracked him down in Indian Territory. He'll be plenty mad, mister, if he come all this way for nothing. A mite short-fused, that Cato."

Stringer glanced toward the man leaning at the far end of the building. Sunlight gleamed against shoulder-length hair glistening with the blue-black sheen of a grackle's wing. Though he held himself casually, there was an air of suppressed strength about him, like a crouching cat ready to pounce.

The sun seemed to burn right through Stringer's hat, kicking up a set of clamoring voices that wouldn't be placated until he either got some sleep, or shut them up with another whiskey. A slight tremor shook his hand as he rubbed it over his mouth.

Perhaps, Stringer thought, considering how he felt at the moment, he shouldn't be so eager to dismiss Cato Crowden's assistance. Or raise his ire. He nodded toward Crowden, and then gripped Jackson's grimy shirt collar and propelled the man toward the storefront.

"You see that tall blond Englishman?" he asked, shaking Jackson in the direction of Hawthorne's retreating back. At Jackson's rapid-fire nod, Stringer explained. "You follow him, but don't let him know you're keeping track of him. He's supposed to be back here in two hours, but I don't want him pulling any surprises on me. You got that?"

"Sure, boss," Jackson stuttered.

Stringer dropped Jackson, who commenced running after Hawthorne the minute his feet touched the ground. Now that he thought on it, this seemed like a pretty fair turn of events. Never before had he dealt with Hawthorne without the benefit of bullwhip and horse and a handful of rogues backing him up. With a squeamish turn of his stomach, he thought of the bloodstained cabin near Caldwell, and matched the man against the deed.

Afoot, with little more than a wooden sidewalk separating them, Hawthorne had loomed larger, his shoulders broader, his overall demeanor more confident than cowed. Stringer cast a surreptitious glance back toward the waiting Cato Crowden. A mite short-fused, Jackson had called him, but perhaps he would make a valuable ally, if Stringer could keep him from exploding.

Besides, Hawthorne had already committed to bringing the warden's daughter back to travel with Mrs. Murrow. If, by some accident, Hawthorne caught sight of him, Stringer knew he'd change plans at once. But if Stringer kept out of his way, Hawthorne wouldn't suspect his recapture was imminent, even if that idiot Jackson all but plastered himself to his shadow.

Yes, a pretty fair turn of events. Stringer tugged his hat brim into place, and headed over to make the acquaintance of Mr. Cato Crowden.

The boy who'd delivered Ellie's bathtub the night before raised his battered felt hat a respectable two inches, his face alight with self-conscious pleasure. "Yore husband asked me to escort you into town, ma'am, and meet up with yore neighbor."

There it was—the proof that Tremayne would

honor his word to set her free. Now she must honor hers and find someone to marry. Somehow she must banish the memory of Tremayne's touch, and despite what he'd said, try to forget what had passed between them, try to stop anticipating another meeting.

For in sending the boy to escort her away, he'd silently told her he never meant to see her again.

"I'll have to ask you to get a move on, ma'am," the boy said. His chest puffed importantly. "I'm the only man around here, Ma bein' a widow and all."

"Did your father pass away recently?" Ellie asked, grateful for any conversation that would distract her thoughts from the night before.

"Naw. He died in the war. Don't even remember my pa. He left this vale a' sadness when I didn't know my butt from a turnip, pardon my language, ma'am. Ma lit out West when she heard she could claim homestead land, bein' a widow. Folks've been right respectful of us since we settled in."

Sarah Reynolds's plans hadn't differed much from her own—she'd settled her land, developed a thriving business, succeeded in staking her independence. Ironic, how widowhood had enhanced Sarah's position in the community; Ellie doubted either she or Lauretta would have much of a reputation left if it became known that single men slept beneath their barn roof.

And sometimes slept in the same pallet.

Ellie cast the proud boy a distracted smile, tentative because there was no joy lending it strength, though there should have been, now that she'd been temporarily freed. She passed a trembling hand over

her hair, embarrassed now to think how she'd struggled to tame its wild thickness without benefit of the
comb Tremayne had carried away in his saddlebags.
How she'd carefully shaken the worst of the dust
from her pink gown and thought, as she struggled
with the buttons, "This covers the places where he
touched me." Hoping, all the while, that his parting
words meant she would see him once more, and that
maybe, just maybe, he would realize that her protes-
tations of the night before had been in response to his
obvious disinterest, that she'd really been hoping he
might suggest that she become *his* wife.

"Are you all right, ma'am? You look a little peaked."

"I'm fine." She cast a look behind her to the rum-
pled pallet, and felt the blush rising from her neck
to stain her cheeks. The boy, farm lad that he was,
added to her embarrassment with a cocky, approv-
ing grin that told her in a few years he meant to
sample the pleasures to be found in this corncrib
with a woman of his own. She hurried to the waiting horses, head down, eager to escape his too-
knowing eyes. Thank goodness he and his
respectable widowed mother assumed she and
Tremayne were husband and wife; it eased the
embarrassment somewhat.

Husband and wife. Husband and wife. She turned
the phrase in her mind, disturbed by its appeal, and
then an idea struck her, an idea so dangerous and yet
inescapable that she nearly lost the precarious
foothold she'd gained in her stirrup.

The boy tossed her into the saddle; she landed with
a soft thump, all the while thinking, "I shall simply

tell everyone I am married to Tremayne, even though I'm not."

She gave less than half an ear to her companion, who seemed torn between nonstop chatter and sudden bouts of adolescent shyness. Her mind was awhirl with her circumstances, and this scheme for gathering the mess into a tidy, endurable heap.

She couldn't marry anyone. The mere thought of allowing any of the men she'd met in Magnolia to hold her, touch her, as Tremayne had done, was intolerable. And in the harsh light of day it seemed a blessing that Tremayne had spurned her embarrassed offer. Any man daring to wed Jonathan McKittrick's daughter risked a bullet between the eyes, regardless of whether he faced the man or not. She could not, in good conscience, permit any man to risk his life in exchange for her freedom.

So, what better phantom husband than Tremayne Hawthorne, a murderer bent upon some mysterious, dangerous mission, who, even if he survived, meant to travel to England to spend the rest of his life upon ancestral lands? At any moment he could be killed, or captured, or succeed in his various quests and sail for England, leaving her blessedly and unquestionably alone. Why, it would be almost as good as being a widow.

She would have no marriage certificate. Had Sarah ever been asked to produce one? she wondered. It wasn't difficult to imagine how Sarah would react if someone dared to ask to see such a personal item. Ellie had spent most of her life pretending to be the pleasant, complaisant daughter; she could assume the air of an offended widow. And if that failed, she could claim an itinerant preacher traveling with the cow herds had done the deed with no paper on hand to sign. There would be no witnesses; again, she could fabricate names of cowboys who'd passed through Wichita with the herd. Why, she could even use the herd's presence to explain Tremayne's absence, saying he'd signed on to earn money. Folks would think he'd run out on her and feel sorry for her when he failed to return, but she could endure the whispers and averted eyes in exchange for her independence. She could even declare him dead after a decent interval.

And there was always the possibility of a child. A tawny-haired, blue-eyed son or daughter who would never know the father living across the sea.

"It could work." She didn't realize she'd muttered the words aloud until the boy said, "Ma'am?" and shot her a questioning look. She treated him to a full-fledged smile in return, a dazzling one, subduing him to sudden red-faced embarrassment. By then they'd drawn up in front of Woodman's elegant dry goods store, where Mattie Murrow was comfortably seated upon a bench, basking in the reflective splendor of the glass entry.

"Thank you!" Ellie cried to the boy, forgetting, until her feet were on the traffic-churned mud street, that she didn't really know much about dismounting from a horse. "Mattie! Oh, let's hurry. I can't wait to get home."

Mattie indicated a narrow space along the bench not taken up by her own ample hips. "Yew sit alongside me here, Ellie. My boy's got delayed some at the rail yard, and I don't see our Tremayne anywheres around yet."

"He's not coming with us." Ellie felt breathless after saying the words, as if she'd run the two miles from the corncrib to the dry goods store. At any moment Mattie would begin to pry into Tremayne's whereabouts, and the scheme that had seemed so simple and foolproof moments ago now sounded nonsensical and doomed to failure. But Mattie just nodded, as if she'd expected Tremayne to stay behind, and shifted back and forth, as if she'd forgotten she sat on a hard wooden bench instead of a comfortable rocking chair.

What to do? All her life Ellie'd found it best to hold her tongue and offer as little information as possible, doling it out in minute portions as need demanded. That strategy might not work in the case of her fictional marriage. She thought of the girls she'd known before her father had terminated all her friendships; even estranged, news of their betrothals and weddings had filtered back to her. Women loved talking about weddings. Wouldn't Mattie think it strange that Ellie had kept such a momentous secret? Following her natural inclination might doom her lie to failure.

"We got married last night," Ellie blurted before habit and caution overcame the impulse.

Mattie stopped her rocking motion for a moment, and sent a swift, appraising glance from Ellie's still-swollen lips to a loose button dangling near her waist. "Uh-huh, last night he was too busy to talk, and this morning he said yew might be wantin' to talk about marriage and such. Can't say as I blame yew, wantin' to marry up with a fella looks like him, but he'll be bound to break yer heart unless yew keep a close watch over him. He sent May Lou into a tizzy over them blue eyes a' his."

How well she understood May Lou's predicament. "He does that without really meaning to," Ellie said lamely, her heart racing, her mouth dry, as if Mattie had doubted her word and even now demanded proof of her nonexistent wedding. *And he's already broken my heart,* she added silently.

"Don't see no weddin' band."

Ellie hadn't thought of a ring. She ran her thumb over her bare finger. "He . . . he signed on with the herd to make money to buy one."

"Now, that's a shame." Mattie shook her head, a sorrowful frown creasing her forehead. "Thinkin' a' that man eatin' dust when yew could be honey-moonin' with him." She commenced the rocking motion again, and then nudged Ellie with her elbow. "One good thing about him starin' at cow rumps for a couple months, he'll sure be powerful glad to see yew when he gets back home."

Her full-throated laugh, bawdy and boisterous, raised an answering giggle from Ellie. She hoped Mattie didn't notice that she sounded a little wild, a little hysterical, that her laughter was more of a release from fear than humor. Mattie believed her! Curious townsfolk glanced at them with broad smiles, and Ellie stared back, knowing she laughed too loud and too long, praying none of them would ask for an explanation of their merriment and make her dredge up more lies to support lies already told.

A running man, his head looking odd and somehow malformed, hurtled past their bench without sparing them a glance. Ellie swung her gaze to follow him a scant thirty feet to the edge of the building, where he joined two men who were staring at her with narrow, speculative intensity. One, tall and excruciatingly thin, was dressed all in black; the other had long, wind-tossed hair that gleamed blue-black where a few strands met the sunlight. The storefront shaded their faces, shrouding them in eerie mystery. Their darkness, their lack of humor, sent a warning prickle skittering down her spine. For a moment, she envisioned them stomping down the street, demanding to see her marriage certificate, her wedding ring, to prove that what she said was true. And then the running man jabbered something, inaudible save for the high-pitched nature of his voice, and the three of them disappeared into the alley that ran alongside the building.

Ellie sagged against the bench back, relieved at their departure. They'd only been staring at the sight of two grown women cackling like a couple of silly old hens on a public bench smack in front of Wichita's most elegant establishment.

Mattie continued chuckling with an earthy edge that left no doubt her thoughts still dwelled upon Ellie's postponed honeymoon. Ellie tucked her ringless hand into her pocket, and fought down the urge to cry.

*   *   *

Silas Stringer venting his rage was some sight to see. Cato simply watched, impressed beyond words. Venom seemed to ooze from Stringer's mottled complexion, poisoning the air so it felt hard to breathe. His lips receded, baring teeth that rivaled any slavering wolf's. His eyes narrowed into slits, predatory, ruthless, so focused and intent that the rest of him seemed to swell larger in comparison.

"You useless freak!" Stringer advanced upon the luckless Half-Scalped Jackson. Sunlight sparked from Stringer's curled fist. There was another thing to like about the man—he favored Cato's weapon of choice. A good three inches of honed steel knife blade protruded from a fist that looked ready to strike.

"I'm gonna carve up the rest of your head, you no-good son of a bitch."

"Boss! Boss!" Jackson babbled, doing little to help his cause by getting his feet hopelessly entangled with each other. "I did what you said. I followed the Englishman. When I saw what he meant to do I figured you'd want to know straight off. Hell, he's twice my size—I couldn't have stopped him if I'd tried. But I know where he went."

Stringer stopped advancing. No words, only a grunt, came from him, but nobody standing in the immediate vicinity could have mistaken the sound for anything but an order to explain, in great detail, what Jackson had seen.

"He bought hisself supplies and told the livery man he needed to trade for a horse to carry him clear to Caldwell," Jackson said.

"Caldwell! He's heading back to his homestead!" Cato exclaimed.

"Shee-it! I just came from there." Stringer added a string of colorful curses. With one fluid, overhead motion, the dagger he held ended up buried blade first in the hard-packed dust at Jackson's twitching feet.

"Guess you'll have to go back." Cato, worried that Hawthorne had headed closer to his part of the world, hoped Stringer might light out after Hawthorne. For himself, a temporary relocation seemed in order. "I'll be heading North myself, away from Indian Territory. Pleased to make your acquaintance, Stringer."

Stringer issued another grunt, one that raised the hackles along Cato's neck.

"Figured you with having some sense," Stringer said, a derisive curl to his lips.

"More than most." Cato ignored the disbelieving snort from Half-Scalped Jackson, who chose that moment to back away, leaving Cato and Stringer facing each other like rams squaring off to butt heads.

"He ain't going back to Caldwell to help his neighbors bring in the harvest," Stringer said. "I'm guessing he's going back to find you."

"He don't know me. He don't know nothing about me." Cato spoke with more conviction than he felt; Darla Hawthorne had sworn to keep his name secret, but she'd turned powerful mouthy near the end. Who knew what she'd blabbed to her husband?

"You saying you ain't done nothing to set that man looking for revenge against you?"

"Didn't seem like it at the time."

"Then you ain't got nothing to worry about, do you?"

Cato wanted to answer, "No." Wanted to turn on a jaunty heel and head far away from Caldwell and give Tremayne Hawthorne even less thought than he'd done over the past five months. Devote the rest of his life to chasing good whiskey and bad women, the same way he'd spent the time between Darla's violent death and Hawthorne's suddenly appearing to take Cato to account for the part he'd played in it. How the hell was he supposed to enjoy himself now, knowing Hawthorne meant to stalk him down?

"Me, I don't like leavin' loose ends." Stringer squatted to fetch his knife and wiped the blade against his knee. "Never know when one's gonna snare you around the leg and pull you down into the dirt."

Cato snorted. "I thought I had this particular loose end tied up. Hawthorne was locked up in the jailhouse, wasn't he?"

"Yeah, well he's out now."

Cato didn't care for the tone Stringer affected, as though he'd said out loud that Cato could do what he wanted, but Stringer thought him a fool for turning away.

"Aw, hell, I'll go with you and finish him off. I don't want to spend the rest of my life looking behind me."

A triumphant smile curled Stringer's lip. "No sense in tiring ourselves out by chasing after him. That's hard, thirsty work. You heard the lady over there say they're married. Son of a bitch is slyer than I gave him credit for. He might be laying false tracks, might not be heading to Caldwell at all. But one thing's for sure—he's got to take her back to her pa, and he figgered out a way to sample the goods along the way."

"You're mighty good at figuring strategy," Cato said, admiring Stringer's savvy. His sour mood lifted a little. "The hell with him doing all the sampling. I'll go grab her right now."

For a moment, it looked as though Stringer meant to go along with the idea. But then he shook his head. "Let her go about her business. He'll be easier to take if we catch him unawares. Shouldn't be too hard keeping track of the new Mrs. Hawthorne. She'll lure him to us like a bee to honey."

That struck Cato as funny, thinking of the troublesome Hawthorne buzzing around like a lightning bug trapped in a jar. It struck him as funny, too, to think that a woman—Hawthorne's second wife—would be the cause of his second downfall. Served Hawthorne right; a man ought to know better than to keep on coming after someone, once the past was past.

"You want to partner up with me and get this business finished?" Stringer asked. "I don't think I ought to get too close to the lady. There's an outside chance she might recognize me."

"She ain't never seen me. Neither has he, for a fact," Cato said, nodding his agreement to the plan, more pleased than he cared to admit that a man of Stringer's caliber would consider him a partner.

And with such a man guarding his back, he dared indulge another thought that struck him as so funny he laughed out loud.

"I'm gonna keep *real* close watch over this new wife and see if she wants to play," Cato explained when Stringer grunted a wordless question. "Had me some fine times with the first one before she got too pushy. With Hawthorne being locked up, I doubt he's learned much about keeping a woman happy."

"Some men run into all kinds of trouble on account of women," Stringer said, an obscene smile spreading his lips.

14

"*Up there.*" Lauretta peered through the lower branches of a wind-bent cottonwood tree. She sent a silent prayer of thanks heavenward that the buzzing, cone-shaped swarm hadn't anchored itself forty feet above her head. And another thank-you for helping her find a swarm at all, this late past the spring swarming season. And still another, begging God to watch over Ellie.

"I'll get it." Hiram tried charging past her, but Lauretta laid a restraining hand on his arm. She withdrew it so quickly she might not have touched him, so conscious was she of the feel of his flesh through the rough homespun he wore.

"You're not dressed right," she said, running a hand down her own gown for emphasis. "You have to wear smooth, tight-woven cotton. Bees don't like fuzzy clothes. I guess their little legs get caught in the hairs so they can't fly off, but they sure can sting."

Hiram's sun-bronzed face settled into determined lines. "I ain't gonna let you climb up after that swarm, that's for sure."

"Just watch me."

Before he could protest, Lauretta skinned up the side of the tree. Not very ladylike behavior, she knew, but what did that matter out here? She liked climbing trees, and she climbed better than most boys, surely better than any grown man. Clinging to a branch with one hand, she pulled her special bottle from a pouch at her waist. Years ago, she'd poked holes through a piece of uncured cowhide and let it harden like a caul fastened over the bottle top. The homemade sprinkler top slipped on and off easily, but with a string wrapped around it just below the lip, it stuck tight as anything. Before leaving the dugout this morning, she'd filled the bottle with a syrupy solution of sugar water, which she now shook liberally over the pulsing swarm.

The bees quieted, interested in investigating this manna from heaven.

Lauretta tucked her bottle away and withdrew a set of pruning shears. Taking care not to disturb the feeding swarm, she trimmed off twigs and small branches surrounding it so nothing would deflect it away from where she wanted it to fall.

"Hold that box right up underneath them, Hire," she called in a hoarse whisper.

Hiram hefted a crate to his shoulders. A light sweat sprang up on his brow; she didn't know whether it meant a return of his ague, or a fear of bees.

"Turn your head away! You don't want them flying into your eyes." Her warning ought to give him a chance to back away without losing any pride if the insects frightened him. Some people had a fear of bees. Sometimes with good reason.

"Hire, maybe you ought not be helping me. You could be sensitive to bee stings and swell up like one of them hot-air balloons. Or worse. Folks die from bee stings. I'd hate to see you keeling over with a heart attack."

"I been stung plenty. I ain't floated off, and I'm still livin'."

"You can just set the box down. You don't have to catch them."

Expressing more stubbornness than she cared to argue with, he continued staring up at the swarm. Maybe he hadn't heard her warning. Loss of hearing could mean the fever was taking him again.

She asked, straight out. "Are you coming down with the ague again, Hire?"

"Don't you worry about me while you're up in a tree, missy."

Lauretta gripped the slender branch the swarm had attached itself to and gave it a sharp, sudden shake. Again. And again. The swarm fell like a cluster of ripe crabapples, landing with a surprisingly loud thud in Hiram's crate.

"Get the lid!" he shouted, easing the crate to the ground and stepping gingerly away.

"Not yet." A little breathless from scrambling out of the tree, Lauretta knelt beside the crate, studying the angry bees. "We can't close them up until I see if we caught the queen."

"How're you gonna know that? There's too many of them to tell apart."

Hiram stood a safe pace away from the crate, so maybe it was only her imagination that made it seem like he was shivering beneath the hot sun.

"If they fly back out of the box, we don't have her. If they start fanning their wings and sticking their little hind ends up in the air, they're ready to set up housekeeping."

"Is that what you did when you caught sight of this place—stuck your butt up in the air and did a little dance?" Hiram shot her a mischievous grin that made a mockery of her fears for his health.

"Hiram Espy!"

"Tell you what, since you're so all-fired set against lettin' me see your face, maybe you ought to give me a little glimpse of the way you flapped your arms and . . ." His teasing trailed off as a low, bawling sound drifted across the open spaces. He lifted his chin and stared over the prairie. "Looks like we got company, Laurie."

We got company. Miss Malvern, back in Arkansas, would never have approved such grammar, but no properly constructed sentence could have warmed Lauretta's heart the way this one did. If there was anything that could restore her spirits after watching Ellie ride away with Tremayne, it was Hiram's presence. She felt so right, so comfortable, and yet so shivery and confused, with Hiram at her side, including her in everything he did.

If only he would stop asking to see her face.

If only she felt safe to bare it to him, without fearing she'd see repugnance and pity cross his own.

As always, she tamped down her regrets when these thoughts entered her mind. She glanced toward the approaching company, glad that it offered such an easy way to break off what could have become another battle of wills. Recognized the shade of pink worn by the woman riding with two others at the rear of a small herd of calves. Recognized the fine-boned bay mare.

"Ellie!" She shrieked, another unladylike action, and shrieked again for good measure. "Ellie's come home!"

Abandoning all thoughts of containing the swarm, she lifted her skirts and darted past the wagon that had hauled them to the trees. Lucky thing Hire had unharnessed the mules to graze, because she surely wasn't about to waste time doing it now, with Ellie on her way to the dugout. Somehow, Lauretta maintained her footing on the slippery grass as she ran full tilt across the prairie. Her heart soared when Ellie's features took shape, and soared even higher when she heard Hiram's strides thumping right behind her.

Ellie wanted to scream.

Lauretta, who hated being the object of stares, hadn't stopped staring at her for one single minute. She'd stared the whole, interminable time it had taken to say good-bye to the Murrows. She'd stared through another eternity while Hiram shared a cup of coffee before heading off to his bunk in the barn. Somehow, she'd managed to keep staring while she discarded her bee bonnet and they made their preparations for the night. And still she stared from her seat on her nail keg, silently, expectantly, her arms crossed over her chest, watching every movement Ellie made while clearing away the coffee things.

A solitary candle flickered atop the table, its flame doing little more than softening the dugout's darkness.

"You're different," Lauretta said just as Ellie thought she couldn't stand another minute of her silent staring.

She could tell! Oh, God, it was true, all those tales girls told about being able to spot a woman who'd given herself to a man without benefit of wedlock. Ellie wondered where it showed. On her skin, which still tingled from his touch? Her lips, which seemed fuller and more sensitive than ever before? In the way she walked, her legs and body remembering the feel of him, and what he'd done, and plaguing her with the desire for more?

"Sadder," Lauretta continued, her voice breaking as if just saying the word made her want to cry. "You should be happy he let you go, Ellie. *We* were so happy to see you we lost a good swarm and left the wagon out on the prairie. What is it you aren't telling me?"

"Everything," Ellie whispered. She sat on the edge of the bed, a simple, thoughtless act that nonetheless brought Tremayne into the forefront of her mind, remembering how he'd lain upon it that day she'd shot him, his long limbs hanging beyond the edge, his fine-honed, muscular body dwarfing a space big enough for two. "I couldn't tell you, Lauretta, not with other people around."

"Tell me now."

And so she did, the words spilling from her in an unfamiliar torrent. She told everything, or almost everything, save for the wild sensations he'd roused within her, for she had no words adequate to describe the wanton, sensual creature his touch created. Nor did she tell her how often he'd claimed her, and how he'd left her. *Never forget you were mine first.* As if he'd grown resigned to losing the things he'd claimed, this man who'd told her his intentions never produced the desired results.

"And we struck a bargain," she concluded. "I swore to him that I'd wed, so my father could have no claim upon me. But I can't marry anyone, not after . . . Even if I wanted to marry, what man would have me now? Besides, my father is a threat to any man who might marry me. So I told Mattie Murrow that Tremayne Hawthorne is my husband. Her son said she'd have it spread all over town in no time, but I don't see how that could be since we left Wichita right after I told her."

"Ellie!" Though she sounded shocked, a mischievous twinkle soon lighted Lauretta's eyes. "I thought Mattie Murrow looked fit to burst. How'd you get her to keep quiet about this in front of me and Hire?"

"I told her it was a big surprise, and I wanted to tell you myself, with us being such close friends and all. She seemed to understand."

"How did you think of such a clever scheme?"

"Clever?"

"Well, of course it's clever. You know Hire and I

will back you up if anyone asks rude questions. There isn't a soul who could call you a liar except Tremayne, and he's long gone."

"That's more or less the way I figured it," Ellie said. She touched a finger to her breastbone, where a nagging, unremitting pain had lodged itself. It flared at the thought of Tremayne vanishing across the sea, and she pressed against the pain, but it subsided only a whit, as if it meant to take up permanent residence beneath her heart.

"If your father doesn't go back on his word, Tremayne will have his title and his place in society, but you'll be free," Lauretta said.

"I . . . Tremayne didn't seem worried about my father changing his mind," Ellie whispered, stunned to think she'd been so intent upon her own freedom that she'd given little thought to the risk Tremayne had assumed.

"Well, you don't want any part of a murderer anyway."

"He's not a murderer." The words came out with no conscious thought.

"He's not?" Lauretta leaned forward, avid interest stamped all over her. "Oh, Lordy, except for being sad about him taking you home, I've been dying to know what he did. He must've told you all about it."

"No. He never mentioned it." Ellie wished she'd never broached the subject, never given voice to the wordless certainty that she'd developed, based on little more than his gentle attempts at comforting her when he'd found her cowering in the dark, the way he'd left the door ajar as he left her side forever. The

way he'd kissed her and held her and possessed her
with such infinite tenderness—such a man could not
be capable of the terrible things he stood accused of.
It hurt to think how implicitly she believed in his
innocence, when he obviously cared nothing about
what she thought. If he'd cared, he'd have explained
things to her without forcing her to ask.

"Well, then, he told you he's innocent."

"No."

"Then you asked him flat-out?"

"No."

"Ellie . . ."

"It doesn't matter. As you said, he's long gone."

Lauretta fixed her with a sharp, assessing glance.
"But what if he comes back?"

Ellie drew in her breath so hard it sounded like a
gasp. She hadn't told Lauretta about the shameful
way she'd tried to lead Tremayne into offering to
marry her, and the aching, tear-choked sensation that
plagued her even now, remembering how he'd
ignored her unsubtle hints and tears, how even the
suggestion that he lead her down the aisle as her
father's proxy hadn't roused a speck of jealousy
within him.

"He won't come back."

"If he does, you could be in trouble," Lauretta said.
"He already killed one wife, Ellie. And a child! An
innocent child! Maybe he doesn't like being married."

"A man needn't kill his family to rid himself of the
responsibility." Ellie shook her head, torn between
defending Tremayne and knowing that each word she
spoke on his behalf betrayed feelings she meant to stifle.

"There's something else." Lauretta frowned, leaning back on her nail keg. "Maybe this isn't such a good idea after all. If you're calling yourself his wife, that means he can do anything he wants with you if he comes back, even take you back to your father, no matter what he promised. Maybe you ought to really marry someone else real quick."

"Sure, I'll marry the next man who pokes his head through our door." Neither of them laughed at her quip. "Laurie, you know I never intended to marry. Only sheer desperation placed the thought into my head."

"I've heard some women say it isn't so bad, being married." Lauretta ducked her head, suddenly intent upon her mending while a blush suffused her cheeks.

Ellie hid a smile. "I've seen for myself that women can succeed out here without a man, and I mean to do it, too. Somehow I believe in my heart that Tremayne Hawthorne is an honorable man. All I can do is hope that he honors his word, and that my father will treat him fairly. Tremayne wouldn't come back just to hurt me."

After a long moment, Lauretta sighed. "Well, just to be safe, you'd better not admit what you've done if he *does* come back. Don't give him any ideas of the power he holds over you. Now, we'd better get some sleep." With a smooth motion, she reached across the table and pinched the candle out, plunging the dugout into nearly impenetrable darkness. From habit, Ellie loosed a small cry of dismay.

"Oh, Lordy, Ellie, I'm sorry! I'm so flustered by all your news that I forgot how much you hate the dark. Let me find the matches."

Ellie heard Lauretta searching for the matches and sat stock-still on the bed, waiting for the familiar, crushing sense of oppression that always settled over her in the dark and robbed her of her breath, her will to live. Waited for the fear to grip her as it had just the night before, holding her immobile in the frigid bath water until Tremayne had flung the corncrib door open and gathered her into his arms.

"Ellie, I'm having trouble finding the matches. I'll move aside the buffalo robe to let in some light—"

Before, the darkness had always pressed in at once, the pressure immediately closing her ears until she could hear nothing but the pounding of her heart. So why could she hear Lauretta's feet scraping over the hard-packed dirt floor? And the cricket's lusty chirping from beneath the window? And the breeze, so ever-present one scarcely noticed it during the light of day? She heard everything now; she took a huge breath and felt her lungs fill with fresh, sweet night air.

"Don't worry about the light, Laurie. I'm fine."

Even if Lauretta doubted her words, there was no mistaking the calm in Ellie's voice. She laughed a little, surprised at herself. "It seems I'm not afraid of the dark anymore. Not at all."

She felt no fear. Only an overwhelming loneliness.

15

Caldwell

The cabin looked so small. Entirely too small to have sheltered so much bitterness and violence. Death. Tremayne took a long, shuddering breath, glancing away from the neglected wooden structure toward where the Chikaskia River meandered in the distance, wondering if Chedgrave Manor, too, would assume such insignificant proportions once he joined his father.

It would. Buckingham Palace itself would seem less than a hovel, given that his mind could spare it only the slightest attention, being so thoroughly filled with thoughts of Ellie.

She haunted him. Even now, with more than eighty miles of prairie separating them, he felt the pull to return and take her in his arms before she pledged herself to another man. Turn his back on this insignificant cabin and deeds long done, thumb his nose in his father's direction and build a new life somewhere, with Ellie. Two souls, battered and scarred—could they heal each other?

"No." He said it aloud, to the accompanying twitter of a sparrow nesting in a mulberry tree Darla had planted years ago. Unless he resolved the unfinished business of his past, he could never be a whole man for Ellie. And she needed a whole man, now, to carry out her audacious, sensible plan, so that when he faced Jonathan McKittrick again, the news of her marriage would keep her safe.

He concentrated once more on the cabin. Inside, if Gus had kept vandals away, Darla's journal would be lying tucked beneath the mattress. Tremayne had never violated her privacy by reading it while she lived, and the law had come after him too soon after she'd died for him to page through it to learn her secrets. Pray God the journal still rested there, and pray it contained what he sought: the name of Darla's lover. When he tracked down that man and settled the score, then he would be worthy of Ellie's love.

But by then she would be long married, perhaps a mother several times over. If a vulture had descended from the sky and set about making a meal of Tremayne's entrails, it couldn't hurt any worse than the thought of Ellie's slender belly swollen with another man's seed.

He couldn't bring himself to enter the cabin just then and immerse himself in the past, not with Ellie so much on his mind. With a glance toward the sun, he mounted the nag he'd rented in Wichita and headed for Gus Zinn's place.

Tremayne knew a mounted man couldn't hope to approach Gus unnoticed. Self-sufficient Pennsylvania Dutchmen like Gus had flocked in great numbers to Kansas. Lured by the promise of free land, they had settled with as little as twenty-five cents in their pockets, vowing to make their way through the strength of their backs. Few men owned horses, and fewer still rode them. One good horse could pull a wagonload, and it offended their sensibilities to waste any animal's strength on hauling one man around.

Sure enough, the sound of Tremayne's horse drew Gus's attention away from the patch he'd been hoeing.

"*Mein Gott.* Tremayne!"

"Gus."

Gus dropped his hoe and made his way across his garden plot, mumbling accented words of disbelief. The months had weathered his skin and added a layer of aloofness Tremayne didn't remember. He had only himself to blame, moving through his arrest like a somnambulist, expecting the support of his friends and neighbors but giving them nothing to believe in in return.

"My land looks in good heart," Tremayne said when Gus stood before him. "I thank you for looking after it. I wouldn't have blamed you if you'd let it go, since I didn't think I'd ever be back here again."

Awkwardness had never been a part of their relationship, but Tremayne felt it between them now. His hand twitched; he realized he'd been anticipating Gus's hearty handshake, which hadn't been offered.

"I didn't do so good with the cabin," Gus said.

"I shouldn't have imposed upon you," he muttered, feeling a new desolation of spirit settling over him.

And then Gus's strong hands were gripping his shoulders. "*Mein Gott,* Tremayne," his friend repeated. "When you come before me, I am thinking I am seeing a ghost. You'll not be blaming me for being surprised to see you. Not four days ago that man told me he'd be taking your things to you at the jailhouse. He didn't say nothing about you being set loose, or I wouldn't have let him take your things."

"I don't understand. Someone came after my things?" Dread crept through him.

"*Ja.* It wasn't until I am learning he didn't take the razor and saw how he nosed into places that were not his business that I am thinking I made a big mistake and realized this fellow wasn't too trustworthy."

"Gus—" Tremayne stopped himself from roaring at Gus to stop dithering about razors. "If someone was here looking for me, there might be trouble. Bad trouble."

Gus's good eye narrowed, and Tremayne hoped it meant his concentration focused commensurately.

"You come with me, Tremayne. Your horse, it needs a rest from carrying you such a long way. My Anna, she's busy with her chickens, but we can help ourselves to a nice slice of *schnitz* pie and coffee. I am thinking there is much we must talk about."

*   *   *

Stringer agitated the whiskey bottle, peeved to see so little liquid swirling against the deep-amber glass. He'd thought he'd laid in an ample supply to outlast the finding of Hawthorne—one more thing to hold against the jumped-up jailbird.

Of course, he hadn't counted on Cato Crowden guzzling more than his share. Stringer regretted now the impulse that had led him to seek out the no-account drifter. Any fool could see Cato had no guts.

Cato sulked, angry at being deprived of a woman's companionship to while away the three days they'd spent so far in watching the McKittrick girl's homestead. He whined, swatting at black flies and mosquitoes, complaining that the Kansas prairie lacked the comforts of his Indian Territory hideout. He questioned Stringer's judgment and cautious watchfulness, not understanding that Hawthorne might well be holed up on the homestead, ready to come out with shotgun blasting the minute they poked their noses near his woman. Worst of all, Stringer suspected Cato's polished exterior hid the guts of a yellow-bellied coward, a man willing to exploit women to the fullest, but turning tail and heading back to his hideout the minute a real man rose to challenge him.

He muttered beneath his breath, cursing the day he'd mentioned Cato Crowden's name to that idiot Half-Scalped Jackson. Better had he gunned Hawthorne down when he spotted him in Wichita, instead of relishing the crow he'd force McKittrick to eat once he hauled both Hawthorne and McKittrick's daughter back.

"What're you mumbling about?" Cato interrupted his thoughts.

"Just thinking we need more supplies." Stringer tilted the bottle and reluctantly let the last few drops trickle down his throat. Another day on this prairie without whiskey to numb the effect of Cato Crowden sounded well-nigh unendurable. "Maybe I'll scout around and see if any of these farmers got some homemade corn liquor for sale."

Cato cast him a derisive snort. "I got more refined tastes. Don't go hunting rotgut on my account."

"Oh, well, yes sir, Mr. Cato Crowden, sir, I'll just ride all the way to Wichita and back to fetch you some aged whiskey." Stringer leaned back against his bedroll, relishing his snappy rejoinder, when he wondered, *Why not?*

Why not ride into Wichita and gain a precious day or two away from Cato's cloying company? Why not revel in a repeat visit to that Delano whore in her snug little hotel room? Hawthorne wasn't hiding out in the dugout or barn; if he was, he hadn't so much as visited the outhouse to take a piss. Hawthorne's woman shared the dugout with another female, and a skinny man lived in their barn. Weak and helpless, the lot of them. Even Cato Crowden seemed capable of keeping an eye on things.

"How much bounty money you fixing to collect once we catch them both?" Cato asked, fanning a persistent fly from his face.

"Ain't no bounty money. Just doing a favor."

And then Stringer's mind started chewing over Cato's idle question.

Money.

He'd been so worked up over McKittrick doubting his abilities that he'd set off like a schoolboy eager to please his headmaster. All these days his gut had been churning over the injustice of the warden entrusting his job, *his job,* to a criminal, just because McKittrick didn't hold with a man taking a few drinks. That, and the certainty that McKittrick would be watching him sideways from now on, just waiting for another chance to call him a drunken whoremonger.

But with McKittrick's money in *his* pocket, Stringer could strike out fresh and seek someone who might hold a better opinion of his unique skills.

He could snatch the girl and then set it all up in Wichita. Send one of those telegraphs demanding a hefty ransom; hell, force McKittrick to haul his fat ass to Wichita and deliver it himself. Now, that would make up for a lot of insults.   Stringer felt his skin stretch in a wide smile at the thought of McKittrick handing over a nice wad of greenbacks; that ought to wipe the self-righteous smirk off McKittrick's face. Damn it all if that idiot Cato hadn't come up with one fine idea.

But Cato would expect a cut.

Better to let Cato stay here, guarding Eleanor McKittrick, and then blow off his sulky, whining, cowardly head once the deal was set. And if Hawthorne showed up in the meantime, hell, his rifle held enough bullets to deal with them both. He would forgo a ransom for Hawthorne for the sheer satisfaction of killing the man responsible for putting all those doubts in McKittrick's head and casting him in a bad light.

Counting on Cato's lazy inclinations to fall in with his plan, Stringer suggested, "Why don't you ride into Wichita for some whiskey, Cato?"

"Why don't we just grab the girl and be done with it?" Cato countered.

"Naw. Hawthorne's got to be part of the deal." Stringer pretended great concentration. "Tell you what—I'll go. It'll give me a chance to ask around town whether anyone's seen him or not."

"You want to waste time riding back and forth to Wichita, you be my guest." Cato shrugged, but his apparent indifference was offset by a sudden snake-like gleam in his eyes. Stringer didn't care for the look.

"You stick close to camp. And stay away from the girl. If Hawthorne's around you could ruin everything, er, and maybe get hurt."

"I ain't scared of Hawthorne," Cato muttered. "I'm more worried over what you're up to all of a sudden."

Stringer quelled a shiver of surprise. How the hell had Cato gotten suspicious? "I'll be back in a day or two." He felt Cato's speculative glance studying his every move as he saddled his horse and rode toward Wichita.

Neither Tremayne nor Gus touched the hearty slices of dried-apple pie, but Tremayne took a quick swallow of Anna's hot coffee. It trickled down his throat like a burning trail of acid, the bitterness caused by what he was hearing rather than from the coffee itself.

"Almost as tall as you," Gus described the stranger he'd found in Tremayne's cabin. "Greasy gray hair. Dressed all in black, like he is fancying himself a bounty man. Claimed he is meaning to meet up with you back at the Fort Smith jail. Said he was looking forward to seeing you there."

Stringer. If Stringer had come looking for him in Caldwell, it meant McKittrick had broken his word. Farnsworth might be dead, and Tremayne already blamed, the quarry in a territory-wide bounty hunt. Worse, Stringer had disappeared right after meeting Gus. If he'd figured out Tremayne had bypassed Caldwell and gone straight to Magnolia, he might even now be stalking Ellie. "That relentless swine," he muttered.

"You are knowing this man?" Gus asked, sounding surprised.

"I know him well enough to realize I must find him at once," Tremayne said. He set his coffee mug down carefully, giving no hint of the violent urgency he felt.

"You have a score to settle with him." Gus nodded.

"Perhaps. But more importantly, there is a woman. She is very important to me, Gus. I fear he means her harm."

"Again, this man means your woman harm? Was not poor Darla enough for this monster?"

Five months in prison had dulled some of Tremayne's social skills, but he'd managed to communicate well enough with Ellie and Lauretta and Hiram. Why was it that Gus's comments were so often incomprehensible to him?

"He didn't make my acquaintance until after Darla's murder," Tremayne said.

"Then this man is not Cato Crowden?"

"Who in God's name is Cato Crowden?" Tremayne couldn't help it; he roared the question, his instincts urging him to rush back to Magnolia to check on Ellie, his mind cautioning him to learn every scrap of information Gus might possess in his rambling brain.

Gus didn't appear eager to spill any information. He studied the scarred wooden table top with rapt attention, his face suffused with a remarkable shade of red.

"Gus?"

Flushing a deeper scarlet, Gus mumbled, "I have made a mess of things. You know I never took a thing from your cabin."

"Gus?"

"The winters here, they're long. Not much to do."

"Gus?" With each repetition of his friend's name, Tremayne's voice honed a sharper edge.

Gus craned his head, searching each corner of the room. "Anna, she is still outside with her chickens?"

Tremayne glowered at him.

Gus waved a hand in defeat. "I'll tell you. Everything you own in your cabin, I am knowing it. I had to make an accounting, you see, if ever you come back, like now, and asked me what happened to such and so. Do you understand?"

Tremayne jumped on that bit of information. "If you made an accounting, then you can tell me what Stringer took."

"His name is Stringer?"

"Gus . . ."

"Yes, yes. He took a silver coin. Two fine lawn

handkerchiefs. And a small book, Tremayne. A hand-written journal hidden beneath the mattress."

Tremayne's shoulders sagged, but just for the space of a heartbeat. He'd been so certain that the journal would reveal the name of Darla's lover. He'd been hoping Darla had entrusted its pages with enough information to help him earn an acquittal from Judge Parker. If Stringer had read the journal and realized how important it was to Tremayne's defense, he might have destroyed it by now, considering the antipathy between them.

The blush deepened Gus's complexion to a brick red. "So you see why I thought he was Cato Crowden."

"No, I don't," Tremayne said, gripping the table edge to lever himself to his feet. "But it doesn't mat—"

"I read the journal, Tremayne. You remember how long was that winter. And then spring storms are hitting after they took you away, blizzard following blizzard. Anna and I could not stand each other's company, and so during one calm spell I moved my pallet over there and bunked down in your place for a few nights. I soon found I was missing the arguing with Anna. I am ashamed to say it, but for something to do, I read the book from cover to cover. You never read it, Tremayne?"

Tremayne understood Gus's embarrassment now; his friend was hesitant to inform him he'd been cuckolded by his wife. "I know she wasn't faithful to me, Gus. I'd hoped to learn the identity of her lover by reading the journal. Sounds as though you've saved me the trouble."

Gus gave him a rueful smile. "I am happy the news

is not breaking your heart. I thought many times of sending it to you. But I am thinking, surely Tremayne will write and ask for this journal if it can prove his innocence. But you are not writing, and I am afraid that in sending it to you I will put a weapon in your enemies' hands.''

"I wasn't thinking too clearly for a long time, Gus."

The Dutchman nodded. "So I am telling you now: This Cato Crowden was her lover. Darla described him in great detail as a very handsome man. When I am realizing this greasy fellow took the journal, I am wondering who would be interested enough to steal it and I am thinking—only Cato Crowden. But the man who came did not look like such a handsome man to me. So I am thinking sometimes infatuation shields a woman's eyes, and sometimes even five months can make a great difference in a man's appearance."

Gus painted a quick verbal sketch for Tremayne of Cato Crowden as Darla had described him, a tall, well-built sweettalker, with a mane of blue-black hair and features impossible to pin to any one ethnic background. "I do not know this man, by name or description. I am thinking he made the best of the situation to sneak out of town after you were arrested."

"Cato Crowden." Tremayne rolled the name over his tongue, feeling the way the hard consonant sounds exploded against the back of his throat. For so long he'd hated a nameless man. Now he had a name, but could no longer summon the hatred. Instead, he felt the weary resignation of a man charged with completing an unpleasant task. Cato Crowden. Darla's lover.

"I am thinking that if the lawman had found the

journal and sought out this Cato Crowden your Darla
wrote so much about, you might never have been
arrested, hmm?"

"The sheriff did what he thought was right,"
Tremayne said.

"Only because you refused to defend yourself,"
Gus retorted.

"And admit my wife tied the horns to my head?
And that I didn't care enough even to wonder who
the man might be, until she bore his child and passed
him off as mine?"

"No man would have condemned you for calling
her an adulteress."

"But what of the child, Gus? The child of an adulteress can only be branded a bastard. And I . . . I
could never do that to a child."

Tremayne's father had not shared such scruples;
indeed, the earl of Chedgrave had shown no remorse
for branding the mark of bastardy upon Tremayne.
Tremayne closed his eyes, his mind taking him back
to that day in the cabin, when he'd held Darla's newborn son in his arms. Tremayne had stared into those
innocent, unfocused baby eyes and felt an unexpected, overwhelming surge of protectiveness. He'd
sworn he would never let the child know the humiliation he had endured. Standing before judge and jury,
admitting the child had not been his, condemning
him to eternity as a bastard, would have meant a
breach of that oath.

Gus stared at him for a long moment. "I am thinking that at last I am understanding the reason for your
behavior."

Tremayne gave a shaky laugh. For so many years, he'd kept his memories and emotions firmly locked away. Bringing them into the open had a surprisingly cleansing effect on his spirit. Gus had never believed him guilty; perhaps that was what made it easier now to speak of what had happened.

"I'm not certain I understood it then—or now. He was such a tiny, helpless thing, Gus. Had I loved his mother, he might have been mine. In my heart, there was no difference. She refused to give him a name. I gave him mine. Nothing on God's earth could induce me to take it back.

"Three months after the child was born, she told me she wanted to leave, to go away with the child's father. Cato Crowden, though she didn't name him. She said she meant to go that very afternoon. God help me, Gus, though by then the child had wrapped its little fingers round my heart, I couldn't deny her a chance to find true love. Darla was my friend, not my lover. I gave her my blessing and wished her well. I made certain my chores kept me busy all day at the far end of the claim so she wouldn't feel guilty over leaving me alone. I came home well past dark, certain they'd be gone, and I found them . . . dead." He shuddered, nauseated by the memory of what the murderer had done to Darla and the boy.

"*Mein Gott*, Tremayne."

Gus's voice was scarcely more than a whisper; his weather-beaten face was creased with lines of sorrowful concern.

"*He* did it, Gus. Cato Crowden. I figure leaving me was all Darla's idea, and when she tried pressing him into taking her away, he killed them for it. Goddamn him. He brutalized them both in ways that still cause me nightmares from witnessing. I fear my wits deserted me when I saw them. I could think only of burying them, hiding them away from prying eyes. And then, before I could whip myself back into action, the law found me."

"Did you know, Tremayne, that Sheriff Davis admits a fancy lady from Caldwell told him he should be going to your cabin. There is something suspicious in that."

"I knew. But it seemed like God's punishment at the time. I told you I wasn't thinking clearly. I felt I should be the one to pay for their deaths, because my lack of passion for her is what led to her seeking a lover."

"There is plenty men and women live together all their lives without much passion," Gus said. "You cannot blame yourself alone if Darla could not find contentment in your arrangement."

"Perhaps not. I sorted things out in my head and realized I'd done the wrong thing in holding my tongue, but by then I was in jail and it was too late. My fellow inmates warned me against sending for the journal. They said evidence has a way of disappearing unless the guards are well bribed, and I didn't have the money. My only hope was to appear before Judge Parker and tell him about the journal, and pray that he'd send a trustworthy marshal to fetch it. I swore that somehow, someday, I'd set things right."

"This woman you are worried about—does she know you are innocent of murder?"

Ellie. He remembered her struggles, her attempts to escape him on the prairie, her eagerness to wed someone else without giving him even a passing consideration. *You just kill the women who cause you trouble.*

"She thinks I'm guilty."

"You are certain? Did she ask you if you did it?"

"If she loved me, she wouldn't have to ask."

"Ach, you men, so thickheaded like a buffalo."

Tremayne and Gus swiveled their heads at the sound of Anna's exasperated voice. Unlike most good cooks, Anna Zinn was rail thin. No stray splashes of food ever marred her starched aprons, and hours spent over boiling kettles never seemed to frizzle her tidy, faded blond hair. Still, she managed to convey a maternal warmth that reached out now to enfold Tremayne within a cocoon of loving concern.

"Why shouldn't she expect an explanation from you?" Anna demanded, forging into conversation with him as if they hadn't spent the past five months apart. "You are reading her mind, I suppose?"

Muttering, Anna helped herself to a cup of coffee and joined the men at the table. "If I was this girl, I am thinking here is a man accused of murder. An innocent man brays his innocence like a mule to anyone who will listen. A guilty man, he is keeping his mouth clamped shut. If I was this girl, and I am thinking this man is guilty, I am running away from him. But if I am thinking he is innocent, I am uncertain whether I should tell him so. For if he is truly innocent, he feels insulted that I need to say it. If he is guilty, he will laugh at my stupidity."

She took a swallow of her coffee and leaned across

the table. Her crinkle-edged eyes bore straight into his. "If I am this girl, I am thinking, if this man cares about me, he will not make me ask. So I will show him what I believe in other ways."

"Anna." Her simple logic smote Tremayne with the strength of one of Silas Stringer's well-aimed kicks. Ellie had no reason to trust any man, let alone one who'd towered over her, deliberately seeking to intimidate by telling her he'd been accused of murdering his wife and child. And yet she'd lain with him, whispered she'd never been afraid of him, telling him in a thousand wordless ways that she trusted and believed in him.

He would go to his grave wondering what she might have said if he'd told her he was innocent, and asked her to wait for him, so they could brave her father together.

"Tremayne," Anna answered him. She placed a work-worn hand on his shoulder. "You are so like the buffalo. Hardheaded and stubborn and brave enough to clash horns with another beast such as yourself. But running in fear should a butterfly's wing stroke your nose. It is time for you to stop running. You run so fast and far from your soft feelings that you do not allow the joy to touch you."

"I have no soft feelings left, Anna," he said. He'd abandoned them, hardened his heart against them. "I've frittered them all away. And now—the horse hasn't rested long enough, but I must return and warn her about Stringer."

"How long will it take you to get back to her?" Gus asked.

"Sixty miles to Wichita. Another twenty-three to Magnolia." Tremayne shook his head. "Two days, if I could find a fresh horse and ride nonstop. Otherwise, three."

"You will reach her in time to save her from this evil Stringer," Anna said, softly patting his hand for reassurance. "Then you will have the rest of your lives to rediscover your soft feelings."

Tremayne shook his head in denial. It had taken three days to reach Caldwell, with each passing mile taunting him with the knowledge that she would be selecting her mate while he drew farther away from her. Another three days to return, and by then she surely would be wed. She wouldn't risk remaining unwed—he had forced the promise from her himself.

It was now her new husband's responsibility to protect her from Stringer.

With the journal gone, Tremayne could feel justified in spending the next few days seeking Cato Crowden. He could turn himself in to Sheriff Davis at Caldwell once he had Crowden in tow, and maybe, just maybe, escape with Farnsworth's life and his own good name intact. Impossible. He would not draw an easy breath until he saw for himself that Ellie was safe.

"I'll save her from Stringer," Tremayne said. For the first time in his life, the act of speaking created physical pain. "I'm afraid it's too late for anything more."

16

Cato felt the sting of Stringer's contempt more sharply with each passing day. How could he have ever felt honored that Stringer wanted his help? Every move Stringer made, every look he directed Cato's way, revealed his attitude of superiority. Lucky thing for Stringer he'd headed off to Wichita. More than once during the past few hours Cato's fingers had positively itched to whip out his knife and slit the smug bastard's throat.

He cursed the day he'd hooked up with Stringer. He'd hoped to get rid of Hawthorne—they couldn't even find him. He'd hoped to have a little fun— Stringer had ordered him to stay put. Hadn't Stringer flat-out laughed and agreed when Cato said he meant to play with Hawthorne's woman? How the hell did a man have fun with a woman if he had to stay three miles away from her? False promises, that's all he'd gotten out of this deal, along with a bucket of sweat and a thousand mosquito bites.

Goddamned smug, superior Stringer. Cato would show him who knew how to capture and return one small but delectable girl—and what to do with her in the meantime. Cato saddled his horse and headed toward Hawthorne's woman's homestead.

He hid his revulsion as he drew near the place. It was the exact sort of strength-draining hovel he had grown up on and sworn never to set foot upon again. During these endless days of watching, he'd noticed their puny hired hand halfheartedly whacking away at the tough prairie sod. A clean, strong-looking individual like himself, showing up and asking for a day's work, ought to be welcomed with open arms.

"'Morning, ma'am," he said to the bee-bonneted woman who greeted him in the yard. "My mama always told me to watch myself around a woman who knows how to handle bees."

"Oh, you," she said, giggling, just as women always did.

"I'm lookin' for work, ma'am. Lots of hard work, and I'd be willin' to trade my labor for a little bit of your home cooking—maybe a slab of corn bread spread with honey."

And she believed him, just as women always did.

That's all it took, a moment's observation to see what meant the most to a woman, a bit of flattery, a big smile with eyes riveted upon her as if she were the only dish of peach ice cream at a Fourth of July picnic.

She said her name was Lauretta Myers and positively shook with delight at the thought of him spending time in her proximity. She giggled now and leaned forward, her stance wordlessly asking him to smile again, which wasn't exactly fair of her, since he couldn't get a glimpse of her face. Must be pretty awful, he thought, the way she kept it all swathed up in bee veiling. Maybe he'd investigate it for himself before this was all over.

But at least she liked his smile, which was more than could be said for the two sobersides who'd joined them and now stood on either side of her.

"I'm tellin' you, Laurie, I mean to build it on my own," insisted their gaunt, sweat-slicked hired hand.

"It's my place, Hiram, and I'll hire extra help if I think we need it."

Cato stared at Hiram with sour dislike. He carried himself with a stringy toughness that just might prove troublesome. Eleanor, now, was almost too much of a pleasure to look at. He liked delicate, soft-looking skin like hers, pale, creamy skin that disappeared beneath the modest collar of her gray gown. He wondered if her tits would be pink or brown around the nipples. He'd always been partial to long thick hair curling down a woman's back, and it was a pure pleasure to see a woman wearing hers that way in broad daylight. With Hiram in the picture, though, it seemed smart to reluctantly cast aside his plan to kidnap Eleanor straight off, and wait until Stringer returned to back him up.

"I can do it myself," Hiram stated again.

Cato issued a delicate snort of disbelief, just enough to keep Lauretta on his side, and not so much that they would all realize he didn't mean to carve up a single foot of sod.

"We could help Hiram ourselves," said Eleanor.

"Ma'am!" Cato injected a strong measure of horror into his exclamation. "It takes a man to build a sod house. You lovely ladies are much too delicate to even think of helping."

"He's right, Ellie," Lauretta said. "I've heard those sod blocks weigh a hundred pounds or more."

"Hunnert pounds is like liftin' a feather," Hiram muttered.

"We don't have to build the soddie right away. We can wait until Hiram feels stronger," Eleanor said, a stubborn tilt to her chin as she stared at Cato with cold dislike.

Bitch.

Cato hooked his thumb into his belt buckle to stifle the impulse he felt to wallop her across the jaw. It'd be a shame to bruise her, though. Yessir, despite her bossy ways, she was a sight better looking than the first Mrs. Hawthorne. Maybe she wasn't in the mood to play today, but there was always tomorrow.

He broadened his peach-ice-cream smile, pretending she had every right to interfere with his plans, all the while imagining what she might feel like squirming around underneath him. Damn, but he should have gone into playacting. He'd swear not a one of them sensed the raging anger brought on by her resistance.

"You promised we'd have a sod house, Ellie," Lauretta said, her voice wobbling with profound disappointment. "I don't see why you're both so upset about this. It'll only take a couple of days to build. We can afford to pay Mr. Crowden for two days' wages."

So, they had money somewhere around the place. It shouldn't be too hard to find. Cato nodded pleasantly. "I'd work awful cheap, ma'am."

"Ellie?" Lauretta whispered.

Hawthorne's woman's stern disapproval melted at Lauretta's entreaty; her hand reached out to give Lauretta a reassuring pat. It cheered Cato to see how susceptible she was to Lauretta's whims. With a little training, she might improve her attitude toward him as well. And if she didn't—well, he knew how to handle women who forgot their place.

"It's too late to start anything today. You can bunk down in the barn with Hiram, Mr. Crowden," she said, no trace of hospitality marking her offer. "There's a pallet in there that's no longer being used."

"If it's all the same to you, ma'am, I'll lay out my bedroll along the creek. It's in my blood, sleeping out in the open." A lie, since he much preferred the comfort of sleeping indoors, but camping outdoors would make it easier to meet with Stringer and rub his nose in it that Cato now had the right to ride up to Hawthorne's woman bold as brass without anyone thinking anything of it. And he had no intention of doing one minute's work. Watching Espy's ague-driven shivering had inspired him; he could claim to have caught a fever while sleeping next to their creek, thus postponing the start of building while making her feel too guilty to chase him away.

"Suit yourself." She turned on her heel and disappeared into the dugout.

"Oh, I always do," he answered, softly. Espy shot him a startled look, but Lauretta, sketching imaginary sod houses in the air, was too busy hopping around like a starving chicken at feeding time to pay him any attention.

It occurred to him later, while he sat throwing pebbles into the creek and anticipating Stringer's grudging admiration, that none of them had said a word about Eleanor's husband returning to build the house.

"You were downright rude to him." Lauretta chided once they were alone, each of them mending their spare dresses by candlelight.

"I don't care," Ellie answered. "I don't like him. With the way men keep showing up on our doorstep, we could have waited another day or two for someone better to come along."

"Better in what way? Don't tell me you were serious about marrying the next man to poke his head through our door!"

"Of course not, silly. I don't know. He reminds me of someone I saw in Wichita, someone rather . . . frightening."

Lauretta snorted. "Frightening? The man has a *way* about him that'd turn any woman's innards to mush. I never saw such black hair, and them soft, wicked eyes. Didn't you see him smile at you? You're just mixing up your, er, unmentionable feelings with fear."

"There's something sneaky about him," Ellie persisted.

"Sneaky? Lordy, Ellie, he rode up in broad daylight, introduced himself and asked for a job. What's so sneaky about that?"

Nothing, unless you counted the way his eyes shifted from side to side when he claimed how hard he meant to work. The lewd, speculative stare he'd fixed on her bosom. Or the quick flash of hostility, quickly dampened, that had darkened his face for the space of a heartbeat when she'd offered to help Hiram herself rather than take him on.

"He makes me nervous," Ellie contented herself with saying aloud.

"Well, that's no surprise. Everyone makes you nervous. And besides, his good looks are enough to make any girl feel out of sorts."

He's not as handsome as Tremayne. Deliberately, Ellie quelled the little rush of pleasure that suffused her at the involuntary thought of Tremayne. For days now, since he'd left her in Wichita, she'd managed to blank him from her memory. Nights, of course, were a different matter. Her dreams, unfettered by her iron-willed control, tormented her with images and sensations that roused her from sleep flushed and aching, and lonely in the dark.

The needle pricked her finger. A tiny drop of blood welled in its wake. She pressed her thumb against it. By morning, the pain diminished, she wouldn't be able to find the spot where she'd been pierced and bled. Would that all her body could so easily resume its unmarked state, and forget the pain.

"I can tell Hiram doesn't like Cato much, either," Ellie said.

"Hiram doesn't take kindly to any other men spending time around here." Though Lauretta bent to bite off the end of her thread, she wasn't quick enough to hide her self-satisfied smile from Ellie.

"Why is that, I wonder?" Ellie teased. Odd, how it was possible that her heart, which felt happy watching Lauretta and Hiram bloom with unacknowledged love for each other, turned frozen with grief at the thought of loving anyone herself. "I'm happy for you, Laurie," she said impulsively.

Lauretta blushed. "There's not much to be happy about. Things have gone about as far as they can between Hire and me."

"Because of your skin?"

"He's always after me to take off my veil!" Lauretta guided a new thread through the eye of her needle. "He doesn't understand. I can't let him see me. I know it would ruin everything."

"Maybe you're misjudging him." Ellie spoke gently. It wouldn't do to remind Lauretta that she bared her face to Ellie every day; Lauretta was convinced nobody but Ellie could look upon her with anything besides abhorrence and pity.

"You're a fine one to talk about misjudging people," Lauretta shot out, a tiny hitch in her voice diluting the sharpness of her words. "You're no judge of character. You didn't like Hiram at all when you first met him, and look what a gentleman he turned out to be. Meanwhile, you took to that lying, murdering Tremayne Hawthorne, and he—he *fornicated* with you and ran off, leaving you to face the consequences on your own."

"Oh, Laurie." Ellie could barely whisper. Her dress slipped from her fingers; her hands fell to her lap, deadened, incapable of movement. She knew, in her heart, that Lauretta had struck out to cover her own pain, but her barbs sank deep. She quivered, closing her eyes against the truth of what Lauretta said.

A moment later she felt Lauretta's fluttering presence at her knee, felt the hot sting of tears soak through her dress. "I didn't mean it." Lauretta sobbed, her fingers clutching Ellie's skirt. "He must have loved you, or he wouldn't have let you come home."

"No, Laurie, you were right. I misjudged him. Because if he loved me, he would have never let me go."

Her observation prompted a fresh torrent of tears from Lauretta. Ellie listened to her cry, her own throat tight and aching, her frozen heart thudding painfully against her ribs.

"Why does it have to hurt so much to be in love?" Lauretta said in a choked voice.

"I don't know."

"Do you . . . do you hate me now, Ellie?"

"I could never hate you. You're my best friend. It's your job to make me face the truth. Maybe now I can quit moping around and get to something important, like making curtains for that new sod house of ours."

The feeling slowly seeped back into Ellie's hands. While Lauretta rose, sniffling and dabbing the tears from her eyes, Ellie gathered up the folds of her fallen dress. The pink dress, the one she'd worn while waiting for Tremayne to come back to the corncrib. She doubted she would ever be able to wear it again without remembering his touch, her wanton response, her disappointment when she'd realized he'd gone away forever.

"You know," she mused, "now that I think on it, I'm rather glad we hired Cato Crowden. It will be nice to get out of this dark old dugout."

"It will," Lauretta agreed fervently. "Oh, Lordy, Ellie, maybe it wasn't such a good idea for you to tell everyone you're married to Tremayne Hawthorne. What if you start liking Cato?"

A shiver of revulsion coursed along Ellie's spine, and she started to protest, but stopped herself. She *had* misjudged Hiram right from the start, and—she could admit it now—she'd been drawn to Tremayne like a hummingbird seduced by the red flowers of a trumpet vine. Maybe Cato's presence would become tolerable after a day or two. And if not, so what? Hiram had told them it would take only a couple of days to cut the sod squares, and that the walls would rise in another day or so. Cato would soon be on his way.

"I like Hiram now, and it doesn't matter that he thinks I'm married to Tremayne," Ellie said.

"You don't like Hiram the way I do." Lauretta's face reddened. "Oh, Ellie, you know he's the one so set on proving himself by building that darned sod house. Yesterday he went and picked up the wagon we left out on the prairie that day you came home. I've had the devil of a time holding him back from starting work on the soddie. I'm worried about him. He's been shaking and sweating something awful, and he barely ate a bite tonight."

"You know how the ague comes and goes, Laurie. You're a good nurse. If anyone can get him through, it'll be you."

"I didn't pull Michael through."

At first Ellie didn't understand why Lauretta's agonized admission brought forth the memory of the day they'd visited Hiram's claim and Ellie had seen the mirage. And then it came to her—the mirage had been a trick of the sun, convincing Ellie that she saw a lake rather than parched prairie grass. Just as the mirror reflected Lauretta's ravaged face and convinced her that it was her disfigurement, rather than her unspoken fear of losing Hiram to sickness, that kept them apart.

People are forever imagining they see things that aren't really there, Tremayne had told her. Hadn't she imagined some caring, some true feeling, on Tremayne's part? Ellie shook the feeling away, pouncing upon Lauretta's problem for distraction.

"You're not being fair to Hiram, Laurie. I think he loves you. You should give him a chance."

"I'll give him a chance if you give Cato a chance." At Ellie's appalled expression, Lauretta continued. "Oh, you don't have to like him in *that* way. Just be polite. For my sake, so I won't have to worry about Hiram working too hard."

Perhaps extending some courtesy to Cato Crowden would teach her to stop reacting from impulse. Ellie laughed, shaking her head. "You win. After all, God wouldn't saddle us with two murderers intent upon taking me back to my father, would He?"

*   *   *

Tremayne knocked on Sarah Reynolds's door, but his attention wandered to where the corncrib stood behind the house.

"Who is it?" Sarah demanded.

She'd slid open a narrow slot in the door, but he knew she couldn't see him. Not on this pitch-dark night. He'd cursed the darkness long and loud. No moon. No stars. Only an impenetrable layer of midnight black clouds that seemed bent on hovering over Wichita all night long, making it impossible for any man, no matter how determined, to ride the twenty-three miles to Magnolia without risking his mount's legs.

"Tremayne Hawthorne. You remember, Mrs. Reynolds, we spent the night in your corncrib last week. I was wondering if you might have any available accommodations. I'd rather spend the night here than in town."

"Why, come right in, Mr. Hawthorne." Sarah flung her door wide, sending a golden shaft of light spilling onto her wooden porch. "Is your wife with you?"

"She's not—" Tremayne stopped himself from correcting her, remembering the unacknowledged misunderstanding that had protected Ellie's reputation. Wichita was a large town—perhaps it shouldn't surprise him that Sarah Reynolds hadn't yet learned that Ellie had never been his wife, that, by now, Ellie belonged to someone else. But he didn't feel up to meeting the censure he felt sure Sarah would direct his way if he admitted now to the deception.

"She's not here," he repeated, in answer to Sarah's question.

"Pardon the heat," Sarah apologized as she ushered him into the kitchen. "I try to put off my baking until night, when everyone's asleep and it's cooler, but that durned stove sure heats things up. I swear if I just set the baking pans out on the table the cookies would bake same as in the oven. If you can bear the heat, you're welcome to a cup of coffee and a couple of cookies."

Tremayne ignored the eager rumbling of his stomach as he shook his head. Despite his hunger, he knew he wouldn't be able to force a single mouthful past the urgency tightening his throat. "Just a bed for a few hours, Mrs. Reynolds. I must be on my way to Magnolia as soon as it's light enough to travel."

To his amazement, Sarah Reynolds burst into full-bodied, bawdy laughter. "I'll bet you can't wait. Just look at you—that beard ain't seen a razor for nigh unto a week, and I never saw a man look so wild-eyed and anxious and just bristling with . . . well, just bristling. Shouldn't a' gone with that herd right off, Mr. Hawthorne, not the day after."

Bewildered, Tremayne began, "Mrs. Reynolds, I apologize for not under—"

"You should apologize, not telling me it was your wedding night. To think I put the two of you in my corncrib! If I'd a' known you two were celebrating your marriage, I'd a' kicked a couple of them cowboys out of a room quicker 'n' booting a dog away from my young 'un's dinner pail."

Her comments began to make a somewhat preposterous kind of sense. A curl of excitement unfolded within him as he probed for more information.

"Ellie told you it was our wedding night?"

"Didn't I just holler at you for not telling me yourself? The two of you is closemouthed as a couple a' ticks. I had to hear it from Bessie Engel, and *she* told me Mattie Murrow knew all about it, too."

"Did they tell anyone else?"

"Well, Mattie told Bessie she helped Ellie open an account at Woodman's. I swear that between them, Bessie and Mattie could teach Mr. Edison a thing or two about spreading news without none of them telegraph lines."

"Everyone knows we're, er, married?"

He sounded like a dolt; her exasperated expression confirmed it, but he didn't care.

"If you think Mattie missed someone, you might want to stop by the newspaper office and place a classified advertisement."

"And everyone believed her?"

The indulgent smile momentarily faded from Sarah's lips, replaced with wary curiosity.

Tremayne sought to repair any damage his probing questions might have caused. "With my going off so fast—we worried about how it would look, whether we should wait to announce our marriage until I returned."

Sarah's smile reappeared. "Let's just say that if I were you, I wouldn't try telling Mr. Woodman that you ain't going to be responsible for Ellie Hawthorne's dry-goods bills."

A low buzzing seemed to lodge itself in Tremayne's brain. Hunger could bring on such a sensation, or exhaustion, and God knows he suffered from both.

So why did he feel so euphoric, so gripped by a name-less joy that he wanted to squash Sarah Reynolds in a massive bear hug and toss her up into the air?

Because Ellie had claimed to be married to him. Going around opening store accounts and calling her-self Ellie *Hawthorne*, without benefit, as yet, of a preacher's blessing. What a foolhardy plan, ignoring his sound advice! Curse that little minx for taking such a risk by twisting her promise around, and his knees would wear out before he ever thanked God sufficiently for putting the idea into her head.

He almost laughed aloud. And then, as if stirring one emotion rekindled another, he felt a resurgence of dread. Silas Stringer. While Tremayne stood in Sarah Reynolds's hot, cinnamon-scented kitchen, grinning like a matchmaker with satisfaction over a marriage that didn't really exist, Stringer might even now have Ellie in his clutches.

"About that room, Mr. Hawthorne. There ain't no herds in town, so I got plenty of space."

"I've had second thoughts, Mrs. Reynolds. I'll accept that coffee you offered and then I'll be on my way."

"You can't ride out on the prairie in this black dark."

"No, but I can lead the horse until dawn."

"You're sure in a powerful hurry, Mr. Hawthorne." She poured his coffee, her suddenly solemn, search-ing look telling him she'd picked up on his sudden apprehension.

"As never before." Tremayne gulped the strong, scalding coffee.

"Mr. Hawthorne?"

He quirked a questioning brow at her.

"Don't go running into the night. You look powerful tired. You won't go any distance in the dark that your horse can't beat at first light. If something bad's waiting for you, you'd be better off having gotten a little rest. And if it's something good you're looking for, why, it'll be all the sweeter if you're not so tired you collapse in a heap the minute you get home."

She was right. The strong coffee hadn't dissipated his exhaustion one whit. He'd stand no chance facing Stringer in such a depleted condition. And if his fears were unfounded, he wanted a joyous reunion with Ellie. He would show her a side of himself she'd never seen. He would tease her until she smiled, laugh with her, joke, cast aside all his gloomy predilections and wallow in delight, knowing that for once the fates had looked kindly upon him.

"Two hours," he compromised.

"I'll wake you before sun-up." She wrapped a handful of golden-brown cookies in a clean cloth. "You give these to your wife as a wedding present from me. I hope the two of you spend a nice, quiet evening enjoying them."

Tremayne tucked the still-warm bundle into his shirt. "So do I, Mrs. Reynolds. So do I."

17

Storm clouds hid the sun from view, but Ellie knew it was well past sunrise when Cato Crowden showed up for work. She'd hoped his failure to appear at first light had meant a change of mind on his part; instead, it just confirmed him as a lazy sluggard whose heart wasn't really set upon doing the work he'd promised to do. She stiffened her spine to greet him.

"We normally start our day at an earlier hour."

"So do I, ma'am, so do I. But . . ." He winced and rolled a shoulder. For a brief moment, Ellie could almost see the boyish charm Lauretta found so appealing. He did have a rather nice smile. "Seems like I caught a touch of the fever sleeping out by the creek."

Much as she'd have liked to reinforce her initial bad opinion of him, she couldn't hold illness against him, especially when Hiram Espy, too, had turned up sick that day. Hiram lay in the barn, thrashing with fever atop his pallet, where they'd found him when he hadn't shown up for breakfast. Ellie knew Lauretta hovered over him, murmuring comforting words, encouraging him to sip life-sustaining fluids. Lauretta's diagnosis had been correct in gauging Hiram's illness. Ellie could not discount Lauretta's belief that Hiram would overtax himself without another man around to help him. So she couldn't send Cato on his way.

But she didn't like the way Cato surveyed the homestead from the back of his horse. More than curiosity marked his attention. Though he seemed to be concentrating solely upon her, she couldn't shake the feeling that he stared around, seeking weaknesses, searching for something that might be hidden. His predatory stance made her reluctant to admit to Cato that Hiram lay helpless with fever, and she longed to get rid of him. "It's too late to start anything now. We'll try again tomorrow."

"Is Miss Lauretta around?"

"She's busy just now."

At her words, Cato's features altered, shifting from apparent admiration to a sly insolence that sent warnings skittering down her spine.

"That's a shame. She's much nicer to me than you. My mama always taught me to treat like with like. I can be real nice to ladies who like me."

Ellie doubted whether she'd ever heard more menacing words. Cato seemed suddenly transformed from a glib, smooth-talking ladies' man to a villain, someone easily capable of causing her harm. "I like you fine, Cato," Ellie forced herself to say. "But I have chores to do and you're holding me back."

"What about my breakfast?"

She'd forgotten that they'd promised he could share their meals. "Breakfast is served at sunup. You can stop back later and pick up a dinner pail."

"Well, then, if we have all day to rest . . ." His voice, low with insinuation, might have come from a satyr's throat. "Maybe you'd like me to come into that there dugout with you so you can nurse me over the fever."

When she'd shot Tremayne, she'd practically begged him to stay in the dugout so she could tend him. The thought of Cato Crowden crossing the threshold into her home turned her stomach. "Get out of here," she ordered.

"Whatever you say . . . for now. I might be back for that dinner pail if the weather holds out."

Silence hung like a pall over the homestead once his horse's drumming hooves passed beyond hearing, leaving her shaking and scarcely able to believe she'd braved his wrath. The weather complemented her mood. All day long the clouds had churned overhead, like the layer of smoke hovering over a cauldron, promising rain but giving up none. The clouds seemed to stifle all normal sound. Birdsong, always rare, hadn't sounded all day. The mules and mare rolled nervous, twitchy eyes skyward between quick snatches of grass, but the heavy air muted their grinding teeth, dulled the sound of their hooves whenever they moved.

How strange that on such an oppressive, sunless day, a mirage should strike her eyes.

From the direction of Wichita, where her willful glances had strayed again and again over the past days, it came. What she'd secretly dreamed of seeing, what she knew couldn't possibly be there. Tremayne Hawthorne, mounted upon a sleek, galloping steed, his tawny hair streaming behind him in motion with the horse's racing stride.

His long, muscular legs, legs that had once entwined with hers, now urged the phantom horse to greater speed. His shoulders, impossibly wide, loomed broad behind the horse's straining neck. His shirt flapped, the buttons all undone so that his ridged, golden chest gleamed with the light layer of sweat a real man might work up, riding a real horse so hard. A mirage, for she heard only a loud roaring in her ears; no thundering hooves shook the ground, no snorting breath sounded from the horse's heaving chest. And proof positive that it was a mirage: When he saw her, the mirage's lips parted in a wide smile, his teeth dazzling white against beard-roughened skin.

Tremayne Hawthorne had never smiled at her like that.

He started dismounting before the horse skidded to a stop, managing somehow to keep his eyes fixed upon hers. His feet hit the ground with a few quick, running steps, which soon lengthened into his familiar, ground-eating stride. In no time he stood before her, only a handspan separating them. It was like being stalked by an oven, the heat he threw off, bathing her in a warmth completely unlike the suffocating humidity that had so addled her brain. His arms reached around and enfolded her with astonishing gentleness.

"Thank God I'm not too late." His voice, his raspy breathing, pierced the leaden quiet, and then all of her senses clamored for his attention.

Let me touch. Her shaking fingers traced the ridge of bone at the juncture of his shoulder.

Let me breathe in his scent. She leaned toward him and breathed in his essence, nearly swooning at the memories her mind conjured.

Let me taste his skin. Her tongue, wayward beyond control, touched the pulsating base of his throat.

"Ellie." He groaned her name, and caught her to him in a way she'd never been held. One powerful arm wrapped itself around her waist and lifted; his other hand forged a path along her spine, pressing every inch of her against his heaving chest with force enough to crush some sort of packet tucked in his belt.

She'd been so certain she'd never see him again that she'd refused to imagine another meeting between them. How she wished now that she'd indulged the urge to drown in such thoughts, allowing her mind to develop witty phrases, her heart to construct a toughened layer not so susceptible to the wild thumping his touch created.

"I can't believe you're really here," she said, not at all witty, not at all tough, her exultant whisper betraying every minute she'd endured of secret, silent longing.

And then Tremayne was laughing, *laughing*, his great shoulders shaking, his vibrating chest tormenting her suddenly sensitive nipples. "I shall endeavor to convince you of my presence," he said, claiming her lips in a kiss as he kicked aside the buffalo robe and carried her into the dugout.

It was close to suppertime before Cato found Stringer's horse standing with gloomy resignation near a bare-trampled wallow. A quick look revealed why the animal hadn't moved off to graze—the reins stretched taut between it and Silas Stringer's clenched hand.

A ragged snore, almost deafening in the prestorm calm, dispelled any notion that Stringer might be dead.

The sight of Stringer stretched out in the mud offended Cato's fastidious sensibilities. Stringer's left cheek lay mashed into the dirt, which meant his skin and hair would be caked with mud once he woke up. A layer of dust covered him from head to toe, but even the fine-powdered brown grit couldn't hide multicolored stains hinting at food and liquor and God alone knew what else. The stench of stale cigar smoke, raw whiskey, and beer drifted off him like stink from a fishboat.

Cato's lip curled. His horse sidled nervously, probably sensing the rage flooding through him. This was the man who thought himself so superior? Cato congratulated himself on the premonition he'd had that Stringer might be planning some sort of doublecross.

The man was a no-good drunk. It was just pure bad luck that Cato had met up with him on a day when Stringer had projected the image of a ruthless, savvy agent of retribution, capable of ending this threat Tremayne Hawthorne posed to Cato's well-being.

If Stringer hadn't sent Half-Scalped Jackson looking for him, Cato would have been safely holed up in his Indian Territory hideaway, not giving two farts about the goings-on in Magnolia, Kansas. Well, he was here now, and annoyed that the pretty little Mrs. Hawthorne seemed immune to his charms, and Stringer was by God going to help him tame her.

He dismounted and approached the prone figure. Stringer deserved a quick kick in his whiskey-soaked guts. Cato got one foot set and was just ready to draw back the brass-tipped toe of the other boot when, striking quick as a snake, Stringer's hand clamped around his ankle and pulled.

"You sneaky vulture!" Cato shrieked on his way to joining Stringer facedown in the mud.

The fall knocked Cato's wind from him, so he had no choice but to lie there, fighting the sensation of suffocation, while Stringer's drunken chortling rang against his ears.

"You were supposed to bring the booze back to the creek, not drink it on the way," he gasped when he could breathe again.

"I brought plenty back. Never said I didn't intend to stoke up on a personal supply before I left town."

Cato levered himself up, mimicking Stringer's sitting position. Hatred knifed through him; but Stringer's quick reflexes and ruthless attitude made it

seem prudent that Cato hide how much respect he'd
lost for the man.

"You were supposed to come straight back, not
leave me here twiddling my thumbs for three days. I
shouldn't have had to spend all afternoon searching
this goddamned prairie for you."

"Lazy as you are, I never expected you to put
yourself out so much. Fact is, your company's wearing thin and I was hoping you'd head back to Indian
Territory if I left you on your own. I never imagined
you'd take it into your head to come looking for me."

"I'll bet that's the truth. I'll bet you were planning
to sleep it off overnight and give me a nasty surprise
in the morning, weren't you?" Cato fixed a venomous
glare on Stringer, who flushed a dull red, confirming
Cato's suspicions. "I couldn't let you sleep straight
through Hawthorne's visit to his woman."

"The hell you say!" Stringer's hand froze in the act
of scraping mud from the side of his head. "Don't tell
me that jailbird was hiding out in the dugout all this
time after all?"

"Naw. I told you it was a mistake for men of action
like us to sit back and wait. I went to the homestead
and looked around. He must've been watching from
somewhere today and got spooked—no sooner did I
get out of sight than he came riding in. You could've
picked him off without even using the sights on that
cannon of yours."

"Well, hell, you should a' just shot him yourself, Cato,
and got this over with. I don't care about Hawthorne
anymore; all I want's the girl."

"I ain't no marksman." *That's why I kept you alive*

instead of laying a knife across your throat just now.
The admission came hard. Someone in his hodge-
podge of ancestors had passed along a set of dim eyeballs. No matter how Cato squinted over a gun barrel,
he flat-out couldn't see far enough to aim with any
certainty of hitting his target. Which didn't prevent
him from carrying and using his Colt, but with the
target being Tremayne Hawthorne, it seemed to him a
degree of certainty was all-important. With the man
within range, it made simple good sense to end his
threat once and for all.

"Prefer closer work, do you?" Stringer asked, his
gaze narrowing with speculation.

"A knife feels good in a man's hand."

"Heard the first Mrs. Hawthorne made more than
a passing acquaintance with some man's knife."
Stringer's red-rimmed gaze flicked speculatively over
the knife hanging at Cato's belt. "Seems Hawthorne
didn't deny slashing her, but he didn't take the blame,
either. Didn't hardly have time to make up a lie or
think up an alibi, 'cause the law busted in on him
before the blood was even dry. You know anything
about that?"

Cato wished he had his fingers wrapped around
the handle of his well-honed bowie right now. A
know-it-all smirk twisted Stringer's narrow features.
Cato didn't like it. "Don't tell me you're starting to
worry over whether he's guilty or not."

"Hell, I don't care whether he's innocent as a newborn babe. That British bastard made me look bad.
He horned in on a job I had a powerful hankering to
do, and now he's in my way again."

As Stringer groped through the mud and trampled grass for his hat, Cato noted a tremor in Stringer's hand, his gun hand. "You got the whiskey shakes. I wouldn't trust you to rope Half-Scalped Jackson in your condition."

"Well, I don't trust you at all, so I guess that evens things up."

"We'll get even later," Cato said, his promise backed up by the click of his gun hammer locking into position. Stringer's whiskey-blurred features shifted with alarm. Cato laughed and waved the gun. "I ain't no marksman, but I don't think I'll miss at this range. So why don't you tell me, *partner,* what you've got going for you that's made you so all-fired anxious to get rid of me?"

Stringer regained his composure. He heaved a sigh and gave a derisive shake of his head. "Aw, go on back to Indian Territory, Cato."

Cato squeezed the trigger and pumped a bullet into Stringer's foot.

"Shee-it!" Stringer staggered, reflexively wrapping his arms around his startled horse's neck to keep from falling. He stared with pain-wracked dismay at the oozing, gaping hole where the right side of his boot used to be. "You shot my goddamned little toe off, Cato. I'm apt to bleed to death. What the hell did you do that for?"

Cato realigned the gun barrel until it pointed at a spot due south of Stringer's navel. "Don't need all them little toes. You only got one of what I'm aiming for now, Stringer. You ready to explain?"

Stringer managed to turn pale beneath the layers of

mud and sunburn. "I should've shot you when you rode up."

Cato cocked the hammer again.

He could feel the subtle shift in power take place between them. More than half drunk, crazed with pain, Stringer seemed to shrivel in stature. Sort of like old Half-Scalped, shrinking back when his sweetheart wrapped her arms around Cato instead. Cato doubted he'd be the butt of any more of Stringer's sneering remarks.

"I never gave a thought to reward money until you brought it up," Stringer said, choking over the words as if he'd swallowed them straight after prying them out of a lard barrel. "Her pa's got more than his share of money and power. I sent him a telegram, made a few demands. He should be on his way to Wichita right now with a big wad of greenbacks stuffed in his money belt, ready to make a trade for his girl."

"Bind up your foot, Silas," Cato said, magnanimous in his victory. "It'll take us a good couple hours of hard riding to get back to that homestead, and then we got some work to do."

"Bless Sarah Reynolds," Tremayne said as he lowered Ellie onto the low, narrow bed.

"Sarah Reynolds? The lady with the . . . the corncrib?"

Tremayne loved her stammering shyness. "The lady with the corncrib. I stayed at her establishment again last night."

"Then you didn't spend the night in one of the Wichita establishments?"

He shook his head, drawing forth a sigh of relief from her. Did he dare to hope it meant she felt jealous at thinking he might have spent the night wrapped in a Wichita whore's arms?

"You didn't eat dinner in Wichita? You didn't go to the dry goods store . . . any of the stores?"

He understood, then, her line of questioning. Ellie McKittrick sought to discover whether he'd found out she was passing herself off as Ellie Hawthorne.

His thumb traced a path down her pert nose to the lip she was chewing in consternation. She seemed far too nervous over such a small deception. He wondered if this might be the right moment to tell her that his father's repudiation, the wrenching away from his Caldwell homestead, all took on crystal-clear purpose as steps in the journey leading him here, to Ellie. Perhaps he should wait before introducing such a weighty topic. He remembered his silent pledge to show her a man who could joke, who could laugh, who could play, and decided to let her present her news at her own pace.

"I patronized nothing in Wichita except the livery, Ellie. And bless Sarah Reynolds, because she tricked me into sleeping longer than I'd intended, which means I've arrived here fresh, and hearty, and sorely missing the feel of your skin against mine."

Her lustrous eyes widened into deep chocolate pools when his fingers hovered near her neckline.

"But Lauretta's tending to Hiram in the barn," Ellie said. Her eyes, already dark with passion, clouded even more. "I'm supposed to relieve her at six o'clock—"

"Excellent. Then we needn't fear interruption for another two hours or more." Tremayne silenced her protest with a kiss and busied himself with divesting her of her clothing. "Enough about Hiram and Lauretta. I'm more interested in hearing how many strangers you've noticed lurking about. I seem to remember you complaining about men dropping in every five minutes." He asked the question with deliberate lightness, not wanting to frighten her.

"Strangers? Why, no more than usual."

That figured nicely with the sketchy information he'd been able to amass. Though he hadn't lied to her about not patronizing any Wichita establishments, he had spent some time asking people if they'd seen anyone matching Stringer's description. Nobody he'd questioned admitted to seeing him, and there'd been no sight of Stringer along the way. But Wichita was too big, the prairie too immense, for Tremayne to search completely. Simply finding Ellie safe and unmolested had put his apprehension over Stringer temporarily to rest. Had Stringer been around, he would have swooped in and grabbed Ellie while she'd been alone and vulnerable. His relief created a lightheartedness within him that he hadn't felt in years.

"In fact, you just missed one of the men," Ellie added with an reflexive shudder that led Tremayne to think she might be making up the information to save face. "He rode off a few minutes before you arrived. I'm surprised you didn't pass each other on the prairie."

"Men passing to and fro. It mustn't have been difficult for you to find someone to marry, then," he teased.

"Oh!" Her eyes widened. Her chin tilted at a proud angle. "Not at all. I found the whole process ridiculously easy."

He felt strangely euphoric, almost giddy, at holding her and touching her, knowing the secret she was doing such a poor job of hiding. "We can discuss your . . . husband later," he stated. "Now, no more talking. No questions. No what-ifs."

"No explanations?"

"No explanations." He buried his lips in her hair, hiding his smile. She seemed enormously relieved at the chance to postpone telling him she'd claimed to be married to him.

Time enough for words later, for all the explanations he owed her, for all those she sought to avoid. For now, there was only Ellie, and the frenzy to possess her sizzling through his veins.

Deep, velvet darkness had sheltered their first lovemaking; afternoon sunlight should have lit this one, but gathering storm clouds cast them in a false twilight gloom. Not so dark, though, that he couldn't drink in her beauty. His hands, his lips, had stroked and memorized her body in the dark, but that possession had brought him only a pale understanding of the porcelain purity of her skin, the proud thrusting of her breasts, the gentle contours of her waist and hips.

Her hair tumbled all over, down her back, over her shoulders, tendrils curling over her face and resting against her breasts, as he laid her on the bed. He loved the way her hair caressed her skin; he wanted to follow every strand, tracing the paths with fingers and tongue.

"You are so beautiful," he whispered.

"I want to look at you the way you're looking at me."

Her voice, low and husky, resonated somewhere low in his loins. No woman had ever asked to look at him, not the whores he'd bought as a youth, certainly not Darla. Ellie's eyes stared at him through thick, sooty lashes, warm and desirous. He'd expended his measure of control when removing her clothes and had none to spare for his own garments; he rent his shirt from neck to waist, heedless of the popping buttons.

A small cloth packet dropped onto the bed next to Ellie's thigh.

He stared at it a moment, so consumed by desire for her that he couldn't recall what he'd carried in his shirt. And then he remembered: Sarah Reynolds's wedding gift of cookies.

"For you," he murmured, intending to set the packet aside for later. But when he lifted it, it felt all wrong. Crumbs trickled from the twisted fold—the cookies must have gotten crushed when he molded Ellie's body against his. He set the packet down, brushing his hand against his thigh to rid himself of the crumbs, and Ellie caught his hand between hers.

"It can wait for later, Tremayne. Come to me now."

Her invitation, eerily echoing his deepest desires, shattered his self-control. His lips found her breasts, sweet, delicious. Her thighs drew up around his waist and he plunged into her, losing himself in her heated depths. Again, and again, murmuring her name against her lips, shuddering and losing a tiny bit of himself each time she whispered his.

Not losing himself . . . coming home.

18

False twilight, deepened by the storm clouds thickening the sky, darkened the room before Tremayne dulled the edge of his appetite for Ellie.

Explanations should be easier in the dark, he thought when his mind reluctantly returned to its normal state, telling him he couldn't stay abed with her any longer with nothing more than passion between them. Lauretta, expecting relief from her nursing duties, could burst in upon them at any time. But more importantly, there were so many things Ellie had to know, so many plans they had to make.

He'd never found words so difficult to fashion.

She lay against him, light and soft, her breath stroking his skin, her hair caressing his cheek. So infinitely precious to him; how to explain the emptiness of his past and convince her he treasured her above all else? He tightened his arm around her shoulders, silently giving her his oath never to let her come to harm.

Her claim to be already married to him—perhaps they should begin there, exploring a circumstance that, God willing, they both found highly agreeable.

Ellie. His wife. The notion stirred all manner of unfamiliar feelings, thickening his throat with an almost pleasurable ache that roughened his voice to a texture resembling riverbed gravel. He closed his hand over the packet of cookies Sarah Reynolds had sent along.

"I know what you've done, Ellie. I know you're not married."

Tremayne's quiet tones sounded an awakening alarm that pierced Ellie's love-dazed contentment. Where were her senses, to have forgotten that her father had sent him? In a moment of weakness, he'd gallantly set her free, but it hadn't taken him long to regret his decision. She should have known, should have sensed the danger, when he'd come racing over the prairie as if demons were snapping at his horse's heels.

Lauretta had warned her he might return. Urged her to be cautious around him. And what had Ellie done? Gushed her happiness at having him back. Pressed against him like a wanton. She'd thrilled to his smile, to his eager embrace. "Thank God I'm not too late," he'd said. Her girlish, romantic head had spun at his words, missing entirely that his behavior indicated nothing more than relief at finding her still at his mercy.

And she had only herself to blame for this

dilemma. If she'd ignored her conscience and married, played the role of good girl instead of self-righteous, headstrong smart aleck, she could be laughing right now instead of fighting back tears.

He shifted their positions without losing hold of her, so that she found herself lying atop him, his fingers wrapped around her wrists like steel manacles.

The intimacy of their position sent waves of embarrassment shuddering through her. His chest rose and fell beneath hers, her lungs unconsciously matching their rhythm to his. The crisp, golden hair adorning his chest tickled her breasts into swollen buds. Her thighs rested upon his, and against their tender, sensitive inner skin she felt him stir and harden. The sensation made an erratic mess of her heartbeat and sent her blood roaring into her head. In that moment she hated him, but hated herself even more, for she knew she would never be free of her overpowering attraction to him.

He knew it, too, which had lent him the audacity to storm into her home and make love to her, completely certain she would welcome his embrace. Such total disregard for propriety, such supreme confidence that she would permit him such liberties, and she had, oh, God, she had . . .

"Well?" His question rumbled low in his chest, vibrating into her own.

How could she lie to him, when she was so completely open and vulnerable to him in every way? The tears she refused to shed blurred her eyes, but she forced herself to meet his gaze. He gave her a lazy, satisfied smile, his eyes darkening with remembered pleasure, the fine skin framing them crinkling with good humor.

His smile was her undoing. She couldn't believe—didn't want to believe—that a man who looked at her so possessively, who commanded her body's wanton response and answered it with such care for her pleasure, could be so heartless and unfeeling. She felt an almost desperate need to tell him *yes,* she'd claimed to be his wife, and an equally desperate fear that he would exult in hearing her tale, relishing the notion that she'd placed herself completely and utterly in his control without forcing him to do a single thing.

And she knew with soul-deep certainty that she loved him.

There could be no secrets between two who loved, no deceptions. If he did not love her in return, better she should know it now, for her heart would surely crack into a thousand irreparable shards, and then it wouldn't matter at all whether she spent the rest of her loveless, bereft life beneath her father's roof.

Tremayne's smile turned perplexed at her hesitation. "Ellie? Sarah Reynolds told me you'd spread word in town that you and I were married. The cookies were her wedding gift to us. Is it true? Did you really claim to be my wife?"

"If I had married another man, do you think I would be lying here like this with you, Tremayne?"

He drew her against him with bold possessiveness, at the same time expelling a sharp, deep breath that hinted at pain she hadn't suspected. Or perhaps she'd just unwittingly poked him in the ribs and made him flinch, because if she'd thought for another moment she would never have asked such a witless question. Any woman, knowing the heaven to be found in Tremayne's arms, would be tempted by his touch.

He released his proprietary hold and let his fingers trace along her upper arm before entangling in her hair. "You know, Ellie, you and I never discussed my . . . my past. My wife died because she took a lover."

Deep within, Ellie felt her heart twist and turn at the thought of Tremayne so enraged by jealousy, so consumed with love for another woman that he'd taken her life rather than see her with another.

She didn't believe it. It hurt too much to believe it. "You didn't kill her," she whispered, lowering her face until her forehead brushed the muscled wall of his chest. She felt his thundering heart quicken its pace, and then firm fingers lifted her chin until her gaze met his once again.

"There is so much we must discuss, Ellie, but first we must clear up the past. My marriage was not a love match. It was a business arrangement, to enable me to claim free homestead land as head of a household before I reached the legal age of twenty-one. We tried living together as man and wife at first. A brief time only, because it was apparent at once that we were destined to be nothing more than friends. She could have gone at any time during our years together and I would have given her my blessing. I didn't kill her. I didn't kill the child planted in her belly by another man. There was no passion between us, ever, that would have goaded me into killing her for finding true love in the arms of another."

Wild, undiluted joy suffused Ellie until she thought she might shake apart from it. Tremayne hadn't loved another woman, hadn't sired her child, and he wasn't a murderer! Her instincts had been proven right.

"Then you don't mind that I borrowed your name?" she asked.

"You took a foolish, dangerous chance, but oh, Ellie, if you knew how I ached to ask you to wait for me, if you knew the rage that held me in its grip each night when I imagined you in another man's arms." The low, husky timbre of his voice, his passionate declarations, set her insides vibrating like a gong. "My head tells me our love is nothing more than a rash, foolish dream. My heart tells me to keep you by my side and strike for the West, before the law comes after me."

"Why not run straight to England? Surely, with a title and wealth to protect you—"

Tremayne shook his head, and she fancied she read despair clouding his expression. "Murder demands justice, Ellie, whether the perpetrator is a penniless bastard or the acknowledged son of an earl. I could be extradited from England easily enough. The proof I needed to clear my name for Darla's murder has been stolen by S—by someone in league with your father. And I learned in Caldwell that Farnsworth has likely been killed, no doubt in a way to implicate me. Your father's fixed it so that the law on both sides of the ocean will be demanding my head."

And there, amid the ecstasy of hearing Tremayne declare his love, a harsh splash of reality sharpened her thoughts, thoroughly dousing her elation.

What had she done?

Tremayne Hawthorne stood to inherit a title, and lands, and wealth beyond imagining. For once, reward beckoned for this man whose intentions never produced the desired results, who'd endured a lifetime of losing everything he held dear.

He could claim none of it, because of her.

Because Tremayne had not taken her back to Arkansas, her father's henchman had stolen and destroyed Tremayne's proof of innocence; her father had ordered Farnsworth murdered, with the blame affixed to Tremayne. By allowing Ellie to remain free, Tremayne had condemned himself to a lifetime on the run. To pay for taking Ellie McKittrick as his wife, the glittering future which might have been his would shimmer into nothingness, like a mirage dissipating beneath the relentless eye of the sun. How long before Tremayne regretted casting aside all hope for vindication, all chance at reclaiming his birthright, in favor of a fugitive's life with her in the West?

He'd grown aroused again; the very air seemed charged with his vibrancy. Within her, everything that was woman responded to his blatant desire. She'd heard that such passions quickly extinguished themselves. But ancestral lands, the restoration of his good name, would endure a lifetime. And she had the power to give these things to him, simply by returning to her father and exchanging her future for Tremayne's.

She would go . . . home, provided her father fixed things so Tremayne could go free. Ellie's hard-schooled defenses for shielding her feelings and emotions stirred from their resting places and erected her

protective shell, but this time with the intent of pre-
serving someone else's hopes and dreams.

A dull, ominous roll of thunder shook the air,
causing the fine hair along her skin to stand on
edge. Raindrops spattered against the window; a
damp chilly breeze lifted the edges of the buffalo-
robe door. It seemed appropriate that the long-
awaited rain should fall now, drowning her dreams.
She eased herself away from him, feeling lightheaded with relief when he made no effort to hold
her in place but let his hand trail along her bare
skin as she rose from the bed. She turned away and
hurriedly pulled her gown into place, fastening buttons wherever possible, conscious all the while of
his scrutiny.

She whirled to face him and fixed a bright, worldly
smile upon her face, noting with detached surprise
that every part of her, even her teeth, hurt from the
effort. "I'm sorry to disappoint you, Tremayne, but as
I said, I only borrowed your name. If you're not going
to become the earl of Chedgrave, I'm not interested in
marrying you. There's someone else, you see."

He settled himself deeper into the grass-stuffed
mattress, arranging Lauretta's down pillow beneath
his head as if he meant to stay the night.

"Tremayne, I'm serious—you must be gone. Go.
Tend to your affairs before it's too late."

Tremayne propped himself on one elbow. The
waning light cast parts of him in shadow and high-
lighted his lean, muscled length lying so gloriously
nude upon her bed.

He extended his hand to her, his fingers curling in

invitation. His eyes seemed to glow with radiant heat. "I'm not leaving here without you," he said.

She could not stop herself from placing her hand in his and reveling one last time in the touch of his skin against hers. She pressed her lips together to avoid crying out when his fingers meshed with hers and his thumb rubbed light, erotic circles against her wrist. She could imagine no sweeter heaven than a lifetime spent with her hand clasped in his.

Oh, Tremayne, her heart cried, its aching quickly stifled when his grin broadened and his hand tightened around hers.

She closed her eyes before speaking the words she hoped would convince him. "My betrothed might have something to say about that. His name . . . is Crowden. I am to become Mrs. Cato Crowden."

Hiram groaned, sick to death of pretending to be sick. He'd almost given up the pretense an endless hour or two ago when he'd heard a horse outside and figured that no-account Cato Crowden must have come back for dinner. He hadn't heard the horse leave, which meant Crowden must still be hanging around. He hoped Ellie had found some particularly nasty chore to set him to doing. He couldn't stop a little satisfied snort at the notion.

"Hire? You awake?" Lauretta bent forward anxiously.

He groaned again with mingled self-recrimination and resignation. When he'd conjured up this idea of faking a bad bout of ague, he'd never considered how rough it would be on Lauretta. He'd hoped she'd hover over him, as she'd done, tempting him with sips of broth and cool cloths over his forehead. But he'd never imagined the handwringing worry she'd bring to his sickbed, or the stark fear that emanated from her as clearly as if he saw it written on her face.

Her face. What he'd hoped was that she'd forget all about hiding her face while she tended him, thinking him unconscious. And then once she'd revealed herself to him, he'd meant to leap up and give her a hearty kiss, right before he said, "There you are, Miss Lauretta Myers. I told you those pockmarks wouldn't make a lick of difference to me."

But that damned veil seemed anchored over her head. It hadn't budged by so much as a flutter during this whole interminable time while he'd feigned unconsciousness and lay wracked with guilt for making Lauretta feel so scared for him. God, how he hated that veil! His heart ached, wondering how a body accommodated itself to something so confining, something that interfered with sight and smell, and made it impossible for a fellow to kiss his girl.

He groaned again when she bent over him with an anxious murmur. She'd been a nurse; what the heck did she see—or not see—that had her so concerned? As an afterthought, he thrashed his feet around and moaned a little more. He figured a genuinely sick person would make a gradual return to consciousness. He felt her fingers, cool and slim against his forehead, and then his eyes flew wide open in response to the walloping slap she laid across his jaw.

"You faker!" she shrieked. She was all puffed up in

her rage like a banty rooster. "Just what in botheration were you trying to prove by scaring me half to death?"

"Aw, Laurie." Hiram sat up, gingerly probing his jaw. "How'd you figure it out?"

"How'd *you* manage to keep your skin so hot all the time?" she challenged back. "I thought sure you had a fever, you lying skunk. You ought to have broken out in a sweat before coming to, that's how I knew you were faking. So how'd you keep your skin all flushed?"

If she'd thought it was flushed before, what would she think now, with the heat coursing up his neck over his face. Hell, he was blushing like a schoolboy. "I ain't never had a woman sitting so close to me for so long before, that's why I'm hot."

"I can't believe you carried on pretending to get a little bit sicker and sicker for days—*days*, Hiram Espy—just so I'd sit next to you for a while."

"I didn't just want you to sit next to me, Miss High and Mighty Lauretta Myers—I wanted you to take off your goddamned hat."

She seemed to deflate. "Oh, Lordy, Hiram, don't start that again."

"I'm not starting—I'm keeping it up. And I'm going to keep on keeping it up until you give me a chance."

"I'm not going to listen to this again." She turned on her heel and began scurrying from the barn.

"You're going to listen to me this time," Hiram warned, stalking determinedly after her.

He clapped his hand over her shoulder. She

wrenched herself free, but not before her gown gave at the shoulder seam with a sharp, rending tear. With an annoyed exclamation, she pulled the gaping cloth together.

Hiram knew he would forever wonder whether he'd caused it on purpose. Or whether it was the combination of the strained angle of her head, the relaxed tension at her torn neckline, and, perhaps, a little nudge from the hand of God, that sent her hat and bee veil toppling from her head.

Her hair, her yellow cornsilk hair, tumbled free of its loose topknot, framing wide eyes the exact shade of a blue topaz he'd once seen in Texas.

Hiram had always known he carried the soul of an artist within him. It seemed a fair trade that a man fated to spending endless hours sweating beneath a scorching sun could take uncommon pleasure in the sight of freshly plowed earth spilling in inky dark rows. That a man compelled to chop wood to keep his family warm could stand mesmerized by the exquisitely tortuous twists of the cottonwood bough he struggled to fell.

He saw Lauretta's face, and his artist's soul whispered, *perfection*. Perfect bone structure, curving cheeks, a tip-tilted nose, all etched in exquisite shades of pink and white and gold.

The man who loved Lauretta grieved, *destruction*. Unfair, the close-packed pockmarks that pitted alabaster-pale skin. Cruel, the thickening of the eyelids meant to shield those shimmering, blue, blue eyes.

Her tears spilled and filled the pockmarks, so that

in the barn's uncertain light her skin looked silvery smooth, beautiful.

Much too late, Hiram realized he'd been staring. Staring. Staring without saying a word, his lips frozen in the act of speaking, his eyes riveted upon her own without offering one hint of the kiss he'd meant to proffer, the assurances he'd meant to swear.

"I knew it."

The dull, defeated voice sounded nothing like his Lauretta.

"Laurie, I—"

"Don't say anything, Hiram. It'd only make things worse." She scooped her hat and veil from the floor and set it back in place with a practiced ease that make his heart lurch. "I'd like you to be on your way now," she said, her words ever so slightly muffled, now that he'd been privileged to hear her speak without the barrier of the veil. "You have your own homestead to tend. Ellie and I can keep Cato on until we get the house built."

"Now, just you hold on there!" He caught her arm and clung tight when she tried to jerk free. "You got no call to be sending me on my way and giving my job to another man because I lost my tongue for a couple minutes."

"You didn't lose it—you didn't know what to do with it," Lauretta shot back. "You're an honest man, Hiram Espy, and that old tongue of yours wouldn't cooperate when you tried to get it to tell a lie, that's all."

"What in blazes are you talking about?"

"'Beauty's but skin deep, Miss Lauretta.' 'Your

eyes are so pretty they make up for all the rest, Miss Lauretta.' 'It's what's inside that counts, Miss Lauretta, not the package it's wrapped up in.'" He knew by the sharp-edged sarcasm that tinged her words that she mimicked phrases uttered by others. "Which lie did you mean to spout, Hiram? I assure you, I've heard them all, right up until the fellow walked away and never looked back."

"Can't say as I blame them, if this is the way you treated them."

That struck her speechless, Hiram noted with satisfaction. He pressed his advantage.

"I was wrong to think it wouldn't bother me," he told her, feeling a pang in his gut when she flinched. "But you were wrong to think it would change my feelings for you. Hell, Laurie, how could I love you without it affecting me? If I come in from the fields some day with my face all red and swole up with bee stings, are you gonna look me in the eye and say, Hiram Espy, I'm leaving you because something created by God made a mess of your face? Or are you gonna shriek and holler and feel bad and kiss me to make it feel better?"

"I imagine I'd feel bad," she whispered, a quiver in her veil hinting that she struggled with amusement. "I don't know about the kissing part."

"Or if I'm shoeing them mules and one of them kicks me in the face so that for the rest of my life my nose faces north when I'm walking east, does that mean you're gonna get sick every time you look at me, or are you gonna get used to it?"

"Well, I suppose I'd get used to it."

"Then maybe it's time you start getting used to yourself. This bee bonnet keeps you hidden from everyone, including your own self." He drew her closer and then released his grip on her arm, holding his breath, waiting to see if she would run, but she didn't. With infinite gentleness, he unfastened the hasty knot she'd tied and folded the veiling back over her hat, and then removed the hat altogether. He studied this time, rather than stared. This was Lauretta—tart, sweet, juicy, tempting—like a woodland apple, its delicious, life-sustaining flesh shielded by a rough, scaly skin. A good farmer knew such fruit was worth any amount of trouble it took to gather it in.

"Don't you dare tell me I look beautiful to you," she shouted, obviously in an agony of embarrassment.

"Naw." He bit back those very words, which had just been about to tumble from his lips, and contented himself with touching what he'd so long been denied, her ravaged skin supple and yielding beneath his rough-callused fingers.

"If you try saying one single nice thing about me, I'll . . . I'll punch you right in the stomach."

"Then I guess I'd better keep my mouth shut. Or mostly shut." With that, he grabbed her to him and kissed her soundly.

She swayed like a ripe-headed wheat stalk when he set her free long moments later.

"You know, Lauretta, I hope none of our young 'uns take after me. Because that means they'll look like angels."

And the woman who wouldn't believe she could

look beautiful to him, who wouldn't stand for anything nice being said about her, gifted him with the
earth's most radiant smile.

A scuffling sound near the doorway caused her to
clap the veiling over her head again, but Hiram made
no objection. "It's probably Cato," he said.

Lauretta sniffed. "It's about time he got here."

"He's been here awhile. I heard his horse a couple
hours ago."

Lauretta shook her head. "Maybe you're sick after
all. I just heard two horses ride in not five minutes
ago."

Hiram didn't feel like arguing such a small point,
not with the memory of her kiss still on his lips. He
added the inopportune interruption to his list of reasons for disliking Cato Crowden when the drifter
poked his head into the barn. Hiram cast a longing
glance toward the shotgun propped against the wall.
Thanks to Tremayne Hawthorne, he'd spent half a
day searching for the shotgun on the prairie. Cato
should count his blessings that nobody'd gotten
around to reloading the weapon.

"Just the two of you in here?" Cato asked. He leaned
into the barn and raked his gaze over Lauretta's
disheveled bee veiling with a knowing smirk that
annoyed Hiram even more.

"Get on out of here, Cato," Hiram ordered.

Cato shook his head. "Now, that makes three times
today people been trying to send me on my way. I
can't understand why you folks seem so set against
my company. Might as well give you a good reason."

Hiram saw Cato's motion toward his gun belt. He

moved toward the shotgun—Cato wouldn't know it wasn't loaded—but not quickly enough. The deadly bore of Cato's gun aimed square at Lauretta's midsection, and the three of them locked into position as if a sudden winter storm had encased them in ice.

"Kick the shotgun over toward me, farmer," Cato said.

Seeing no way out, Hiram did as he was told.

"All in all, this is a lucky day for you," Cato's voice sounded gratingly cheerful. "I'm not real eager to fire this gun just now. The friend I have waiting outside will be powerful annoyed with me if I raise too much of a commotion. You see, he's going after whoever's in the dugout if they don't soon poke their heads out—"

With a strangled cry of rage, Hiram moved toward Cato, but came up short at the warning click of a hammer being cocked into firing position.

"I've had about enough of you." Only menace could be heard in Cato's voice now. "Miz' Lauretta, you gather some of that rope in the corner and tie up good old Hiram before he gets himself into trouble. Do a good job, too, because if I think it's too loose when I check it, I'm liable to tighten the knots so the blood can't flow, and that does cruel things to a man's limbs."

Lauretta fumbled with the rope. Cato encouraged her. "Do it right and I'll be real gentle when it's your turn."

"Don't hurt her," Hiram begged, his voice ragged. "Don't hurt the women."

"Who, me? Hell, ain't no man on this earth

sweeter to women, long as they don't turn all bossy."
Cato rested his hand over the knife belted to his waist
and smiled. "Kind of sours my nature when a woman
tries to push me around."

He held her; there was no doubt, for Tremayne could
feel Ellie's pulse fluttering against his thumb. But he
could feel nothing else. His lungs ceased their unconscious quest for air, his heart pounded to a stop, no
sound reached his ears—or so it seemed, his spirit so
thoroughly numbed by her announcement that it dis-
associated itself from his body.

And Ellie, though he gripped her hand, had disappeared as well, displaced by the vaguely smiling,
agreeable stranger whose eyes were careful blanks
giving no hint of her true feelings.

"You lie," he stated flatly. "I felt your love, Ellie, in
the way you touched me, the way you cried my name.
I don't believe you have such an avid interest in my
expectations, or that the man called Cato Crowden is
anywhere near here."

He thought, for the space of a heartbeat, that he'd
caught her in the midst of a jest, the humor of which
escaped him just now. Consternation creased her forehead and her lips parted with chagrin, before a bland
sort of relief smoothed her features again. "Believe
what you will about my avarice. As for Cato—he's
down near the creek if you care to ride out and meet
him."

It couldn't be true. She couldn't have hidden such
an avaricious streak from him. And not Cato Crowden.

Oh, God, not Cato Crowden. Somehow, some way, she must have learned the name of his nemesis and sought to tease him with it. A plot, concocted between her and Sarah Reynolds to play him for a fool, to repay him for riding away when he should have stayed by her side. It had to be something of that nature. The fates could not be so cruel as to shatter his dreams like Sarah's cookie crumbs.

He found no humor in her claim; nor, looking at her, did he think her anything other than utterly, completely serious.

"You're lying." He found himself repeating his words as he rose to his feet, towering over her, his hands gripping her delicate shoulders, grateful for once for possessing a physique that might frighten a woman into admitting the truth. He wanted to shake her until her eyes kindled once again with the love he'd seen shining for him . . . for him!

She turned amiable, helpful, as any woman might be in explaining her future husband's whereabouts to an inquiring friend. "He might be back in time for supper. Depends on the weather, he said."

"Describe him to me," he interrupted, fiercely determined to believe she played some elaborate jest.

Her eyes widened slightly at the absurd request, but she complied with a description far too close to the one Gus had quoted from Darla's journal to doubt its veracity. "Well, he's almost as tall as you. Long black hair hanging down beyond his shoulders. Actually, though I didn't want to admit it at first, he's quite good-looking, and charming, too."

A lion plucked from the jungle and incarcerated

within a circus cage could feel no greater urge to roar its anguish. Just so had Darla described what drew her to Cato. Now Ellie was lost to him—the claws gouged deep within, threatening to tear out his heart. That Cato Crowden was the man she had turned to suffused him with a desire for unholy vengeance that imperiled his very soul.

"You're hurting me," she said in a calm, reasonable manner that broke the fragile barrier of his control.

"*I'm* hurting you?" He set her away from him because he feared that very thing. Bitter rage consumed him, making him doubt his ability to stop short of crushing her to death against him rather than share her with Cato Crowden. Heart-pounding fear, too, coursed through him at the thought of what she could suffer at Cato Crowden's sadistic hands. While he'd gone off looking for the proof to save his illegitimate hide, she'd found Cato. Oh, God, Cato Crowden—if it had been any other, he swore he could have mastered his torment. "You dare speak of my hurting you when you intend to submit to Cato Crowden—I can't even say it."

He found himself dressed with no memory of jerking on his clothes; he found himself looming before her once more, enraged beyond measure by the pleasant, polite way she stared past him.

He found himself lifting her within his arms, molding her resistant body against his, stamping every inch of her as his, waiting, waiting, for a sigh, a sweet trembling, to tell him he'd penetrated her defenses.

He swore when she stayed rigid and unyielding. "I

suspect the man is a murderer. You can't marry him. Come with me, Ellie. It doesn't matter if you've . . . if he's lured you into feeling some fondness for him. I can turn my back on the past, and so can you. I may never become earl of Chedgrave, but I swear I'll make it up to you somehow."

A gentle tremor coursed through her. "I'd rather just shrivel up and die. You get yourself out of here before anyone sees you. You don't know how much your earldom means to me."

And then it seemed her shield extended to his heart, encasing all its incipient soft feelings in a stone-like shroud.

"Very well." At her words, his walled-off heart ceased taking pleasure in the feel of her against him. He pushed her away and spun toward the door, yanking at the buffalo robe with such force that it tore from the nails with a hideous, rending sound.

He strode two dozens steps into the eerie, prestorm gloom. Found himself across the yard and ready to mount his horse before he realized he'd done exactly what Anna had cautioned him against doing. His damnable pride was causing him to run away. Again.

He could see now that he'd taken the easy way by fleeing England rather than endure the humiliation brought by his father's actions. He'd turned an easy, tolerant eye to his wife's infidelity without assuring himself that the man who'd seduced her deserved her affections. He'd endured the hell of Jonathan McKittrick's jailhouse because he couldn't admit his failures. How much anguish might have been prevented had he only probed beyond the obvious to find what had prompted such hurtful results?

Ellie's turning away, straight into Cato Crowden's arms with her lips still swollen from his kisses, her core still warm from Tremayne's possession, made no sense. Unless she pursued this course with good intent, fueled by faulty logic. Only one thing was certain: There had been many doubts and misunderstandings between them. If he left her now, he would never know the truth.

He brought himself up short and then turned back to the dugout, determined to demand an explanation.

Ellie stood clutching the torn buffalo robe, her face a white mask of anguish. A woman who loved another man would have retained a disinterested facade. A woman who loved him, but feared the outcome of that love, might look like Ellie.

"Ellie." He held his hand out to her again, knowing that if only she would touch him again he would never, ever let her go. She spoke, but a sharp clap of thunder exploded above him, roaring on interminably so that he couldn't hear her. "El—" He meant to say her name again when the thunder struck once more and something pounded him hard below his left shoulder. He parted his lips to call her name when thunder cracked and he was struck again, and a garbled sound of pain burst from him. She screamed, pointing to his chest. A low buzzing sound filled his head as he looked down and noted with detached surprise that somehow his shirt had gotten torn, that jagged edges of his flesh mingled with the shredded homespun that was quickly turning bright, burning red.

He tried to smile at her, to tell her he loved her, oh, God, how he loved her. Another booming thud brought him to his knees. Pain blossomed, searing, almost blinding, but he kept his swimming vision locked upon her. He wanted to make sure she knew everything would be all right, joke that he would help her smooth the tangled path she'd created for them. But there was no time. How unutterably, unbearably sad, to have everything within his grasp and run out of time. *No time, no time, no time,* his mind kept repeating as everything dimmed into black.

19

Rain pelted down with such sudden force that it staggered Ellie as she tried to run to him. "Tremayne!" She cried his name, desperate for some sign that he heard, but the gusting wind tore the sound from her lips, rendering it an impotent whimper against the storm's raging fury.

"Don't die," she sobbed. "Please don't die." Her head spun with a thousand things she ached to tell him, a recanting of her lies, the admission that she was so inexperienced with love that she'd thought she was doing the right thing, the noble thing, to send him away.

But her throat seemed paralyzed beyond calling his name and pleading with him to live. There were barely a dozen feet separating them but her legs could not carry her swiftly enough. The wind buffeted her, setting her back a single pace. She howled her frustration, feeling his eyes upon her and watching their wondrous glow dim as his hand fell limply into the mud.

She almost reached him. She had only to regain the step she'd lost before sinking to her knees and taking his hand, when the ground thundered beneath her feet and she was swept up in the relentless grip of a mounted horseman.

"No!" She fought the arm that encircled her like a steel band, gouging at it with her fingernails, drumming her feet against the horse's heaving sides. Screaming in wordless, inarticulate shrieks, she twisted and tore at her captor's flesh. Somehow, she managed to keep her eyes riveted upon Tremayne. The deluge molded his hair against his scalp, his clothes against his prone body, revealing skin a shade too pale, outlining a chest that didn't seem to rise with life-giving breath. The rain darkened the ground; the area surrounding Tremayne seemed blacker still, enriched with his life's blood coursing from his mangled shoulder.

He would die without ever knowing how much she loved him.

The horse slowed and her captor hauled her up in front of him. Dull with despair, Ellie lacked the strength to look up and identify him, but a harsh, sinister voice solved the puzzle for her.

"Goddamn you, Cato, put her down!"

"And let you get a clear shot at me? She's gonna be sitting right here, Stringer, in front of my vitals, until we divvy up what's waiting for us in Wichita."

Silas Stringer. Her father's tracker. Though numb

with grief, a shudder passed through her, and every nightmare she'd ever dreamed threatened to replay in her mind. Her instincts had been right all along. It *had* been Cato and Stringer watching her that day she'd sat and laughed with Mattie in front of Woodman's store.

And Cato Crowden. She would get no satisfaction in telling Lauretta that this time Ellie McKittrick had judged a man's character correctly.

"Well, you stupid, suspicious son of a bitch, you put us into a fine mess." Stringer pulled alongside Cato's horse and cast an assessing look at Ellie. "Why the hell did you have to pick her up and go charging away? All we had to do was kill the other two and we could have had ourselves a dry night's sleep in that dugout before heading for Wichita in the morning."

Cato's hold on her tightened. "You're talking about killing people in front of a witness and you call *me* stupid? I'll tell you what's stupid—you're the one had to shoot Hawthorne three times, you're so whiskey-pissed you can't even aim."

"My aim's off because you shot my toe and it's messing up the way I get set for a shot. Besides, I got him, didn't I?"

"He'll come after you and make you pay for this." Ellie spoke quietly, reassuring herself, but it brought Stringer's startled regard upon her—and a hearty chuckle from Cato Crowden.

"If he lives, he might show up in five months or so. That's how long it took him to come after me for killing his first wife."

"I knew it," Stringer muttered, while Ellie mouthed a silent denial. Cato Crowden—and Tremayne's dead wife. Cato Crowden—and moments ago she'd taunted Tremayne, claiming she wanted to become Cato's bride. Oh, God, Tremayne might even now lie dying, his last sight that of Cato Crowden swooping Ellie into his arms and laughing as they rode away.

Cato's hand, holding her in her unsteady perch in front of him, began roaming over her body, as if the intimacy he'd shared with Tremayne's dead wife entitled him to enjoy the same with Ellie.

At his too-bold touch a jolt of revulsion stiffened her backbone, and then instinct, long-honed to shield her from reality, sent icy tendrils coiling through her to numb her emotions. *Endure,* the shield said seductively. *It will end.*

"No more!" Her full-throated shout shattered the shield. She caught Cato's hand in her own and bit him, hard, in the tender flesh between thumb and forefinger. She gouged backward with her elbows, seeking some vulnerability in the vitals he meant for her to protect. Her riding skills, uncertain at best, deserted her in her sudden frenzy; the drenching rain made everything slippery, and she dared for a moment to think she might slip through his arms and off the horse's back.

But he stopped her. He simply wrapped his bleeding hand in the sodden neckline of her gown and twisted, choking her as if she were a leashed puppy.

"Bitch," he snarled in her ear. "You'll pay."

Ellie clawed at Cato's hand. Her vision swam; her hearing faded; it seemed as though a huge claw had worked itself beneath her breastbone to squeeze the last breath of air from her lungs.

"Dear God, help me," she silently prayed. "Mama, please, please help me." She steeled her heart against more pain, every ounce of her will fighting against the thought that Tremayne might have joined her mother and could hear her prayers. Whether he lived or died, her body had known the ecstacy of his touch, her heart had thrilled to the beat of his, her woman's soul had reveled in the passions neither had been able to resist. Never had two people risked so much in order to love, or come so close before having it all stolen away, by lies, by misunderstandings, by ancient wounds that had left crippling emotional scars. *Tremayne, you told me how dangerous the prairie could be. Make something happen now.*

Only the stinging slash of rain acknowledged her plea.

And then Stringer said, "Her father ain't gonna turn over the ransom if she's dead when we get her to Wichita."

"Probably drown in this rain anyway," Cato muttered, but he loosened his hold.

So Stringer expected her father to meet them in Wichita. Reprieve from strangulation, at the cost of being returned to her father for ransom. Greed drove Cato and Stringer; perhaps she could exploit their base natures.

"You should go back to the homestead." Ellie's bruised throat limited her volume to a whisper, and she spoke hesitantly, not from the pain, but from the certainty that the next words she spoke could mean a chance at life for the man she loved. "If it's ransom you're after, you've left the biggest prize lying back there in the yard."

Cato bent his head low to hear, and the rain poured from his hat brim to splash cold against her skin.

"Tremayne Hawthorne," she rasped. "He's the heir to a substantial fortune and title in England. My father holds a hostage who would be willing to pay well for Tremayne. You must keep him alive. You can load him into the back of our wagon and take him with us to Wichita."

"Is she telling the truth?" Cato demanded.

Stringer gave a terse nod. "Except the hostage got away."

"What—were you responsible for holding onto the hostage?" Cato jeered. Stringer's hand flexed toward his gun belt, and Ellie knew only her position in front of Cato prevented the tracker from avenging the insult.

"My father will redeem us both."

"I doubt that," Stringer countered. "He's getting what he wants."

"He'll know how to put you in touch with people in England who would pay," Ellie promised, hoping Stringer's anger and Cato's greed would dull their ears to the desperation in her voice. "Tremayne's family will pay a fortune for his safe return, an immense fortune." Anything, she would promise anything, to give Tremayne a chance to live.

"Hell, let's go back," Cato said. "It'll be pitch dark soon. I'd like to think over what she said. And I don't feel like traveling all night in this rain with a she-demon biting and hissing at me, when there are better ways to pass the time."

Though her skin shuddered at his words, Ellie couldn't prevent sagging back against Cato in relief when he wheeled his horse around, heading them back to the homestead.

Rain prevented Tremayne from completely sinking into the oblivion that would obliterate the pain. It struck cold against his face and paradoxically white hot on his torn and bleeding shoulder. His mind, not so vulnerable to the rain's physical touch, wandered in a state of benumbed recrimination. He'd bungled everything, teasing when he should have been forthright, seducing when he should have been explaining, storming away when he should have been gathering Ellie in his arms. If ever a man deserved to be shot, it was he—and he would tell her so, as soon as his depleted strength seeped back into his limbs so he could rescue her.

The pain must have blanked his mind for a moment, for the rain had ended when, from nowhere, came ungentle hands peeling him from the muddy earth and flinging his unresisting body into a sodden wagonbed. A frenzied buzzing started when his head struck the back of the wagon seat. Oh, God—not another concussion! Physical agony such as he'd never experienced wracked through him. He twisted against it and found a sharper torment when his unsteady gaze settled upon Ellie struggling in the embrace of a man who could only be Cato Crowden.

Struggling. She didn't want to rest there. Tremayne might have laughed, did it not hurt so much to breathe. Like a cat clawing free from the paws of a hound, Ellie flailed and kicked her way loose. She lost her balance in the mud but stopped her fall with braced hands. The odd buzzing sound stepped up its fury when he tried lifting his head away from the wagon seat. The low, droning hum increased its pitch when the wagonbed sagged beneath her weight, and she gained Tremayne's side.

He had so much to tell her. Humbly grateful for the chance to profess his love, he sent his scattered wits in search of the words he meant to say while she cradled the back of his buzzing head in one hand. Tears coursed down her face so that for a moment he thought the rain had resumed. "I can't touch your wound until I wash the mud from my hands. I didn't mean anything I said. Don't die, my love, please don't die."

Words of love, reassurances, explanations—there were so many—which to say first? The most important.

"Buzz," he croaked.

Her face paled at his witless utterance. Her expression firmed into brisk efficiency, wiping away the tender concern she'd shown. With her free hand she probed gently through his shirt, avoiding the torn, exposed flesh.

He tried speaking again, knowing he'd disappointed her. Small wonder—it had been too long since he'd tried speaking words of love, but he'd fashion a full book of poetry for her once he got them out of this mess.

"Buzz . . . buzzing."

"You've lost blood, but it could have been much worse."

Ellie tried to speak soothingly, as Lauretta had told her a nurse must do. For it was obvious Tremayne considered her nothing more than a nurse. *Buzzing* at her, for heaven's sake, while she called him her love and implored him to live. Even so, she felt grateful that Cato's accusation had proven true: Stringer's vaunted skill had indeed been diminished by alcohol. A better aim, a steadier hand, might have sent the bullets tearing through Tremayne's chest instead of carving a couple of nasty, but nonfatal, gouges close to his collarbone. The worst wound appeared to have caught Tremayne between the juncture of arm and chest wall, only inches from his beating heart. Judging by the look of the wound, the bullet might have passed through, but not altogether harmlessly. It had damaged something within because his arm dangled uselessly at his side.

"Buzzing," he repeated pointing vaguely to the back of his head with his right hand.

Her own pulse raced with anxiety over the steady seeping away of his life's blood. She could waste no time before cleaning and binding his wounds, but he seemed so agitated she deemed it important to spare a moment to reassure him. "Lauretta told me wounded men often hear a humming noise . . ." Her voice trailed off and she cocked her head toward the wagon seat his head had so recently cracked. Impossible, but it seemed the buzzing that fascinated him so sounded in her own ears.

"My God, Tremayne—there's a bee colony nesting under the wagon seat!"

Ellie remembered Lauretta telling her how she and Hiram had abandoned a newly captured bee swarm and left the wagon sitting out on the prairie in their excitement over her unexpected return. Apparently, the disturbed swarm had found a tiny opening in the boxed-in wagon seat and set up housekeeping. When Stringer and Cato flung Tremayne into the back of the wagon, they'd done so with enough force to jar the backboard loose, exposing the bee colony.

"A weapon . . . for us?" Tremayne asked in a thready whisper.

Ellie's heart soared to hear him say, "for us."

"God knows we could use a weapon. But these are just bugs."

"They sting."

Ellie couldn't repress a tiny shiver. "If only they would do so on command."

"Coffee, Ellie. Very sweet. Thick with sugar. Spill it on them somehow, and I will toss the bees in their direction, gently, as my tutor taught me to do with a ball when playing bowls."

He might be delirious, speaking of throwing bees and lawn bowling at a time like this. Such a ridiculous plan couldn't possibly work—one weeping, tremulous woman and one wounded, crippled man attacking two murderous cutthroats with sugar and honeybees. He had some nerve, expecting her to risk their lives. *For us.* They couldn't do it. They would fail. Everything she had ever tried in the throes of desperation had failed. *For us.*

"Ellie . . . you wouldn't truly marry him, would you?"

He asked it with a husky tremor that made it sound as if learning the truth meant more to him than surviving Cato's and Stringer's plans. His eyes, glorious blue, fixed on hers with mute appeal that tore straight through the cool detachment she'd tried to hide behind.

"How could I marry him, Tremayne, when I belonged to you first and always?"

There—she'd said what was in her heart, stripping herself defenseless.

And then Tremayne turned a supremely radiant grin on her and flexed the fingers of his good hand. "Then trust me, Ellie," he said. "Trust me."

One couldn't merely say the words, "I trust you," to make it so. A person proved her trust by thinking up a reasonable explanation for brewing a pot of coffee at a time like this. By dumping it over the heads of killers and somehow managing to sneak into the barn to set her friends free instead of staying in the wagonbed alongside Tremayne and holding him tight. A person proved her trust by doing all those things, knowing it didn't matter whether she lived or died, only that she'd found someone she could trust enough to do those things with.

She touched her fingers to Tremayne's heart before sliding from the wagon. She hurried to intercept Stringer and Cato before they got close enough to see the milling bees.

"His wounds need tending before he can be moved." She hoped they would credit her breathlessness to her short burst of speed rather than the nervousness that shook her from toes to teeth. "I must boil water and fashion some sort of bandage. Would you release Lauretta from the barn? She's a nurse—"

"Boil the goddamned water," Cato ordered.

"Hold on—what if she has a gun somewhere in the dugout?" Stringer asked.

"If you'd paid any attention while we were staking them out, you'd know they only had the one shotgun, and I took it from Espy when I tied him up in the barn." Cato motioned toward the dugout with his chin. "Boil the water."

"Fine." She pressed her lips together for strength, and then added, "I'll set a pot of coffee on to boil while I'm at it."

Neither made an objection, obviously so secure in their belief that they held everyone helpless that they didn't mind sipping a cup of coffee after the downpour. She'd feared Cato might follow her into the dugout, but he didn't, and she felt a grim satisfaction at finding the havoc wreaked within by the storm. Stringer and Cato would find the dugout a comfortless shelter. Although several cloudbursts had passed overhead since she and Lauretta had taken possession, the recently ended storm was the first deluge of any duration to strike. Inky runnels coursed down the earthen walls. Fat, muddy droplets seeped through the ceiling planks to fall and add their moisture to the quagmire the water had made of the hard-packed dirt floor.

At any other time she might have despaired at witnessing the dugout's inability to fend off the elements, but for now she merely cursed the dragging weight of mud against her hem as she tried to balance completing her task against the irresistible urge to run to the door again and again for a glimpse of Tremayne.

Only the hearth, no doubt fortified by her more experienced predecessors, managed to retain its normal shape and function. She coaxed the banked embers into life, and filled the kettle and coffeepot from their water barrel. By habit she reached for the can of Freeman's Coffee Essence and measured it into the cups, even though what she brewed was not meant for drinking.

And while the water heated, she divided every bit of their sugar and molasses and honey between two tin cups.

The coffeepot, holding less water, was the first vessel to come to a boil. She carefully poured water over the sticky mess in the cups and stirred, holding her breath when at first it seemed nothing but sludge would result—and then the sweeteners dissolved in the steaming water.

She added a little cold water to the murky liquid, so Stringer and Cato wouldn't react so quickly to the boiling temperature that they leaped away before being thoroughly soaked. She tucked a small paring knife into the hem of her sleeve, and gripped the cup handles.

Tremayne watched her bearing the battered tin cups as though they were the finest Sevres porcelain. She managed to take a course that coaxed her quarry to within a few steps of the wagon without letting them see the bee colony, walking with the regal bearing of the countess he meant to make her.

Love and pride stirred within him as he summoned his strength for the greatest effort of his life.

Odd, to think that one possessed of his formidable physique should find inching his fingers along a wooden board a task nearly beyond his capabilities. The effort left him gasping for breath. He steeled himself when he plunged his hand into the swarming mass of bees, and gritted his teeth against the needle-sharp stings that greeted his intrusion. He found the waxy mass of their incipient hive and wrenched it loose just as Ellie flawlessly replayed the slight fall she'd experienced earlier. She flung the coffee cups toward Stringer and Cato, drenching them, crying out with pretended dismay while her fall carried her below Tremayne's line of sight.

Tremayne held the alien-feeling mass in his hand, feeling the fanning of their wings, the sharp prickle of their feet, almost relishing a sting that caught him on the pad of his thumb. His instincts urged him to rid himself of it at once; his hatred for both men demanded that he try hurling the angrily buzzing mass at them with force enough to maim, though he knew that was impossible. He ignored both impulses, knowing that any rash action on his part could doom their plan to failure. Strange creatures, bees, to form such a tight, defensive ball around the wax they'd created to shelter their young that one could toss them lightly, gently, to land at the feet of one's enemies. Stifling a cry against the pain each time movement jarred his injured shoulder, Tremayne somehow hauled himself upright in the wagonbed and, calling forth long-disused skills, he tossed the bees.

Nothing happened for the longest of moments. Stringer and Cato hadn't even noticed what he'd done, being so busy wiping irritatedly at the stickiness soaking their clothing. Ellie's spilled coffee had merely increased the sogginess, not discernible to human eyes, of their already sodden garments.

The angry bees, however, developed an intense interest in investigating whether this strange nectar had been the cause of the violation of their new home.

Cato muttered a few imprecations and stomped his foot against the ground when the first insects crawled over his boots to his britches. Stringer's aversion exploded with more colorful obscenities. Ellie, with a furtive glance that Tremayne found oddly reassuring, rose and bolted to the barn while Cato and Stringer were distracted. Both men tried brushing the bees from their clothing, and began a curious, shambling sort of dance that escalated into a shouting frenzy when the insects clung—and stung.

"Them things kill! Get them *off* me!" Stringer's shriek carried the edge of terror.

Cato greeted Stringer's plea with laughter. "'Fraid of a couple a' bugs, Silas?"

"Damn things bit my pa till he swole up and died. Damn bees are worse than snakes for us Stringers. My ma always told me to stay away from them. Get them *off* me!"

Cato's mirthful chuckling soon turned into sharp yelps of pain.

It seemed an eternity but no more than a couple of minutes passed before Ellie wriggled into the wagonbed. "I cut Hiram and Lauretta loose. Hiram says he'll take their guns—Lauretta taught him how to work around bees." She glanced toward Cato and Stringer and shuddered, her eyes wide with guilty excitement and the terrible knowledge that she'd helped instigate the punishment now unfolding.

"Don't feel guilty," Tremayne said. "Remember what they meant to do to you."

She nodded, swallowing hard. She made a slight jerking motion, as if she wanted to curl close against him, but something held her back. He pulled her closer yet with his good arm, and then pressed her against the wooden floor, exposing his back to shield her from any stray angry bees, whispering words of love he doubted she could hear over the screaming.

20

Ellie sat on her nail keg with her back braced against the dugout's wall. The mud-caked roots and grassy fibers had dried quickly once the sullen, late-day sun reappeared, and the wall's knobby protrusions pressed through the thin stuff of her dress. She'd worked so hard to develop a similar exterior for herself, and that tough and bristling part of her watched without emotion as Hiram Espy loaded Stringer's grotesquely bloated corpse and a moaning Cato Crowden into the wagonbed. A weeping woman, a wounded man, and a fistful of irritated honeybees had proven to be formidable foes indeed against the two ruffians.

She should be savoring the day's triumphs; instead, her thoughts taunted her that while she'd told Tremayne she belonged to him first and always, no similar sentiment had crossed his lips. Had she imagined the love shining in his eyes, or had it been only their desperate situation that made it seem their souls were in accord? She had sent him away, wounded him with deliberate cruelty, though with the best of intentions. Could a man whose intentions never seemed to produce the desired results understand—or forgive her?

These silent insecurities urged her to retreat. But she would not, never again, even though this new, firm resolve didn't make it easier to wait, and wonder, until she could be alone with Tremayne.

Tremayne balanced upon their other nail keg, enduring Lauretta's ministrations. She had tied his hair back more tightly than Tremayne usually wore it, revealing the determined set to his jaw. He sat bare from the waist up, the power implicit in the firm, ridged contours of his stomach and chest diminished not at all by the snowy white bandage Lauretta skillfully wrapped around his shoulder and upper arm.

Grateful as she was for Lauretta's medical skills, and delighted as she felt that Lauretta had finally decided to bare her face to them all, Ellie nonetheless wished she'd quit fussing. She craved privacy with Tremayne with an almost paralyzing ache.

Tremayne seemed to sense her thoughts. He swung a lazy glance in her direction, a glance that traveled from her hem to her neckline, and tiny shivers of excitement sprang to life in response to his visual caress.

"There," Lauretta said with a satisfied pat to Tremayne's shoulder. "You're set to travel. Though I don't mind telling you I won't rest easy until the two of you get word back and let us know you've arrived somewhere safely. Oh, Lordy, all those western places sound so far away."

Tremayne leaned forward and picked up the plain leather-bound journal they'd found in Stringer's saddlebags. He turned it over and over, riffling the edges of the pages with his thumb.

"Now that I have Cato Crowden and this journal, I'm not so sure I want Ellie to accompany me," Tremayne said, drawing a gasp from Lauretta. "I'm not going West."

Ellie stared at him with mute distress. She'd succeeded too well in convincing him that she wanted his title, and not him, and now that he held the means of proving his innocence, he was flinging it back in her face. It felt as if her heart crumbled into a thousand weighty particles, trickling down to settle like a layer of molten lead over her hopes and dreams.

"You have to go West!" Lauretta found her tongue and hopped about in her agitation. "Ellie told you what that Stringer and Cato had planned! Her father's probably waiting in Wichita right now! Either the warden or Sheriff Walker would clap you into jail for the rest of your life! They'll drag Ellie home and lock her up and she'll never get away! You and Ellie could be separated and never see each other again!"

Lauretta continued her excited litany, enumerating every one of Ellie's secret fears. Somehow, though, Lauretta's shrill voice faded and the threat of those fears diminished when Tremayne's eyes locked upon Ellie's. Rising to his full height, he tucked the journal into his waistband, and then he extended his hand toward her.

"The road I prefer to take holds no guarantees," he said. "Your father's wrath could still force me into jail and ensnare you within his grasp. I shouldn't allow you to take that risk. But there's a chance, Ellie, a hope that we can overcome it all. Will you take that chance with me, beloved?"

Ellie sat rigidly, feeling physical agony as she tore her glance away from his to stare at her clasped hands. Intertwining her fingers helped disguise their trembling; perhaps it was no accident that this gesture formed the attitude of prayer. Tremayne's pose, his words, told her that he forgave the hurt she'd caused him. She could say no. She could admit her fears for herself, and his self-sacrificing love for her would send them on the run, away from all their demons.

She wondered, though, how many sleepless nights he'd spend staring across the ocean, his proud blue eyes dimmed with remorse for failing to clear his name and claim what should have been his from birth. Many years from now, he'd stand before her with his back not quite so straight, his hand not quite as steady, and she'd never know whether merciless age alone had taken its toll or long-nourished regret weighed harder upon him.

She rose to meet him, a bit unsteady on her feet. "If we leave at first light, we can be in Wichita by late afternoon. I was sometimes permitted to help father with his correspondence. I remember the Wichita sheriff, Walt Walker, often wrote asking after the fate of those he'd sent on to Fort Smith. Perhaps Sheriff Walker would be interested in our story." She felt herself wondrously strengthened when her hand became tucked snugly within Tremayne's.

"There seems to be something missing from this finger," he teased, his thumb brushing over the place where she'd never thought to see a wedding ring. "There's bound to be a church where we can stop and rectify this situation."

"I don't know—will the church sell rings?" She didn't know how the light, playful rejoinder worked its way past the excited hammering of her heart.

Tremayne's eyes crinkled with delight. "I don't mean to get there and be disappointed. If it suits you, I'll raid your kitchen and fashion a temporary one from the bent handle of a spoon. And then I will replace it with something a bit more elegant—if we ever reach England. I can see it in my dreams, Ellie, the achievement of all I've ever wanted, but I can't imagine it coming true without you at my side."

"Dreams and imagination." Ellie smiled when he pulled her into his embrace, where she could feel his heartbeat thundering in concert with her own. "Do you know, Tremayne, that sometimes a mirage turns out to be the real thing, a paradise on Earth."

Ellie had never entered the building Magnolia's homesteaders used as a church. Little larger than a shed, it was constructed of weathered gray cottonwood trunks that ran up and down instead of sideways. It tilted ominously toward the rear, looking as though a hearty chorus of "Bringing in the Sheaves" could set it on its backside. A luxuriously embroidered lace curtain flapped incongruously over a square hole that had never been finished properly into a window. Gaps between boards loomed wide enough to admit a bird or snake; the handful of human worshipers who could squeeze into its narrow confines must surely find the building uncomfortably hot during summer, bone-chillingly cold during the winter.

A crudely lettered sign announced, "Alle welcum. R. Culhane, Pastor. P.S. Try the barn if I aint in the hows."

"I'll track him down," Hiram said. "Let him know he got two weddin's to preach."

Ellie smiled at Lauretta's joyously shivering reaction to Hiram's comment. Even though Lauretta had cast off her bonnet, her whole body continued to show the emotions most people expressed only with their faces. Ellie hoped she would never change.

Ellie thought that later she'd ask Lauretta if she could imagine a finer wedding chapel than this sorry excuse for a house of God.

Of course, she might not have felt such fondness for the ramshackle structure, had any man besides Tremayne Hawthorne held her elbow in a possessive, anticipatory grip while they waited.

"Your pulse is racing." Tremayne's low voice whispered against her ear and promptly set her blood to boiling at an even faster rate.

"I'm . . . I'm a little nervous," she admitted. "What could be taking Hiram so long?"

"Don't worry, Ellie. I won't be leaving this place until we've been declared man and wife."

His assurance both warmed and amused her. He sought to convince her that he meant to go through with this marriage, as if she couldn't recognize the love shining from his eyes, the desire he barely kept at bay. She squeezed his hand to show him she understood.

Maybe someday, after they were safely married and had straightened out all the problems surrounding them, she could admit the real cause of her nervous, fretful worrying.

She would tell him that the breath-draining heat, the lace curtain stirring at the window, had somehow carried her back to that day when she'd sat shivering at her father's breakfast table, intent upon escape. She would tell him that when she heard footsteps shuffling outside the church door, she'd remembered how her father had paused in the hallway, checking his timepiece against the clock. How each moment had dragged endlessly, stretching her nerves to the breaking point, until she'd feared some impending doom would bring all her plans and dreams crashing around her, splintering them so thoroughly that she would never truly live.

She knew Jonathan McKittrick had been summoned to Wichita by Silas Stringer. Even now her father might be pacing the floor in Sheriff Walt Walker's jailhouse. Or perhaps he'd grown impatient waiting for Stringer and he'd already arranged for a posse to come after Tremayne, making plans to exert his legal right to force her back to Arkansas.

And then Hiram returned with Pastor Culhane.

She leaned against Tremayne, the reassuring sound of his steady heartbeat thrumming into her, completely obscuring the preacher's earnest words. *Hurry! Hurry!* her mind screamed when Culhane solemnly licked his forefinger to turn a page in the worn prayerbook he read from. She wanted to scream when a wisp of grass fell from Culhane's forehead and the preacher made fussing, embarrassed tidying motions, as if he'd only then realized he'd run in straight from plowing, that his hair spiked up from the friction of pulling off his straw hat. He droned on, his words no more intelligible than the buzzing of a pesky fly.

He stopped speaking suddenly, his mouth a startled O of surprise. Tremayne swiveled away and Ellie could hear, then, the sounds that had distracted them. Male voices exclaiming, harnesses jingling, horses stamping. The new arrivals clustered around their wagon, just visible through the propped-open door. Ellie knew what caught their attention: Stringer's corpse and Cato's bound form lay in the wagonbed.

The doorway darkened. Ellie stifled a scream, pressing her hand hard against her mouth lest she cry out, for she knew before it actually happened that her father would step through the door.

"Finish!" Tremayne ordered the preacher.

Culhane stuttered. "I—I—I—"

Hiram gave the preacher a shove, jarring the rest of the words loose.

"Pronounce you man and wife!"

It couldn't be called silence, that moment of breathless tension that followed Culhane's pronouncement.

Jonathan McKittrick shattered the stormlike calm. "The Lord guided me in telling me to make speed here rather than wait in Wichita. I have the sheriff and a half-dozen men backing me up. Put a ring on her finger, and I'll see to it you don't leave this place alive," he warned.

Tremayne quelled him into silence with a single, determined glance, and slid the wide spoon ring into place.

And Jonathan McKittrick suddenly seemed diminished.

Ellie touched the crude ring with the pad of her thumb and studied her father openly, wondering if all those years of averting her gaze had altered her memory of him. He couldn't have changed so much in just a couple of weeks. He seemed tall as ever, and maybe a bit more fleshy, which should have lent him greater stature. Perhaps she found him less formidable because now she could compare the beardless swell of his cheek, the plump curve of his breast and buttocks, against her intimate knowledge of Tremayne's nearly overwhelming masculinity.

No, it was more than a keener understanding of his physical disability. Her father hadn't changed; the difference was entirely within herself. She'd been only half alive without Tremayne's love to lend her strength and confidence. Whole, secure in her husband's love, she knew she would no longer fear her father, no matter what happened after this moment.

"Eleanor," McKittrick began, using his most

pompous, thundering voice, the mean gleam in his small eyes telling her he had noted her hesitation and now expected his sharp tongue to cow her into submission.

He must have sensed the change within her, for his tone turned wheedling, his posture becoming that of an anxious father eager to prevent his beloved daughter from making a mistake. "This travesty of a marriage is easily annulled. You have no idea of the heartache this man will bring you. I know you couldn't have turned to him out of love. Perhaps my . . . my overprotective nature forced you into this. As these people are my witness, I will permit you to live as you choose, without interference. Do you hear me, Eleanor?"

She felt Tremayne's body grow rigid, his breathing catch, at hearing her father say the words that rendered Tremayne's presence in her life superfluous—if she didn't love him. And then her father turned to Tremayne.

"Farnsworth is safe, Hawthorne. He ran off before coming to grief. Now, just admit you married my daughter to stop me from throwing you back into jail and I'll consider our score evened. You have my word on it. You'll walk out of here a free man and reclaim your heritage, with no fear of any of this coming back to haunt you. Keeping Eleanor with you will only drag you down."

Satan himself could not have resurrected Ellie's fears so unerringly.

"My wife is all that's important in my life," said Tremayne, shattering her fears.

"Eleanor—" her father began.

"My name is Ellie." She placed her hand upon Tremayne's forearm, and gloried in the feel of his hand clasping hers. "Ellie Hawthorne. And my husband and I have a most interesting tale to tell that sheriff you've brought along."

Epilogue

England, March 1878

Fog had settled in on the uncommonly warm, early-spring day they buried Reginald Bavington, the late earl of Chedgrave. Five days later it continued hovering over Chedgrave lands, softening the skeletal appearance of still-leafless trees, obscuring the new earl of Chedgrave's vision as he stood before the bedroom window, staring out toward the sea.

Tremayne smiled when Ellie came up next to him at the window and rested her head against his shoulder. The long hours he'd spent flexing the bullet-torn muscles proved their worth by making it a matter of no effort to encircle his wife within his arms.

She laughed softly against his shirt. "I never thought to see you looking back over the ocean once we cleared your name and you reconciled with your father."

"Mmm."

"Mmm, indeed," she retorted, pulling his head down for a quick kiss. "All this fog is dulling your conversational skills, Tremayne. We should do something . . . earl-like, or lordly . . ."

Her voice trailed away, and Tremayne knew the word had prompted memories of Lauretta. He understood, for he'd been spending entirely too much time thinking about the treasured friends, the hard-won lands, they'd left behind.

Sighing, he gazed about them at the richly appointed stateroom. The carved oak bed, the embroidered silk hangings, the priceless furnishings—all his. And yet not his, for he'd done nothing to earn it. A wry smile twisted his lips. Had he spent so many years trying to prove his worth that he'd developed a workman's attitude? It seemed so—nothing else explained why he unfavorably compared such luxury to the primitive existence found in a dirt-walled dugout, or why he found himself pining for the grassy scent of a prairie feather mattress he'd filled himself.

Ellie would think him a fool beyond equal if he confessed that he wanted to return to America after all he'd done to get here. No power on earth could induce a woman to choose the wild and spare Kansas frontier over the lush English countryside. Scarcities even wealth couldn't overcome. Back-breaking labor over servants anxious to coddle every whim. A trip to the general store the source of excitement, when here she had a world at her feet.

"What do you like best about this place?" Ellie asked, eerily in accordance with his own thoughts.

"Dressing you in silks and satins," he said at once. "And then peeling it off, layer by layer, all the way down to—"

"Tremayne! Your sister might hear!"

He buried his face in Ellie's sweet-scented hair, laughing at her red-faced embarrassment but casting a suspicious eye around the room, searching for a tawny-haired, blue-eyed minx. He caught a flash of blue muslin burrowing deep into a drapery fold.

"Out with you, Miranda," he ordered.

His eight-year-old half sister presented herself, dusty and disheveled, and he fought to hide the indulgent grin her presence always seemed to prompt. Tremayne had anticipated the constrained relationship that had marked the brief reunion with his father and which had continued up to his death. He hadn't expected to like and respect Katherine, his stepmother, and he certainly hadn't envisioned the doting fondness he felt for young Miranda.

No doubt all of England whispered about his sudden good fortune and speculated on his failure to order his father's second family to the dower house. Let them whistle in the wind, as Lauretta would say.

Nonetheless, he would have to school himself to overcome this defenselessness against winsome females, in the event the child swelling Ellie's belly proved to be a little girl and he found himself hopelessly, but delightfully, outnumbered.

"He looks a bit sad again today, Ellie," Miranda confided, speaking to Ellie as if he wasn't there.

"He has a gloomy nature." Ellie bent down to the child's level, and the two of them peered up at him.

Miranda's eyes, blue as his own, reflected solemn concern. Ellie's chocolate brown gaze twinkled with humor. "Or, he might be sorry for breaking his promise to me."

"Tremayne wouldn't break a promise!"

Amused as he was by Miranda's stout defense of his character, Tremayne couldn't help being intrigued by Ellie's statement.

"He promised to build me a sod house, and he never did."

"He didn't?" Shock held Miranda silent for all of two seconds. "What's a sod house?" A flood of questions burst from her. Ellie patiently answered them all, describing a sod house, making a word sketch of the Kansas prairie, rousing a homesickness within Tremayne so severe it left him weak-kneed with longing.

"We must return," he said, awed that she understood the ache he'd refused to acknowledge.

"The *Silver Gryphon* sails Tuesday at sunrise," Ellie said. At the questioning quirk of his brow, she added, "I've been memorizing the departure tables at the beginning of each month ever since we arrived here. What took you so long, Tremayne?"

He couldn't speak over the fullness in his heart.

"The sod house sounds rather nice," Miranda said, "but I much prefer Chedgrave Manor."

"Excellent." Tremayne found his tongue. "You and your mother shall stay on here to watch over things while I tend to Ellie's sod house."

Undiluted joy lit Ellie's lustrous eyes.

"Does that mean you're leaving, Tremayne? You

aven't been here nearly long enough. It's been such
un having a big brother around." Miranda's piping
'oice trembled alarmingly.

"We'll make frequent visits," Ellie promised.

"Oh! I must tell Mama. She's packing everything. I
hink she feared *we* might have to go live in some-
hing like a sod house." She bounded to the doorway
ind turned back to them. "Shall I ask the servants to
send Mama's trunks in to you instead?"

"How much of Chedgrave do you want to take
vith us, Ellie?" Tremayne asked.

The muscles banding his waist had gone suddenly
igid; his breath seemed lodged somewhere below his
oreastbone. It was as though his body had taken his
soul captive, awaiting her response.

Ellie wrapped her arm about his waist, and placed
nis hand against her soft belly, wrapping the two of
them together, yet somehow setting him free.

"I have everything right here, Tremayne."

"One trunk," Tremayne called to Miranda, though
he, too, held everything he wanted within the circle of
his arms. "A big trunk, roomy enough to hold a lifetime supply of silks and satins."

COMING NEXT MONTH

ONE NIGHT by Debbie Macomber
A wild, romantic adventure from bestselling and much-loved author Debbie Macomber. When their boss sends them to a convention in Dallas together, Carrie Jamison, a vibrant and witty radio deejay for KUTE in Kansas City, Kansas, and Kyle Harris, an arrogant, strait-laced KUTE reporter, are in for the ride of their lives, until one night . . . "Debbie Macomber writes delightful, heartwarming romances that touch the emotions and leave the reader feeling good."—Jayne Ann Krentz

MAIL-ORDER OUTLAW by Millie Criswell
From the award-winning author of *Phantom Lover* and *Diamond in the Rough*, a historical romance filled with passion, fun, and adventure about a beautiful New York socialite who found herself married to a mail-order outlaw. "Excellent! Once you pick it up, you won't put it down."—Dorothy Garlock, bestselling author of *Sins of Summer*

THE SKY LORD by Emma Harrington
When Dallas MacDonald discovered that his ward and betrothed had run off and married his enemy, Ian MacDougall, he was determined to fetch his unfaithful charge even if it meant war. But on entering Inverlocky Castle, Dallas found more pleasure in abducting MacDougall's enchanting sister, Isobel, than in securing his own former betrothed.

WILLOW CREEK by Carolyn Lampman
The final book in the Cheyenne Trilogy. Given her father's ill health during the hot, dry summer of 1886, Nicki Chandler had no choice but to take responsibility for their Wyoming homestead. But when her father hired handsome drifter Levi Cantrell to relieve some of her burdens, the last thing Nicki and Levi ever wanted was to fall in love.

PEGGY SUE GOT MURDERED by Tess Gerritsen
Medical examiner M. J. Novak, M.D., has a problem: Too many bodies are rolling into the local morgue. She teams up with the handsome, aristocratic president of a pharmaceutical company, who has his own agenda. Their search for the truth takes them from glittering ballrooms to perilous back alleys and into a romance that neither ever dreamed would happen.

PIRATE'S PRIZE by Venita Helton
A humorous and heartwarming romance set against the backdrop of the War of 1812. Beautiful Loire Chartier and dashing Dominique Youx were meant for each other. But when Loire learned that Dominique was the half brother of the infamous pirate, Jean Lafitte, and that he once plundered her father's cargo ship, all hell broke loose.

Harper **The Mark of Distinctive**
Monogram **Women's Fiction**